THEIR FATHERS' GOD

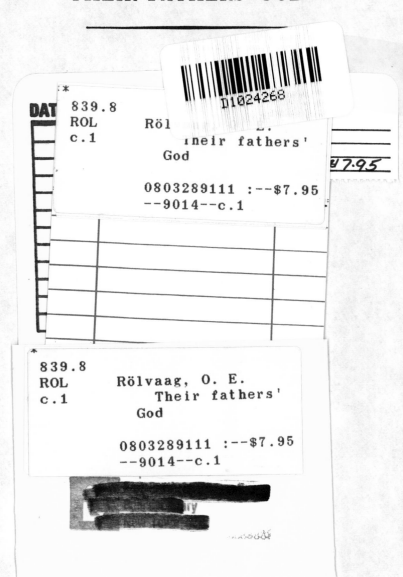

Their Fathers' God

by

O. E. Rölvaag

Translated by Trygve M. Ager

9014

University of Nebraska Press
Lincoln and London

First Bison Book printing: March 1983

Most recent printing indicated by the first digit below:
1   2   3   4   5   6   7   8   9   10

Library of Congress Cataloging in Publication Data

Rölvaag, Ole Edvart, 1876–1931.
  Their fathers' God.

  Translation of: Den signede dag.
  Reprint. Originally published: New York : Harper, 1931.
  "Bison book"—T.p. verso.
  I. Title.
PT9150.R55S513 1983   839.8'2372   82-17636
ISBN 0-8032-8911-1 (pbk.)

Published by arrangement with Harper & Row, Publishers, Inc.

Translator's Foreword

In this translation I have frequently found myself in positions where it has been necessary to commit assault and battery on both literature and language. Certainly all translation is a most difficult task and all translators are criminals, if not at heart at least in deed.

In any translation it is the original mood of the story that suffers most—*i.e.*, its art. Wary of this, Mr. Rölvaag gave me all the liberties a translator could ask, instructing me to "translate mood and let the story take care of itself."

The original text of this novel is richly spiced with Norwegian dialects, particularly the *Nordlandsk* of northern Norway. These dialects, in turn, possess no end of idioms, full of flavour and significance. Few of them have equivalents in English; the rest are virtually untranslatable, for the simple reason that if rendered literally, they will not be understood, and if rendered freely, the necessary modifications rob them of their lustre and casual terseness. In either case much if not all of the psychological background will go by the board.

Idioms, with their peculiar ability of often revealing in a flash an entire thought-complex, are not public property. They grow into a language and there they belong and stay. They need no laws to protect them. To attempt to translate them from one language to another is to invite trouble. Regardless of consequences, I have in some instances done that very thing.

An effort has been made to put Beret's *Nordlandsk* into a natural English. For the sake of differentiation her speeches in English have been allowed a certain stiffness and a sprinkling of Norwegian idioms, characteristic of one with but a scant knowledge of the language.

Translator's Foreword

It should be remembered that Nikoline speaks a colourful, romantic, often allegorical *Nordlandsk*.

I am deeply indebted to Evelyn Trip Berdahl of Urbana, Illinois, for her kind and expert assistance in the preparation of this manuscript. I need hardly say that Mr. Rölvaag's own suggestions have been invaluable.

TRYGVE M. AGER

CONTENTS

THEIR FATHERS' GOD

I. "—A Cloud Like a Man's Hand"

NO HOPE for rain to-night, either. Oh, no, it took pains to stay away, wherever it was!

To the west gold-fringed clouds floated in the still evening. Alive. Magnificent. What was their cargo? Where were they bound? Only mocking impotent man! Not here did they have an errand. Oh no, breathe it not! And no matter, since they bore no trace of rain. . . . For months now, at every eventide the clouds had hovered out there . . . grey, a tint of blue in them . . . all around them, flaming billows of yellow and gold against a background of indigo blue . . . billows that blushed against the oncoming night. . . . Surely this must be witchery of some other world? troll-stuff of the supernatural? . . . Long-faced the people went about . . . only famine and starvation wherever you looked. How would this end? Who dared prophesy? . . . But who could have believed that the end of all things was to be brought about through fair weather? . . . Doesn't the Good Book tell of signs in the sun and in the moon? Now all signs were gone!

Fair weather and a dead calm. Molten sun and a quivering sky. Day after day the same. All alike. And always when evening came on, vagabond clouds drifted together out in the west . . . bathed in a sea of red . . . got fringes of gold. The gold died slowly away in the amber dusk. . . . God alone knew whence these apparitions came, and where they were going. Each morning found the heavens swept clean and glistening. Not a sign of rain in the whole dried-up sky!

Since the coming of spring the drought had been severe.

Their Fathers' God

With every hour it was getting worse. Throughout the long day the sun baked and burnt, each day to the very end. Godless men swore that fire had broken out on the moon, too, because no sooner had the last drops of dew disappeared in the morning than the ground was drier and browner than it had been yesterday.

Though June was only half spent, the fields lay parched and sallow. And the earth's crust shrank; long cracks appeared, running in all directions, like the wrinkles in an old man's face. . . . The cattle stood gasping in the heat. When a cow dragged herself from one place to another her shanks dangled spiritless. . . . The small birds, the few that still remained, lifted their heads to sing with parched throats . . . their songs shrivelled into nothing. . . . Now at nightfall the prairie was like an eeried wasteland. Under the green eye of the moon the flat reaches turned into a goblin haunt.

"The hand of God lay heavy upon all"—age-old words that had now become real. Pious people sought out their closets in secret and there, behind shut doors, sobbed for mercy from the lash of the Lord's wrath. At every Sunday service the shepherds entreated for rain. Prayer-meetings ended always with fervent supplications to Him Who feeds the fowls of the air and clothes the lilies of the field. . . . He must not forget the lambs themselves when they are lost in the night!

But the God of Mercy turned a deaf ear to the supplications. No rainfall of any kind since early last winter. The flood-gates of blessing had been locked tight. The Keeper of the Key did not see the travail of His people. . . . Not even the darkest of the clouds held so much as a cupful of water!

Word came from counties farther west that conditions among the new settlers out there were even worse. Many a man, it was said, had been forced to bundle wife and children into wagons and strike back to civilization. Destitute people, out on a burnt-up prairie, cannot live on sunshine and a scorching southwind! Back East there was at least food to be had, even though one did not have the ready cash to pay for

"—A Cloud Like a Man's Hand"

it. In Miner County, so the rumours went, a man could now for a mere song get a half-section of land with buildings and broken fields. Most of the settlers had neither the faith nor the courage to face crop failures and starvation. One after another they were pulling up stakes.

Yesterday a canvassed wagon, on its way East, had passed through the Spring Creek settlement, now following the same trail it had taken three years ago when the course lay on Sunset Land. In huge yellow letters on the canvas the owner had painted his defiant farewell:

> *Fifty miles from water*
> *One hundred miles from wood*
> *To Hell with South Dakota,*
> *We're leaving you for good!*

Three famished milk cows straggled along behind the wagon. Their duty now, as on the westward trip, was to sustain life in those riding. The sight of the woebegone caravan stung like scorpions all who saw it. Wherever it halted the driver left behind the same grim story: The whole country was scorched . . . every field burnt up . . . settlers had abandoned all hope of ever establishing homes in that cursed place. . . . As for him, he wouldn't give a cent for the whole God damn prairie! The man raged, desperation burnt in his eyes. Only two weeks ago, he said, he had driven southward for one whole day, trying to get a little seed and some porridge meal on credit. All he had brought back were four measly ears of corn! What else was there to do but pull out? The kids couldn't live on dried-up gophers and hot air! Everything he had struggled for for the last three years was out there. Whoever wanted it was welcome to go and take it! . . . A woman with a face pale and drawn sat in the wagon listening to him. She had nothing to say, showed no emotion. Whenever the wagon stopped beside a farmhouse a tangle of barefooted children would scramble to the ground, rush pell-mell through the door, and crowd about the table. Nor did they have anything to say.

The caravan shambled along, kindling new uneasiness on

3

its way. It made Tönseten so hopping mad that he had to explode to anyone who would listen. . . . That man was a blubbering baby! Good God, think of a home-seeker quitting such a country!

II

June 18, 1894. The evening chores were finished and the young boss on the Holm farm stood by the pigsty gazing at the clouds which floated lazily in the sunset. He leaned forward on the gate-post; now and then he pushed his foot between the rails to rub at grimy backs that came near. His young face was uncommonly sober.

Slowly, imperceptibly the twilight deepened into blue, dark night. The stillness was full and unfathomable, with a pricked-up ear on every blade of grass. Listening. Questioning. What would the night bring?

Suddenly there drifted down the road snatches of a song; Peder Holm quickly raised his head to listen. It was the rusty voice of an old man scuffing along with a cane. He was so intent upon his song that whenever the words slipped, his memory he would rest himself on ponderous and long-drawn *la-ha-ums*. As soon as the lost words were caught, he would go on again with the song, thumping up the roadway that led into the Holm farmyard.

Peder Holm tilted his head and listened more intently.

—Well, there was godfather coming!

The voice out in the darkness adventured into the song again, now more coherently:

> "The twilight fades to dark of night
> And journeyed has the day to its last hour
> La-um . . . la-ha . . . to its last hour.
> And towards that evil, darker night
> I find the Moth now guides my weary steps
> La-um . . . my weary steps.
> Where worms at last will wallow in my skin
> And cleanse this flesh of all its lust and sin.
> La-ha, um-um . . .
> And cleanse this flesh of all its lust and sin."

4

"—A Cloud Like a Man's Hand"

"Is it you, Syvert Tönseten?" shouted Peder in his broad Nordland dialect.

"Gosh, how you scared me!" The old man came hobbling towards the sty.

Peder laughed. He and Tönseten were the best of friends, usually.

"What was that ditty you were singing? It's a new one to me."

"Ditty, your grandmother! That's no ditty, child!" said Tönseten firmly and jabbed his cane into the ground for added emphasis. "That's an old evening hymn. You seem to have forgotten all about church and Christianity since you turned heathen and got to be the pope's right-hand man!"

"Now you're trying to string me!"

"Oh no, I ain't! It is a hymn, and a good one at that. You'll find it in the Synod's old Hymnal. We used to sing it in the good old days down in Kaskeland.[1] I've half forgotten it." Tönseten looked about him, puzzled. "What are you doing out here so late? Young warblers like you ought to be at home in their nests with their mates at this time of night!" He shook his cane at Peder reprovingly.

"I was just standing here wondering about the weather."

"Well, don't you worry any more about the weather. It'll be changing pretty soon now," added Tönseten with confidence.

"Sure it will. Ha! I can see it changing!"

"Yes-sir-ree, you can bet your last dime on it! Just wait until we set that rainmaker working. I was to town to-day; people weren't talking about anything else; I never saw the like of such excitement. Just so those commissioners don't get pig-headed and throw a monkey-wrench into the machinery. They're voting on it to-morrow."

"You don't believe in that foolishness, Syvert?" Peder stood erect.

"Me believe in it? Well . . . heh-heh! . . . Guess I'd bet-

---

[1] Kaskeland: Norwegian-American for Koshkonong, one of the first Norwegian settlements in the State of Wisconsin.

ter believe what honest people have seen with their own eyes, hadn't I?"

"It's a damned swindle and nothing else!" said Peder, hotly.

"That's not for a young fellow like you to say. Here in America we do what's got to be done. If we need rain we go and make it. Must be a lot easier to milk a few buckets of rain out of the atmosphere than to dig thousands of feet into the bowels of the earth after all the coal you use." Tönseten spoke with the finality of long experience.

Peder remained silent. Into his face had come a look of contempt. And finally he asked:

"Is the County Board going to hire him?"

"Sure thing! Can't you see the fields and pastures getting worse burnt up every day? If we don't get rain, and that damn soon, it's good-bye forever to the whole country. The grasshoppers wasn't half as bad as this. They didn't hurt the hay any. Hmn. We'd have to butcher all our live stock and then where would we be?" Again Peder remained silent. Tönseten talked on, bent on reporting the gist of what he had heard in town. "The Board wants to hire him, all right; Gjermund is the only commissioner bucking it. That jackass has always been stubborn as a mule. Well, he'll have to give in this time. If I wasn't so dead tired, I'd go over and tell him a thing or two right now . . . by God, if I wouldn't!"

"How much does that fellow want for his rain?" asked Peder, quietly.

"He says for seven hundred dollars he'll drench the whole county."

Peder let fly a sharp kick at the snout that came up to sniff at his toe; a mad grunt flared up in the darkness:

"You said they were going to meet to-morrow?"

"Yup. To-morrow morning."

"And you think they'll hire him?" Peder asked. Now his thoughts began to take shape.

"Ho—I'm positive of it! I talked with two of the commissioners to-day; both of them told me they would never dare to turn him down now. If they did, they'd be lynched.

"—A Cloud Like a Man's Hand"

And sure as the devil they would! People won't hear of it. This man Jewell, they say, is a real wizard. Down in Iowa he gave them a shower that came mighty near washing a whole county right off the map. He's got the papers to prove it. . . . Is your mother home? I've got a little errand to do for Kjersti."

"You'll find 'em both in the kitchen."

Tönseten thanked him and walked to the house. Peder turned toward the barn, walking uncertainly. But before he reached the door he had broken into a run.

He darted in, and a moment later he came out leading a horse which he had quickly bridled. Mounting it, he rode to the house. There, at the doorstep, he stopped and called to his wife.

Susie opened the door and looked out into the dark. Her surprise at seeing him on horseback at this hour of the night carried her down the steps. . . . What was he up to now? . . .

"Listen, Susie"—he talked low and fast—"I have to run off on a little errand. Don't sit up and wait for me!"

"But it's bedtime now? Where in the world are you going?" There was uneasiness in her voice. She came close to him.

"I have to ride over and see Charley for a minute. Please be a good girl now and go in and go to bed."

"Oh, take the buggy; then I can go along, too!" Her voice had a pleading note. "I haven't been over home for ages; I've almost forgotten what the old place looks like." Her hands clasped his knee and she shook it imploringly.

"Now-now! Is that any way for a nice little Irish girleen to behave? Susie, be reasonable, won't you? Listen: Charley and I have something very, very important to do to-night. We can't be bothered with any girls . . . not to-night! It won't take me long, Susie. At least I don't think it will."

"Oh, you Norwegians! You're all so selfish and hard-hearted. Why won't you tell me what you boys are up to? Is it such a secret?"

Peder laughed. Unnecessarily loud that laugh was.

7

Their Fathers' God

"Wait until afterwards and I'll tell you all about it. Now if you'll be a real good girl, I'll give you two great big kisses when I come back."

"Only two?"

"Well, make it two and a half, then. How's that?"

"You're mean to-night, Peder. That's the Norwegian in you." Her voice was full of tenderness.

"You're right, Susie. And it's all because the Norwegians never had a lot of saints and such fellows to look after them."

"That's just why they're so hard to manage! Why can't you take the buggy? Won't I ever get a chance to see the folks again? Do you think I'm going to sit around here and listen to you and your mother talk Norwegian all the rest of my life?"

Peder did not answer; instead he tightened his reins and turned the horse. "I won't be gone long, Susie!" he cried over his shoulder as the horse at a brisk trot carried him down the roadway.

Not until he entered the farmyard of his father-in-law did Peder slacken the pace. There he tied the horse near the door and walked quickly in without stopping to rap. No time for formalities now.

Charley, the brother-in-law, was on his feet before Peder had opened the door. For a moment the two stared at each other, then both laughed heartily.

"Well, here's old Paul Revere himself. How are you, you highway robber?"

Peder grinned.

"Had to drop in to see if you'd join me in the ride."

There was banter in the eyes of both, more marked in Charley's because they were more inflammable.

"Is your father at home?"

"What's it to you? He hasn't got any more daughters to give away."

"Is that so? Now watch out what you're saying, Mr. Charley Doheny, or I'll bump you one on the nose!" Peder growled, and slammed his fist into his open hand to underscore the threat.

"—A Cloud Like a Man's Hand"

"So that's why you've come to-night? You certainly wasted plenty of time in letting us know about it." Charley clenched his fists, threw out his chest, and strode about pompously.

"Yes, sir. I'm all keyed up for a scrap. And the more of a two-fisted knock-down-and-drag-out affair it is the better I'll like it. Come on; we're in a hurry!"

"Oh! So you're going to crawl out of it again?" asked Charley, laughingly.

"That's exactly what I'm not going to do. Shake the lead out of your pants and get ready. We've wasted too much time already."

"You seem to be in a big rush to get your licking."

"To *give* it!" Peder corrected. "All fooling aside. Haven't you heard about that crook who breezed into town the other day with an offer to punch a hole in the sky for us?"

"Ah-ha—it's Mr. Jewell's scalp you're after?"

"—And that the county is going to plank down seven hundred honest American dollars for letting him do it? Have you heard that, too?"

"Oh, he'll never get that much."

"Those seven hundred dollars will be added to your taxes," Peder continued, unhalted.

"Say, are you crazy?"

"Absolutely not. Where else do you suppose the money would be coming from?"

"But what if he can make it rain?" Charley asked.

"Oh, bosh! And I thought you were a good orthodox Catholic?"

"What does that have to do with the rain? Besides, we believe in miracles."

"Yes, but not in this sort of foolishness. Imagine anybody in this day and age ass enough to fall for such talk!"

"What makes you think I've fallen for it?"

"You're crazy enough. . . . I can see it in your face you believe it."

At that both of the boys laughed.

"Come along and we'll see if we can't ring in a little fun

9

Their Fathers' God

for the money." Peder told his plan: "Gjermund Dahl is chairman of the County Board. We'll ride over to his place and make a protest. We'll get Dennis O'Hara to go along; that will make three of us. Too bad your father isn't home! They say that Dahl is against hiring Jewell, but he'll never be able to stop it single-handed. We'll see what he has to say. If he thinks it will be of any use, we'll all go to town to-morrow and raise hell at the meeting. By God—no County Board is going to squander my money like that and get by with it!"

Charley stared at his brother-in-law:

"Gosh, man! Why don't you go in for politics? That's where you belong."

Peder grunted and clutched the back of a chair beside him.

"Huh!" he said, "a fellow can't let himself be babied along forever. Those old die-hards on the Board carry on as if they owned the whole county. How old do we have to be before we can tell 'em where to get off? Listen—I've decided that from now on I'm going to have a hand in these affairs. Come on; let's get going!"

"Do you think it will help any?"

"How can I tell? It'll at least give the people something new to talk about. Already I've got all the gossips in the county talking, and take it from me, I'll give 'em plenty more!" Involuntarily he squared his shoulders and stood erect. Hot defiance reddened his boyish face.

"And you want to get me tangled up in this mess, too?"

"Rot, Charley! Are you going to wait until your whiskers fall out before you start taking an interest in things that really are your business? Don't you see that you'll be running up against things of this kind the rest of your life?"

"If there's going to be some fun in it, I'm with you. A little circus won't hurt this dry spell any."

Presently they were riding down the road, side by side. For a while neither spoke. It was Charley who broke the silence.

"How's Susie, anyhow?"

"—A Cloud Like a Man's Hand"

"What do you mean?" Peder wrestled for a moment with the reply before he gave it voice.

"I don't suppose she talks anything but Norwegian now?"

His remark irritated Peder:

"You're right. There's not a single Irish sound left in her mouth." Peder rode so fast that Charley had to urge his horse on in order to keep pace with him.

"I was talking with Father Williams the other day," Charley said when he had caught up again. "He wanted to know all about Susie. Guess what he said?"

"I'm no good at guessing riddles," answered Peder sulkily. "I'd have to be all-knowing in order to divine the mysteries of a priest."

"He said that it wasn't so bad, after all, that Susie had married a Norwegian. 'The people of Norway,' he said, 'hadn't separated from the True Church because they wanted to. Some foreign king came along and made them change their religion.' . . . Isn't that right?"

Peder checked the pace of his horse.

"I don't know much about that," he said. "And I care less." His voice was cold and bitter. "You and I are Americans, Charley. Popes and kings don't mean a darn to us. Tell that to Father Williams."

"You'll get a good chance to do that yourself. He's coming to see you one of these days," chuckled the brother-in-law.

"To see *me*?"

"Sure he is. He baptized Susie, you know . . . prepared her for confirmation, too. She's almost like a daughter to him. Father Williams is as good a man as you'll find anywhere. You be nice to him!"

"I'll bet he told you more than that?" Peder asked, darkly.

"That wouldn't be strange, would it? He's our priest, you know. But why worry about that now? We're out gunning for rainmakers to-night."

Peder's laugh was bitter.

"Promise me, Charley, that you won't get married until

Their Fathers' God

you've talked the thing over with every doggone old woman in the county. *Freedom?* The idea makes me laugh!"

"I promise you to go slow!" the other assured him, heartily. "Not much danger of a calamity like that as long as the drought hangs on."

A silence settled over the two riders, disturbed only by the even clop-clop of the horses' hoofs.

"Oh, damn it all, I can't stand this much longer! All winter long, every Norwegian for miles around has been meddling in my affairs. Now if the Irish, too, begin, I'm going to clear out. To hell with the whole caboodle! . . . Wherever I go there's sure to be somebody popping up with a smart remark. If they're afraid to say it, they just stand around grinning. And that's worse. It seems that I've committed a crime by marrying your sister!"

"Don't let it bother you," said Charley, good-heartedly. "During a drought like this people have to have something to talk about. Anyway, don't slam the door in Father Williams' face when he comes to call on you folks. I tell you, Peder, he is the kindest man I know . . . as big-hearted as they make 'em. Why, he'd give a man the shirt off his back! I bet you'll like him."

"At least as long as he stays away!" said Peder, dryly.

III

Dennis O'Hara had no quarrel to pick with rainmakers. Why should he? Maybe Mr. Jewell really had discovered some way of making rain . . . who could tell? At any rate, it would be great sport to watch him try. But if Peder and Charley were going to stir up some excitement before the main show began, then Dennis certainly wanted to be in on that, too!

It was late when the three Apostles of Truth reached the home of the chairman of the County Board. They found Gjermund Dahl sitting barefooted and alone in the parlour; all around him lay scattered the newspapers he had been reading. The rest of the household was in bed. When the three entered he struggled to his feet and offered them chairs.

Peder acted as spokesman. Excitement got the better of him; here he was, a mere youngster, face to face with the chairman of the County Board, telling him what he ought to do and what he ought not to do. . . . Was it he that was running the county? His agitation jumbled his thoughts and tangled up his words. He tried to calm down . . . he must steady himself . . . be clear . . . talk like a grown-up man! He looked Gjermund straight in the eye, and there was a warm ring in his voice, his head thrown back.

The older man heard him out, observing him half cynically, half in wonder. . . . Here was an unknown force. . . . Is this young man a harbinger of spring? Gjermund wondered. He said:

"I see! . . . So you boys would like to see me strung up in order to save the county seven hundred dollars? Well, that shows a mighty fine public spirit, but it strikes me that the milk of human kindness in you is running kind of blue. The whole affair won't cost you, Peder, more than a few cents. Can't you afford that much when you realize the life of a neighbour is at stake?" Gjermund placed his feet on a chair, the right leg carefully over the left; his long shapeless face cocked sidewise and the lower lip thrust forward. His eyes were fixed on Peder.

"You don't believe in this humbug any more than I do!" Peder shot back at him. His natural voice had returned, and all traces of discomfiture were gone.

"No-o, I'm not that ignorant, thank God. But how are you going to handle a lot of crazy people? Tell me that?"

"Well, are you going to let them run the county?"

"Pshaw! They'll do that no matter what I say or do. This drought is driving everybody horn-mad. Nothing strange about that; if it hangs on much longer, it will mean the worst crop failure in the history of the Northwest. Last year the panic sent the prices way down; the farmer came away from the market poorer than he went to it. This year we won't have a thing to sell, no matter what the prices are. Do you

13

wonder that people are catching at straws? There are lots right around here who are talking seriously about moving to some other part of the country. Not all of them will be satisfied with just talking—you can be sure of that. Hunger has the power to perform miracles." There was a quiet resignation in Gjermund's words. He stroked his chin and studied Peder.

"You mean to say, then, that there's nothing to be done about it?"

"No; not that I can see. But if you have anything to suggest, I'd like to hear it."

Dennis interrupted:

"Peder is hankering for a good fight. Peder Holm *versus* Jewell. He invited us to come along and see the fun. Can't you help him? They surely can't add that to our taxes."

"It would draw a big crowd, all right," Charley suggested, good-naturedly. "Nobody has a thing to do nowadays, anyway; out our way we've quit cultivating."

All but Peder laughed. He stood there silent, his eyes afire.

"If you boys show up at the Town Hall eleven o'clock to-morrow morning, you can have all the fighting you want."

"You mean, then, that it's useless to try to stop this foolishness?" Peder asked, indignantly.

"It looks that way." Gjermund was silent for a moment; then continued, deliberately: "I was in town to-day; I talked to farmers and townspeople. The word had gone around that I am against the rainmaker, and folks weren't at all bashful about letting me know what would happen if I didn't give in. You take my word for it, any commissioner who dares to vote against the rainmaker to-morrow is simply gambling with the noose. To try to talk sense to people now would be like trying to scratch your way through a barn wall; you'd only run your fingers full of slivers." Gjermund wiggled the toes on his right foot, bent the big one far back and gazed at it meditatively. Now and then he looked up at Peder. . . . "How big an army could you three fellows scare up by to-morrow morning if you went right after them? . . . What does your father say about it, Charley?"

"Oh, he's all right. Maybe he could even get Father Williams to come along."

"You mean the priest?"

"Sure. . . . But I'm not sure if he'd come."

Gjermund laughed, dropped his hand from his chin and sat up in the chair.

"How about you, Dennis?"

Dennis scratched the back of his neck and grinned:

"If I promise Tor Helgeson a drink or two, there's nothing on earth that'll keep him away. And there isn't a stronger man in this corner of the state," he added, assuringly.

Gjermund Dahl got up and paced the floor. An uneasiness had come over him. Involuntarily he straightened his back, raised his head.

"Nix, boys! Rough stuff will never get us anywhere. Our job is to go out and round up all the sane people left in the county and get them to attend that meeting to-morrow. . . . Gosh—it would be a treat to see common sense come out on top for once!" Gjermund was half muttering to himself, although the words were meant for the boys. "How about old Tallaksen, Peder? He's the biggest taxpayer around here. Do you think you could rout him out? And the ministers . . . if anyone ought to get up and witness against the rain-maker's black art, they're the boys who should do it. You'd better have both the ministers on hand." Gjermund looked at the boys; the fight shone in his eyes.

Peder reddened and laughed:

"I guess you'd better have somebody else go after those fellows!"

"All right," agreed Gjermund, "leave them to me. I'll see both of them the first thing in the morning. I haven't met our new minister yet. They tell me he's a man of good sense." Suddenly his words came faster: "You'll have to pry loose your neighbours over West. Get Rognaldsen, and your brother, and—well, get every taxpayer who's able to swing a battle-axe! Understand? . . . If we only had a little more

time. Why in thunder didn't you boys come around before?
Hadn't you heard about it? You ought to have come last
night."

All three stared at him. Here was another man facing
them:

"All right, boys, if there's going to be a battle, let's have
a real one! But get this straight: There will have to be
miracles performed between now and eleven o'clock to-morrow morning, and it's up to you fellows to go out and perform them. If you don't succeed, you might just as well go
right home and stay there. But we can't have any rough
stuff . . . we got plenty foolishness already. Next fall the
county will be looking for help and rich people aren't in the
habit of loaning money to half-wits. The more men you
can bring to the meeting to-morrow, the better our chances
will be of chasing this man Jewell back to where he came
from. . . . Now get started. I'll be needing a little rest
before the battle starts. And God help us if you don't show
up to-morrow a thousand strong!"

IV

Outside, the boys held a brief council. It took them but
a few minutes to agree on which neighbours might possibly
be enlisted for the cause and which of these they might reasonably expect to find awake at this late hour. It was now
long past ten o'clock.

"All right," said Peder, clinching the agreement. "Now
let's get started. You fellows go for the Irish and I'll take
the Norwegians. Remember, we're out to perform miracles!"

With that he mounted his horse and was gone into the
night. He took the road that led northward straight to Tallaksen's. Henry, the oldest of the sons, was still awake, and
to him Peder explained the plan. He heard the ring of authority in his own voice and it cheered him. Everyone who
didn't want to see this county become the laughing-stock for
all the world must be at the meeting to-morrow to protest!
He had just been over to see Gjermund Dahl and Dahl had

"—A Cloud Like a Man's Hand"

said that something might be done if only the people with
some wits in their heads would bestir themselves. Could
Henry and his brothers come? And Dahl was especially
anxious that Henry's father should be there. "I tell you,
Henry, it's just about time for us young fellows to get up
and do a little hollering . . . we've got to let the old codgers
know we're growing up." He added, confidentially: "Here's
what I've been thinking—five years from now you and I will
be harvesting the reward or the punishment for what is being
done around here to-day!"

Henry showed no enthusiasm. He said he could not answer for his father. It might be that they would all turn out
. . . things were rather dead around the farm nowadays
. . . he had heard the boys speak about going to town
soon . . . yes, they might be there. . . . Henry yawned
sleepily.

Peder said good night and set out for his brother's farm.
. . . Good old Store-Hans! Hadn't seen him now for a
dog's age . . . to be exact, only once since the wedding just
before Christmas . . . and then only for a minute. Plain
that Hans objected to his marriage to Susie . . . that it
had been a hard pill for him to swallow. For weeks Peder
had purposely been avoiding his brother; he trusted that by
leaving Hans alone long enough the injuries would gradually
heal and be forgotten. . . . Time would certainly fix it! All
storms roll over . . . sometime!

The horse slowed down, almost to a walk. Peder did not
notice it. A multitude of thoughts buzzed in his mind. These
months since Christmas had been happy, golden ones. All
the time he had kept himself at home, close with Susie. Yes,
he had drunk deeply of love's cup. Not that he had forgotten
the world of men and reality! No, sir. Every day it had
beckoned to him, challenging him, as it passed by his door.
At times he had been forced to summon all his will to be
able to turn his back to it, to say "Get thee behind me!" It
was true that he had not escaped suffering some burns and
bruises from his self-imposed bonds. Half a year now since he
had married her. The gossip had lately been going stronger,

17

no denying that. People had stared at him, smiled knowingly as if to say that they understood everything perfectly:
"Young man, you don't see it yet . . . just wait. We know
what we're talking about." . . . That's what their smiles
meant. How he had ached to paste their faces for them!
. . . What reason did people have for carrying on like this?
The thought was as puzzling now as ever: I've done nothing
worse than marry a neighbour girl I've known all my life
. . . not a soul can say a bad word about her. Yet everybody
is acting as if I had committed the worst crime thinkable.
It's a queer old world . . . damned queer!

The horse jogged along. Peder's thoughts were running
amuck:

. . . Just take that fathead Gabrielsen, for instance . . .
a pretty preacher, he is! Why did he have to go down to
Godmother Kjersti and sit around shedding tears over me?
Telling her that I had brought on my own ruin. Said that
I had hardened my heart and that I had sold myself to the
devil by letting myself be married by a Catholic priest. . . .
Oh well, that jackass isn't around here any more—thank God
for that! . . . Those half-witted jokes that people are always slinging in my face! Just as if I were a little kid who
has done something wrong and is going home to mother to
get spanked. . . . Peder squared his shoulders: Just hold
on, you fools . . . he who laughs last laughs best! . . . He
felt a new power well up within him; it made his body tingle
with strength. . . . Let them step up now and he'd pound
the whole county to a jelly. . . . Still, he might have been
a fool for going to Father Nolan to get married? . . . Oh
well, what's done is done!

. . . Glad I've got this errand to do over here to-night. If
my big brother has anything against me, I'll give him a
chance to get it out of his system. Until he does, we two will
have tough sliding. . . . Hans was always that way . . .
Sofie and Susie got to become friends. Can't tell what might
happen to mother if Store-Hans doesn't show up at home
pretty soon. . . . Anybody can see how she goes around
fretting over his kids. . . . Suddenly Peder burst into a

loud laugh: It won't be long now before she'll have one right there in the house—foolish old mother!

The house was dark and still when Peder rode into his brother's yard. He was well acquainted here. Quickly he tied the horse to the post near the porch, went straight to the bedroom window, and rapped loudly on the screen.

"Don't shoot," he cried gaily. "It's only me! Get up, Hans; I've got something important to tell you. I'll be waiting for you on the porch."

Soon his brother came out, barefooted and in his night-shirt.

"What brings you here at this time of the night?" he asked, sullenly, in Norwegian.

Peder answered in English:

"Sit down and I'll tell you all about it." He spoke slowly, as though he were weighing every word: He was sent here by Gjermund Dahl to ask Store-Hans to come to the meeting at the Town Hall to-morrow. And he must be sure to bring two or three dependable men with him. . . . Word for word Peder repeated what Gjermund had said about the famine and the hard times that would strike the county before winter. That's why it was so important that the rainmaker be chased out of town. "Well, that's what I came here to tell you. And now I guess it's about time for me to hustle home to my wife!" He rose to go.

Store-Hans had listened without a word. As his brother got up he said, darkly:

"Yes, by God—it's just about time!" His voice trembled under a load of scorn, yet it sounded as if he were laughing. "No need to worry about the future as long as we've got fellows like you coming around in the middle of the night playing politician!"

Peder whipped around and stepped up close to his brother, his whole body shaking; there was a smile on his face. He spoke in Norwegian:

"You'd better keep your mouth shut, Hans, or I might forget that you're my brother." He looked Store-Hans straight in the eye. "As far back as I can remember you've

been making it your duty to take care of me. But now you're
going to cut it out . . . for *good*, you understand?"

"Looks like you still need it!"

Hans stood leaning against the wall. Peder laid his hands
heavily on his brother's shoulders:

"Just what are you driving at, old boy? Out with it, I
say!"

"You'd grab hold of me, would you?" Hans straightened
himself. His voice was hoarse, his face drawn with anger.

"Darn right I would!" Peder thrust Hans' shoulders
against the wall and there was a dull sound. "I feel like giving you the thrashing of your life, Hans. . . . You ought
to be ashamed to talk like this to your own brother. And
you who's supposed to have so much good sense! . . . Guess
I'm not the only one who needs somebody to take care of
him. . . . Listen, Hans, if I've ever wronged you, you're
going to tell me right now. I won't stand for this sort of
thing any longer. . . . Here you've been sulking around all
winter long, sour as green apples. You haven't even been over
to see your own mother. Aren't you ashamed of yourself?"
Peder's words, half-choked by tears and anger, fell on Hans
in spurts.

"Look out now!" Hans tried to get loose from the vise
holding him to the wall. His voice was thick:

"Every place I go people pounce on me, asking me how
the Nordlænding is getting along with his Irish wife. They
all grin wickedly . . . want to know how it feels to be related to a lot of Catholics . . . how much the pope is taxing
you . . . when you're joining in the war on the Protestants ——" For a moment Hans could not go on. "You've
disgraced the whole family . . . that's what you've done!"

"Aw, hell! Is that all that's ailing you? What a silly old
fool you are!" cried Peder, relieved, his voice boyish and
joyful. "So that's all that's bothering you?" He released his
hold. "Just tell 'em to come to me. I'll show 'em what's
what!"

There was a pause. Then his brother spoke again:

"That's the way you've always been . . . always diving

"—A Cloud Like a Man's Hand"

headlong into one thing after another without ever stopping
to think of consequences. You hardly get out of one scrape
before you plunge neck-deep into another. Ever since you
started school folks have been gossiping about you. . . . God
alone knows what you're up to now!"

Peder laughed uproariously:

"Only dead people lie around and never stir; they just
can't help themselves because they are dead, plumb dead!"
His voice dropped, then continued, teasingly: "After all,
Hans, you're just an ordinary beetlehead . . . just like all
the rest of them. Why, you haven't got one-third the sense
we've given you credit for!"

Peder's joking missed its mark. His brother still leaned
against the wall . . . silent, glowering, unthawed. But his
body had lost much of its tautness of a moment ago, and
Peder noticed it. It's beginning to sink in, he thought . . .
soon he'll be all right. Then with his customary cheerfulness
he said:

"Well, so much for that! Tell Gjermund when you see
him that I was here." With that he went down the steps and
started towards his horse. Halfway there he stopped suddenly and about-faced: "If you don't come over to see us
before long, Hans, I'll have to come and drag you over.
And be sure you bring Sofie along. Then you can both see
for yourselves how swell the Irish and the Norwegians can
get along together. Good night!"

Without a word the brother turned, opened the door, and
went into the house.

v

In the best of spirits Peder rode homeward. The evening
clouds had disappeared. Over him lay the deep summer
night. Stars and a great stillness. Before him an empty country road. He caught a faint amber glow above the horizon in
the west. Over there the stars were not shining so brightly.
Clouds? To-night he didn't care much.

Now he was one worry poorer . . . the boil had broken

at last! Soon all the poison that had been rankling in his brother for so long would be oozing out. . . . His strength leaped and lilted within him. . . . Yes, sir! Here is one man who knows how to handle the grumblers! Soon it would be all right again between him and his brother . . . all Hans needs now is a little time for thinking things over. At heart he's a good boy . . . one in a thousand. . . . Funny that a grown-up man should be so sensitive to woman-talk. Was it a streak running in the family? Now and then Peder had felt it in himself. . . . Certainly people must have said all there was to say by this time. Peder chuckled to himself. . . . Maybe he could bestir himself a little and give them something new to talk about?

A light from an upper window shone down on him as he rode into the yard at home. He saluted it gaily: Aha, so some one's still up? . . . Without wasting any time he brought his horse to the stall, chucked hay in the manger, and went to the house. On the porch he paused to pull off his boots. Quietly he opened the door and tiptoed across the kitchen floor, stopping for a moment at his mother's bedroom door to listen. She must have gone to bed hours ago. Noiselessly he hurried upstairs. Outside their room he stopped for breath. Then he opened the door slowly and went in.

"Good evening!" he bubbled, gaily. The light blinded him so that for a moment he stood blinking.

Susie was seated on the edge of the bed, in her nightgown. Her hair had been gathered into two heavy braids that hung down, resting on her breasts. She was startled, for he had come so quietly that she had not heard him until he opened the door. One hand darted furtively under the pillow; with an effort she came towards him.

He opened his arms to her, but did not move.

"You little rascal! Here you haven't gone to bed yet?" he whispered. To show his anger he made a frown so deep that it devoured his whole face. "Didn't I tell you to go to bed early to-night?"

She snuggled up to him, close. Warmly she pressed him

to her, as if he were returning after a long, long absence. For a while they stood thus, neither of them speaking. "I thought you'd never come!" she said at last. "It's nearly morning, isn't it?" Her arms were around his neck; now she let her head drop back so that her eyes could find his. "Peder," her voice was soft and sweet, "he's been kicking so to-night. I'm sure it's a boy! Just imagine, pretty soon you'll be the proud daddy of a wee little red-headed Irishman. Put your arms around the small of my back, Peder. There—that feels so good!"

"Hmn," said Peder, and he kissed her under her ear. Then without warning he lifted her in his arms and carried her to the bed. There he laid her down tenderly, but he did not let go of her. "By rights you should have a spanking for not minding your lord and master! . . . What was that thing I saw you push under the pillow?"

Her arm was about his neck; she drew his head down to hers.

"Don't be mean to me!" she pleaded. "You were gone so long. I was alone and didn't have a thing to do. So I said my prayers to the Blessed Virgin . . . for rain, and for the little roughneck who won't let me sleep! Are you mad at me now? Let me look at you." She placed her hands on his cheeks and turned his head until she could look straight into his eyes.

Gently Peder freed himself from her hold; with one hand he groped about under the pillow. "Here's your Black Magic. . . . Oh, Susie, Susie! . . . Aren't you ever going to grow up?" In his hand he held a necklace of small white beads. At the center of the string was a gilt heart; from this was hung the gilded crucifix on a short string of five beads. Peder held the rosary in his hand and laughed. "Yes, sir, I'll stake my money on this hocus-pocus of yours. If the county would only spend those seven hundred dollars on you and that Virgin of yours, I'll bet we'd get all the rain we want. Keep up the good work, little girl."

"Peder, you mustn't talk like that!"

He laughed good-naturedly. "Oh, Susie, when are you going to start using your brains?" He laid the beads on the commode and then picked up the alarm clock, setting it for half past four. Before shaking off his overalls and putting out the light he combed his crop of blond hair meticulously. Then he got into bed.

"Aren't you going to tell me where you've been to-night?" she asked, cuddling close to him.

"That's soon done." He turned his back to her. . . . Now he must get to sleep quickly . . . no time for foolishness to-night. "I was over to my brother's and gave him the beating of his life. Don't be surprised if we get visitors before long."

"Was that where you were?"

"Um-huh."

"Is he still mad at me?"

"He's never been mad at you."

"Oh yes, he has! He thinks I led you astray, or something . . . I can tell it in his eyes. I know he hates me! Heavens! it wasn't my fault you wanted to marry me. And that wife of his is just like him. What did they say?"

"Nothing."

"You're fibbing."

"No, I'm not."

"Oh, come on, tell me! Do you s'pose I care about those Norskies?"

"He didn't even peep," Peder assured her. "I asked him to come over and bring his wife, so they could see for themselves how nicely the Catholic and the Lutheran are getting along."

"You didn't, either!"

" 'Course I did."

"Are they coming?" Susie asked, eagerly. "What will I say to them . . . when they won't even talk?"

"Don't be so silly, Susie." But immediately he yielded, turned and patted her. "Just show Sofie that the chickens lay eggs and the cows give milk on our farm exactly as they do on hers. Use your good sense and you'll be all right. Now we'll have to see about getting some sleep. Gosh—I'm tired!"

Peder could feel that she was lying awake, thinking. He was sorry for her and mumbled sleepily:

"Guess Father Williams will be around to see you one of these days."

"Really?" Susie raised herself on her elbow and shook him. "You aren't fooling me? Who told you so?"

"Charley."

"Where did you see Charley?"

"Just stopped in for a minute. He and I have to be off to town early to-morrow. If you don't keep still now, I'll have to go and sleep in the haymow! I've got to get up at four-thirty—it's past one already."

Obediently Susie lay down again. . . . Peder was so unreasonable. How could she fall asleep now?

"Has Charley seen him?" She breathed the question softly as if releasing a sigh she could no longer hold.

"Um-huh."

"Oh, I'm so happy!" She placed her arm about him snugly to assure him that now she was all through asking questions. But she talked on, her voice hushed and soothing: "You have no idea how kind Father Williams is. He has always liked me . . . I used to be his pet girl."

"Um-huh," he mumbled, faintly.

"He certainly must be disgusted with me!" she murmured. . . . "We went to Father Nolan to be married. And I haven't been to Confession for ages . . . not to Mass, either . . . I haven't taken any gifts for the altar. . . ." Her voice grew plaintive: "Pretty soon I'll have a baby. . . . No wonder we don't get any rain!"

Peder sat up with a start. He gripped her arm tightly.

"Now cut out that whimpering!" He felt her body tremble under his hand. And instantly he was sorry, lifted her in his arm, and pleaded, warmly: "Oh Susie, Susie! If you would only use common sense we could live together like two birds in a tree." He patted her encouragingly. "You don't have to go off and tell a strange man about anything you've done . . . you're not guilty of any wrong. Can't you see that it's all a lot of poppycock? As if a priest should have anything to say about us and our lives!"

"Oh, but you don't understand!" Her voice was quivering with anguish.

"Do you mean to tell me that I can't add two and two?" His impatience was again on the verge of bursting into flame.

She saw it coming and tried to stop it:

"No, no, Peder; don't get angry at me. Of course you know lots . . . it's just that you can't understand. Now lie down and go to sleep." She lay down, turning away from him. To prove that she meant what she had said, she reached back and patted him.

Peder turned towards her, found her hand and held it tightly. There were other things that he wanted to say . . . things that he would have to tell her sometime . . . and, by God! she'd have to hear him out! But not to-night. Can't waste time and thought in trying to reason with half-sick women. . . . Matters of far greater importance demanded his attention now . . . people gone crazy with the heat . . . horn-mad. . . .

Soon he was fast asleep.

Susie lay for a long time listening to the quiet breathing behind her. Wide awake and fearful, she remained motionless until she was confident that Peder was sound asleep. Then she slipped out of bed and tiptoed to the commode; there she groped about in the darkness until her hand fell on the rosary. She picked it up cautiously and stole back to the bed. Her head sank down on the pillow; her lips moved silently; in one hand she held the rosary . . . the fingers of the other moved slowly from bead to bead. The great mystery that the Blessed Virgin had bestowed on her was so vitally alive to-night. And each time it stirred she had a sweet pain that lingered on and on.

"Dear Mother of God, be Thou merciful to me!"

"—A Cloud Like a Man's Hand"

VI

Just as the day was peeping over the eastern prairies the bright tinkle of the clock sent Peder tumbling out of bed, befuddled with unfinished sleep. Every limb was stiff and heavy as lead. Susie only turned her head and slept on. She was lying on her side with both hands tucked under her cheek; around her little finger were three white beads. Her upturned cheek was flushed; looked almost as if she were laughing. Wary lest he make any unnecessary noise, Peder picked up his shoes and socks and went barefooted down the stairs.

In the kitchen stove a fire was already burning and the coffee-pot had been set forward. The door to his mother's bedroom stood ajar; Peder peeped in. She was not there.

Outside, a fresh trail in the heavy morning dew led towards the henhouse. Peder followed it all the way, but found no one. He went to the barn, paused when he reached the door, and listened.

"Mother? . . . Are you here?" he called, softly.

An elderly, slightly stooped woman with a basket on her arm came out from one of the stalls. The lines of worry that lay about her mouth robbed her face of much of its beauty. Beret Holm raised her head to look at her son, and it was as if a gentle hand had stroked out some of the lines.

"You're up early." Peder went into the nearest stall and began feeding the horses.

"What was it that kept you out so late last night? You were gone a long time."

"Had a little errand to do over at Hans'." Peder did not pause at his work.

"Was there anything special going on over there?"

"I forgot to ask." He went into the second stall. "I guess they're planning to come over before long."

The mother approached the stall where Peder was working.

"Then there will be something happening hereabouts . . .

if such strangers are coming!" Her voice was sweet with happiness. "You aren't fooling me?"

Peder ignored her question.

Beret went to the door. There she turned and came back to him:

"You should tell Susie to quit turning the separator. She isn't so strong now, and needs to take good care of herself . . . I can do the separating."

Peder turned crimson; this was the first time Susie's condition had been mentioned between him and his mother.

"Yes . . . maybe that's a good idea." Then he changed the subject. "Doesn't look much like rain to-day, either," he ventured as he came out of the stall. "Just set the basket down and I'll bring it in for you."

"It isn't heavy."

"But I haven't anything to carry."

For a moment their eyes met; his shy and quick, hers warm with maternal concern. Peder smiled to himself and walked out of the barn.

Not until the milking was done and he had had a bite of breakfast did Peder tell his mother (Susie had not yet come down) that to-day he would have to go to town. Maybe it would be late before he got back. For fear that she might worry while he was gone, he told her about the rainmaker, adding that the County Board was to decide to-day about hiring him. . . . He s'posed he'd better go. . . . Last night he had seen Gjermund Dahl who had urged him to be sure to show up at the meeting.

"I can't believe it, Permand![1] How can anyone want to attempt such a blasphemous act? For blasphemy it is."

"I don't know. Sounds crazy to me."

Fixedly Beret looked at her son.

"But such things are outright sin. You must not agree to it. It's your duty to try to prevent it."

"That's just what we're trying to do!" said Peder, all aglow.

"Is Hans going with you?"

[1] Beret's pet name for Peder.

28

"—A Cloud Like a Man's Hand"

"I told him to come." Peder rose quickly from his chair, shoving it back noisily. "You'd better tell Susie where I've gone . . . I'll have to get started right away."

A few minutes later he was in the buggy, racing down the road so fast that a long cloud of dust lay in his wake. But even this speed was not fast enough. To-day he wanted to fly.

Now everything would come out all right. Mother was on his side. . . . Strange about mother . . . she understood everything . . . sometimes. . . . She'd take care of Susie, all right! . . . Poor kid . . . goes around there making a big fuss about nothing at all. She'd get over it, though . . . he'd see to that! In time. Best to take such things easy . . . especially now. . . . "C'mon!" he shouted at the horse and reached for the whip. "Get some more speed in your legs!"

Reaching Tambur-Ola first, Peder told him of the meeting and urged him to be sure to be there. . . . No telling how it might turn out. But one thing was certain, there'd be enough rumpus to pay him for coming.

The old drummer-boy needed no great urging.

From Tambur-Ola's Peder set out eastward. At Rognaldsen's they were still busy with the milking. Rognaldsen himself had barely got into his overalls. He yawned and wouldn't say much at first. One eye was half closed. . . . Might be that he'd come . . . he'd have to wait until after breakfast, and then see. . . . Most likely it wasn't so dry over Peder's way? . . . That so? . . . What was that rainmaker asking for a good shower? . . . Seven hundred? That's all? Not so unreasonable. Wouldn't take much wheat to pay for that! Who cares, anyway? Let the fools who stay on foot the bill! He for his part was figuring on moving back to Minnesota. . . . And how were things getting along with Peder and that little Irish girl of his? Was he going to quit the church now . . . and turn Catholic? So that he could tear around and sin all he damn pleased? The pope, you know, he's got plenty of forgiveness to peddle out to sinners! . . . Rognaldsen held onto the buggy, his squinting face close to Peder's. Peder was seized by a mad desire to jump out and smash him good and plenty.

At Johannes Mörstad's he was met with a different reception. Here everything promised to go smoothly. . . . Yes, sir. You betcha. Johannes would get ready and go right away. Sure he would. Catch him paying good money for such humbug! No, sir. Not Johannes Mörstad! . . . But then he happened to ask if Tönseten would be at the meeting. Peder was not at all sure about the advisability of inviting his godfather to come; Tönseten might not be quite orthodox in this question of what power was to govern the rainfall in South Dakota. At that Mörstad knitted his brow and grew ruminative. Well . . . just the same, it would be a good idea to talk it over first with some of the older settlers. That man Tönseten was like a grand-dad to this whole county. Johannes, for one, would want to drop in and hear what he had to say about it . . . there was a man who understood politics!

When he drove away from Mörstad's, Peder's blood was boiling. Earlier in the morning Tambur-Ola had stood by the buggy and chuckled up into his face: "I guess the fields ain't the only things that's drying up out here in South Dakota! . . . If that was all, we wouldn't have much to worry about." Peder kept turning the words over in his mind—certainly Tambur-Ola must have meant Mörstad. Worse fools!

At the crossroad by the Tallaksen school he slowed down, uncertain whether he should take the roundabout way northwards. . . . What's the use of trying to stir up these deadheads? What's dead is dead, and there's nothing to do about it! But when Dolly objected to turning north he slapped her sharply with the reins: "Get up, will you!"

The next stop was at Andrew Holte's. Peder found Andrew mending a fence and he wasted no time in stating his errand:

"Chuck that hammer, Andrew, and come along. You can get people to listen to you—I mean just what I say."

Peder's open praise struck home. Andrew's honest face met his in gratitude. He asked, timidly:

"—A Cloud Like a Man's Hand"

"Do you think it will be of any use?"

"I don't know; that remains to be seen. But doesn't it strike you that it's just about time that we younger farmers around here had some say? It's a cinch we'll have to pay the taxes. We certainly have the right to say how the tax money is to be spent. Why shouldn't we exercise that right? There are people around here who have a lot of confidence in you; they're waiting for you to take the lead; that's why you've got greater responsibilities than some of the rest of us." Peder was encouraged by his own frankness.

"Aw—I guess that can't be right."

"But I know it's right!"

Andrew looked at him wonderingly; his big face opened; his whole being seemed to swell with honest frankness:

"Do you know," he confessed, bashfully, "sometimes I get afraid of myself. . . . At times these worldly matters get such a grip on me. In a way I'd rather like to get into politics; I think I could do quite a bit of good."

Peder jumped down from the buggy and grasped Andrew's hand.

"Thanks for saying that, Andrew! That's exactly how I feel. I can't see any sin in it—no, I can't. You're born into this world and I think it's because you're supposed to be here. You must try to do what you see and what you feel to be right, that's the lamp God has given you to go by. If you find people carrying on foolishly, it's your duty to tell them. You didn't get your talents to bury them in the ground."

"No. . . . But they might have been given me just to tempt me . . . so that I might fight and overcome the temptations and grow strong thereby," said Andrew, meekly.

"That's all hokum, pure and simple!" insisted Peder. "You can see that yourself. If everybody should figure that way, life would be empty . . . there'd be nothing to it. No progress . . . nothing to fight for . . . no victories. The only thing to do would be to go out into the badlands and sit down and suck your thumb. You remember the story of the fool who buried his talent in the ground? What if Lincoln had reasoned that way?" Peder slapped him on the shoulder. "Now hustle and get ready. And be sure to bring a couple others along with you. You're acquainted up this way, you know the neighbours it would do any good to ask."

"But I've never had any experience in things like this," Andrew objected, hesitatingly.

"You can't get it any younger!" laughed Peder. Then his voice grew serious: "Here's your chance now. The country and the future are ours; we're going to be held responsible for what is done to-day—you can't deny that. Right now we're fumbling; we haven't a goal. Our biggest trouble is we haven't a ghost of an idea what we're about. You can see it in our politics. Same thing in our church life, too. We simply trudge along in the same old ruts, thinking that it's always been this way, and so it's always got to be the same way for ever. Now it's about time we woke up and rubbed the sleep out of our eyes."

"We are all bound for heaven," said Andrew, quietly; a full smile cast sunshine over his rugged face.

"That's just why we've got to get things in order here on earth," said Peder, strongly. "Because others will come and take our places." He kicked at a lump of dirt. "I wonder, Andrew, if we sometimes aren't looking at things upside down? . . . If our whole outlook on life hasn't been all jumbled up because we've been afraid. . . . We've come into the world—that's an indisputable fact. Here we are. Isn't it here, then, that we have our greatest responsibilities? And believe me, there are plenty of things here that need looking after!"

"Our ultimate object is to know God," said Andrew, kindly.

Peder looked at him earnestly.

"That may be so, but surely our present duty is to live. . . . Oh well, so much for that. Now I won't take up any more of your time, or neither of us will ever get to the meeting!"

"You go and talk for the rest of us," Andrew suggested. "In this matter I agree with you fully."

"I'm going, all right . . . you can depend on that! But

"—A Cloud Like a Man's Hand"

I'm no good at speech-making, that's where you shine. Listen, can't you get Nils Nilsen and your minister to come along?"

"I suppose I could try," agreed Andrew.

Again Peder grasped his hand and shook it heartily.

"Thanks for that! No one shall say that the farmers around here aren't showing any interest . . . the commissioners will not have that for an excuse!"

VII

As soon as Peder drove into town, he felt the excitement in the air. Not even on a fine Saturday afternoon between seasons had he seen the streets so crowded. He considered himself lucky when at last he found an empty space on the hitching-bar behind Johnson's general store.

He went straightway to the Town Hall. Although the meeting had not yet begun, the place was jammed; many were still loitering outside. Only men, all of them in their overalls; most of them middle-aged. Scattered about were groups individually tangled up in hot dispute. Threats and curses broke the tranquil day. On nearing the Hall Peder walked more slowly, every sense taut. Here were carefree sunshine faces, men who took things as they came; drought or no drought, it was all the same to them; they could stand starvation as long as the next fellow. But there were also dark storm-cloud faces whose sullen words foreboded trouble. . . . Let them scowl! thought Peder, and walked on. A boyish delight was upon him. He smiled knowingly at every face he met. He belonged here. He was a part of this thing that bristled all around him . . . unseen it was, yet so threateningly alive, so heavily breathing. . . . This meeting somehow was his, belonged to him. Perhaps he ought to stop and talk with some of these men? Win them over as this morning he had won Andrew? . . . No, no time for that now. The meeting would soon begin, and he'd better be getting inside. There the fireworks would go off, and he wouldn't miss out on them.

33

Their Fathers' God

He elbowed his way through the crowded doorway. Just inside the Hall he brushed against his brother.

"Glad you're here, Hans!" he beamed. "Mother's expecting you next Sunday. You come and stay awhile." His brother said nothing. Peder squeezed in beside him and there he remained standing. . . . They could start any time now!

A noisy group of young farmers on the other side of the room attracted his attention; he forgot all about his brother. Over there stood Charley, Dennis, Tor Helgesen, and a whole army of Irishmen. Tor, in high spirits, with a grin as big as his ruddy face, towered a full head above the rest. His jolly tongue was running loose to-day; evidently there was no stopping it. Peder's glance left the group to wander curiously about the Hall. . . . Every seat taken . . . the commissioners in their chairs around the long table that stretched across the front of the room. Gjermund, tall and thoughtful, alone at the upper end; the clerk at the other. The confused babble that rose in all parts of the Hall steadily made the suspense more compressed and combustible. . . . Where were all the Norwegians? Peder's brow darkened.

It was well past eleven o'clock when Gjermund got up and rapped for order. A breathless hush settled over the crowd. Peder could hear the violent thumping of his own heart; the suspense was choking him.

Half in fun, half in earnest, Gjermund began in his customary unemotional, rambling way to explain the purpose of the meeting:

—They'd all heard about the drought . . . no use making any further announcements about that. It would surely change for the better soon; certainly it couldn't become much worse. Even the Ark had finally stranded on Mount Ararat! . . . He s'posed that everybody present had heard about the public benefactor who had come into the county . . . a Lord Almighty No. 2 who claimed that he could make rain fall on both the just and the unjust whensoever and wheresoever it pleased him. . . . Too bad that there should be a fly in the ointment! This Lord Almighty the Second asked a handsome thank-offering before he would throw open the spill-

ways of heaven. Seven hundred dollars was what this blessing would cost the county. . . . Gjermund's lower lip shot
forward as he glared at the audience. . . . Never before in
all its history had this county paid a nickel for either rain or
sunshine. That's why the Board believed it fair to lay this
matter before the taxpayers. Would they be in the market
for a few bucketfuls of rain? In order that they might have
first-hand information on how this miracle of miracles was
to happen, the Board had invited the miracle-man himself to
be present. Did the audience wish to hear from him?

The ominous *yea* which thundered through the Hall indicated clearly that Gjermund's words had not fallen on too
good a ground.

When silence finally returned, Gjermund nodded to a man
in one of the front seats and all heads stretched to see.
Slowly and pompously there rose a small man, smooth-
shaven and well dressed, his nose big and sharply pointed,
his eyes restless and spying; he possessed the self-assurance
gained by those who must win the confidence of strangers.
First he made a polite bow to the chairman and the Board
members, then a more generous one to the audience.

The man began his speech by admitting humbly that he
might be a Lord Almighty No. 2—here he bowed to Gjermund—but could they expect help from a lesser source? He
paused, self-possessed. Then he confessed frankly that he had
been deeply touched by the nature of this meeting. His listeners must pardon him for taking a moment of their time to
congratulate the county on its excellent Board of Commissioners. Here for the first time in all his long experience had
he encountered an example of real, genuine democracy. What
a wondrous land this would be if all people, in all parts of
it, were given similar opportunity of letting their will be
known when matters of importance were up for settlement!
To be here to-day was truly a memorable adventure; he
would carry tidings of this meeting wherever his travels
might take him.

His theme was the onward march of science. His right
hand, white and delicate, moved in a series of gently executed

Their Fathers' God

gesticulations, much in the manner of an orchestra director beating time, his left hand was pressed flat against his loin.

—Science, the unconquerable David of the present day, each morning sallied forth to do battle with the giant of the Philistines. This new warrior never rested, never wearied. All the mighty strongholds of the hell-born forces of darkness and ignorance were tottering and tumbling before his hand, one after another. Soon all humanity could repose in peace and safety, each man under his own fig tree. Science was the never-failing servitor of man.

The maze of allusions to the Bible sent one listener into a violent coughing spell. Peder's glance flew over the audience and found Tambur-Ola's grinning face. Satisfied, Peder went back to the speaker.

—See what science had done for the medical profession! Mr. Jewell went on. Nowadays doctors could put a glass eye in your head; for winking purposes this eye was fully as good as the original! To-day any man so unfortunate as to lose a leg needs only to go to a doctor and be fitted for a new one; he need not give up dancing and good times for a little thing like that! When a woman grows so old that all her teeth fall out she has only to go to a dentist and have a new outfit installed, and then go on kissing just as heartily as before. And as for hair? . . . Well, why need he waste their time talking about anything so commonplace as hair? But a warning might not be out of place: The Romeos of to-day had better look twice before they leaped; otherwise they might have a rude awakening the morning after!—The speaker held out his hand while he waited for the laughter to die down. Meanwhile his eagle beak lifted higher, a new confidence in his eyes.

—So it was in every walk of life, he continued. Amazing things were being done these days. Here he could sit down in this little Dakota town and chat with his wife in far-away Chicago. A farmer boy had only to put a stamp on his love letter, drop it in a box and say, "Now go!" and no matter whether the object of his affections lived back in Old Erin or among the mountains and fiords of distant Norway, the

"—A Cloud Like a Man's Hand"

letter would go straight to her. . . . Old humpbacked grand-dad used to poke around with his scythe on a patch of land not much larger than a kitchen floor . . . here the speaker stooped over imitating grandfather cutting hay . . . but now his grandson sits enthroned on a majestic self-binder, mow-ing down miles upon miles of the golden wheat while the bundles, neatly tied, roll out from the machine like sausages from a sausage-machine. . . . Talk about progress! Mother in her girlhood would milk a cow long before anyone ever thought of making love to her; but the cream wouldn't be ready for the churn until long after she had become grand-mother . . . imagine what kind of butter that made! Nowa-days the milk was no sooner taken from the cow than the butter was on the table ready for use. . . . Every day brought out new wonders in inventions. To-day men were going miles down into the bowels of the earth for all the gold, silver, and the coal that mankind needed; only a matter of time now be-fore people would be warming their homes with heat tapped from the heart of the earth! Why not? Was that any more impossible than supplying a large city with light by simply setting some wheels in motion?

—And here was the strangest thing of all: Not one of these inventions he had named but that it had at some time or other been looked upon as the blackest witchcraft. Each inventor had been forced to run the gauntlet of ridicule. In every instance the masses had cried unto the heavens: "Hum-bug! Humbug!" This bitter experience he had had himself long ago and this was how it had happened: As a boy he had once told his grandfather that now it required only a few minutes to send a message from Chicago to Ireland; as a reward for the information he had been given the whaling of his life! All of these miracles, he explained with a tremolo, had been accomplished by God-fearing persons who had been single-minded enough to take the good Lord at His word when He said, "Go out and subdue the earth and have do-minion over it."

—His own little success was, of course, insignificant com-pared with that of others. The eagle face became modest.

Their Fathers' God

Everyone knew that the rain was drifting about in the upper regions of the atmosphere. Why should man not draw some of it down whenever he stood in need of moisture? Was there any mystery about getting water from above? He liked to think of the process as milking the atmosphere. Surely they had read about the man who drew lightning down from the sky? The rain was up there, too. The trick was simply to knock the bung out of the barrel. He admitted frankly that there was one difficulty not yet solved—the downpour could not be regulated. Sometimes, like in Iowa a few weeks ago, there came a bit too much, which wasn't his fault; some fool druggist had sold him the wrong kind of chemicals! When Mr. Jewell threatened to go into details of his Iowa experiment Gjermund cut him short:

—Wouldn't he explain to the audience just how he went about this stunt of "milking the atmosphere"?

Mr. Jewell would be only too glad to witness unto them about the truth.

It was the simplest thing in the world, he frankly assured Gjermund. Just as natural, in fact, as that night must follow day; all he did was to work hand in hand with the laws of nature. He paused as if intending to go no further.

"But how?" insisted Gjermund.

—The principle was so downright simple, smiled the speaker, that he would not insult grown-up people by explaining it. He merely shot a charge of chemicals up into space; up there they exploded and created a vacuum . . . a vast, empty room he'd call it. The thick, moist air coming by would rush down into the room . . . "and then, my dear friends, you had better see to it that the women-folks don't step outside without their umbrellas!" And the one thing, he continued, that made all this possible was the fact the moist, rainy air was heavier than the dry.—He smiled benignantly at the audience: Certainly nobody could question so simple a process!

From all parts of the hall faces beamed at him like those of children who hear rare promises of unbelievable gifts.

"—A Cloud Like a Man's Hand"

"What chemicals have this magic power?" Gjermund
wanted to know.

Mr. Jewell shook his head with a knowing smile.

—No, that was his secret! For him to divulge it would
be suicidal. The best years of his life he had spent in ceaseless toil in his laboratory; not a red cent in pay had he received. Now that his process had been perfected and he was
giving it to the world, it was only fair that he should receive
compensation. . . . And no one could say that he was ex-
tortionate in his demands. Seven hundred dollars for drench-
ing a dried-up county could hardly be called exorbitant!

"We have no complaint to make about the price,"
Gjermund retorted, "but we have to ask some kind of guarantee. You admit you cannot regulate the downpour. What
if your sky-busting should bring down a cloudburst in the
neighbouring county, too? And suppose the farmers there
should take it into their stubborn heads not to like it? What
if a couple of them should get too much rain? And what if
they should sue our county for damages?"

The man raised his head and sniffed; then let it sink
again, submissively:

"Do you really believe there can be danger of too much
rain, the way things are looking in South Dakota now?" The
artlessness of the question gave it a sting.

"But you admit that it can happen?"

"If the farmers over there were that foolish, yes," he
granted readily.

"We're not discussing people's foolishness. As a responsible county administration we must make certain about these
things. To the north it's only a short way from here to the
county line; up there they've had enough rain to last them
awhile. Suppose some farmers up that way should get too
much of your cloud-tapping, and they actually could prove
their crops had been damaged? what if each of them should
sue us for three or four thousand dollars? That's one catch
I see. The other is that you cannot make the rainfall even
throughout the county; the Lord Himself isn't always able
to do that. Some farmers will be getting too much, others

39

not enough. Won't all of them have equal cause to sue? You must remember that we are buying this rain out of county funds!" In Gjermund's words lay a quiet scorn.

In the middle of the hall a man of gigantic size sprang up, bellowing out:

"Any commissioner who sees the way things are out here, and won't take help when he can get it, we should get rid of!"

With this threat the giant slumped back into his chair. Stillness fell on the crowd. Over by the wall Tor Helgesen lifted himself on his toes, looked in the direction of the giant, and laughed gleefully. Gjermund busied himself with some papers, pretending that he had not heard what the man had said. He announced calmly that there was now a chance for questions; the meeting would soon be adjourned.

Impatiently Peder's toe kicked the floor. Suddenly the words were pouring out of him—he was surprised at the warmth in his voice:

"I'd like to know a little more about that 'empty room' of Mr. Jewell's. Just how long will it stay empty?"

"Until it fills up!" snapped the eagle face. It lifted high enough to catch a glimpse of the boy who had asked the question. Mr. Jewell gave a chuckle that spread contagiously throughout the hall.

A thing unseen had Peder about the throat, threatening to choke him. Whatever it was he must grapple with it! Involuntarily he pushed through the crowd towards the front of the room. After a few steps, he stopped to look back. But a shove like the roll of a heavy ocean surf sent him all the way to the commissioners' table. When he now looked back he met a blank stare from all over the hall; here and there he heard snickers that might at any moment break out into loud laughter.

"It's a good thing we can afford to laugh," he flung into the faces. "That gives us something to fill the 'empty room' with!"

Mr. Jewell sprang to his feet, a deep flush on his thin cheeks:

"—A Cloud Like a Man's Hand"

"May I ask is this boy a taxpayer? We aren't going to waste our time listening to children?"

The audience pitched and seethed. Out of it rose Tor Helgesen's uproarious laugh and the coarse applause of men who were getting the fun they had come for.

Gjermund rapped loudly for order:

"Peder Holm has the floor!"

"We farmers out here aren't much posted on science," Peder went on. "Until to-day we didn't know about the 'empty rooms' drifting in the air and waiting for rain to come along and fill them. We've got to admit that's doggone interesting nature study! Suppose the rain clouds we're waiting for are still far away, let's say, at this moment floating over China? Or Palestine? Or that they're hanging over Mount Carmel where once upon a time soothsayers and false prophets tried their tricks at rainmaking? What I want to know is, will this 'empty room' of Mr. Jewell's stay here, right above the centre of our county, until these clouds have come all the way to fill it? As a new gospel, this is a corker!" Peder breathed heavily. "But the funniest thing of all is that we are being asked to fork out seven hundred dollars without getting a chance to see what we're buying. If I was a commissioner, I'd ask for a sample before paying out good money."

In a flash Mr. Jewell was on his feet, his arm making a dramatic sweep:

"Gentlemen," he said, unctuously, "I wish to inform the young man that the rain will be wet, *sopping wet*, if you please, just like ordinary decent rain!" He laughed maliciously: "In all the years I've been experimenting with the mysteries of the upper atmosphere, I've never yet found *dry* rain!"

A wave of laughter rolled through the room, subsiding slowly despite Gjermund's impatient rapping.

"Makes no difference whether your rain is wet or dry, Mr. Jewell; you keep your mouth shut till it's your turn to talk. Peder Holm has the floor," growled Gjermund.

—It's queer, Peder thought, the faces can't hurt me any.

41

Their Fathers' God

. . . Great sport to stand here teasing the monster. . . .
Coolly he waited for a chance to continue.

"If this Baal's prophet would only step outside and tap us
a bucketful, we'd make him take fourteen hundred dollars
instead of seven. He doesn't even have the sense to value his
own moisture high enough. Anyone with an ounce of intelli-
gence must see that the fellow is here to fleece us; an honest
man with an honest proposition would be down on his knees
begging for a chance to show us the goods. If this man could
'milk the atmosphere,'" Peder repeated the phrase mockingly, "he'd be the eighth wonder of the world! Instead of
chasing around the prairie, swindling simple-minded folks,
he'd now be the main attraction of Barnum's circus; people
would be flocking there, paying big money to get a look
at him! . . . Why should we make him a present of seven
hundred dollars? Instead we ought to chase him to Jericho.
That's most likely where he came from. If we let ourselves
be hornswoggled by this rascal, we're worse than fools!"

Peder started to walk back to his place, looking neither
right nor left. Down by the door his eyes found a face—
there stood his brother, his good old Store-Hans, beaming
at him. Straight down the aisle he went, deaf to all the hullabaloo that rose about him. A great joy threatened to break
through the walls of his breast, and he felt a sudden desire
to cry and wasn't so sure that tears were not already in his
eyes, because he was seeing his brother through a mist. He
clutched his brother's hand eagerly and held it, inarticulate
sounds rising in his throat.

"Let him make it rain!" . . . "We want the rain right
away!" . . . "You're damn right! We've been drying up
long enough!" The last was a taunting challenge from Tor
Telgesen; the joy of victory was in it.

Minutes passed before Gjermund could make himself
heard:

—It wouldn't hurt to act on Mr. Holm's suggestion.
They'd do wisely in looking at the goods before they bought.

Instantly Mr. Jewell was on his feet:

—Did the chairman really mean what he was saying? To

42

"—A Cloud Like a Man's Hand"

him it sounded like jesting. He would take the liberty to reply in the same vein . . . assuming, of course, that he would be granted permission to defend himself? He wanted to make it clear that the rain would be wet, just as wet as when the Almighty Himself caused it to fall! But the laughter did not last long this time; it faltered, and failed to take fire. When he spoke again the man was all sincerity:

"This idea of demanding the rain first and letting the pay go until afterwards is altogether too childish for grownups. I repeat to you what I said awhile ago: I cannot check the flood when once it starts. Now suppose that I go outside and start co-operating with the laws of nature, which is precisely what you do yourself every time you make use of an invention. All right; soon it starts raining; maybe it keeps on for days, as is often the case when it rains in the old-fashioned way. Then how about me? The County Board need only say, 'Bah! You didn't bring this rain; we would have had it anyhow; get out of here!' . . . I don't mean to insinuate that you gentlemen would do a thing so dishonest, but you can all see if I should comply with such a request here, I'd have to do the same at the next place. I know what I'm talking about! Once I drenched half of the state of Texas and didn't get a red herring for my trouble. I don't want to be made the goat a second time. If you men have any serious questions to ask, I'll be more than pleased to answer them. But I don't want to waste my time with unreasonable children!"

Again the audience was in confusion; out of the tumult rose a jumble of cries and threats: "We want rain!" . . . "Give him a chance!" . . . "We can afford it!" . . . "Sure!" . . . "We don't have to pay the taxes until next spring, anyhow!" And all the while man-to-man disputes were going on loud-voiced and angry. Gjermund made no effort to restore order.

But by and by men stood up to ask questions and gradually order returned. One man wanted to know how much the taxes would amount to per quarter section? Another: Since Mr. Jewell could not stop the downpour, mightn't there be some danger of a second Flood? And a third: How long would it take for the rain to come? The giant in the centre of the hall who had hurled the threats at Gjermund a few minutes before, got to his feet once more, dark and ominous: What were the commissioners monkeying about? Were they stone blind? Couldn't they see how everything was burning up? Hadn't they heard of the hordes of starving settlers leaving the state every day? Why under the heaven hadn't they hired Mr. Jewell long ago?

Dryly Gjermund invited the rainmaker to answer the questions.

Sure and self-possessed, Mr. Jewell came slowly to his feet:

—How long it would take? He could not say exactly. It would not be less than six hours; nor more than two days. On one occasion it had taken one day and two nights. As to the cost per farm, he had figured it out roughly and had found that the tax would amount to a little over twenty cents per quarter-section, or, in other words, about a nickel per forty. If there was any farmer present who couldn't afford to pay a nickel per forty, with a whole year to pay it in, he'd be glad to help that man out! . . . He looked around, smiling pleasantly. For a minute he stood thus.

A heavy-set man, black-cassocked, rose from his seat near the front and asked quietly if a layman might be permitted to say a few words here. As he faced the audience a whisper went over the hall: "Father Williams!"—Peder's heart stopped beating. He stood on his toes to get a better view of the man. The first impression grew stronger as he looked: this smooth-shaven face, this hair of rusty-yellow, these eyes yellowish-blue and gentle—it was the kindliest face he had seen on any man. . . . So that's how her priest looked! Where were the Lutheran ministers to-day? He saw Andrew Holte and Nils Nilsen standing by the rear wall, the latter with a doomsday look on his face. None of the Lutheran ministers were there.

More important matters to attend to now—Father Williams was speaking. The priest's voice deepened the impression that his face gave—he is kindness personified:

"I am not a farmer, but many of those entrusted to my care are tillers of the soil. I see several of them here. I am glad they have come. To them I want to address a few words of advice. This man's claim of being able to draw rain from the skies sounds unreasonable to us; he will have to bear with our skepticism! On the other hand, we would do well to keep in mind that God's mercy is constantly performing miracles among us, and always through the medium of human agencies. The young man who spoke a few minutes ago might well remember that fact.

"This man Jewell comes to us declaring that God has revealed to him one of nature's great secrets. He has called on me and has shown me letters of introduction and testimonials; they seem genuine and honest. If he wittingly is deceiving us, he is the most brazen of all imposters. And if such be the case, we can rest assured that God's judgment will eventually find him out.

"The price is fair enough; the assessment on each farm will be so small that it can embarrass no one. We all realize that difficult times will follow unless the drought is soon broken. Therefore I advise my people to vote in favour of giving Mr. Jewell an opportunity. It seems to me that we can afford to risk being defrauded. But none of us can afford a total crop failure. Mr. Jewell's insistence upon receiving the pay in advance is only reasonable. Consequently there are but two ways open to us. We may either believe that God through this man is sending us the succour that we so sorely need, and this would be nothing new in His great Kingdom of Mercy. Did He not do the same through His servant Elijah? If we believe in Mr. Jewell, we should pay him his price and let him proceed with his work. On the other hand, we can brand him a swindler, keep our money, and tell him to be on his way. This is precisely the situation that always develops when the Lord offers help through human skill and wisdom. Always there is some doubt, some hesitation, because we are fearful of fraud. But

Their Fathers' God

we are now sorely distressed; let us therefore act honourably
and in good faith. Once more, however, I must remind Mr.
Jewell that if he wilfully is betraying a stricken people, he
is an arch-Judas. Though he might escape the punishment
of men, there is One who rules supreme in heaven from
Whose Omnipotent Hand he can never escape!

"I sincerely advise our County Board to engage him. In
so doing I am reminded of an incident recorded in sacred
history: God's chosen people wandering in the desert were
sorely in need of water, when the Lord addressed Moses,
instructing him to speak unto a rock. This seemed to Moses
an impossible means of securing water, and because of his
lack of faith he was disobedient unto God. For that one sin
Moses paid dearly; he was not permitted to enter into the
Promised Land. Let us to-day be on our guard lest Holy
Writ repeat itself among us!"

Father Williams had voiced the opinion of the majority
and now the audience sat back relieved. Shucks, only five
cents per forty! And not payable until next year's taxes
come due. . . . No harm in letting the man try!

A strange dizziness had come over Peder. He had to lean
against the wall in order to keep on his feet. His brother
whispered to him in Norwegian, there was no trace of bitterness in his voice: "That's the kind of help you can expect
from the crowd you've married into!" Peder could not answer him; he had to follow in what was going on.

Gjermund was speaking once more:

"Now that we have received the benediction of the Church
I suggest that we go out and get a bite to eat. I am beginning
to feel hungry. Anyone else wishing to speak before we
adjourn the meeting? Better make use of the opportunity
while you have it. The Board meets again this afternoon,
but that'll be a closed session."

Michael Doheny stood up and suggested a trial vote in
order to help the commissioners decide.

Gjermund scratched his chin, reluctant to put the question
to a vote. His hesitancy stirred the audience uneasily.

"All right," he laughed. "Let's see how many of you

farmers want to borrow seven hundred dollars at ten per cent interest to buy rain with?" The attitude of the crowd kindled his ire. "As a responsible public servant I ask you to consider certain things: Mr. Jewell cannot give us the faintest shadow of a guarantee. He's dishing up a lot of cheap talk. I make no bones about telling you that your decision is madness! This foolishness may cost our county seven times seven hundred dollars before we're through with it. If this man could make rain fall whenever and wherever he pleased, he'd certainly be a member of the President's Cabinet! I agree with Peder Holm: his omnipotence would make him the world's wonder-child. I'm too jealous of the honour of my county to want to see it pilloried before the whole world. I call it a dirty shame. But let the will of the people rule. Go ahead and vote!"

Gjermund took the defeat calmly. He did not even call for an opposition vote.

"Now you can go home and eat," he said. "The Board will take care of the rest."

VIII

Noisily the crowd broke up, pushed out into the sunlight, and scattered. Some left straightway for home, but most of the men were in no particular hurry. Here and there they collected in small groups to laugh and talk; many loitered about, bent on keeping an eye open for further developments. . . . Was the row over now? What would the Board do about it? . . . It would be sport to watch the man make rain. Those who could afford a meal could also afford a glass of beer. Others let the food go for the sake of the beer. Along the bar of "The Golden Eagle" the hubbub was already at high tide and a man could hardly hear his own voice—"*Skaal, karer!*"[1] "Here's to you and for lots of rain!"

With the rest Peder had come out of the Hall. Disgusted and glum, he looked about for his brother, but couldn't find him. . . . Where could he have gone?

[1] Skaal, karer—Here's to you, fellows.

. . . What was that? . . . In a near-by group he thought
he heard his name and he moved cautiously. But when the
men became aware of him they stopped talking and soon
scattered. He knew none of them. A bitter defiance surged
up in him: Well, here he was! If anyone had any bones to
pick with him, let him come on! . . . The passion so over-
powered him that he could neither hear nor see.

Suddenly a big hand slapped down on his shoulder and
Charley's merry voice sang out:

"Where in thunder have you been hiding?"

Peder kept his eyes to the ground . . . couldn't stand to
look at Charley now . . . couldn't stop and talk. . . . He
walked along grimly, Charley at his side.

"Father Williams wants you to come over to the parsonage
for dinner. Dad's there already."

"Father Williams?" Peder couldn't believe his ears.

"Sure; he's waiting for you."

"Did he send you to tell me?"

"Don't you hear me say so? I've been looking all over
town for you. You'll have to come right away."

"No," said Peder, gruffly, "not by a damn sight!"

"Aw, what the devil's the matter with you? Father Williams isn't poison; he's the best-hearted man alive. You're
sure to like him!"

Peder continued to walk along in the same direction . . .
inaccessible, silent, his body bristling.

"Oh, come on!" urged Charley.

"Huh! . . . What you take me for? Eat with that crazy
old fool? T'hell with him! Tell him I said so!"

"Don't be a baby, Peder!" Charley was irritated and made
no effort to conceal it. "You can't expect everybody to agree
with you all the time."

"No, I see I can't."

They came to a street corner and stopped. Peder was
unrelenting; over his eyes the wrinkles drew together in
knots.

"Only an ass can talk the way your Father Williams did

"—A Cloud Like a Man's Hand"

to-day. You folks can sure feel proud of having a leader like him!" He started to cross the street.

Charley gripped him firmly about the arm.

"Now listen! You've got to come with me . . . or I'll pick you up and carry you!"

"Oh no, you won't, Charley Doheny!" Peder stopped and laughed coldly. "It's the first time I've ever seen grown-up people falling for anything so damn silly. And you"—his voice cracked—"*you* voted with them! You deserted us. Why didn't you say so last night? . . . But of course you had to side with your 'big-hearted' Father Williams, the chicken-headed leader of all the asses in this county!"

"Now you shut up!" snapped Charley.

"I've said it and I'm going to stand by it," returned Peder, kicking his toe into the ground. "It's the damnest performance I've ever seen!"

"You're a fool, Peder!" Charley wheeled around and recrossed the street.

Peder watched him go. Dark anger and hot hatred blazed in him. . . . Let him go—the idiot!

From the other side of the street Charley called back:

"I said you were a fool!" But now all the anger was gone from his voice.

"I heard you the first time," said Peder. Black-browed, he walked away in the opposite direction. But soon he lifted his head high and threw back his shoulders defiantly. . . . They needn't think they could rope him in that way!

He did not turn until he was sure that Charley was out of sight. Then he came sauntering back. . . . Why was he loafing around here? . . . He was beaten . . . the humbug had won out. . . . Why didn't he go home and go to bed?

Suddenly he saw a group of men in front of "The Golden Eagle." Angry cries and wild hooting came from the group. Small boys, popping up from nowhere and lining the opposite walk, stared wide-eyed at the impending fight.

Peder quickened his pace. In the centre of the crowd he caught sight of Tor Helgesen and Dennis O'Hara, both in their shirt sleeves, with arms bared to the elbows and with

Their Fathers' God

hats atilt. In front of them was the giant who a short while before had threatened Gjermund. The bully stood silent, his jaw set, his cheeks slightly puffed, and his eyes had a dangerous look. The circle closed around them. Inside the saloon a few minutes ago they had clashed in an argument over who had made the better speech, Peder or the priest; Tor, the eager, self-appointed champion of the former, had been so cocksure and so positive of the superiority of the Norwegian that he had challenged the giant to come outside and let a wrestling match decide the argument.

No sooner did Tor see Peder among the onlookers than he forgot all else.

"Judas priest!" he shouted. "There he stands! Where have you been keeping yourself? . . . C'mon, fellows, let's go and have one more round. Then I'll sing you a nice little song!—You"—Tor turned to the giant—"you just stand right there until it begins to rain! I am so doggone happy because soon I can wash my neck, that right now I'd just as soon wrestle anybody! . . . Hi, fellows!" He spat in his hands and made a *Hallingkast*.[1] But as he came down, his foot slipped, and only Dennis' strong arm saved him from plunging headlong into the dusty street.

"There the pig went down. Now we won't have to listen to his grunting for a while!" the man growled.

Tor stood dead still, glaring at the giant. Suddenly he had clutched both his shoulders.

"Did I hear you call me a pig? Well, now let's hear who'll do the grunting! . . . Here's where I turn you into pork sausages . . . right now!"

The circle of onlookers widened to make room for the wrestlers. Tor, bending himself into a mighty bow, forced his bulky adversary back slowly, their bodies taut like steel springs. So evenly matched were they that the moment the giant found a slight foothold, Tor could not budge him an inch and was forced to give ground himself. Not until his foot struck the edge of the sidewalk was he able to check

[1] A kick or fling into the air by which the kicker aims to touch the beam of a ceiling or some object in the air, and come down standing.

the fierce onslaught. But then he held his foe. Pumping more strength into his arms—his breath coming in short, hot puffs, his cheeks redder than ripe tomatoes—and hurling himself forward in one superhuman effort, he compelled the giant to yield. With new confidence Tor pressed on. The big man was forced back, back, back, and could not stop until he had been pushed all the way across the street. He did not see the sidewalk, tripped against the edge of it and sat down with a heavy thud.

. . . "There you are!" Tor beamed, breathing hard. "Now you sit there and rest yourself while you look for the rain. Don't ever again let me catch you tackling a grown-up man!" Tor was still holding onto his foe. To the onlookers it appeared as if he were about to butt the giant's head with his own.

Then Peder stepped in:

"That's enough, Tor! It'll soon be raining. Come here and let me talk to you."

Tor loosed his hold and straightened up.

"Did you see how easily I handled that baby?" he cried, delighted. "Thank God, I still got some juice left in my old joints! . . . Now, Peder, you tell him some more about the rain clouds over Mount Carmel. That's the smartest thing I ever heard! . . . You see"—he lowered his voice—"those clouds might even be snagged in the mountains back home in Telemark . . . and if they are, we won't be getting the rain for weeks yet. . . . Not for weeks! . . . I guess I know how long it takes to get here!" Tor was so taken by the thought that he forgot all about the giant. "C'mon, Dennis, old boy! You know you and me . . . we could lick this whole country!" With one arm about Dennis and the other about Peder he led them into the saloon.

Tor was in a rollicking humour:

"You know what Dennis and I have been talking about? No, I know you don't . . . because when we looked for you we couldn't find you anywhere. Well sir-ree, when fall comes we're going to elect you county commissioner . . . doggone right, we are! . . . Maybe governor! . . . Hi there, Mr.

Their Fathers' God

Bartender, fill us up three big schooners plumb full of the
wettest beer in the house . . . we've got to have a little drink
on this!" Tor leaned against the bar, keeping his left arm
about Peder. "You see," he whispered in Norwegian, "if us
Norwegians would only stick together, we could lick the
whole county easy as pie . . . and the whole state along
with it, if we wanted to! . . . Old Gjermund is a good
man, but he's a little too scared of the Catholics. Did you
notice how long his face got when the priest was preaching?"

Tor talked on, softly and confidentially. Peder reddened
and felt uneasy. He listened to only half of what Tor was
saying. . . . Most likely Dennis was wondering what kind
of deviltry he and Tor were up to now. He reached for his
glass, touched it to Tor's and Dennis's, and emptied it in
one draught. No sooner had he set it back than he tossed
out a dollar and called for three more.

On Peder's left side gaped an unoccupied space, but farther up, the bar was crowded; many could not even get near
the rail. More people came in, yet the space on his left remained empty. The bartenders bustled about, tapped glasses
full of foaming beer and marshalled them out on the counter.
An arm would press through the row of thirsty men, drop
a nickel, pick up a full glass, and carry it away. Out on the
floor men stood in large and small groups, drinking and
talking.

Peder puzzled over the vacant space between him and
the others. . . . Were they avoiding him? When he turned,
people seemed to be eyeing him queerly? . . . What was the
matter? He recognized only a few faces; most of the men
he didn't know.

The room was a steady buzz of many voices, the stamp
and scuffle of heavy shoes, tobacco smoke, and the stale
stench of beer. . . . Fun to be here, thought Peder. He had
not tasted food since early morning; he was exhausted by
the many hours of tense excitement; now the strong beer
put him in a cheerful mood. . . . Pleasant to be here . . .
to feel a part of this life that stirred all around him . . .
that hummed and talked, clinked glasses and drained them,

laughed and swore without fear—he was an inseparable part of it.

As Peder's hand reached out for his glass, Dennis spoke to him, but got no answer. Somewhere behind him Peder heard his own name rise out of the hubbub, spoken by a voice that was full and clear, and he felt his ears grow large and hot.

. . . "Just before last Christmas he married this Doheny girl. . . . Had to marry her, I suppose. Anyhow, it had to be done in a big hurry. . . . They tell me that old man Doheny isn't exactly pleased about having his ——" The voice drowned in the shuffle of two men passing near-by. Peder hardly dared to breathe. His ears stretched through the hubbub to get what the men were saying.

. . . "Isn't he the son of that Norwegian widow over by the creek? The woman who built that big barn a few years ago? Let's see, what's her name now again? Can't remember these Norwegian names!" . . . "Yes, that's the one," the clear voice affirmed. "At one time she was a little off . . . you know, bats in the belfry ——" The voice slipped away, but soon bobbed up again. "A shame the way the young people are throwing themselves away these days. Father Williams was telling us just the other day ——"

Were they leaving now? Quickly Peder turned his head, searching the crowd. A little apart from the rest he saw two faces close together in confidential talk, the one black-whiskered and calm, the other big-featured. In a cold sweat Peder turned again to Tor and Dennis, who were rocking in each other's arms, laughing so hard that tears had come. "Hi there!" he shouted at the bartender. "We're dying of thirst waiting for the rain! Bring us something wet, and be quick about it!—Step up here, fellows!" Peder moved over into the empty space.

Tor was not too far lost to hear the invitation.

"Hurray—Peder you're a brick! Yessir-ree. . . . See for yourself how this everlasting drought has stripped me of every penny." Tor pulled Dennis with him in order to throw his free arm about Peder: "Now listen to what Dennis and

Their Fathers' God

I have been figuring out: When that Baal's prophet goes out to do his stunt we three'll thrash the daylight out of him! We'll be doing a good turn for the county . . . understand? Not that I couldn't do it alone . . . cripes, no! . . . Old Gjermund is too scared of the Catholics. Now I ask you, Is it fair that the Catholics should lord it over us for ever and ever? Dennis here is all right. I've converted him. . . . Oh, Dennis! My Dennis!" Lovingly Tor drew the Irishman to him.

Peder again emptied his glass in a single draught. Tor did likewise. "Fill them up," cried Peder. "Here's the money!"

Tor could not possibly allow such generosity to pass without showing his gratitude. Clapping his big hands, he began singing the old ballad *"Per Spillemand,"* jigging as he sang. "How's that!" he cried when he had finished singing.

Tor's performance made the men come closer: a packed semicircle formed about the three. No sooner had he ended than boisterous applause and cheers urged him to go on. The praise sent his spirits soaring higher. With glowing eyes, he cocked his head and sang the ballad of *"Anne Knutsdotter."* Because of its merrier tempo he could put still more exuberance into the performance.

His audience laughed loudly and cried for more.

"Not on your life, fellows, not till I've moistened my Adam's apple! . . . Peder, you scamp! Here you stand doing nothing but drink, drink, drink. Now get busy and tell the boys where the rain clouds are, and I'll be trying to think of another song." He gripped Peder's shoulder and turned him toward the circle. "Now tell 'em about the clouds!"

Rows of faces, packed together, stood close upon Peder, regarding him with questioning looks. "Throw him out!" cried one. "That's the bird who doesn't want the rain!"

Peder flung back his head defiantly. Dense mists floated before his eyes. He saw words spring out of them and stand in the air, clear, intelligible words. . . . That's funny, he thought. Before he realized it, he was saying the words to himself. Slowly at first. . . . He was surprised at hearing himself speak. In the same instant his eye fell on two craning

54

"—A Cloud Like a Man's Hand"

faces; one was black-whiskered. . . . I must have it out with that fellow . . . life will be impossible unless I can smash that grin!

. . . "We're just like a flock of sheep," Peder heard himself say. "We let ourselves be led by crooks and old women. It's sad, but it's true. It's no joke, I tell you, to be made fun of by school children . . . to have little boys spit in your face and yell 'Baa!' That's what will happen to all of us now." He saw the words clearer, and he put greater force into saying them. "But it's a lot worse for us to go around harbouring bad thoughts about one another and to say bad things about our neighbours when their backs are turned. Gossip will never get us anywhere!" He paused to see whether that face was hearing him.

. . . "Here we are . . . a big prairie full of people gathered from all parts of the earth . . . Tor from Norway; Dennis from Ireland; some of us have sprung up right out of the sod. . . . No matter where we've come from, we all have the same job—to push together for the goal that mankind has been seeking ever since it was morning the first day. Our task is here to build up a happiness so great and so wonderful that the glory of it will brighten up the far corners of the world. But before we can hope to reach that goal we've got to clear the road of a lot of worm-eaten barriers. I mean all those silly superstitions and prejudices that centuries ago should have been dumped into the sea. These prairies will never be beautiful until we finish that job. Isn't that right?" . . . He looked about him.

. . . "I married an Irish girl; she belongs to the Catholic Church; and here you people are talking about me as if I were the worst criminal on earth! Instead of getting rid of our prejudices we are burying ourselves deeper in them. Or else we build them up into high walls and paint warning signs: 'Woe to the man who peeps over!' The Norwegians must keep on being Norwegians, and the Catholics must keep on being Catholics! So has it been since Adam wore diapers, and so it must remain throughout all the ages, world without end! . . . That shows how ignorant we are . . . and

55

how wicked we are, too! Did my father figure that way when he flung his trunk aboard a boat to cross the ocean? and stake his all in the wilderness of a strange land? Did you men figure that way when you hitched your oxen to a rickety ox-cart and set out for the Land of Nowhere?" Unspeakable ecstasy was upon him as he hurled the words straight into the wall of faces. "We've quit using oxen because they moved too slow. We've thrown the ox-cart on the junk pile because it was too lumbersome an outfit. Who'd think of using it to-day? Now it's about time we got the sugar teats out of our mouths. We need to look about to see what time of day it's getting to be. Things have been happening down through the centuries . . . men have had ideas and have dared to speak them!" Like a wild animal he scented the air and drew a deep breath, the strained faces tugged at him with the force of a great undertow. He felt the power and braced himself against it.

. . . "Right outside our door there is big, bright day waiting for us. Do we dare to walk out into it? . . . For old women it may be all right to bring a pound of butter and a rooster to the minister or to the priest and trade these things for forgiveness of sins. We men have tasks vastly more important than that. We're here to build for a greater justice among men. Prejudices and superstitions will have to go. A people in bondage can neither hear nor see, and are afraid to think thoughts that can be used in the building! . . . Once upon a time when drought and famine had struck the land the people flocked to Mount Carmel. It isn't a pleasant story to read. Priests and magicians were called upon to do their tricks. The crowd, afraid of the spell of unearthly forces, lay prostrate on the ground. Why? Simply because people at that time didn't know any better. The lightning flashed, and they trembled; in the rumblings of the thunder they heard God's voice; His anger was in the storm. The only way to get rain was to make peace with an angry God." Peder studied the terrified faces. How were they taking it? "We ourselves aren't much better. To-day we have listened

"—A Cloud Like a Man's Hand"

to the council of superstitious old fools . . . we are paying tribute to magicians. In order to get rain we——"

A noisy group from the street crowded through the door. "Everybody out! . . . Hurry! . . . Jewell's getting ready to start! . . . Yes—three o'clock over on the hill! . . . Quick, bartender! Where'd you hide all the beer?"

The saloon was in a turmoil. Peder turned toward the bar, his body shaking, his face dark and forbidding. The men emptied their glasses and hurried out. When he looked around, Tor and Dennis had vanished.

He planked both elbows down on the bar.

"Whisky!" he said, huskily. "Give me some whisky!"

The bartender set out the glass, filled it, and left the bottle standing there while he went to serve others.

Peder drank one glass after another.

—This must be water, he thought, pouring out another glass. The saloon was now nearly empty. Heavy stillness filled the big room. The undertow was gone. Peder felt himself floating away on the silence . . . floating, floating . . . vanishing . . . out into a grey nothingness.

After a while the bartender came back, lifted the bottle and held it against the light.

"You must 'ave been thirsty? . . . Fine speech you made. . . . Better not make too much fun of ordinary people. They can't see farther than their noses, and that ain't their fault. . . . Sounded as if you were sore at the preachers? I didn't like that. There ain't no smarter man in all Dakota than Father Williams." He looked at the bottle once more. "How many did you have, anyhow? . . . You better hustle along home!" he admonished. "'Tain't just ordinary pump water you been drinking . . . it's good *old rye*, this is!"

IX

Peder shambled through the door and came to a stop out on the sidewalk. For a while he stood there, blinking at the sun.

"And the people answered him not a word," he mumbled.

57

Their Fathers' God

"Nossir, not a doggone word!" . . . Faces, faces . . .
scores and scores of them . . . vaguely they swam before
him in the sun's glare. Were they grinning again? . . . He
searched for a placid one with black whiskers, but couldn't
find it. That's a shame . . . a dirty, low-down shame . . .
ought to have a few words man-to-man with that face!

He walked a short way, but stopped abruptly, close up
against a high wall of red brick. . . . Hmm, he was mumbling to himself. . . . Now you'd better hustle along home!
. . . Straight home. . . . The bartender's warning kept repeating itself in his mind. . . . That's right! Why, isn't that
what I've been standing here saying all the time? . . . No,
by God! to-day I'm going to Mount Carmel, damned if I'm
not! He smashed his fist against the wall so that blood
trickled from his knuckles. The pain sobered him for a moment, and he pulled himself together: Got to hurry home!
. . . Susie'll be waiting for me . . . poor little Susie! She
just can't get used to living with us 'Norskies' . . . always
worrying and whimpering . . . always so scared!

Warily he picked his way down the quiet, abandoned street.
. . . Funny I can't make my feet mind me . . . get them to
go where I want them to? . . . Can't let Hans see me now
. . . if he finds me drunk, he'd be sore again. . . . Let's see
now . . . hmm . . . the horse is tied behind Johnson & Son's.
. . . The going was difficult, but he plugged along, sometimes on one side of the sidewalk, sometimes on the other.
At last he laid his hand on the bar to which his horse was
tied. After pulling the knot loose and getting the halter off
he clambered up into the buggy, wound the reins carefully
about his right hand, and clucked to the horse. Somehow his
tongue wasn't working as it should and this puzzled him.

No sooner had he got the horse started than his thoughts
went back to Susie. He was muttering to himself:

Can't see what she's whimpering about. . . . She wanted
to get married just as much I did . . . only one condition,
she said . . . we'd have to be married by a priest. . . .
Well, did I refuse her . . . I did not . . . that's how big a
fool I was! Oh, Susie, why did we go to a priest? . . .

"—A Cloud Like a Man's Hand"

Funny she can't understand that it wouldn't be any better if we lived with her folks? . . . She'd never make an Irishman out of me. Nossir, I'm Norwegian, I am! . . . Tor was right, we Norwegians could clean up the whole county easily. Show me a man, pope or priest, that can scare me!

With one eye Peder peered into the thick mist that hung just in front of the horse's nose; the other eye would not open all the way.

. . . That speech of mine was a fizzle . . . t'hell with it all! . . . Wait till I'm governor . . . then I'll tell 'em a thing or two! . . . The buggy was swaying so perilously that he had to clutch the braces supporting the top. Was some one playing the devil with him? He could not figure this thing out: Inside his head a wheel was spinning around and around; everything he looked at spun with it . . . around and around. There was no let-up; the whirling hurt him and made him dizzy. He gritted his teeth and braced his right foot against the dashboard to stop the spinning, but every time he stirred, some one thumped him in the neck and nearly sent him tumbling out of the buggy.

. . . A shame he couldn't get any peace! He was tired and needed rest. Far out in the mist drifted a thought that he could read faintly with his one good eye. . . . Ah, it was coming nearer . . . now he could see it plainly: "If you were any kind of a man at all, you'd go back now and settle with them!" Peder nodded in agreement: Hurry back to Mount Carmel and have it out with the prophets of Baal! Tell old Black Whiskers a thing or two from the Lord God of Hosts! . . . Peder chuckled: "C'mon, Dolly! We're not afraid of 'em! Let's go straight over to Carmel!"

With both hands clutching tightly to the buggy braces he peered out ahead for the side road. . . . Hmm. That's funny . . . he certainly knew where that road took off. There were deep ruts there . . . black gumbo . . . the ruts had been made early this spring. . . . You're plumb crazy! he snarled back at some one who contradicted him. . . . Don't you s'pose I know the way to Mount Carmel? I know my Bible better than any priest or minister!

Their Fathers' God

Soon he found a wagon track that turned west, and he broke into a tittering laugh: See, didn't I tell you?

But Dolly objected to the road. The horse stopped and whinnied.

And that made him laugh again:

What's that, Obodja? You won't go? Ha, I don't blame you! . . . That Ahab is an old son-of-a-bitch of a fellow . . . I know him! But he sha'n't hurt you . . . not as long as —— He smacked his lips and tried to coax the horse: Don't be afraid, Obodja! The famine is great in Samaria. Mother's afraid . . . she thinks the drought is punishment come over us because I married Susie Doheny . . . what you think of that now? Punishment because I married the girl I loved!

Cautiously and unwillingly the horse left the road to follow the wagon track. Peder had forgotten all about the road. Again he was struggling to untangle something in the thick mist up ahead, but his effort only seemed to drive it farther and farther back; it became distant and dim. Finally it disappeared altogether in deep, woolly darkness. . . . Hm— that's funny! He would go out there after it . . . darned right, he'd! . . . He groped, pawing about with his arms . . . muddled . . . pawed . . . catching hold of nothing at all . . . not a thing . . . ever . . . he fell . . . throughout all time and eternity he was falling.

At last he came out of the everlasting nothingness; a hard fist had been pounding him relentlessly in the back. For ages and ages he had been lying there begging the fist to let him alone. So long had his tormentor persisted that Peder's whole body had been pounded into jelly; there was no feeling left in him. All around him pitch darkness. The tiny lanterns up under the ceiling weren't nearly strong enough to light up the room. He was sitting on a floor that was large and wet, trying to locate certain points in reality. . . . Sh! what was that? Out of the darkness came a lowing, sombre and long-drawn, rumbling like distant thunder and dying slowly.

"—A Cloud Like a Man's Hand"

He tugged at himself. . . . Mount Carmel . . . aha . . .
eouf! . . . Still too early to get up. . . . Move over, Susie,
and give me some of the quilts! . . . I'm freezing to death
. . . can't you hear what I'm saying—oh, Susie?

The moaning night wind soughing over the prairies chilled
him. Suddenly he realized that he was sitting in wet grass
. . . couldn't understand that the grass should be wet and
began to grope around with his hands. Everything wet, sopping wet . . . rain? . . . Wet rain? . . . I've never seen
rain any wetter! . . . He struck his fist in the ground—
there's no just God in heaven! Slowly he struggled to his
knees . . . remained thus for a while. Some one whispered
in his ear: "You dirty pig! You're drunk, dead drunk!
You've lost your way . . . you don't know where you are!
. . . Must've been raining for ages and ages!"

Peder toppled over and lay there, his self-pity knowing no
bounds. . . . All for nothing. You've made a fool of yourself . . . the prophets of Baal have won . . . now the Irish
will have plenty to talk about!

His misery changed to nauseating disgust with himself:
Peder Victorious, you're the biggest fool that ever walked
on two feet! . . . You got drunk because you were ashamed
to take the licking you had deserved . . . you poor, poor
simp! . . . Your wife is waiting for you at home . . . your
mother is lying awake, worrying herself to death about you!

—Yes sir, it's true . . . every word of it! hiccoughed
Peder. He began to cry, sobbing at first, the sobs gaining
momentum until he was gasping for breath.

. . . Now he must die . . . he couldn't live after this
. . . this *was* death! . . . The thought brought him comfort.
. . . Death would help him escape from it all! His grief
lifted somewhat and his sobs came easier. Afterwards followed a heavy drowsiness; his whole body like a lump of
lead, he again sank together in unconsciousness.

Eventually he was roused from the stupor by a persistent
tugging at his arm. He had no idea of how long he had
been lying there. Frightened, he struggled to his feet, and
was greatly surprised to discover that he had the reins wound

about his hand. Dolly had detected signs of life in him and
had grown restless. Now she neighed . . . she hadn't the
strength to stand here any longer!

Peder's sympathy for the horse was instant. Not a thing
had he given the poor beast to eat or drink since yesterday
morning—God, what a brute he was! . . . He picked his
way forward, feeling along the buggy shafts until he could
put his arms about the mare's neck. With his face pressed
against her muzzle he gave himself over to repentance and
affection. The horse whinnied and pawed the ground, rubbing her soft nose in his face, begging him to start right
away. A fence had blocked her path.

By and by he had untangled the reins and crawled into
the buggy. He peered up to locate the North Star in order
to get his bearings. Carefully he turned Dolly away from
the fence and let her take her own way. A single idea possessed him: Flee, flee, flee! Before the day should break he
must be so far away from here that nobody would recognize
him. The thought made him cautious. . . . First of all he
must make certain where he was.

Dolly readily found her way back to the main road, and
at once Peder knew where he was. West of town lay a wide
expanse of low land, unused save for haying. The horse
had followed an old wagon track leading far out into the
field and ending abruptly against a barbed-wire fence.

Peder followed the main road until he reached the first
crossroad. There he turned, laying his course to the west.
Again he had to coax the horse before she would obey. But
all he could get out of her was a weary amble, and he had
not the heart to use the whip.

He had not gone far before a greyish light crept into the
skyline of the east. Out of the grey dawn flowed a chilling
breeze. Peder sat huddled up, his face ashen, his teeth
clenched. . . . I'd better get out and run, he thought. That'll
warm me up, and it'll make it easier for Dolly. . . . We got
to hurry. . . . Pretty soon it'll be light . . . we got to go
faster!

Shivering, faint, he climbed out of the buggy. At first it

"—A Cloud Like a Man's Hand"

was as if he had no feet at all. An unbearable nausea filled him; he tried to vomit, but couldn't. Running over the bumpy road helped him; warmth came into his body and he began to feel better. Day neared rapidly. The flood of light grew fuller and brighter as the mammoth red ball rose out of the abyss between the wall of the sky and the edge of the prairie. The coming of the sun cheered him. The fields lay so quiet that the stillness made his ears ring. He listened for sound, but not a straw stirred. The sun gained in brilliance. Two meadow larks, each on a fence-post, trilled to one another their "Good morning!" Their song disturbed him. . . . He must move faster . . . still faster!

Peder could run no farther. Without stopping the horse he scrambled into the buggy. . . . Terrible how Dolly was dragging her hoofs along! . . . The Black Hills were a long way off. . . . If only he could get far enough so that he dared drive in at some farm and water the horse. . . . Plenty of grass here in the lowlands . . . he'd have to rest a few hours and let her graze awhile.

Peder, wide awake now, kept an eye on the country about him. His lifeless body slumped forward in the seat. With a start he sat up straight, his eyes narrowing. An unreasonable phenomenon was bewildering his senses . . . this was all wrong . . . contrary to the laws of nature: There couldn't have been any rain around here! . . . Look! The dust lay thick and heavy on the road and along the side of it. . . . He couldn't have gone very far yet from the place where he had spent the night? . . . It wasn't much of a rain the rainmaker had given them! This was worse than nothing. Life suddenly looked brighter. Peder felt an irresistible desire to whistle, to sing a song of praise, to shout. Over the prairie was spread a heavy blanket of dew. Morning freshness everywhere. The vast expanse lay sparkling with countless thousands of diamonds which caught and held the light of a red yellow sun. . . . Twinkle, twinkle . . . as far as your eye could reach. The song of the meadow lark rose in jubilant ecstasy. And with it broad, bright day! Peder gaped

63

wide-eyed at this wonder. . . . What had become of the rain?

He jerked in the reins so sharply that the horse reared. . . . What in thunder? Then he broke into a hoarse, boisterous laugh. What an idiot I am! . . . It hasn't rained a drop —God Almighty, not a drop! . . . Father Williams is no Elijah the Second, not by a long shot! . . . His eye swept the sky for signs of rain clouds. . . . Not a speck of a cloud anywhere. He cried and laughed at the same time, hiccoughing: I don't care what happens, if that rain will only hold off for two more days, I'll slip the Lord the first ten-dollar bill I get! . . . He turned the horse around and shouted in Norwegian to her:

"Now switch your tail and strike for home!"

x

Susie and Beret were busy with the milking when Peder came. Quickly he unharnessed Dolly and watered her; he took care not to let her drink her fill all at once. . . . Whoa there, little girl! You got to have something to eat before you drink any more. . . . He patted the animal tenderly. . . . Don't be afraid that you won't get enough. He took his time in caring for the horse.

Afterwards he went out into the yard where his mother sat milking, whistling in order to announce the fact that he was there.

"Well, I don't suppose you got much sleep last night?" he asked, lightly, his eyes on Susie's back; she was milking a cow only a few steps away.

Beret shot a glance up at him. His grey face compelled her to look once more:

"Aren't you well?"

"Me? Ha-ha! What are you talking about? . . . Have you looked at the weather to-day? What do you think about it?"

Beret answered in a low voice without looking up:

"To me it looks strange that a married man stays away

64

from home night after night. Have you no thought for the responsibilities you have taken upon yourself? . . . Here we are sitting up waiting night after night. We have no idea of where you are or of what you are up to. You might be dead, for all we know."

"Aw, that'll be all right!" he forced a laugh. "From now on I'm going to stay right here . . . all summer long. . . . I had to wait and see how the rainmaking turned out. A circus like that we don't have every week . . . lots of people didn't see their beds last night!" His voice was quite jovial.

"We better let the Lord mind His business, and try to take care of our own!" said Beret with dark warning in her voice. "Rolling stones gather no moss."

Peder paid no more attention to his mother; while he had been talking with her he had kept his eyes on Susie, who sat with her forehead pressed against the loin of the cow. She had made no move indicating that she knew he had come back.

He went to her and laid one hand on her shoulder; with the other he stroked her cheek:

"Be a good girl and let me do the milking. Then you go in and cook me three breakfasts and a couple of dinners!" His voice was low and warm and he continued to caress her cheek. She said nothing, but under his hand he felt her trembling. She laughed ever so little, which struck him queerly. . . . Why did she laugh now? She wasn't angry with him, then? His mother had finished the cow she was milking when he came in, had moved to another, and sat with her back towards them. Peder bent down and kissed the cheek he had been stroking.

Then Susie spoke in a cold, indifferent voice:

"You go on with making rain . . . your mother and I will stay here and run the farm."

He chuckled at her words and felt better because of her peevishness. . . . She ought to be a bit angry with him . . . entirely all right . . . he wouldn't blame her in the least!

Their Fathers' God

"Little Susie girl," he coaxed, "it isn't good for you to sit stooped over like this . . . I know all about such things!"

"It's fun to milk," she answered, curtly.

"But it's not good for you. You've got to take better care of our little Irishman."

Suddenly hot words, soaked in tears, were pouring out of her:

"You must have been wallowing in whisky? Gosh! how you stink! Can't you get away from me? . . . Here you come home at this hour pretending ——" Her voice drowned in a sob that arched her back dangerously.

With bent head he walked away. He saw things in a haze; stood a moment wondering how far along they were with the milking. Not knowing what else to do, he ran in after a pail, grabbed a stool, and sat down by the first unmilked cow he found.

The strong odor of the barnyard, the friendly breathing of the cows, the squirting of the sweet-smelling milk into the pail, and the song of a meadow lark calling its mate to-day affected him strangely. . . . Mother hopping mad. . . . Susie crying. . . . Oh well—all the same, life was good . . . an endless green meadow where there was naught but kindness. He belonged to the meadow and it to him. Above him lay the blue lofts of the heavens . . . one above the other . . . seven in all—he had heard Susie say. . . . Seven? . . . It didn't much matter. Except for the gnawing at the pit of his stomach, life was good and kind. A warm sun shed beneficent light down upon every creeping thing. . . . Clear, bright day. . . . Rain? Not enough to wet your finger tips in! He sat there weeping, and couldn't stop, and even the crying felt good. Incoherently he mumbled: "I've witnessed unto the truth. . . . He that loveth father or mother more than me is not worthy of me!"

When Peder came into the house Susie had gone upstairs, and she remained there as long as he was indoors. He sat down to the table and drained the first cup of coffee, then the second, and soon was asking for the third. But he was not particularly hungry. . . . Besides, he hadn't much time

66

to waste in eating. Yesterday had been fooled away with a lot of nonsense . . . he better show these women that he could hold up his end . . . let them do the same! . . . What were they kicking about? A man must do a man's work. . . . How old must he be before he could go out and prophesy?

All day long he worked outside, first making the rounds of the farm, going from field to field. Everything on the high ground was burnt brown. Beret's potato patch had fared worst of all, because it lay at the top of the slope and had been set early.

When he came back he hitched the horses to the breaking-plough and drove down toward the creek, where he set to work breaking a new field of bottom-land. Here the mould was still moist and so black that it glistened in the sun.

In the afternoon Beret came down to see what he was doing.

"I was thinking it might be a good idea to have a few potatoes for winter," he answered, briefly, paying no more attention to her. By evening he had the field pulverized and fenced in, ready for the planting. With satisfaction he stood looking at his work. . . . I'll show 'em I am good for something. . . . Sitting around with half-sick women I'm not cut out for. . . . They'll have to get used to it!

That evening Susie did not help with the milking. When Peder and Beret came in, the food stood ready on the table —fried potatoes, fried eggs, fried salt pork, and tea. Beret could not bear fried food. "It must be a real Irish supper you have cooked for us to-night," she said, quietly, as she set the coffee-pot forward on the stove and boiled an egg for herself.

The kitchen lamp had not yet been lit; the late afterglow flooding through the windows gave the women sufficient light to work in. After washing hurriedly Peder slumped into the rocking-chair, his eyes glazed with drowsiness, his legs bars of lead. Good God how tired he was! Though his mother's words had been spoken so quietly, they lingered in the air. He sat listening to them repeating themselves and observing how Susie took them. She, too, must be hearing them. Pretty soon he got up and paced the floor. . . . This probably wouldn't have happened if he had come home last night . . . no, most likely not.

He took his usual place at the table and ate his supper. Susie did not sit down; as soon as she had poured out his tea she went upstairs. When he was sure she didn't intend to come down again he got up and emptied his tea into the slop-pail, held his cup out to his mother:

"That coffee smells good. Can you spare me a cup?"

As soon as he had finished eating he left the room. The purple twilight which hung over the prairies deepened his gloom. . . . It was his fault . . . all his fault. . . . Doggone such a life!

Mechanically he went to the barn and tended the horses for the night. When he had finished he stopped by Dolly's stall. . . . Poor Dolly! She was hanging her head as if all life had gone out of her. He slipped into the stall and patted her, his heart so full that he could have cried. He found some extra fine bedding and spread under her. . . . Now lie down and rest yourself!

Coming out of the stall, he stopped by the post. Pulling out his pocket knife he cut an X into the front side of it. As he cut, four words stood before him, one for each arm of the X: *Never—Touch—Booze—Again!* the words said; he could see them clearly and cut still deeper into the wood.

Meditatively he looked at the carving. . . . Let this remind you that from now on you're through with all kinds of foolishness! . . . You're no longer a boy. . . . Never do things that you need feel ashamed of. . . . Now you go to bed!

Halfway to the house he stopped to study the western sky. . . . No signs of rain . . . thank God for that! His face brightened.

Peder turned quickly . . . the screen door to the kitchen had slammed shut with a sharp bang. . . . Now what's up? . . . There came Susie in her white Sunday dress and her new hat she had bought this spring. Peder stared until his eyes blurred.

"Haven't you gone to bed yet?" he asked, in an unsteady voice.

She was near him in the dusk.

"Hitch up the horse for me, will you?" she said, cheerfully.

"Going anywhere?"

"Sure."

"At this time of night?" asked Peder, incredulously.

"It's the regular time for people around here, isn't it?"

"Susie!"

"I only have a little errand at father's. I can go by myself if you're too tired to come along."

Peder had become wide awake.

"What will people think when they see you out at this time of night?"

"About me running home for a minute?" she asked, innocently.

"Home?" he repeated, emphasizing the word.

Susie laughed teasingly:

"They can only think that I'm so busy during the day I must run my errands at night. Besides, I don't intend to see an awful lot of people." For a moment she stood there, then started toward the barn.

He followed, dragging his feet.

"Put it off until to-morrow. . . . Then you can stay all day."

"We've got the washing to do to-morrow."

"What will your folks think?"

Susie was already inside the barn, where the darkness was so deep that he could barely discern the outline of her figure.

"Is it more of a scandal for me to run home on an errand than it is for you to be staying away night after night without ever letting me know where you are? . . . I'll take Dolly. Where is her harness?" The brisk cheerfulness of Susie's voice was undisturbed.

Though the night was balmy, chills ran up and down

Peder's back as he went into the barn. He said nothing . . . couldn't have uttered a word just now, not even if his life had depended on it.

"Come along if you're afraid I won't come back! I don't want you to sit at home crying your eyes out!" she went on light-heartedly.

Peder was silent. A bitter emptiness gnawed at his heart. He dragged himself to the post, pulled the harness off the hook and threw it on King. . . . Dolly was going to rest to-night! He heard Susie leave the barn and he took his time about getting the horse ready. . . . Did he really have to go to-night? . . . Couldn't she find any other way of getting even? . . . Didn't she realize he hadn't slept for two nights? . . . Aw hell ——!

When he came out with King, Susie had already pulled out the buggy and climbed into the seat. Without wasting any time, Peder hitched up the horse, jumped in, and started off.

The night was clear and still; on every straw a cricket sat chirping. There was no moon; the heat of the day had left a haze that blurred the stars. For a while they drove along in silence. Peder still felt the cold shivers in his back and clenched his teeth to keep them from chattering. He looked about him, but saw only black emptiness.

Susie was humming snatches of a melody which at first he did not hear. But as the humming went on and on more feeling came into her voice, and the words of the sentimental song, "Where Is My Wandering Boy To-night," grew distinct in Peder's ears. Unrelentingly she sang stanza after stanza, pursuing the sad tale to the end.

The longer Peder listened to it, the colder became his indifference. Impenetrable darkness had engulfed him. . . . Together he and Susie had set out; they had been bound for the End of the World; they must get there because there was no other destination for them, and now, all of a sudden, they were travelling this way! . . . Good God—how cold he was!

II. "And They Shall Call His Name Emmanuel—"

I

THE little red-haired Irishman who about midsummer came to take up permanent quarters on the Holm farm soon tyrannized the whole place, and, henceforth, ruled without fear or favour. Whenever it pleased him to set up a howl, and that might be any hour, day or night, some one had to run and attend to his wants. When his nap time came you'd better be careful lest you make the least bit of a noise. After he had dropped off to sleep you had to walk on tiptoe and talk only in soft whispers; you couldn't even give a decent cough. Woe unto you if you disturbed his slumber and aroused his fury! Though he was so little that you could bed him comfortably in the palm of your hand, he soon bossed the whole farm.

The tyrant soon proved the old saying that red hair and a hot temper go hand in hand. He had made short work of his coming, wasting little time over such simple formalities. During the forenoon of that memorable day his father had been hard at work in a field of dried-up oats, which had to be cut now or there wouldn't even be any straw to feed the cattle. Towards noon Beret had come running to the field, crying that he must go get help . . . at once . . . Susie was getting sick . . . it looked as if it might go fast . . . he mustn't delay a second! . . . Beret had been excited and worried, and was gone before he could ask her a question. Peder had wasted no time. Both to town and back he had driven Dolly at break-neck speed. Well, that trip he might have spared himself. On his return he found the tiniest runt of a red-haired human being he had ever seen, sleeping peacefully in the crook of Susie's arm. There was nothing else for him to do but to take the doctor back again; on top of this wild-goose chase he had to pay out ten dollars in perfectly good money.

It was Susie who had named him. Coming out of a languorous drowsiness, and not immediately realizing where the baby was, she had cried in alarm, "What have you done to my Petie?" The name had clung to him, only that Beret always, and Peder sometimes, called him Pete.

While Susie was confined it fell to Beret to bathe him and give him whatever other attention he required. After Susie got up she tried her hand at the bathing rite, her mother-in-law standing over her to supervise and give instructions; but Susie was so bungling and so clumsy that Beret soon saw that this would never do; the child might tumble to the floor and crack his head any minute! "No, no, not that way, you butter-fingers!" she cried in disgust. "Now let me show you how!" Thereupon she unceremoniously picked him up, ordering Susie to get up from the chair. "You will learn in time," she had added in a milder tone as she sat down to demonstrate.

But no sooner was the bath finished than Susie snatched Petie out of her arms and went upstairs with him. There she sat down to cry.

Beret continued to bathe him every morning. In the beginning, if Susie happened to be near, Beret would give him back to his mother as soon as she had finished with him, but as time went on the ceremony came to take a longer and longer time. . . . The boy must be given a chance to stretch himself a little before you bundled him up. . . . Look at him now! For long spells Beret would sit with him on her lap, letting him kick and sprawl to his heart's content. This, however, was only part of the performance: With her knee swaying to and fro in a cradle-like movement she sang to him strange, sleepy songs, in a language that Susie could not understand; the words low and soft, the melodies so sad that all the world's melancholy blinked wide-eyed out of them.

"They Shall Call His Name Emmanuel"

. . . Was this some dark incantation to spirit her child away and give her a changeling in place? So at least it seemed to Susie. Petie always fell under the spell. First his eyes grew stiff and glazed, the lids turning heavy as lead, gradually shutting. Thereupon Beret would dress him and return him to his mother. Each time Susie gave the baby to the older woman and each time she took him from her, she would secretly make the sign of the cross under his back. As soon as she had him safely in her arms she would carry him straight upstairs and put him in the cradle.

Peder's turn to wait on him came usually at night. Susie's confinement had left her weak and listless and needful of sleep. So he insisted that she rest and sleep . . . he'd get up and render homage whensoever His Majesty demanded it! She needn't stay awake worrying. . . . Wasn't he an expert? What else had he done all his life but take care of bad boys?

For a while everything went well. But eventually there came a night of insurrection when the arrangement refused to work at all. Again and again Petie would wake up and break into lusty howls. What could Peder do? He dragged himself out of bed and walked the floor with him, trying all his tricks to hush him to sleep. But no sooner had Petie touched the pillow and his father blown out the lamp than mad screams would come from the cradle. Repeatedly the same thing happened. At last Peder had no more patience left, not a drop. Furious, he sprang out of bed and grabbed the boy—they weren't going to have this racket all night . . . nothing but original Irish sin cropping out . . . he'd soon teach him a thing or two! . . . Turning Petie over, he spanked him soundly, paying not the slightest heed to the howls.

And all hopes for rest for that night were ruined. Susie, who had been lying half asleep, listening to the goings-on, jumped out of bed; like a tigress she snatched the child away from him, unholy sparks shooting out from the brown in her eyes. . . . What did he mean by striking a new-born

Their Fathers' God

baby? Had he lost his mind? Had he gone crazy? . . . Peder came to and could not say a word.

Little did Petie care about his parents' difficulties. Taking a new start, he screamed so vehemently that he turned the whole house upside down. In her nightclothes and all out of breath Beret came running up into the loft, demanding severely to know what was going on here? . . . If they couldn't mind the dear child at night, she'd be glad to tend him herself! . . . Had they let him fall out of the cradle? . . . Look in his clothes . . . a pin must have come loose.

Without a word Susie pushed her aside.

At that Beret was hurt.

"Then he has wind on his stomach. Turn him over and pat him on his back and he'll soon let go of it. . . . I told you not to eat all that cabbage at noon . . . now you see what you get for it!"

Susie blew her aside, walked around the bed and sat with her back towards the others.

The next morning she herself gave Petie his bath. But she didn't try it again. . . . Grandma had nothing else to do . . . besides, old people were so easily put out when they didn't get their way in everything . . . by and by she'd take care of him herself!

Peder soon forgot his reverses of that fatal night; these days he trained himself as though his highest ambition was to become an expert nursemaid. Whenever he came into the house he would go straight to the baby. If Petie was awake, he would take him in his arms and talk things over with him, so ridiculously funny that the others could not help laughing:

—How much had he grown to-day? . . . Had the women-folks been neglecting him? . . . What—not had enough to eat? He'd see about that . . . to-morrow, by George—he would have to get out and help with the work! Why should he be loafing around the house all day long? Did he figure that he could get anywhere that way? . . . Stretch yourself now so I can see what a giant you're turning out to be. . . . In the evenings he would sit with the boy in his arms, cooing to him and crooning old Norwegian songs until the child

"They Shall Call His Name Emmanuel"

was fast asleep. One night as he sat thus, Susie stood near-by, watching him:

"What kind of deviltry are you teaching my child, any-how? Here you were born and raised in this country, same as I was, and I can't understand a word you're singing. You ought to be ashamed of yourself! . . . I better take him and move over home for a while? How can he ever learn to talk if you keep this up?" The words were spoken in a jesting tone, but underneath was a dead seriousness that was visible in her face.

Peder only laughed. Raising the soft hand of the child, he stroked it against his cheek.

To the neighbours he had not said a word about Susie's confinement, going about his work as though everything was as usual at his place. In the evening of the very day Petie was born old Tönseten came hobbling over to ask how things were. Kjersti had sent him; she had had such a queer dream last night. He found Peder sitting in the doorway of the barn and there joined him in a friendly gossip. When Tönseten said good-bye and went home Peder had not even hinted at the miracle which had befallen his house that day, and because Peder had acted as usual Tönseten had not sus-pected that anything had happened.

Several times while she was in bed Susie suggested that Peder drive over and tell her father the great news. Peder said he would . . . perhaps this evening, anyway as soon as he could find time. She spoke of it again one evening as he sat on the edge of the bed, holding her hand in his and caressing it.

"There's no rush about getting word to your folks," he said. "Just let him grow a while longer. Then there'll be more of him for them to look at. No hurry yet! I can see how he's growing bigger and smarter every day; a week from now you won't find his equal in this county. . . . Lis-ten, little girl, to-day he talked to me! Absolutely. . . . Now I'll tell you how we'll go about it: We'll just put it off a few more days and let him drive us over. Then he can tell 'em himself! Yes, sir, that's exactly what we'll do! . . . You

75

won't catch me hiring extra help for the husking this fall. Why should I when we've got a grown-up son hanging around the house all day long doing nothing?" Peder's words were so bantering and good-natured that Susie laughed herself silly. And the days went on as before without Peder making any effort to bring the news to the Doheny home.

One evening two weeks after the great event had happened—Susie was now on her feet again—Doheny dropped in on his way home from town to see how things were going over here.

Peder heard the buggy approach and went into the yard to receive the visitor. After the two had exchanged greetings and Peder had asked about Charley, Doheny went in to shake hands with his daughter; he said he could stay only a minute or two. Peder waited until his father-in-law was in the house, then he unhitched the horse and put it in the barn. He took his time outside. Finally he sauntered into the kitchen.

Joy, warm and contagious, flooded the room. Beret was busily preparing company supper, laughing to herself at the hilarious chatter going on between the father and daughter. Susie was setting the table; on it had been spread a white clean tablecloth. Doheny, with his grandson snug in his arms, was strutting about, his face all flushed and puffed up with joy.

"Is it because he's a red-headed Irishman you haven't let us know?" Doheny assailed Peder, boisterously.

Peder was washing himself and could not answer right away.

"It's no more red than mine," he said, finally. "Besides, it's turning darker every day. You never saw a real Norwegian with red hair!" He faced his father-in-law.

"Norwegian me eye . . . ha-ha-ha! Can you beat that? Holy God! man, don't you see that his face is a regular map of Ireland?"

"You're wrong there!" Peder's voice was deep and full with pride: "That fellow is neither Irish nor anything else;

76

he's an American; some day he's going to be President, if
you want to know it!"

This brought a laugh from all three of them. . . . Peder
did not touch the baby as long as his father-in-law was with
them.

II

Late in August there came to the Holm farm a visitor
whom Peder had not expected. He was down by the creek
repairing a fence when he saw the buggy drive into the yard,
and he wondered who it could be. He waited until he had
finished the job before he went to find out . . . the folks
knew where he was and could easily call him . . . he
couldn't leave the fence like this. . . . Most likely only a
pedlar, anyway.

When he returned to the house he found the visitor's
horse still tied to the hitching-post. He recognized neither it
nor the buggy.

—Well, that was funny. He'd better go inside and see
who was there.

A slap in the face could not have startled him more. He
gasped and was about to leave. But instantly he realized that
such conduct would never do, not now. So he stood still. To
overcome his embarrassment he began to cough. In his own
place at the table sat Father Williams. He was eating a lunch
that had been set before him; near him stood Susie with
Petie in her arms. Beret was nowhere to be seen.

And that saved Peder.

"Where's mother?" he asked in a low voice. As he spoke
he noticed that the door to her bedroom stood slightly open.

Father Williams looked up and laid his bread on his plate,
but did not rise.

Susie caught Peder's sleeve:

"Now you're going to meet Father Williams!" She tugged
at his arm as if she expected resistance.

From the trill in her voice he knew how happy she was.
Instantly the thought struck him:

77

Their Fathers' God

I'd better be careful . . . there's no telling what might happen here. . . . I can't get out of shaking hands now! He followed her with a swaggering stride.

The priest stood up and grasped Peder's hand firmly. For a moment the two measured each other, Peder mute and cold, a quiver of scorn about his lips; the priest with a benign air of kindness, the reward of countless victories over himself.

"Well," he said, "so you're the man that stole my little Susie?" He shook Peder's hand heartily. "And it was you, too, who wanted to burn the rainmaker . . . and afterwards refused to break bread with me? You shouldn't have refused . . . I meant only well."

In this flood of good will Peder felt uncomfortable, and he was forced to drop his eyes. When he tried to pull his hand away the priest only tightened his grip on it, shaking it with renewed vigour:

"Let me look at you a bit. I like your face," he said, frankly. And turning to Susie: "The Blessed Virgin has certainly been kind to you; you have a good husband." The benign eyes came back to Peder. "There are no falsehoods in this face, I feel sure of that. The Lord bless both of you! Only I can't quite forgive you for running off to Father Nolan to get married. That, I suppose, was your idea, Susie?" He chuckled merrily, dropped Peder's hand, and sat down.

Susie hurried to set a place for Peder.

"You come and eat, too," she urged, sweetly.

Peder slumped down on the chair. . . . Why shouldn't he eat in his own home? Nobody need think that he cared a snap about either priest or pope! Now and then he stole a glance at Father Williams, but the impression was always the same—this is a remarkable face!

And the features were rather singular: The forehead high and imposing above spanning eyebrows, very brushy; the nose thick and lumpy . . . unfinished, and needing further moulding; beneath it and entirely out of proportion with the other features was a wide mouth that cut the face in

78

"They Shall Call His Name Emmanuel"

two; one corner dropped lower than the other, especially when he smiled; the whole face smooth-shaven; on the cheeks was a generous sprinkling of brown freckles; high on the forehead they clustered, resembling big birthmarks, but the eyes gave the lasting impression; whenever the lids raised, a blue, warm light streamed out and swept everything else aside. In that light it was good to be, especially for those who were heavy-laden and in need of comfort.

The priest talked on, good-naturedly, about everyday affairs.

Only an occasional answer from Peder when he couldn't get out of answering. He was hardening himself in silence. . . . If the priest had anything to see him about, he'd better get started! . . . He ate the slice of bread and didn't care for more. The priest, however, reached for another slice and helped himself to more jelly. Peder did likewise. But now he ate more slowly . . . he couldn't very well leave the table before the guest had finished . . . else he might think he had no manners, or that he was running away . . . easier to eat than to just sit there looking at the priest! . . . For Peder the lunch developed into an eating contest; now it was a question of capacity. Who could hold out the longer? Pretty soon the second slice was gone and he took a third, which he buttered in mute defiance and ate with deliberate slowness. . . . It was late afternoon . . . he might as well make it supper while he was about it . . . no one should accuse him of running away from the table before his guest had been satisfied! The eating went on.

Susie, feeling the silence that had fallen between the two men, began talking rapidly. Her voice was different now, irritated and forced; there was a high note in it.

. . . Now I've got her mad at me, thought Peder. But I've nothing to say to this god of hers. . . . I didn't ask him to come here. Never will she play this trick on me again!

At last Father Williams had eaten his fill; he folded his hands and said a brief prayer; then got up and thanked Susie heartily for the lunch. Peder paid no attention to him.

Their Fathers' God

He went to the bedroom door, where he asked, unnecessarily loud, in Norwegian:

"Have you picked in the eggs yet, mother?"

Beret met him in the doorway; she must have been expecting him.

"I'll come right away," she said, low and hurriedly, as she came out of the room. "Wait a moment till I find the basket!" There was a touch of fear in her low voice.

But before they reached the door Father Williams stopped them:

"I'd like to have a few words in private with you, Peder Holm."

"All right, that's easily done." Peder went out and straight down to the priest's carriage, walking fast as if he had stepped into offal and was hurrying away from the stink; when he stopped he threw back his shoulders and faced the priest.

"I only wanted to say, my friend," began Father Williams, "that ever since she was a child Susie has been very dear to me; you would have to search far to find another with a heart like hers. It's pure gold. No doubt you know that already. Please be considerate of her! She comes of a people different from yours; she belongs to a different faith. In all things you must deal fairly with her and give her the same freedom that you reserve for yourself. A stranger she has come into your home; it is your bounden duty to see to it that she attends her Church as often as can be reasonably expected. Susie is of a religious bent; all through her girlhood years she loved the Blessed Virgin and was faithful to the Church. You are to remember also that of the blessings the Lord bestows on you two, her Church is to have a tithe. I remind you of these things because as Susie's priest and father confessor it is my holy duty to do so. And now I shall have to hurry along." Father Williams offered his hand in good-bye.

Peder saw the proffered hand, but did not take it; his fists were plunged deep into his pockets.

"They Shall Call His Name Emmanuel"

The priest stepped up so close that he could lay his hand on Peder's shoulder:

"This saying is not pleasing to you, I see, but that, my young friend, is often the case with God's demands."

Coldly Peder scrutinized the man from head to foot . . . who was he to come here and tell him about the demands of God? . . . On the priest's vest his eyes fell on a lump of jelly, and he gave a long breath of relief. Gone was his defiance and his awe; he wanted to laugh good and hard; his head shot up—now he could look the man of God straight in the eye!

"If Susie wants to go to church, I'll not block her way. Sure she can go!" He paused to put more force into his words: "But I'm telling you to your face that I'll never force her or coax her! We Norwegians aren't built that way. In such matters grown people must do what they themselves believe is right."

"But that's wrong, very wrong, indeed! When you took onto yourself a wife of a different faith you thereby assumed certain obligations which you can never escape." The voice was so mild that Peder wasn't sure whether the man wasn't joking. When he understood the priest meant what he said the muscles in his face went taut and he could feel himself turning pale:

"I advise you for your own good not to mix into matters that don't concern you. Whatever obligations Susie and I have towards each other are our own business and not yours. Furthermore, it was just as much her wish as it was mine that we were married!"

"Control yourself, young man. Getting angry avails you nothing. You are wrong—in any marriage the wife is the weaker vessel. It is your holy duty to lead her aright."

"Poppycock! . . . That's not my duty at all. Go and preach that to the Catholics. . . . My duty, just like hers, is to use common sense so that we can get on together. Why have we got it if it isn't to be used? Just for milking cows?" Peder's voice was icy with scorn.

81

Their Fathers' God

"To enable you to walk obediently in the ways that God has laid out for you."

Peder jumped:

"To what?"

"To walk obediently in God's ways in the humility of the Cross."

"I suppose you've got those ways all mapped out?" he asked, in vibrant defiance.

"That I have," returned Father Williams, earnestly.

"Since when?" Peder could say only those two words.

"Since eternity."

A word leaped before Peder's eyes, a glorious word, a word that would make the priest's hide smell scorched. Darn the fool! He was about to clench it, to shout it out, but he needed more words to go with it and was groping for them. Then Susie came down the lawn with Petie in her arms. Peder heard her steps and turned. . . . "What? Are you bringing a new-born baby out in the cold evening air?" He took a few steps towards her as if to order her back into the house, then whirled about abruptly and sauntered off in the direction of the barn. He did not look back at them. Against the barn wall he noticed the post-hole auger which he had borrowed of Tönseten. . . . By George! he ought to bring that auger back right away! . . . He threw it on his shoulder and strode jauntily down the roadway, his head high in the air, as a soldier strutting on parade.

. . . If they had anything more untalked, he better leave 'em . . . give 'em plenty of chance. . . . The old fool preached the Law to him . . . most likely he had saved the Gospel for her. . . . But if he thought he could play pope with him, he had another guess coming!

Peder stayed a long while with Tönseten. He seemed tired and out of sorts, found it hard to collect his thoughts, and talked on aimlessly. "You can't be feeling right to-night?" inquired Kjersti, solicitously. "Guess I must have eaten something that didn't agree with me," Peder answered. It was nearly dark when he got up to go.

On the way home he took his time. . . . There was no

rush. No rush at all. His head bent thoughtfully. . . . Does that fool really intend to stick himself in between Susie and me? . . . He'd better watch out! . . . He's out to rescue Susie's soul for the pope, I suppose. . . . Suddenly he stopped and laughed aloud: What if Gabrielsen, that sap-head, should get a notion to come around and work on *her*? I too must have a soul that's worth rescuing? Aha, this might turn out to be a first-rate circus!

On entering the yard he made a détour that led back of the outhouses and into the barn from the rear. Cautiously he walked to the front door and looked out. . . . No one in sight—thank God! For safety's sake he went into the yard and peered about. . . . No, the priest had gone. Three cheers for that!

It was late when he finally came into the house; supper had been ready a long time. Near the stove Susie sat nursing the baby. As soon as he had washed and was ready, she arose and set his chair in its usual place at the table. . . . Now they must come and eat right away . . . to-night it was her turn to wait on the table. . . . No, thanks, she wasn't at all hungry! . . . She seemed in high spirits; in every move and in every word she was so sweet and so loving that Peder could not help wondering. In her eyes lay a bright gleam that broke into fire whenever she came near him. Then she had to pat him or give him a pinch.

Hmm! thought Peder, can this be the result of the visit? If so, he's welcome to come again . . . whenever it pleases Our Lady to send him.

After they had gone upstairs she said not a word about Father Williams' visit. This, too, seemed strange to Peder, but he decided that as long as she was not anxious to talk about it, he might as well keep still also. . . . There were things, though, he'd have liked to ask her about.

III

As Peder was tending the horses early the next morning his mother came into the barn, greeting him with her quiet

Their Fathers' God

"Good morning," and stood watching him work. Peder felt that something must be troubling her and waited for her to speak.

When she did, her voice was unusually low and mild:

"Isn't it time pretty soon that you have the child baptized?"

"No big hurry, is there?" Peder laughed.

"Such things are not to be put off too long."

Peder turned and filled the manger. Beret waited for him to get through.

"I hardly know what to name him yet."

"Don't you know what to name him?" She came closer, her voice sweet with kindness: "There surely can be no question about that. Your name is Peder, your father's name was Peder, and so was his father's before him. It's a fine name and has been used in your family since time out of mind. It should be good enough for your first child, too. . . . Don't forget that the God of our fathers watches over us!" she added, admonishingly.

"We'd have to talk to Susie about it first," said Peder, going on with his work.

But then Beret became more serious:

"That's not the way your father reasoned when he brought you to baptism. He didn't stop to ask me what I wanted. . . . You mustn't put this off any longer. Have you forgotten what the Bible says of parents who neglect their children's baptism?"

"All right, all right," said Peder, sulkily. He left the barn and went out to look after the pigs. . . . Good Lord! were they going to raise a fuss over this, too?

This difference between mother and son happened on Wednesday. For the rest of the week Beret went about taciturn and low in spirits, with little interest in things going on about her. When she wasn't working outdoors she retreated to her own room, always careful to shut the door behind her.

On Sunday morning she again came to Peder as he was cleaning the barn. Shifting the egg basket from her right

"They Shall Call His Name Emmanuel"

arm to her left, she brought up the question of Petie's baptism anew, as if she had been thinking of nothing else since she first mentioned it:

"Be careful that you don't neglect a duty which you will later regret!" There was an ominous, mystifying note of warning in her quiet words.

At first Peder did not realize what she was talking about. "Now what's the trouble?"

"You have taken upon yourself responsibilities which you yourself don't understand."

"How so?"

"Do you ask?"

"You heard me, didn't you?"

"You must have the child baptized right away. I'm your mother and have a right to talk to you when I see you do wrong."

"You make me tired!"

She came a step nearer:

"Does it make you tired, Peder, that I want you to do that which is right in the sight of God?"

"It certainly does!"

Beret paused:

"You may be smart, Permand, but you don't see very far. Things might happen here that you would sorrow about all the rest of your life!"

"Oh, you're crazy!"

"Don't say that!" she returned, sharply.

"Yes, I do! . . . Here you're getting yourself worked up over nothing at all. Why, the boy's as hale and hearty as a pirate!" Peder scraped the shovel over the floor. "I might as well tell you right now, that fellow Gabrielsen will never baptize any of my children . . . at least not as long as I have a say in the matter. And now you know it!"

"And I promise you," her voice shook, "that some day you will have to answer for your neglect! It will strike where you least expect it!" There was grim earnestness in her dark prophecy.

"Yo-ho and a bottle of rum!" Peder laughed in anger. He

went out to empty the wheelbarrow and took his time in doing so. When he returned the mother had gone, and the subject was never mentioned between them again.

The fair weather lasted throughout the autumn. And with it the drought. There came October days the like of which no living man had ever before experienced. An everlasting sun shining serenely down on a still earth. No clouds. No breeze. Only a mellow light in a satiated stillness. To the west, in the twilight, trailed a witch's veil. What it was no one knew or dared venture to guess. Clouds? Why risk your soul on clouds when there wasn't a drop of moisture in the whole universe? Into the big moonlight nights floated a haze, tinted with cinnabar brightness; under the haze the eerie prairies, in a sleepful silence, stretched themselves . . . stretched and were lost in the haze. . . . God—what nights these were!

On a morning early in October Peder and Susie left the child with Beret and drove to town. There were many things Susie needed now, for both herself and the baby. Father Williams, too, was expecting her to call. She and Peder had planned the journey many days ahead.

A queer restlessness seized Beret as soon as the buggy had disappeared down the road; she went from one thing to another, little realizing what she was doing. One minute she was out on the porch, absent-mindedly gazing down the road. Then back to her bedroom, where she fell to groping about in her big chest. From it she took out a white garment, handling it with careful fingers. Her hymn book was lying in its usual place on the night table. She turned the pages until she found the right place; there, between the leaves she laid a handkerchief. Finally she donned a Sunday dress, picked up Petie, and went off to Sörine's place.

Flustered and out of breath, she entered her neighbour's house. In her bloodshot eyes was a restless look which refused to meet Sörine's. And she had difficulty in speaking; her voice was husky and low:

"One time, Sörine," she began, awkwardly, stumbling on the words, "you came to me. . . . You couldn't see your way ahead or back. You remember that time, I am sure. . . . Now I come to you because I am in the same fix. I need your help and must have it."

Sörine shrank back at the look in Beret's eyes. She could only stare at her.

Beret came nearer, speaking in the same hushed tone:

"If you see some one committing a sin and if it lies in your power to prevent it, isn't it then your duty to do so?"

"Good Lord—both you and I must know that!"

"Yes . . . we do," nodded Beret as though she felt her burden lightened. "Even if the people for whom we do it should not exactly like it. Isn't that so?"

"What is on your mind, Beret? . . . Won't you sit down?"

"Not to-day. . . . Now you must come home with me!"

"Are you in such a hurry?"

"Yes, I am. This matter I cannot put off any longer."

"What has happened? Is some one sick?"

"I will tell you later."

Beret's strange manner frightened Sörine; hurriedly she tied a kerchief about her head and went with her.

In silence, side by side, the two followed the empty prairie road; in narrow places Beret paused to let Sörine walk ahead, but followed so closely that it looked as if she were chasing the other woman. Sörine thought of turning back. . . . What was Beret up to? . . . Was she queer again?

"Are your folks at home?"

"They went to town to-day," answered Beret, close behind her.

Sörine walked on.

After coming into her own kitchen and laying the baby down Beret opened the front room door and looked in; from there she went to the stairway and listened; at last to the window to look down the road. An unaccountable nervousness marked her every movement; she seemed afraid of making the least noise.

"It is only right," she said, in a hushed voice when she came back to Sörine, "that those who have been given sense

should use it. Now I want you to baptize the child for me.
Your husband baptized his father; you must take pity on
his son!"

Dumbly Sörine stared at her; her frank, kindly face utterly bewildered.

"I don't dare do such a thing!" she quaked. Then she
added, beseechingly: "Make no mistake, now Beret! What
would the parents say? . . . We've the minister right in our
midst; the church is near by!"

"Don't think for a moment that I don't know what I am
doing. My mind never saw clearer, if that is what is bothering you. . . . Mark my words, if we're to wait for the
parents to do it, it's more likely than not that the child will
never see the Kingdom of God. Permand is too kind-hearted
. . . he will do naught to hurt Susie's feelings. She is much
the same way towards him. She wants"—Beret's voice lowered to a hoarse whisper—"the child baptized in the Catholic
Church, and so does her priest—I know what I'm talking
about. Such misfortune is not going to happen to any of
mine as long as I am on my feet and in my right mind!"
Possessed by a secret power, Beret bent menacingly over
her neighbour woman; at this moment she was the stronger
of the two. Suddenly her voice and manner softened. "Before I came to you this morning I told myself that I couldn't
have refused you in case you had come to me in the same
errand. Now you must do what I have asked of you, Sörine!
. . . Come and wash your hands first."

"Why can't you take the child to the minister?"

"No," said Beret, bleakly, "that I cannot do. Permand is
dead set against it. . . . Now we can soon begin."

While Sörine washed her hands Beret made the necessary
preparations. She spread a white cloth on the table; on it she
placed a bowl of water. And she fetched the hymn-book.
Opening it at the place where she had placed the handkerchief, she handed the book to Sörine:

"Read this while I get him ready." She hurried into the
bedroom and from the big chest she took a child's baptismal
gown, yellowed with age, which she slipped on the boy.

"They Shall Call His Name Emmanuel"

Sörine remembered having seen the gown before; it was white and had been used the time Peder was baptized.

When all was ready Beret came with the child.

"You say what the book tells you to say. You know how it is to be done. The name is *Peder Emmanuel*. Permand likes the name; Susie always calls him Petie, and that means the same thing. . . . Now, in God's name, we can start!" Beret's shaking hands, her feverish haste, her low, hushed voice, and the secret power that was upon her cast a spell over the other woman.

Sörine lowered her eyes to the book and in an unsteady voice spoke the words of the baptismal ritual. She came to the act itself and asked, just as she had so often heard the minister ask in church: "What is the child's name?" and slowly and clearly Beret spoke it:

"Peder Emmanuel!"

Sörine let drip handfuls of water on the head of the child, saying, solemnly:

"Peder Emmanuel, I baptize you in the name of the Father, and of the Son, and of the Holy Ghost." As she did so her whole body trembled so violently that she feared she would fall in a faint; she hastened through the Lord's Prayer, said Amen, and threw herself down on a chair. Her face was wet with cold perspiration.

"Praise be to God, now it is *done*. May it be pleasing in His sight!" sighed Beret. "You have done me a kindness that I shall never forget!" She carried the boy into the bedroom, removed the baptismal gown and laid it away. When she reappeared she was walking with her head high; her face beamed happily.

"You sit still, Sörine, while I cook you a cup of chocolate. To-day we will have to do without the porridge."[1] She laid the child in Sörine's lap. "Unless I'm much mistaken, out of this fellow you'll some day see come a man!"

Sörine sat weeping and was unable to utter a word.

[1] Among the common folk in the district of Norway where these people had come from, porridge was a festive dish used at celebrations of baptism, weddings, and funerals; it was cooked of sweet milk and rice, and served with melted butter and cinnamon.

Their Fathers' God

IV

Well pleased, the Lord looked down on Beret's act of Christian solicitude; He could not have expressed his approval more clearly; He had seen the travail of His child and hearkened unto her voice. Shortly after noon on the very day she had had Petie baptized a heavy mantle of clouds was cast over the entire sky. Towards evening there fell a hesitant sprinkle, and before nightfall it was raining, quietly but with unmistakable certainty. At last God had deigned to hold His hand right side down. And now, when the drought had once been broken, there came rain in abundance; during the rest of October and all through November it rained much, often for days at a time. Until long after Christmas the prairie lay bleak and bare and glutted with moisture.

Not even the oldest settlers could recall a winter so mild as this one turned out to be. No snow worth mentioning fell until spring had come in the air, and then it never lasted long; the sun, mounting higher in the sky with every new day, made short work of the snow. All winter long the cattle could rove outside, nipping sustenance wherever they might find it. Despite the hopeless outlook throughout the previous summer and early fall, there was no cattle famine that winter.

Save for necessary trips to town and a few visits at the home of his father-in-law, Peder did not leave the farm during the winter. Outdoors the live stock provided him with plenty of work. Indoors Petie lay waiting for him. . . . No more wild sprees . . . gone all the foolishness of youth! He looked at the X carved by Dolly's stall and laughed. Whenever he came into the house he dallied with Petie until the child dozed off to sleep in the sunshine of the father's happiness. In the evenings he read, often until far out in the night. . . . Pleasant to sit here with Petie and Susie so near! Now and then he might look up from his reading and listen to her peaceful breathing. And always with the same deep contentment.

"They Shall Call His Name Emmanuel"

Much of what he found in the books lingered in his thoughts. More so now than before he was married. Like a traveller in a new country, he was overjoyed by every turn in the road. . . . One Wonderland more fabulous than the next. What a dunce he must be not to have thought of these things himself! So clear, so self-evident . . . why didn't everybody see them? . . . Occasionally he felt impelled to share these newly-found treasures with Susie, and he tried reading aloud to her. But she was always so tired after the day's toil that she listened only with ears full of drowsiness. Although he did not say it, her lack of interest in new ideas vexed him.

On Tambur-Ola's bookshelf Peder had found two remarkable volumes—Thomas Paine's *Age of Reason* and *The Speeches of Robert Ingersoll*. The clear-sightedness of the first bedazzled and overwhelmed him. So strongly did the book grip him that, without effort, he memorized most of it. The night he found the account of the Fall and of how Satan was mixed up in the catastrophe, he jumped from his chair and aroused Susie:

"You've got to listen to this!" Jubilantly he sat down on the edge of the bed and read the episode to her. At first Susie laughed. "Now you're cheating!" she cried. "They don't put things like that into books! How could anyone be so wicked?" But after he had made her read it through for herself she flung the book down and turned away from him. "He means the Protestants and their teachings . . . I knew it all the time!" She pulled the covers well over her head, and in spite of all his teasing and coaxing she would not listen to more. "Please let me go to sleep now," she begged, plaintively.

And it ended the same way when he a few nights later tried her with an excerpt from Ingersoll; she refused point-blank to listen to him. Of a sudden it flashed upon him: She is afraid of these ideas, she doesn't dare let them get hold of her! . . . It touched him deeply and immediately she became dearer to him. Nevertheless, he could not understand her attitude. . . . Strange that she, a sane, sound human being, so happy to be alive, with such a robust love for fun, should be afraid of ideas—the most beautiful things in the whole universe! How could any healthy person be afraid to think and to reason? He stopped abruptly, laid the book aside, and caressed her. But she refused to join him in the love-making. That night he sat up much later than usual. One thing was clear to him now: Susie must be handled carefully . . . he wouldn't push her too fast. . . . If he could only keep her away from that damned priest and all his confounded superstitions!

Then came spring and tore away the chains which for so long had held the forces of life in check. For Peder the days lasted from dawn to dusk. The urge to read was gone. He went about his work intoxicated by the fragrance of sprouting, bursting life and of dank, living earth. He had dreams of wondrous things to be, felt them more than he saw them. Great to be alive! he'd nod brightly at all that was unfolding about him. Wholly and inexorably the forces of life were carrying him along. Where they were taking him he did not know, nor did he care—it was so good to be alive . . . to feel the pulse of life beat in him, that same pulse-beat that quickened every living thing.

. . . Now let's hurry and get done with this field, he'd talk to his horses. . . . Hope they're not forgetting to keep an eye on Petie! . . . Won't this day ever end?

Father Williams had been on the Holm farm once this spring. Peder had not seen him. When Susie afterwards told him about the visit he only laughed and said, "When will you cut out all that foolishness and start using your reason?"

Late one evening Tambur-Ola came strolling up the roadway and sat down with Peder on the threshold of the barn, "to witness onto him"—as he expressed it—"about the sins and shortcomings of priests and parsons." On this subject Tambur-Ola could speak at length and authoritatively.

"This is what I came to ask you: Didn't you have it pounded into your head in parochial school that every single word in the Bible is inspired? Didn't you? Well, do you still believe it? . . . Because if you do, there's something gone wrong in your top story. How much have we got left of the Old Testament? Answer me now, just as if you were standing face to face with God Almighty Himself! Only a few threads that the theologians have pulled out. That's all we hear! They figured they could get these fragments to harmonize with the apostle Paul—that's the God's truth about it! Do you think it's the preachers who've peeled away all the rest? Not on your tintype! And that's what I started out to say: It's science and the course of events, human experience, that must get the credit for that job. Take it from me, that rainmaker wasn't so far wrong. Mankind has quit believing that it's God's damnation that shells the teeth out of women when they get old and wrinkled. There's a lot of other notions doomed to tumble. The tooth of time can crunch mountains into bits. People to-day don't heed the preacher's beck and call like they used to. I don't mean us Norwegians, 'cause we're worse than sheep. Other folks are getting too intelligent and too suspicious to swallow the old yarns that's handed 'em." Tambur-Ola tapped the ashes out of his pipe and refilled it from his pouch.

"Now, by gosh! I want to tell you something funny: Reverend Gabrielsen, poor sucker, stopped in the other day about coffee time to see the old woman and to collect a free pound of butter, and what did I do but go right up to him and ask him, innocent-like, how he'd explain the fact that they've been finding petrified fish out in the Rocky Mountains? And what do you suppose he said?" Tambur-Ola laughed gleefully. "This is what he said: 'Don't you believe the Lord might have placed them there just to test your faith?' Yes sir, by God! that's exactly what he said! Doesn't that make him the champion of all our imbeciles?" As Tambur-Ola stood up and got ready to leave he paused. "Don't know as if in all my life I've seen more than one real Christian, and she doesn't live a million miles from here! . . . Coming over to see me soon?"

Whenever Tambur-Ola launched out on one of his tirades Peder only half listened, neither agreeing nor contradicting.

93

Their Fathers' God

From the strange jumble of his own thoughts he tried to sort out one here and one there and link them together.

To-night he sat for a long time looking at the ideas as they came and went; he had a stick in his hand which he kept thrusting into the ground and digging small holes with.

. . . Anyone could see that the ministers had a screw loose. Either they were stupider than other people or else they preferred their own little world of illusions. . . . Most likely a lot of dead dogmas had been hammered into them . . . and they now had been babbling the same things over and over for so long that their brains had stopped functioning.

. . . "Conceived in sin and born in iniquity and therefore eternally damned." That's what they both taught and preached. Never had a more malicious lie been flung out against life. . . . They had picked out the greatest, the holiest, the most beautiful thing in life and painted it the blackest of all wickedness . . . had branded the divine power itself as the vilest and basest of all transgressions! . . . Hadn't they ever felt the omnipotence of love? Why didn't they rise up in wrath against that lie? . . . Every lie reaps its own revenge and they were getting theirs. Now the ministers were sitting around, scared to death because of desires and passions which they could never fully subdue. . . . What was it Paul meant by a "thorn in the flesh"? Good enough for them! Just so they would keep their frost-killing teachings away from life's glorious springtime! What did they know about life? They themselves, most of them, were only weazened runts afraid of the sunlight. Those who followed them and fell for their imbecility turned into scarecrows, more to be pitied, perhaps, than laughed at. . . . Just take that man Gabrielsen . . . stupid as an ox and raising kids. . . . That bird hadn't denied himself—that's sure!

. . . Were they all stone blind? Couldn't they see that whenever the life force seethed and fermented there would be misfits? Life was far from perfect . . . on every hand full of imperfections. Some cattle were dangerous . . . they were born that way. Some cows were in heat as soon as a

94

ray of warm sunlight struck their hides. . . . There were
mad dogs . . . horses that could not be tamed because you
couldn't teach them kindness. . . . Same way with trees and
flowers . . . there were trees that grew so crooked and
knotty that they could be used only for firewood. . . . And
the wheat . . . some heads runty and dried up long before
harvest. . . . And even the finest, like all other growth it
withered and fell to the ground when its time came. . . .
All life doomed and damned eternally simply because a gulli-
ble woman thousands of years ago fell to gossiping with a
snake? . . . All life cursed, conceived in sin and born in iniquity simply because of the curiosity of that wench. . . . Who
was she? . . . A rib? Fine fish story that was! . . . Such
was divine justice? . . . Oh no! No one was ever going to
pump such lies into his children! . . . Mother would have
to scold as much as she pleased. . . . Peder snapped the
stick in two and flung the pieces away.

No dark misgiving could sink its talons into him that summer. The gossip about him and Susie was subsiding. . . .
Plenty of signs . . . especially in Store-Hans. . . . Shucks!
why bother about gossip, no matter how bad it was? . . .
Fools must have things to fuss over . . . otherwise they'd
soon get sick and die!

One thing was clear to him now: As a rule people were
incapable of seeing beyond the narrow circle marked off by
the experiences of their daily life. They could quarrel about
politics until the sweat fell in bucketfuls because politics was
a part of their everyday life. Likewise about the harvest, the
market, and other economic factors. But never independently; always according to clearly drawn party lines. Beyond
that narrow circle the theologians had arranged and settled
everything for all time to come. . . . Were things going to
go on like this forever? No, and a hundred times *no*! Like a
sweet unction the story of the five talents lingered in his
mind. The time would come when there would be neither
politics nor religion . . . neither potentates nor priests!

Political meetings were held during the summer, but Peder
did not attend them. . . . No rush . . . a long time yet be-

fore you're thirty. Now you go out into the desert and live quietly for a while. . . . You don't see things clearly yet. Don't know enough. Can't accomplish anything. Hold your horses until the new day begins to break over the country!

Often he toiled fourteen hours of the day and still came home in the evening bright and erect. . . . To-night he would be real good to his little colleen! Poor girl, going about scared half to death . . . and she who wanted so much to be happy! . . . What was she afraid of? Weren't all those things she and the priest had such faith in the fruit of human thought? . . . Must not human thinking for ever be changing? . . . He laughed with a chuckle: Guess I'd better get a stick of dynamite and *blow* the witchcraft out of her!

V

Peder's inherent desire to understand led him constantly to arrange his thoughts into series and to build these series up into a unified whole. In so doing he was always amazed at finding how radically his conclusion differed from existing and commonly accepted patterns. This experience made him proceed with greater care and vigilance, like a skilful player picking the cards in a difficult game of solitaire. Occasionally all went well; the structure took on meaning, was firmly grounded, and when completed provided a view that made him dizzy with joy. But there were times when he built and built until the whole structure toppled over in a hopeless ruin, and existence lost all meaning. All things between heaven and earth lay in chaos. At such times the despair over his own impotence might grow so heavy that it threatened to strangle him. Little by little it dawned on him: all that was, had to be. It was life itself that was responsible, and he felt like a man gone astray in the desert. But would it have to remain that way for all time to come? Absolutely not! Again and again it had happened that one man, clear-eyed and alone, had risen to turn all history upside down. After him the stream of existence had flowed in new channels until

"They Shall Call His Name Emmanuel"

another man dared to open a fresh course. Peder felt a restless undertow tugging at him; the idea that life was calling him to other things than milking cows and swilling hogs terrified him.

One evening he sauntered off to Tambur-Ola's to return some books he had borrowed. From the barn he heard a doleful humming and recognized "The Song of Life's Dismay."[1] . . . So this was how matters stood with his neighbour? And, sure enough, tracing the humming to its source, he found Tambur-Ola poking listlessly about with a rake, his hat pulled far down over his left eye, his whole body as slouched and hopeless as that of a man in a death cell. For a while he could not get a word out of Tambur-Ola. At last the man spoke:

"Go home and read Luke, then you'll see! You're going to be a minister; you'll need that gospel!" He went on raking.

Peder waited a few moments, then cautiously asked how things were going here.

Fire shot out of Tambur-Ola's eye, his voice was full of fury:

"Read it like you would any other story-book. Then come back here and tell me what we've left. . . . Over in the Bethel church Nils Nilsen gets up and witnesses until he's got all the old ganders standing on their heads. At ours we get the true doctrine preached so pure and so perfect that any old woman can shoot off the whole doggone rigmarole in her sleep. Just the same, the whole smash is headed straight for hell! . . . It's a pretty mess . . . all humbug and horse dung!"

"You and I better seek the port of missing men and there start up a congregation of our own," said Peder, laughing quietly.

The remark stung Tambur-Ola.

"Then you won't have to go very far!" He was working his rake so furiously that Peder had to jump out of the way. His talk came fitfully:

[1] See *Peder Victorious.*

97

Their Fathers' God

"Oh no, my boy, that's not what He had in mind when He went about on earth trying to teach people goodness, not at all." All at once he stepped up close to Peder, jabbed the rake into the ground and propped himself against it. "And yet He shouted it right in people's ears, using the plainest words there ever was. Not once did He as much as hint at churches and ladies' aids. *Not once!* Understand? With Him only one thing mattered. Go out and be kind to one another; the Kingdom is within you. That's what *He* said. You remember what He did in the temple? Now tell me—don't you think we've cooked a fine soup out of His teachings? We build God up into big churches, and organize Him into congregations and ladies' aids, and the people in these congregations keep on scrapping internally with each other and each congregation with all the other congregations. There ain't ever a let-up, and they don't get tired of it. A fine mess, I call it! There's our St. Luke congregation shipping Bethel off to hell; the Bethel crowd goes around scowling at us as if we were a pack of devils. Your own wife don't dare risk her soul's salvation by putting her foot inside the door of either one, although"—he stopped for breath— "though her sisters in both places sew embroidery by the yard and drink coffee by the barrel, all for the honour and glory of God! Don't you think we've done an intelligent man's job out of following His advice, plain as it was? Wouldn't He be pleased if He came around here now to look us over?" The voice became so thin and high-pitched that it snapped; the face was a sneering grin.

Sombre and out of sorts Peder turned homewards. Still a little daylight left. Out in the dusk floated an amber haze. Low in the western sky hung light purple curtains with fringes of gold. Softly they were fading into deep night.

At home on the porch step sat his mother, resting, her eyes dwelling tranquilly on the lingering afterglow.

"To-night the hand of God is painting beautifully," she said, quietly, without moving.

He went straight upstairs. Susie had already rocked Petie to sleep; the child was slumbering peacefully in his cradle, near the head of the bed. Susie, too, was getting ready for bed.

Peder picked up the Bible, opened it to Luke, and sat down to read. Soon Susie came to him in her nightgown, perched herself on his knee with one arm about his shoulder. That was how she liked to sit, because then she could feel how strong he was and still overpower him, always drawing him until she had him.

"Is it the Bible to-night?" she asked, and glanced curiously at the book.

"The Spirit of the Lord is upon me, because he hath annointed me to preach the gospel to the poor; he hath sent me to heal the broken-hearted, to preach deliverance to the captives, and recovering of sight to the blind, to set at liberty them that are bruised,—To preach the acceptable year of the Lord."

Peder glanced up. "Yes . . . the Bible."

Now he had slipped away again! She laid her hand over the page to make him listen.

"Do all Norwegians do that?"

"Do what?" His arm went around her.

"Do they all read the Bible?"

"Oh, I rather doubt it."

"Of course they don't. They're not all that silly."

"Silly?" he repeated, pushing his other knee under her.

"Certainly," she said, decisively. "Because they don't understand it. They only disagree and quarrel about it. That's how all the different sects get started. Why, look at the Norwegians out here! You've got two churches and two ministers and neither one will have a thing to do with the other. That's how much good it does!"

To Peder this thought was so new and at the same time so correct, and yet so naïvely silly, that he had to laugh.

"Well," he asked, finally, "how about the Irish? Don't they read the Bible?"

"What do you take us for? At least, not very many—I'm sure."

"Then the others ought to get started pretty soon."

Their Fathers' God

"They've got enough to fight about, let alone the holy mysteries of the Bible."

"Reading the Bible would enable them to check up on the queer notions of the priests; they wouldn't be quite so ready to swallow everything." Peder talked good-naturedly, but with a teasing note, all the while stroking her hand.

"You mean that ordinary people should tell the learned how to interpret the mysteries? That would certainly be a nice mess! No, thanks, we've got too much sense. . . . Come on, now we're going to bed!" She had stood up and was tugging at his arm. "To-night I want to be good to you. That's why I waited till you came back. Come now!" Her rich sensuousness lay about her like a halo.

"Not until I've finished Luke!" He laughed pleasantly and sat still. "You pile in; it won't take me long."

She turned from him, her whole being changing colour; in her eyes burned a cold light ominously, flared up, and died slowly. Though she was barefoot, she walked as if she were afraid of making a noise. When she reached the cradle and stood with her back towards him she bent over and made the sign of the cross on the face of the sleeping boy. Then she went to the mirror and took down her hair for the night.

"You should quit that kind of reading," she said, indifferently.

"Why?"

"That's for the priests who know how to interpret it."

"There's the Catholic in you cropping out!"

"Oh, is it?" Her voice was cold; she flung one braid over her shoulder.

"Yes, sir. You folks don't dare to think. You're afraid your souls will be tormented too long if you do." He didn't look up: "All this hell-fire stuff is pure bunkum, made up and peddled by the priests. They use it on you like a whip."

"Is that so!"

He became aware of her haughty manner and spoke jokingly:

"I really mean what I'm saying. You're a good cook, Susie; now answer me this: Just how would you go about roasting a soul—that is, purifying it by fire? And the soul has no substance, it's spirit?"

"That shows how much you understand!" she burst out scornfully. "If you really wanted to understand, you wouldn't sit around making fun of holy things; you'd go to some one prepared to explain them!"

"Take it easy, little girl! That's exactly what I'm doing now. There isn't priest or pope or any other authority who knows more than what's in this book."

"And you, a common farmer, think you can understand it!"

"Do you think the Bible was written only for the Catholic priests?"

"Don't they belong in the succession?"

"What do I care about your apostolic succession? The Bible is as much mine as it is any priest's. Now really, can't you see that? My people have been reading and studying it for hundreds of years. As far back as I can remember I've been hearing the Bible explained; I've read it through from cover to cover, myself, and I know stretches of it by heart. Don't you think I've got as much sense as Father Williams? Why shouldn't I have?" he added, innocently. "We're both human beings. You should have heard what a fool he made of himself at that rainmaker meeting!"

Susie said nothing. She had opened the top drawer of the commode and was hunting for something. Suddenly she spoke up; her voice was harsh:

"You've been eating bread all your life. Can you bake it? You should have better sense than your mother. She bakes it and you eat it!"

"Ha! here's where I corner you!" he cried, cheerfully. "If I had heard as much about dough, if I had read as much about it, if I had struggled as much with it as I have with the Scriptures, I'd be baking biscuits and short cakes for your old saints . . . that's the truth!"

Susie was bending over a small box in the drawer. In it she found the object of her search—a medal on a string which she herself had worn as a child. On her way to the bed she knelt beside the cradle, unbuttoned the child's nightshirt, and slipped the string about his neck, carefully concealing the medal under his shirt. When she was in bed she said:

"You don't know a single priest. Still you say things like that about them . . . and you always talk about fair play!"

His hand quivered slightly as he turned the page. . . . There she was afraid again, poor thing! . . . Just because he had been a little rough with that idol of hers! . . . He rose slowly, went to the bed, and stroked her cheek.

"Now I want to witness onto you, Susie dear: God's spirit, His will and wisdom, are revealed through human beings, not only through certain ones in certain positions, but through everybody, through you and me! You and I are snapshots of His being. The only textbook we've got of God is life itself. Sometime the blindfold is bound to be torn away from your eyes. Then you'll see that human experience is the only guide we have to depend on. . . . Pray to the Virgin Mary for that miracle to happen soon!"

She lay silent and motionless, pretending that she neither heard his words nor felt his caresses. He waited, but she did not speak. In the half-darkness surrounding the bed it was impossible to read her eyes. Receiving no answer, he went back to Luke.

When he at length was ready to crawl into bed he stood for a moment and looked down at her. Now she lay fast asleep with the rosary in her hand. . . . That's to tease me, he thought. . . . Oh Susie, Susie!

VI

One day in August while the Dohenys were putting up hay, Michael, in topping off a stack, happened to step carelessly, lost his balance, and slid to the ground. Charley had placed the stake, which was to be driven into the top, against the side of the stack; his father fell on it and ran it into his thigh. Before Charley got him home and to bed he nearly bled to death.

Susie did not hear about the accident until a week after it had happened. Doheny was then in bed; infection had set in and there was no telling how it would turn out. It was Tönseten who brought the news to the Holm farm.

Immediately Susie wanted to go home and take care of her father. She couldn't for the world understand why Charley had not let her know. She talked crossly about him, felt sorry for herself because she was cut off from her people, and said a good many things in which there was not much sense.

At once Peder made ready to drive her over. When he saw her bundling up Petie and understood that she planned to take him with her, he told her to leave him at home. . . . He and mother would take care of him!

Which only made matters worse:

"Do you think I'd go away and leave the baby?" she flared up. "Can you nurse him? . . . Swell care he'd be getting from you!"

"You should have weaned him last spring, as mother told you."

Susie opened her mouth as if to answer, but turned away and went out.

Not many words passed between them during the drive to the Doheny farm.

There they found things in a mess. The kitchen floor was strewn with milk-pails and cooking-utensils, all of them dirty. On the table were stacked the dishes from breakfast and dinner, unwashed and greasy. A dish-towel, grey, spotted with dirt, had been thrown over the bread-tray and butter-plate. The whole room was so full of flies that you had to fight your way. The front room was in no better order. Overalls and Sunday clothes were thrown about helter-skelter on chairs and the table; one of Charley's Sunday shirts lay on the floor. A stale odour struck you the moment you entered.

In the downstairs bedroom lay Michael, alone, waging war against legions of buzzing flies. Charley had gone to town for a new supply of medicine. Doheny would not hear of getting a doctor all the way out here.

At the door of the bedroom Peder stopped short. In here the air was so foul that he found it hard to breathe. The other two rooms were filthy; this one was worse. On the floor along the edge of the bed were bread crumbs, clumps of dirt, and many dead flies; the slop-pail under the bed was only partly covered with an old newspaper; the sheet Michael used for a covering was soiled with coffee spots and blotches of spilt food.

The sight of his father-in-law made Peder shrink—hair uncombed, beard unshaved, the face pale and drawn with suffering.

When the two entered, the injured man stared for a moment wide-eyed at Susie; her coming affected him; he turned his head towards the wall. Peder thought he saw tears come into his eyes and quietly withdrew to the kitchen in order that father and daughter might be alone. There he set to work shooing flies and putting things in order.

It nauseated him to dig into all this dirt, but the thought of the baby having to sleep here to-night stirred him to action. . . . She certainly could see that it would never do to have the baby here! And he and mother so handy with Petie! . . . Peder rolled up his sleeves. . . . By George! that's how they'd arrange it: He'd hustle and help Susie get things in order so that she and Petie could go back with him . . . no trick to get her back here by breakfast time to-morrow. He'd come back for her in the evening as soon as he was through with the chores. . . . That way she could stay here as long as Doheny needed her.

He made a fire in the stove and heated a kettle of water. When Susie at length came into the kitchen to see what had become of him she found him bending over a steaming pan of dirty dishes.

At a glance she took in the scene, and gave a short, choked laugh. Again she laughed, as if she suddenly had come upon something highly amusing and was enjoying it all by herself. One by one her mother-in-law's many hints at the sin of un-cleanliness flashed on her mind (once Beret had asked her right out if all the Irish were slovenly), and now he was standing there, thinking it was his business to clean up in her father's house, and hers too!

Peder looked up quickly. He knew that short laugh from

"They Shall Call His Name Emmanuel"

former occasions; he had heard it a few times before. Instantly he realized that now she was boiling mad.

"What's the matter?" he asked, perplexed.

"The matter?"

"Sure! What's wrong?"

"Oh, leave those dishes alone, you fool!" she exploded, her body trembling with anger. "I've heard enough about the sloppy Irish. You Norwegians needn't come around here rubbing it in. I'm running this house!"

"It can't do any harm if I help you a little. You see for yourself how things look." As he spoke, his temper caught fire . . . so this was the thanks he got! . . . "Not much to be proud of . . . the house looks like a pig-pen!"

"Once upon a time you didn't mind either the pen or the pigs! Besides, I didn't ask you to come here. You could've stayed at home."

Suddenly he faced her. She had said just about enough! The corners of his mouth twitched; once again he felt that dizziness which made him oblivious to everything.

"You might have left that unsaid!" he answered in a hard, low voice.

"Can't I open my mouth here, either?" She stood facing him, erect and defiant, her eyes glistening. Suddenly she noticed how he was taking it: his face white and drawn, his mouth quivering just like Petie's when he was getting ready for a real howl, and she laughed, and now her laugh sounded wholly natural.

"Funny how little you Norwegians can stand! . . . Since you've started, you might just as well clean up these pails, too. Take all of 'em. . . . Don't see how Charley could turn around in here." As if nothing out of the ordinary had happened, she went back to the bedroom.

Peder had cleaned up most of the mess and thrown the dishrag aside. . . . Never again would he desecrate her holy of holies! . . . For a while he stood motionless out on the steps, looking down the road. . . . I suppose I'd better go in and say good-bye, he thought, bitterly. . . . Haven't even said hello to him yet. . . . Well, the one that has common sense had better use it.

Once more he went into the bedroom. Susie was sitting near the head of the bed, chatting with her father. She had replaced the soiled sheet with a clean one, had washed his face, combed his hair and beard, and righted his clothes. Now and then she struck at a fly. The slop-pail was still standing under the bed.

The eyes of both father and daughter met Peder.

Doheny greeted him cheerfully:

"Doggone it if I can see any way out! You'll just have to lend me Susie until I'm able to be around again. She's better than nothing, I can see that now. If I'd only known how smart she is, you'd never have gotten her—not on your life! . . . Poor girl"—his voice was apologetic—"while she grew up she had no one to teach her the things that most girls learn. . . . I'll soon be on my feet and you can have her back."

"Do you know what?" said Susie, jokingly. "Father didn't want to send for me because he thought you couldn't get along without me."

"Is that so funny?" answered Peder, curtly, keeping his eyes on Doheny. "She better stay as long as you need her; you can't go on like this without help. I'll be back to-morrow night. . . . Is there anything you want me to bring for the baby?" he asked Susie, still without looking at her.

"You know what he needs. It doesn't matter much with me. If I should want anything, I can send Charley over," she said, carelessly.

Peder intended only a hasty glance, but his eyes became riveted to her. . . . Was this Susie? His own wife? By the bed sat a woman whom he recognized but did not know. As for her actions, she might as well have been a stranger: Her father's hand lay in her lap and she was stroking it; in her other arm she held the sleeping boy. . . . What did he have to do with these people? . . . They were only strangers to him . . . of their heart-life he was not a part . . . could never be. For him the pause became painfully awkward.

"They Shall Call His Name Emmanuel"

"Yes, sir," declared Doheny, "you can have her back as soon as I get on my feet!"

To Peder this remark sounded like a hint to leave. He mumbled that he hoped Doheny would soon be all right again and hesitated, fumbling with his hat.

"Well, so-long then." He gave one more look at the sleeping boy and left.

The same evening Charley came over to get a few things for the baby and a dress or two for Susie. "She told me where I could find them if—that is, if you should not happen to be at home." Charley was embarrassed, obviously finding little pleasure in performing his errand.

. . . Well, this was certainly a queer message! "Guess I ought to be able to find my wife's clothes, eh?" He grinned oddly up at his brother-in-law. . . . "Come inside while you wait."

Peder remained upstairs a long time. Just as he was ready to come down a thought struck him. Back he went to the bed, lifted her pillow, picked up the rosary that was lying beneath it, and wrapped it in a piece of paper. On another sheet he wrote, hastily: "Better not forget your prayers! Might as well say a couple for me, too—it'll be kind of lonesome around here to-night with both you and that other girl gone." Thoughtfully he went down the stairs: She surely couldn't have intended that Charley was to find these things for her? The idea of sending him upstairs to muss around in their sanctuary! . . . Why didn't she come over herself? Her time wasn't that valuable?

After supper the next evening he hitched Dolly to the buggy, making ready to go over to Doheny's. This was like the good old days . . . he was off to see his girl! He felt so happy and light of heart that he had to whistle. Although Susie and Petie had been gone only since yesterday, it seemed to Peder that he had not seen them for ages. This afternoon he had thought of many things that he must talk to her about as soon as he could get her alone.

But before Peder got started his brother-in-law arrived with a note from Susie. She listed several things she needed, both for herself and the boy. Finally there was a hasty greeting for him. He must not expect her home soon, it said. And lastly, "As long as you've got your mother, you won't be needing me."

Those last words puzzled him. He read the note over from the beginning, but again that final sentence gave him trouble. He saw the words, read them, but could get no further. . . . And here stood Charley watching him. He had to figure out something to say:

"You didn't get here any too soon. . . . I was just ready to leave; another minute and you wouldn't have found me at home. You tell Susie that I'm getting along fine. She can stay as long as she likes. . . . Just a minute and I'll get those things for you."

When Charley was ready to leave, Beret came out with a package which she handed him:

"Here," she said, slowly, in her broken English, "is a little something for Susie. Now that she has a whole house to take care of, she won't find much time for baking. The cake is fresh; I just baked it this afternoon. Tell her from me that if she needs help, I could maybe come over for a day. Peder will get along alone . . . that is, if she wants me."

Peder thought this magnificent of his mother, but immediately wished that the last had gone unsaid.

The following evening he hurried through the chores and prepared to leave early lest Charley beat him again.

It was not yet dark when he turned up the roadway to his father-in-law's house. He smiled confidently . . . tonight he had won! But the farther he proceeded the more perplexed he became. Not a soul to be seen anywhere; the house was deserted; doors and windows were shut tight. Out in the barnyard the cows were crowding about the fence and lowing for attention. . . . Hm! What do you make of this? Has everybody sunk into the ground? . . . Peder walked around the yard, searching. There was the buggy, but the wagon was missing. . . . They must all have gone to town? Suddenly his anxiety increased. . . . Why the devil doesn't she come home with the kid? Here it's night

already! . . . Some people haven't more sense than they
need!

VII

Susie was back again in her old room upstairs. The second night that she lay there she was kept awake by her
father's low moaning. At last it became so unbearable that
she went downstairs to see if there was anything she could
do for him. She found him tossing in his bed, unable to find
rest because of the severe pain.

Without consulting him she went to the kitchen, started a
fire, and heated a kettle of water; after hunting up some
rags she began applying hot applications to the injured thigh.
This, Beret had told her, was the right treatment for sores.
Gradually the pain subsided and Doheny dozed off. In his
sleep he lay mumbling plaintively; the moaning would not
cease. To Susie the sounds were like those of a child who
has cried so long that it cannot stop. As the minutes passed
she became wide awake with anxiety. The night stood by,
hushed and listening, and gave her good opportunity to
think. And there were many things to think about, once she
began looking around.

From now on Susie took full charge. As soon as Charley
came down in the morning she told him that their father
could not be left like this any longer; they'd have to get him
to a doctor right away. This trouble—she could tell that now
—was no ordinary sore!

"But he'll never consent to it," Charley objected, darkly.
"You know how set he is on having his own way. Perhaps
I'd better try to get a doctor to come out here. I've men-
tioned it to him time and again, but he won't hear of it."

"You do as I say. During the night I figured it all out.
You get the wagon ready, put lots of hay in the bottom;
we'll throw in all the bedding we've got; I'll take Petie and
go along. Just do as I say and we'll get him to go, all right!"

Her determination had a good effect on Charley; he went
out, got the wagon ready and the horses harnessed.

109

Their Fathers' God

To their father they said nothing of their plans until after breakfast. When Susie had finished dressing the baby for the journey she went into the bedroom and announced:

"Well, Michael Doheny, get your Sunday clothes on; we're going out for a ride. Charley is hitching up."

Her father looked up suspiciously:

"Now what sort of deviltry are you up to?"

"Nothing in particular. Except that I want to go along with you to the doctor. I'll have to find out how to take care of you."

"Not on your life! You're doing better already than all the pill-slingers in Christendom."

Susie pretended not to have heard him:

"Wait till you see the bed we've rigged up for you! It's fit for a king. Hurry up now, or I'll take my little Mikey and move back to the Norskies." She laughed, but back of the laughter was a solid wall of resolution.

"Terrible how bossy you've got since you moved away. They must be spoiling you over there?"

"You're quite right, child. All I do from morning to night is going around giving orders. You should see them hop when I snap my fingers! . . . Here's a clean shirt for you. And here is your good suit. Do you want me to help you?"

"Why, you little tike! What do you mean by coming around here ordering your own father about? Aren't you ashamed of yourself?" Doheny scolded and protested until he was beaming with such good humour that Susie could only laugh at him. He pulled the shirt over his head, sputtering: "Begor! that Norwegian of yours had better go find himself a new wife. I'll never let you get away from here again, that's sure. Bring me my overalls—no, not my Sunday pants. That shows how much sense you've got!"

"Be good, now, and dress decently."

"Be damned if I do! How would I ever get that pair over all these bandages? If you don't show any better sense with the Norwegians, they must think I've got a half-wit for a daughter."

"They Shall Call His Name Emmanuel"

Susie saw that he was right this time, and handed him his overalls:

"Well, if you insist on looking like a pig, it's all right with me!"

She pulled and fussed, Doheny expostulating, and it seemed they never before had had so much fun. Finally he was in the wagon, bolstered up by pillows under his head and arms, and well covered with quilts and blankets. When she ran in to get the baby Doheny shouted after her that they'd been waiting for her since long before daybreak. Why all this delay? Didn't she know they were in a hurry? They weren't used to fiddling away precious time waiting for slow-poke Norwegians! "Get started, Charley. Let her stay here and putter around as much as she likes!"

When Susie had settled herself in the seat with the boy on her lap, she laughed happily:

"My mother-in-law should see me now!"

"How are you two getting along?" Charley was as full of good spirits as his father. "Is she really as kind-hearted as she looks? Darn nice of her to send that cake yesterday."

"Kind-hearted? No end of kindness there!" Susie assured him, laughing at the same time. "She'd be fit for sainthood any day . . . it's really hard on an ordinary sinner to live with her." The last came as an afterthought.

Charley laughed uproariously.

"That's nothing to laugh about!" said Susie, reprovingly. "There's just nobody like her when it comes to goodness. The last few weeks before Mikey came"—Susie bent over the child and caressed him—"she wouldn't let me stir. Not to mention doing any work. You should have seen all the attention I got!"

"Do you call him Mikey?"

"Can't I call him whatever I please?"

"You talk as if you'd landed in paradise already!" grumbled Doheny, angrily.

"Isn't that exactly what I'm sitting here telling you?"

"Is that why you never come over to see us?" he asked, sulkily.

Their Fathers' God

"I suppose it is." She held the boy closer to her and looked straight ahead.

"It must be rather tough to live in a house with some one who's always trying to be so holy," mused Charley. "What do you suppose she'd say if I should come around some night and ask you to go to a dance?"

At first Susie did not answer him.

"Old folks aren't always so easy to please. Have you forgotten old grandma? Talk about crazy notions! And wasn't she saying her prayers all the time? It's strange with old people. Why, just take father for instance!" she added, mischievously.

"Have you really quit dancing for good? You used to be so crazy about it?" twitted Charley.

"Come and try me sometime!"

"Begor! that's right," agreed Doheny. "You ought to have a little fun even if you're married. Your father-in-law was no saint, that's certain!"

At once Susie was all eagerness:

"Oh, tell me about him!"

"Sure! What do I know about him?" Doheny shifted himself to a more restful position among the cushions. "I both saw and talked to him many times, but that didn't help me any. He never did learn to speak civilized. You know he lost his life that awful winter—let's see, that'll be fifteen years ago next spring? I remember the day as well as if it was yesterday. Cold and blizzardy. He went off to get a doctor for a neighbour that was dying. Some say he went for a preacher; no one could ever make me believe it. Not that fellow! You can just bet your father-in-law was no saint. The Norwegians had better not try to canonize him!"

Susie had become deeply interested:

—What did Per Hansa look like?[1] Was he handsome? Was he kind? . . . He was quick-tempered, I'll bet? . . . She felt that she shouldn't have asked that question, and added, eagerly: "Do you remember him well?"

"Have you ever heard a worse fool? I certainly can remem-

[1] See *Giants in the Earth*.

112

ber him when I sit here telling you about him! Has the pooken stolen your wits?"

"Well, tell me, then!"

"Ask your mother-in-law."

"She doesn't know how to talk."

"No?—Well, that shows what you've gone and got yourself into. Good enough for you!"

"Did the Irish and Norwegians mix a lot then?"

"What a fool you are! Do you s'pose they knew how to talk then, when she can't even now?"

"They certainly can *talk*!"

"A minute ago you yourself said they couldn't. You are a numskull. Drive up, Charley, and don't listen to her!"

"Were they kind?"

"Kind? My God! how kind they were! No words for it. Why, one time I saw with my own eyes how Mrs. Tonaas' first husband, the huffiest and huskiest bully that ever lived, take Joe Gill and heave him right up into heaven. That's as true as I'm sitting here telling it to you. Your father-in-law was with him that time. Nice relations you've got."

"Are all Norwegians so terribly clean?"

"I guess so! We used to say that they peeled the potatoes both before and after they ate them, and still they didn't get them clean enough to suit them." Suddenly Doheny broke into a jolly laugh. "I'll bet your mother-in-law has been giving you hell for your sloppiness."

"She's done no such thing!"

"Oh yes, she has, child—I can tell it from your back!"

For a while they found great merriment in this new turn of the conversation. The brother teased; the father helped, and that was worse, because he always exaggerated so heartlessly. All three of them laughed together so loudly that Petie woke and joined in. Then Susie had to laugh at him. All about them quivered the bright day. Huge and deep blue the sky floated above and far beyond every living thing. This was the first time in years that they had been out riding together. Father and son were so happy and grateful at having Susie with them once more that they could not help bantering with her. For the time Doheny had forgotten all about his thigh.

VIII

Doctor Green had received his medical degree at Edinburgh University. After having moved here he had soon become known both far and wide for his proficiency as well as for his fiery temper. It was said that if he got angry, he had no scruples about booting a patient into the street. Added to that, he was a notorious freethinker. Nevertheless, he was kept busy both day and night, for a more skilful physician was not to be found in this part of South Dakota.

It was to him that Doheny wished to be taken.

The strong smell of medicines in the waiting-room and the sight of the many faces that lined the walls (on some were stamped marks of long suffering) obliterated with one stroke the gay mood of the three during their journey thither.

From the moment Doctor Green began examining Doheny until they were again out on the street matters went from bad to worse. No sooner had he seen the sore and the bandages Susie had wrapped around than he flew into a violent rage. He called Doheny an old fool and wanted to know what he meant by this? There were easier ways of committing suicide! Didn't he ever read the papers? Or maybe he wanted to make corned beef out of his leg? In that case, it was ready for use any time now! With that he turned his wrath on Charley and Susie. Hadn't they ever gone to school? Hadn't they been raised in America? Did everybody out on the prairie live like pigs?

When he set to work on the wound it was with a hard hand. First he thrust instruments into both sides and tore it wide open; as if that weren't enough, he took his knife and slashed about heartlessly, mostly upwards. Doheny groaned with the pain; Susie gritted her teeth and held the baby so tightly that he began to cry; Charley stood looking on, pale and silent.

"Now that will do for to-day," said the doctor, when he

114

"They Shall Call His Name Emmanuel"

had bandaged the leg. "This would have been no trick at all if you had come right away instead of messing with it yourself. You've about one chance in fifty of saving that leg. And I tell you, that chance looks pretty slim. You're to be back here again at ten to-morrow morning."

"How can I do that?" cried Doheny, terrified. "We live 'way out on the prairie. Can't you give me some medicine to take along?"

"Rent a room some place in town. Your daughter can stay here with you." When he saw how the three stood staring dumbfounded at one another, his anger flared up anew: "Don't you want to live, man? Now listen to me"—he turned menacingly on Charley—"if your father isn't here at ten o'clock to-morrow morning, you needn't bring him around later. You understand?"

With that ominous warning he filled a bottle with medicine and gave it to Charley, together with a package of sterilized bandages, and the instructions to Susie:

"At ten o'clock to-night and at two in the morning you're to change the bandages. Understand? Now get this into your head: first you take a bowl and boil it in water for ten minutes. Do you hear me? I said *boil* it! You're to put the cotton in the bowl and pour enough of the solution on it until it's sopping wet. Now let me look at your hands."

Timidly Susie held forth her right hand.

"When I say hands I mean both. Or have you only one?"

Shifting the baby to her right arm, she extended her other hand. She blushed furiously as the enraged man twisted and examined her hands.

"Nnnh!" he snorted. "It won't hurt if you wash them with soap before you set to work on the sore. There's dirt enough in it already. . . . Here, let me tell you something." His voice lowered to a confidential whisper that trembled with exasperation: "It was old Satan himself who invented dirt. It was dirt that caused the fall of man. You didn't know that, eh? This is how it happened: Eve gave Adam that apple without washing it first!"

With no further formality he opened the door wide and

shoved them out. In the waiting-room sat new faces that met theirs questioningly. Impossible to talk things over in front of all these strangers. The three went out to the wagon, Doheny limping and leaning heavily on Charley.

"We'd better try Flannigan's. Perhaps they'd have a room to spare?" suggested Charley.

"Drive home!" said Doheny, firmly. "No trouble to get me here by ten in the morning as long as the weather stays like this. I don't want to butt in on any strangers."

"We are not going home!" declared Susie, emphatically. "Drive straight over to Father Williams'. He's got a big house. I'll go in and ask him myself."

"You're crazy, Susie! We can't go begging our way into the parsonage," objected Charley, disgusted.

"Who said beg? Can't father pay?"

"Do as your sister says!" commanded Doheny, angrily.

"Because you know how big-hearted the priest is. You remember how he came and looked after mother?"

"That's just why we can't do it!" insisted Charley.

"Shut up and listen when sensible people talk! If he takes me in, he won't be doing it for nothing."

"It's a low-down thing to do," maintained Charley, defiantly, as he untied the horses.

Anyone overhearing them as they stood there quarrelling would have sworn that agreement among them was utterly impossible. The bright sunshine of harmony which a short while before had made their faces beam joyously had now vanished entirely.

Presently the wagon stopped in front of the parsonage; on the way there not a word had been spoken by anyone.

"I sure won't go in," said Charley, curtly.

"Nobody's asked you to. Hold the baby while I get down," Susie commanded.

Through his study window Father Williams had seen the wagon stop. He left his chair and came out to meet Susie.

With a voice like that of an old woman at confession she told about her father's accident and how deathly sick he was. . . . Doctor Green hardly believed he'd be able to pull through . . . and now she would have to stay in town with him . . . to take care of the sore both day and night . . . the doctor wouldn't let them go home again until her father was well. . . . Oh, oh, it was terrible! . . . Could Father Williams help them find a place where they might get a room? . . . When she finished her account she was sobbing bitterly.

"There now, child," the priest sought to quiet her. "You did the right thing in coming to me first. A room? Why, certainly we'll find a room for you! In my house there are all kinds of room. You will be doing me a favour by staying here. And you will stay and take care of your father? That's fine, exactly what a dutiful daughter should do. Come right in!"

In the face of all this kindness Susie could not control herself. Her sobs grew to loud weeping. And yet she was so profoundly happy that she could have thrown herself on the priest's neck and hugged him! She knew now that all their difficulties were as good as ended. Father was to stay at the priest's and the priest was in perfect accord with God and the saints! She eagerly grasped one of Father Williams' hands with both of hers. "Thanks! Oh, thanks ever so much!" She could not go on, and wept some more.

Before Charley went home she instructed him to drive past Holm's and let Peder know what had happened. "Tell him to be sure to stop in when he comes to town. And tell him I need some more clean clothes for the baby. Now don't forget to give him my greetings. Ask him to come soon!"

IX

The house in which Father Williams lived was divided in two by a long hallway that led from the front entrance through to the kitchen door. To the right, at the front, was the priest's study; a pair of sliding doors which were usually left open admitted one from the study to the dining-room; beyond the dining-room, and separated from it by a heavy velvet portière, was the kitchen. On the other side of the

Their Fathers' God

hallway the priest's bedroom was nearest the front; next to it was a guest-room, and beyond this lived old Annie Mc-Bride, the housekeeper, cook, and absolute monarch of the house. For Doheny's convenience Father Williams gave him his own bedroom and Susie and the baby the guest-room adjoining it.

Night had come; they had finished supper and were sitting in the study. Both men were puffing at their pipes. Old Annie had served beer with the meal, and Doheny had not said no to a second glass. He had, for the moment, forgotten the thin thread on which his life was hanging.

But now in the study he was conscious of the pain once more, and he asked the priest if he really believed his condition could be as bad as that crazy doctor had said. Could it, really? It was nothing more than a sore in the thigh? The doctors weren't always right.

Father Williams sent great clouds of smoke ceilingwards before answering. The need for comfort and hope was plain in Doheny's questions.

"Green is a peculiar man, that is sure. And yet, I believe you would have to search far before you would find his equal as a doctor." The priest blew more smoke. "There's one thing you should remember, Michael Doheny: In matters of life and death there is some one else who has the final word. Death does not come until the Lord sends it."

These words put Doheny more at ease. He sat pondering over them for a while and refilled his pipe. When he had lit it he asked about God's interference in man's everyday affairs: Could the drought that ruined all their crops last year have been a kind of punishment? Did the priest think that people out here were any worse than anywhere else? In some parts of the country there had been more than enough rain. Was that because people in those places were better and more deserving? . . . There was no disrespect in Doheny's voice; only a timorous wonderment, like that of the child who feels that his father is in the wrong but doesn't dare gainsay him.

Father Williams let the questions lie for the time being;

he sat quietly in the half-dark, puffing at his pipe. Susie watched him eagerly and waited for his answer; the baby dozed in her lap. After having sat thus awhile the priest began to speak, much in the manner of one who talks aloud to himself about things of which he is certain:

"We know that God is. Let that suffice. That is as far as we can go and as far as we need to go. Trying to reason about Him gets us only into difficulties; it may lead to grievous temptation. He is the Infinite, the Almighty, the All-good, from eternity and to eternity. Isn't it enough to know that? Whatever good we receive comes from His merciful Hand; the ill we must occasionally suffer is inflicted by evil powers which He permits to visit us. For the good we should thank Him earnestly; against the other we should pray the Mother of God and the holy angels to intercede for us." The priest grew quiet, lost in thought.

Petie awoke and became restless; it was his nursing-time and he insisted on attention.

Father Williams turned to Susie:

"You are tired, child; soon you will have to get your father ready for the night. We shall say our evening prayers, and all go to bed."

By the opposite wall was a *prie-dieu,* cushioned with red velvet; above it on the wall hung a crucifix. Father Williams knelt on the stool, folded his hands, and said a prayer in Latin, slowly and with a great serenity. To Susie it was as if she understood all of it. Many of the words she had heard so often that they had become living to her. When the priest had finished he said the Lord's Prayer in English; he remained kneeling for a few moments, his head bowed low. Finally he rose.

Susie's face shone with an unearthly brightness. Her lips were parted and she continued to lull the baby in her lap, swaying her knees in a cradle-like movement. Petie had long since ceased whimpering, but she had not noticed it. Only one thought was in her mind: This simple devotion was the most beautiful thing she had ever experienced. She felt herself surrounded by an impenetrable wall of goodness. Here she sat among her own people, snug and sheltered in the age-old faith of her fathers. She was theirs and they were hers. Countless, unbreakable bonds held them together. Around them were the great things of life, the things that really mattered, secure and never-failing. A burning desire came to her: If Peder had only been here to experience this hour! And suddenly it was as if she were grovelling about in a strange land where everything was grey and grim. She was frightened and bitter cold. Abruptly she went to her room. There she sat down to nurse the boy and to undress him. She could not recall any other time when she had been so fatigued and so hopelessly sick at heart.

After having rocked the child to sleep she laid him on the bed. . . . What was it the doctor wanted her to do? She stretched and yawned, and went to the kitchen where she found old Annie McBride tidying up for the evening. Susie told her what she needed—a bowl about as big as *this*, and a kettle to boil the bowl in. . . . Yes, it has to be boiled, she repeated, sleepily.

The woman looked at her distrustfully.

"You certainly ain't goin' to boil a bowl? A plain bowl? Fine soup that'll make!"

"It sounds silly, I suppose, but I've got to do it. Doctor Green is afraid there might be little bugs on it, 'microbes of sin' he called them. Gosh! how silly that man is!"

Too late Susie realised that she had made a terrible blunder. The old woman took the mention of "little bugs" as a direct insult, black and unforgivable. She flew into a rage, made menacing thrusts with her scrawny arms, while curses leapt from her tongue. Never before had Susie seen such a fury; she was so frightened she did not know where to turn.

"The devil take you and your Doctor Green, and all your damned little bugs! As sure as my name is Annie McBride, conceived and born where the King's Road takes off for Dublin—I want you to know I came by my name in an honourable way!"—she shot a crushing glance at Susie. "The doctor's black soul will be roasted alive! Oh, that salamander out of hell! Just wait till old St. Patrick gets his hands on him!"

Father Williams, who had heard his housekeeper's outburst, left his chair and came to the kitchen.

"What may be going on here?" he asked, appearing in the doorway.

"Going on!" the old woman hissed in his face. "'Don't you suppose that this freethinker, this devil's own black son—God have mercy on my mouth!—that this hell-hound has told her the dishes I wash with soap and lye after every meal, the dishes that you eat from every day, that those dishes have to be boiled for hours before they're clean enough to soak some old rags in?" She was choking with anger. "And to think that for this whoremonger—yes, for *him*!—I've had to bake and fuss till my limbs ached simply because you insist on draggin' all kinds of dirty scoundrels into your house. Begory me soul! I won't stand for it!"

"Be careful of your tongue, Annie!" said Father Williams, admonishingly. "If you refuse to help Susie find the things she needs, I'll do it myself. You're carrying on like a wicked child. How could the doctor know that these people were to stay here to-night?" Then he added, in an assuaging voice: "You must remember that not all people are as cleanly as you, Annie. Go to your room now and stay there until you are yourself again." As if nothing had happened, he turned to Susie and asked what she needed.

Of a sudden the woman lost all control of herself. Planting her gnarly fists into her sides, she bent far forward as if she were about to leap into the priest's face, her thin little braid standing out like a whip:

"Get out of my kitchen and be damned quick about it! I won't have any loose fish out here where I work! Don't you s'pose that I know what all of you men are? Here you stand stickin' up for that pig, that rakehell of a ——"

Her tirade ended abruptly. The priest threw one arm about her back, the other about her knees and picked her up bodily; and kicking the door open, he carried her out of the room. The door across the hall opened and was slammed shut. Then followed shouts, mad howls, curses, and vile out-bursts. Finally the racket died away in hysterical whinings. Susie, struck dumb, stood listening intently.

When the priest returned to the kitchen his face was pale with weariness. He leaned heavily against the cupboard. In a tired voice he asked Susie what she wanted.

She had already found the necessary things and now had the bowl boiling in the kettle according to the doctor's orders. But in the excitement she had forgotten about washing her hands. She did not dare look up at Father Williams now; it was even more difficult than ever to think of something to say to him.

He spoke first; his voice was lower and kinder than usual:

"You must not pay any attention to old Annie. Her soul is not as black as the speech in her mouth. I doubt if you could find a more well-meaning person." The priest coughed. "Sometimes a gust of anger will upset her completely, and she says things of which she herself is not aware. Afterwards she is overcome just as completely with remorse. She is in that stage now. I doubt that she will get much rest to-night."

Susie could think of nothing fitting to say; she only stood there with her eyes downcast. The priest talked on in the same low, kind voice:

"Poor, poor woman! Her life she has lived in the shad-ows. Once she had a husband; he deserted her, and you can't wonder that he did. The son the Lord gave her is also gone; she has no idea what became of him. Later she became an outcast, at the mercy of all that is evil. She sank deeper than I thought possible for a human being to sink. I found her in an asylum and became her father confessor; that's how she came into my house. For six years now I have been strug-gling with her. I never have had a more faithful and capable servant. Except for these spells of uncontrollable anger she is wonderful. I am telling you these things because I want you to be kind to her. She means well; you need not be afraid of her. She never could stand Doctor Green; the rea-son, I think, is that he always wants to argue with me. When you come right down to it there is not a great deal of difference between him and her."

The priest straightened himself and turned to go. "Don't let it frighten you if you should hear disturbance in the house to-night. I expect I shall have to come downstairs after a while to see how the poor thing is getting along. God grant you and yours a good night!"

Before Susie had finished the rebandaging, Father Williams stepped into the room. He laid a thick volume on the table.

"In case you find it necessary to sit up with your father to-night this book will help you shorten the hours." The volume bore the title *The Lives of the Saints*.

After Susie had gone to bed she lay awake, thinking of the episode between Father Williams and Annie McBride. The words which the woman had flung into his face were so unspeakably vile and yet so grotesquely funny that she lay shaking with laughter. She felt a sweet, warm comfort: Here was a woman who had sinned royally, but on that account the priest did not cast her out. With the thought of his kindness and gentleness she dozed off into peaceful unconsciousness.

Suddenly she was wide awake and listening, a cold fear running through her. . . . Sh—there were sounds of footsteps on the stairs, footsteps that treaded stealthily and approached slowly . . . a faint gleam of light showed them the way . . . there they stopped outside the old woman's door! For a brief moment deathly silence. Then a hoarse whisper that pierced the darkness:

"Are you in your right mind now so I can confess you?"

There was a slight noise of a door being opened and the gleam of light disappeared. Thereupon followed heartrending moans that died quickly. The whole house stood on tiptoe, listening. Susie stretched her ears until she was lost in weariness.

Shortly after midnight she sat up with a start, rubbing her eyes, every nerve alert. . . . Heavens! Was it father?

Their Fathers' God

There, beside the bed, stood some one, uttering low moans. The darkness in the room was impenetrable.

"Did you-hou find what you wa-hanted?"

Involuntarily Susie lifted the baby aside, groped in the darkness, and caught hold of a shriveled-up, cold hand.

"Come!" she whispered, and drew the old woman into the bed. "Now lie down and go to sleep. . . . It's easier when there are two in the bed. That's what grandma always used to say. . . . Don't wake the baby!"

Never a word said old Annie. She crawled under the covers, and there rolled herself into a ball from which there arose now and then long, pent-up sobs. The sobs died soon and she lay there snoring profound snores.

But before Susie could again lose herself in sleep she heard her father call to her, and she jumped out of bed. When she came into his room she found him in great pain. So far he had not slept a wink. An unnatural restlessness was upon him.

"How are you now?" asked Susie, in a voice that was thick with sleep.

"Can't you see for yourself how I am?" Doheny turned his face away from her. "If this keeps up, the worms will soon be having a feast!" After a pause he continued, in the same bitter tone: "Never could understand why you should go and throw yourself away on an ungodly heathen . . . just as if there weren't any other men to choose from! . . . You see now the reward I'm reaping. Golly! you've done well by your own father!"

Susie stared at him, intensely awake now. Pretty soon her eyes caught him, and she held them.

"Do you think that's the reason you fell off the haystack?"

"What do *you* think about it? Give me a sip of water." He lay silent awhile. . . . "How will you explain the fact that an old experienced farmer drives the stake into himself instead of the haystack? Such things don't happen without reason!" Again silence. . . . "There's the baby you're letting grow up into a heathen. If this is to keep on, there's

124

"They Shall Call His Name Emmanuel"

no use in me going to a doctor? How long do you intend to keep him a heathen? Haven't we got a priest? That's another thing I lay here thinking about!"

Not a word did Susie answer until she had changed the bandages. Without looking at him she began to speak slowly, feeling her way:

"If it was such a sin for me to marry the man I loved, the punishment should have fallen on me and not you. You, of course, have nothing to answer for!"

"Oh, I'm not sure about that," answered Doheny, glumly. "I might've looked after you better . . . not let you chase out nights. I might've put a stop to it when I saw things were going too far . . . might've guessed how it would all end. Now I'm getting my reward!" Small beads of perspiration had formed on his face; the back of his hand was moist; evidently it had cost him great exertion to say these things to her.

Susie went out to the kitchen; was gone awhile. She returned with a basin of lukewarm water and bathed his face. She said nothing, but the tenderness in the movements of her hand spoke for her. And the treatment seemed to work; when he now spoke his depressed mood had lifted:

"You're an angel, Susie, I don't mind telling you. The saints will not forget you!"

"Do you want me to stay here and read to you awhile?" she asked, timidly.

"You're going right to bed."

"Father Williams said if you couldn't sleep——"

"Go to bed right away!" he ordered, with paternal firmness.

When she had turned down the lamp and was ready to leave, he said, hesitatingly:

"Don't forget what I told you about the boy. Here we've come into the priest's house, and that's your own doings. Strange ways He has found to send us here—that I must say!" He saw her pause in the doorway and spoke more brusquely: "What are you waiting for? See to it that you

get to bed this very minute! . . . Don't you hear what I'm
telling you?"

x

During the days that followed, Doheny found no relief.
The nights were worse than the days, for then the house
got so still that the creaking of the bed as he tossed restlessly and his low agonized groanings could reach Susie's
ears. She always kept the two doors open. Night after night
she lay listening for sounds. She would fight for sleep and
only grow more wakeful. Her eyelids burnt until she was
forced to open them wide. She dreaded the thought of getting
up and going into his room. It was those eyes of his; they
always caught hers, always asking the same thing:

What will you do about it?

They had now lived at Father Williams' house for a full
week. During that time there had been no noticeable change
for either better or worse.

Charley came to see them as often as he could. To-day
he had been there with clean things for the baby. Susie had
taken the clothes from his hands, had looked at them with
absent eyes, had asked about Peder . . . how was he? Like
a fleeting shadow the thought passed through her mind.
Strange he doesn't come? In a moment it was gone. Her
life with him and her days on the Holm farm seemed distant and dim, like memories of a dream dreamt long ago;
now her whole life revolved about her father's bed; she
could see nothing else. . . . Yet, why didn't he come? Last
night she had ached to be in his arms.

Every morning and evening Doctor Green dropped in to
see Doheny. Like a faithful dog Susie followed the doctor's every motion. For, she thought, if there is anyone who
can save father's life, it is Doctor Green . . . and Father
Williams!

One morning as the doctor was about to leave the room
he paused and stood at the bedside, looking down at his
patient. Susie was at the foot of the bed, waiting, and

126

"They Shall Call His Name Emmanuel"

watching intently. Under the doctor's searching eyes Doheny turned his face away:

"Isn't it any better to-day, either?" he asked in a tone of forced resignation.

"Can't say it is." The doctor observed him fixedly.

For a while neither spoke. Suddenly Doheny's hand slapped down on the covers:

"To think that I have to lay around in bed like a bed-ridden old woman!" All his helplessness and suffering found expression in the outburst. It fell hard on Susie's ears.

"I was just thinking," said the doctor, "that it's altogether too risky to let this thing go much longer. Looks like we'll have to amputate. To hide the truth from you would be doing you small kindness." He picked up his hat. "I'll be in to see you this evening. Amputation is nothing to be afraid of. It means, however, that that which is once cut off cannot be glued on again."

Unnoticed, Susie had slipped into the hall, where she stood stark still, listening to what the doctor was saying. Just as he came out she darted into her own room and flung herself down on the bed. Sobs were choking her and she stuffed a pillow corner into her mouth in order to stop the sound. The doors to both rooms stood wide open. From her father came low moans that lashed her pitilessly, each one saying plainly:

"It's your fault! It's all your fault!"

As far back as she could remember she had had a guardian angel who followed her about, always close at hand; at one time she was sure that he was a good friend or close relative of her grandmother's angel, for whenever grandmother lay chatting with her's Susie would be sure to feel her own near-by. She knew exactly what he looked like; she wasn't sure but that she had seen him once or twice. There was that night when she had lain sick and alone, and then the night when her mother had died. Even though the angel did change shape with her changing moods, he remained her constant source of help and her daily refuge. While she was very young she had often played with him

and had had him running errands for her. As she grew
older and acquired knowledge both of the things round
about her and of herself, she did not dare to call him when
she played. One thing she could not understand: he grew
so much faster than she. It was astonishing how fast he
could grow! All at once he was the Mother of God, and
suddenly God's Son, and then God the Father Himself who
sat on a throne up in the skies, scowling at her and demanding that she do just *so*. Afterwards had followed a time
when she had struggled long and diligently to make Him her
angel again. It was good to have Him in reserve whenever
consciousness of guilt troubled her . . . especially when she
came home from a dance, warm and flustered, after she
had been whirled in the arms of strong men; at such times
she was never certain that she might not have sinned a little
bit. She needed only to hold a brief council with the angel,
confiding everything to him, and he'd run quickly to the
Mother of God and say that Susie was all right. After that
she could fall asleep in a wink.

The angel was almost like the thumb of her right hand.
There she had another dear companion! While she was
still a tiny girl that thumb had been dearer to her than any
other part of her body. And so much more useful, too!
She slept with it in her mouth, she talked with it and sang
to it, she could wrap a rag around it and have it for a
doll and give it the funniest names. The thumb, too, was
a sort of guardian. Marvellous how much strength was hidden in that thumb! When she crooked the end of the forefinger around the tip of the thumb she could lift the
heaviest things, even big buckets brimful of water. For a
time she wondered if the angel didn't sleep in her thumb
during the night. She was quite sure he did.

She looked about for the angel now; immediately she
felt him near at hand, and all was well again. She rose from
the bed, looked into the mirror, and prettied her hair. Then
she went back to her father.

In his room she began groping around, as if searching for
some object she could not find right away, always carefully

keeping her face turned from him. After some moments she talked as if the thought had just come into her mind and as if she were wondering about it:

"Don't you think you ought to go to confession?" She bent over to pick up a shred of cotton gauze which she laid on the table. "And receive communion? . . . I can mention it to Father Williams if you want me to?"

"How about yourself?" he asked, irritably.

"Me?"

"Just as if you don't need to go to confession!"

"Never mind about me. . . . There may be lots of things I need to do," she admitted, cheerfully. But she returned to her first suggestion: "You're strong enough to be taken to the church, aren't you? Charley and I could carry you over. It's only a short way."

"Ha, Charley! He's out on the farm."

"Well, I was only asking."

"Besides, he was here yesterday."

"Why shouldn't he come to-day too?"

"He has other things to do! Can't be chasing to town every day."

"But if he should come?" insisted Susie. "He and I could do it easily!"

"Easy me eye! You got less sense than a goose. That's what's the matter with you."

"Can I help it? I'm your daughter," she laughed, teasingly.

Apparently too sick to quibble further, Doheny said no more. Susie puttered about for a few minutes, and, picking up the gauze again, she went out.

A little while later she opened the door to the priest's study and peeped in.

Father Williams looked up from his book.

"Come right in, child, and tell me what you want."

Susie accepted eagerly, as if she had received the very invitation she had come for. At once she began, speaking fast in order to shut off the sobs that threatened to overtake her:

Their Fathers' God

"Everything is so terrible I hardly know which way to turn! Father's much worse . . . the doctor says his leg will have to be cut off . . . and maybe he isn't strong enough to stand it. . . . Don't you think he ought to go to confession? . . . Because, what if he should die?" Susie swallowed heavy lumps. "He thinks he's being punished because I married Peder . . . which isn't his fault at all . . . I'd have done it no matter what he said! . . . Don't you think we could carry him over to the Church? . . . It isn't far. I am sure Charley will be here to-day, too . . . he and I can carry him . . . and . . ." It was no longer possible to check the sobs. . . . "I suppose I ought to have Petie baptized before anything happens to father . . . he thinks the saints are angry with me because I haven't had it done before!" With that she broke down completely. But now the worst of her worries had been shifted to shoulders stronger than her own, and already she felt her load lightened.

"Now it will soon be all right! I guess we got that ugly old tooth out, root and all, that time, didn't we?" The priest came around the table, and placing his arm around her assuringly he led her to the old, leather-covered chair; there he remained standing behind her with one arm resting on the back of the chair. "Now, child, unburden your heart!"

Susie could not go on because of her weeping, and so the priest spoke for her:

"Through the years, as long as I have known him, your father has led a clean, moral life. For all that he may need confession, especially now that he is uncertain of what the future has in store for him. But you, my child, should need it a great deal more. Since your confirmation you have got yourself into serious difficulties. Wilfully you have kept away from the merciful bosom of the Church. Without consulting me you ran off and married a man of another faith. He is a headstrong, wilful man, I can see it plainly. You are not succeeding in bending him your way; instead, you are permitting yourself to be drawn over into his indifference. Again and again you have missed Mass, even though

"They Shall Call His Name Emmanuel"

I have taken special pains to remind you of your neglect. When do you plan to have the child baptized? Do you expect the saints to look with favour on you and yours as long as you turn your back on all your sacred duties? And you who used to be such a faithful little girl!" The paternal kindness in his words made the grievous indictments all the more crushing.

Susie wept helplessly.

"My husband isn't Catholic. . . . He is mad at us . . . no, not mad! I didn't mean that . . . he is the kindest man on earth! . . . I say prayers for him every night. . . . Oh, everything is so terrible! . . . If I baptize the baby without his knowing it, he'll . . . he'll . . . never forgive me . . . I can feel it in me . . . because he doesn't understand." The weeping became so choking that she had to get up and go to the window.

The priest said nothing further until she again was quiet. After a while he continued, slowly and seriously:

"I can well see that you are in a difficult position. Yet as your father confessor I am compelled to tell you that your suffering is the consequence of your own sins. If you had come to me for advice, you would never have married outside the True Church. These mixed marriages are the greatest bane, the greatest danger, confronting the Church. Truly it has been said that 'the carnal mind is enmity against God.' Nevertheless, it is the eternal displeasure of God and not the ill will of man that you must fear and guard yourself against. If you are to wait for your husband's approval, it is doubtful that your child will ever receive sonship with God. It therefore becomes your sacred duty, regardless of what your husband's opinion in the matter may be, to bring your child to holy baptism as soon as you can. 'We should obey God more than man,' thus spake one of the saints."

Susie stood with her back towards the priest. After he had spoken there was only one thing for her to do, only one thing that she could do. It was God Himself who had arranged this opportunity for her. The thought brought with it blissful relief. . . . After this she would be so kind to Peder! . . . And say many prayers to the Mother of God. . . . She would understand her troubles and intercede for her.

Quickly, her face shining, she turned and came straight to Father Williams. She was filled with a great decision: "Could it be done to-day? If my brother comes?"

"There is nothing in the world to prevent it," the priest assured her, firmly. "The holy ceremony can be performed even if he does not come. We can baptize the child in your father's room. He can be the witness, and you carry the child yourself. Nothing could be more appropriate." He spoke quietly and with a deep, almost childlike joy.

Susie reached for his hand. The priest looked at her long and earnestly while he patted her tenderly.

"Since it is your child, Susie, and your first-born, I shall make this sacrament unforgettable both for you and the child." The priest's face was flushed with a deep gladness. "I shall baptize the boy with the same water that was used for the baptism of Our Lord and Saviour. Yes, child, that is exactly what I will do!"

The brown spots in Susie's eyes burnt like two bright tapers. Not a word did she understand of the priest's miraculous promise; she only felt that now there were being arranged for her marvellous things of which she was totally undeserving.

"You see," he continued, "a few years ago I made a pilgrimage to the Holy Land to view those holy scenes and tread on the sacred ground, and I brought back with me a flask of water which I myself took from the River Jordan. And that water we shall use to-day!" He stroked her hand. "Hurry now and prepare yourself and the child for the holy ceremony!"

XI

Through the rest of the forenoon Susie kept a sharp lookout for her brother, though yet it was far too early to expect him. She said her rosary earnestly that he should come, he must come, because this was to be no ordinary, everyday affair. Again she felt the nearness of the angel and she bade him hasten off to tell Charley not to fail her!

What should she name Petie? Oh, if she only knew what Peder wanted! Often when she and Peder had been playing with the boy in the evening she had called him *Patrick*; she had done it for fun and had declared that they would name him Patrick after her grandfather. Susie could not remember her grandfather Patrick, but she had heard her father say many times that a finer man had never walked on two feet; and usually he would add: "That's of course because he was named after the saint." She had repeated this to Peder. But every time she mentioned the name Patrick, Peder was sure to scoff and scold . . . only fooling, most likely. Certainly he couldn't have meant all that! He had even sworn up and down that they'd never disgrace a Norwegian boy by naming him after an Irish idol! She recalled one evening last spring, when they had been joking about the name, that Peder had said: "Don't you suppose we Norwegians have saints, too? . . . You might as well know now as later that his name is going to be St. Olaf! . . . There was the boy that knew something! He needed only to wink and the trolls would burst like bubbles. He christianized half the world, and I guess Ireland along with it!"— "Was he a Catholic, then?" she had asked. "How can you be so foolish, Susie?" he had answered. "How could a *real* saint ever be a Catholic? Maybe you don't believe me? Well, over in Minnesota there's a great college named after him." Peder had said many things that night, but, of course, it was only to tease her. Yet she had noticed a queer undertone which she did not like and which she couldn't quite forget.

No matter what name we choose, she decided, finally, we'll be calling him Petie most of the time, anyhow. . . . Patrick St. Olaf sounds pretty. That'll be two saints instead of one!

She took the boy in her arms and went into the kitchen, where she found Annie McBride at work. There she settled

Their Fathers' God

herself to give Petie a real bath. Her mind was so full that she felt the need to confide in some one. All this about the water from the River Jordan was too good not to tell, and she launched into an account of the great things that were going to take place this afternoon. To get the better of the misgivings which still beset her, she confessed to the old housekeeper that the baptism would have to be performed without the knowledge and consent of the child's father. But she did not worry about that . . . she had such a wonderful husband! Thereupon she had to show what a matchless young man Peder was, heaping proof upon proof. Annie McBride said little. Susie sat in the kitchen visiting until dinner was on the table.

Her premonition proved to be right. A little past two o'clock Charley was at the door of the parsonage. At the sight of him she was filled with a serene joy—the Mother of God had heard her prayers! A wall of great security surrounded her. With both hands she grasped Charley's arm and revealed her plan.

"And now," she finished, happily, "you'll have to go to confession, too, all three of us will go. I shall be churched and Petie baptized! Won't it be grand?"

Charley looked down into his sister's enthusiasm:

"Do you dare? Without letting Peder know about it?"

"Certainly! . . . I *got* to do it. You can see for yourself I got to."

"Have you talked it over with Father Williams?"

"Everything! He says I'm doing right. . . . And Peder is always so kind!" she added, with a passionate assurance. "You and father haven't any idea of what a kind husband I've got."

"Have I ever said he wasn't kind?" He dropped her arms.

"Don't you suppose I can tell it on you?"

Charley scratched his neck.

"Well, no matter how kind he is, he still can get hopping mad. I know him!"

"Yes, mad! What about yourself now and then? Go and get yourself ready. I must go in and take care of Petie."

"They Shall Call His Name Emmanuel"

A little while later Susie and Charley together carried their father in a chair the short way to the church; in her eagerness Susie got out of step with Charley and the going became jerky. Doheny clenched his teeth in terrible pain and held onto the chair.

The church greeted them with the tranquillity of supernal peace. The bright day, sifting through the coloured windows, was in here, in the hallowed stillness, transformed to mellow, subdued light, mysterious and holy; on the altars the candles blinked solemnly, warning all who entered that here one must tread softly, for just above on the high altar hung the crucified Son of God in the last throes of His death struggle.

The service lasted long. First, each one went to confession and was absolved. After that Susie was churched. To her it seemed that each ceremony left her in new and spotless garments, each purer and more resplendent than the one before. The baptismal ceremony, performed chiefly in Latin, made, in a new way, a more profound impression on her than anything she had ever experienced. The priest was no longer Father Williams, that gentle friend in whom she could always confide and feel safe with; before her stood another, a representative of God himself; out of him flowed the secret power of great mysteries. From the moment he had met her in the aisle with, "What do you ask of the Church?" and she had answered, meekly, "The Faith," and until she had stood by the baptismal font, it was as if step by step she had been approaching the very throne of Omnipotence. She could not have explained what happened to her and her child, because it was all so wonderful. She had never studied Latin in school, nevertheless she understood the ancient speech as easily as though it were her mother tongue. Here a higher power was addressing her; she was only a lost child who in humility accepted that which was given her. Her son, flesh of her flesh and blood of her own heart, she presented for holy baptism; the son that she had got in sin, committed in the frivolity of youth, she now surrendered into the hand of Omnipotence. Willingly she deliv-

Their Fathers' God

ered him up, and felt at the same moment a strange pain and unspeakable sweetness.

The priest wetted his thumb on his tongue and touched the child's ears and nostrils, first the right ear, then the left, saying:

"Ephpheta, quod est, Adaperire." As he touched the nostrils he said: *"In odorem suavitatis,"* then he continued to pray: *"Tu autem effugare, diabole; appropinquabit enim judicum Dei."*

When he reached the baptismal act he pronounced the name clearly and unmistakably:

"Patrick St. Olaf, Ego te baptizo in nomine Patris, et Filii, et Spiritus Sancti." He poured the water, the same that he himself had taken from the River Jordan, crosswise over the child's head. Next he dipped his thumb into the holy oil and with it salved a cross on the crown of the head, praying: *Deus omnipotens, Pater Domini nostri Jesu Christi; qui te regeneravit ex aqua et Spiritu Sancto, quique dedit tibi remissionem omnium peccatorum, ipse te liniat Chrismate salutis in eodem Christo Jesu Domino nostro in vitam æternam. Amen. Pax tibi."* And here the priest laid a white cloth on the child's breast and said in English: "Receive this white garment, which mayest thou carry without stain before the judgment seat of our Lord Jesus Christ, that thou mayest have life everlasting. Amen." . . . After the prayer he held forth to Susie a burning candle which she accepted in behalf of the child, and he said, also in English: "Receive this burning light, and keep thy baptism so as to be without blame: observe the commandments of God, that when our Lord shall come to His nuptials, thou mayest meet Him together with all the saints in the heavenly court, and live for ever and ever. Amen. Go in peace, and the Lord be with thee. Amen."

Susie stood with the child in her arms, a great effulgence enfolding her. Her child, her very flesh and blood, had been inducted into the communion of saints and had received sonship from God the Father. Now little child-angels were ringing the bells of heaven in honour of the occasion. Entranced, Susie stood in the doorway of the church; she had forgotten all about the others. In the western sky shone the bright afterglow of a great sun that had just now sunk into the prairie. . . . Out there were all the fairy angels . . . now they were hurrying home, back to their sweet mysteries!

When Doctor Green called that evening he stood for a long time observing Doheny. Now what the devil was loose here? The pulse was rapid and irregular; his cheeks burned with red spots; the back of his hand was wet with perspiration. The sick man had his pipe lit and was blowing out clouds of smoke; in everything he said was a gay recklessness.

"How do you feel?" asked the doctor, curtly, narrowing his eyes.

"Can't you see for yourself? Aren't you the doctor? Not that I mind telling you!" Doheny pulled himself higher up on his pillow. "If you don't get the hell out of here with your black bag and all your crazy talk about amputation, I'll get up and *throw* you out! That's providing you don't pull up a chair and light your pipe and act sociable. I'm good and sick of your hanging around here."

"Hm! Is that all that's troubling you?"

"That's plenty, isn't it? Now don't let me hear you say a word about chopping the legs off an honest man. I'm not planning to go limping around either here or in the hereafter."

Doctor Green joined in the raillery:

"Better men than you have been forced to limp here in order to dance in the hereafter."

"No real Irishman, as far as I know!"

"It's Ulster folk I'm talking about!" said the doctor, dryly.

"Then you don't know much about them. Begor! they limp both here and in the hereafter!"

"Just as you'll be doing, yourself, if you don't look out! Let's have a look at that good-for-nothing leg of yours."

"Guess you better. You've got a few things left to learn yet, all right."

The sore did not appear to be any worse. The bandages

were full of matter, which the doctor interpreted as a good sign. He rebandaged the leg, then took Doheny's pulse a second time while he sat regarding the patient intently. When he got up he asked, in an angry voice:

"What have you been doing to-day? Jigging?"

"Eh-heh!" nodded Doheny, secretively.

"I'm telling you, my dear man," snarled the doctor, "that unless you stay quiet and do as I say you'll have to take the consequences! There's no necessity of sucking that pipe quite so hard; inside of you there's filth enough already. You haven't been drinking?"

"Oh, drat it! You wait till to-morrow, and you'll see!"

"See what? Some miracle going to be pulled off?"

"Bet your life! To-morrow I toss the old bed on my back and hike for home. If you've got a confinement case to look after out my way, I'll give you a free ride!" Doheny broke into a boisterous laugh. "We'll go so fast we'll catch on to the tail of the wind that blows before us, and the wind coming behind can never catch up. Not in all your life will you have another chance for such a ride!"

The doctor said no more. He was utterly at a loss how to explain the strange exaltation in his patient's mood, and did not dare question him further for fear of exciting him. . . . What the devil had the man been up to to-day?

The doctor was barely out of the door before Doheny reached under the bed and brought out a pint bottle of whisky; he had had Charley get the bottle shortly after they had returned from the church, and already he had sampled it once. Now he smiled slyly and took a few deep draughts. Then he returned it to its hiding-place under the bed.

So puzzled over his patient's condition was Doctor Green that he stepped into the priest's study in quest of information. He had a suspicion—no mortal could ever guess what kind of mischief that darned priest might be up to! Black-browed and ready for a fight, he entered the study. And in no uncertain terms he informed the priest that Doheny was worse to-day; he was in a critical condition and required absolute quiet; the least mental disturbance might bring about a change for the worse.

"By the grace of God, I think we will soon see a change for the better," said the priest, with confidence. "This afternoon he has unburdened his soul in confession. In addition he has experienced the great joy of witnessing the baptism of his grandson. He is exceedingly fond of the child. Do you wonder that he is glad now that he has seen the little one made a citizen in the great Kingdom of God and a member of the true Church? He himself stood sponsor for the child. Let it not disturb you if Michael Doheny to-night feels happy." The thick clouds of tobacco smoke which the priest was blowing out hung about his head like the nimbus of a burnt offering, pleasing in the sight of God.

"So that is it!" thundered the doctor. "I might have guessed that you had been practising your black art on him!" Suddenly his voice was sweet with insinuating scorn: "Tell me, have you no sense at all? Oh, I don't suppose you need any in your work!" Here the voice darkened: "But, anyway, what do you mean, just what do you mean by dragging a poor devil whose life hangs on a thread out of bed and sending him through one emotional crisis after another? God have mercy—and this thing you call Christianity!"

The surge of the onslaught had lifted the priest from his chair. Steadying himself with his hands flat on the table, he leaned forward; his voice, though it had not lost its kindness, was blurred:

"You scoff at God's holy ways with His children because the god of unbelief has darkened your understanding! Your duty is to care for this man's body. Mine it is to prepare his immortal soul for whatever might happen to him."

The doctor came so close that he could burn the priest with his eyes:

"The devil take you and all your superstitions! Go in and feel of the man's pulse and see what you've done. Just go in and see! If you for one minute think your old, dried-up saints and all that sort of hocus-pocus can heal a badly festering wound, you've got less sense than a two-year-old child. You look out for *tetanus*, look out, I tell you! If this ends in tetanus, I'll have you arrested for murder, yes, for *murder!* Do you hear me?" With this dire threat the doctor turned and left the room.

But while he had been pouring out his wrath upon the priest old Annie McBride had approached the room with her tea-tray. Each evening she found pleasure in performing this act of charity, for, she thought, no one who has worked all day long can possibly continue until long past midnight without a bit of extra nourishment. Through the half-open door she heard the voice of her archenemy denouncing the man whom she idolized, and at once she was in a fit of fury. The moment the doctor stepped through the door she sprang at him with the tray.

"Hisss!" she fumed . . . "Crrr!" A frightful crash resounded through the house. Before the doctor could gain the outer door the tea-tray crashed furiously against his neck, and tray, teapot, tarts, and dishes clattered to the floor; a hissing, pent-up: "The devil take your dirty hide!" was followed by the sharp bang of the door as it slammed shut after him.

The priest rushed into the hallway, where he stood speechless until he grasped the situation.

"Now, now Annie!" He went to her and patted her paternally on the shoulder. "Have things gone wrong with you again?" He placed an arm about her crooked back and led her towards the kitchen. "And the tea that I would have enjoyed so much! Ha-ha-ha!" he chuckled. "Would you believe it? I feel so hungry that I could eat a whole ox, horns and all!"

"God bless your soul!" sobbed Annie. "You're not going to go hungry in your own house. Go lock the door so that salamander can't come back. Did he hurt you?"

Susie had heard the uproar in the hall, and when she had found out what had happened she gave her father the details. Both had laughed until the tears came. Now she sat undressed for bed in her room, combing her hair. It was late

"They Shall Call His Name Emmanuel"

and the house was still. Her lips moved . . . *Ego te absolvo* . . . *a peccatis tuis* . . . *Ego te* ——

Suddenly Annie McBride poked her head through the door.

"He was here this afternoon!" Her voice was bubbling with malicious glee.

"Doctor Green? Was he here this afternoon, too?"

"No-o-o. Your husband!"

"What?" Susie stood up, holding on to the table, pallor spreading over her face.

"Sure thing." Annie stepped into the room, closing the door behind her. "He asked for you. And you can bet your last penny I told him!" The old stub of a woman was so pleased that she perched herself on the edge of the bed and dangled her feet like a little child who cannot sit still.

"What time?" Susie was shivering and threw her arms about her shoulders.

"While you were in church. Or you'd have seen him yourself, wouldn't you? Good-looking husband you hooked. But not easy to convert; stubborn like the devil: I could tell it on his face. You must get Father Williams to help you."

"Did you tell him where we were?" Susie leant against the edge of the table.

"I should say not! No, that job I left for you!" Evidently Annie McBride was finding no end of fun in Susie's predicament.

"What did you tell him?"

"Nothing but the gospel truth! I said you were out. That wasn't lying, was it? I didn't think you cared to see him just then! You didn't, did you?"

"Did he leave right away? Don't talk so loud; father won't be able to sleep."

"I should say he left—ha-ha-ha! He went down the street as if his rump was on fire. I wouldn't want to be in your boots when you tell him what you was up to to-day! You bet I wouldn't. He's good-looking, that's sure."

"Did—did you—well, did you hint anything?"

Their Fathers' God

"No, child. And if I was you, I would be in no hurry, either! That much I could see on his face."

Susie sat down and began combing her hair once more.

"You said he left right away?"

"Why, I reckon he did. I sure didn't ask him to stay. I'll bet he's hard to get along with? My husband was a beast when he got mad. Feared neither God nor the devil himself. He, too, was a Protestant. God have mercy on his soul! He was a devil of a fellow, that's sure, but better than no man at all." The woman chatted on, dangling her feet back and forth, always in opposite directions.

Susie listened absently while she braided her hair. She finished, and tossed the left braid over her shoulder; the other she held and stroked in her hand.

"My husband's both nice and kind; you have no idea of how nice he can be. I'm going to tell him everything as soon as I get home. I only did what was right."

Annie McBride stood up to leave. She squinted at Susie:

"I wouldn't be in too much of a hurry about telling him! You don't know men yet. What's done is done; it won't get any worse if you wait. That's how it always was with my husband."

Susie followed her to the door.

"You're certain that he didn't come to the church?" And at the same moment she gave a short laugh as though she were only joking. But coming back into the room her face sobered and she mumbled passionately: *"Ego te absolvo! . . . Ego te ——!"*

142

III. "And They Shall Be One Flesh"

TWICE while Susie was at Father Williams' did Peder think up excuses for going to town. The first time he took it leisurely; instead of going directly to the priest's house he loitered along Main Street, stopped and chatted with anyone he knew well enough to talk to, and stood for a long time watching some men at work on a new store building. His business at the general store might have been transacted in three minutes, but he let it take him an hour, thinking that she might show up. Darkness was coming on before he finally set out for home. Then he felt disgusted and decidedly out of sorts. . . . Wasn't this affair ever going to end?

The second time, a good two weeks ago, he told himself on the way down that to-day he was going to drive straight to the priest's house! . . . Bet your life he was! . . . Hadn't seen her now for a dog's age. No telling what this might lead to? No, sir, he couldn't put it off any longer; he must have a good heart-to-heart talk with her . . . must have it to-day, without fail! . . . Man alive! she was his wife, wasn't she? . . . What did he have to be ashamed about? Hadn't they been married fairly and squarely and according to all the rules and hocus-pocus of the Catholic Church?

Peder whipped up the horse. . . . T'hell with that now! It would have been all the same if they'd gone to some other church. . . . Well, anyway, pretty soon he'd have a grown-up son! . . . He laughed at the thought and grew firmer in his purpose. . . . You're going straight to the parsonage, yes, you are! No need of going in. You're man enough to say *no* to whatever he asks you . . . show him once and for all that he can't make a Catholic out of a good Lutheran. . . . If he invites you in, you only have to tell him that you're in a hurry, that you haven't the time. That'd be no lie to-day, anyhow. You only wanted to drop in and see how your wife and the boy were getting along. . . . Peder's face beamed happily. . . . And when she comes out, you ask, so loud that anyone who wants to can hear it: What in thunder have you done with Petie? I don't see him. Then she'll laugh and run in and get the boy. . . . Peder sat chuckling to himself. . . . And as soon as you get him up in the buggy you tell her: Now you've had him all to yourself for so long, you better let me take him for a while. Since you two left me the old house has been gloomy as a graveyard. . . . You can come along, too, can't you? We can hire some one to take care of your father. That won't cost such an awful lot. Now show a little action! Get your clothes and we'll gallop straight for home! . . . Can't you see that I can't go on living without you? At night I just lay tossing around; I've worn the bed down to a frazzle and now I've got to buy a new one. Sure I have; that's why I had to come to town to-day! Hurry, now. Just wait till you hear all the surprising things I've got to tell you!

This time, too, he was destined to turn homeward without having seen either Susie or the boy. As he drove up Main Street, Andrew Holte was tying his horse to the post where Peder usually left his own. Andrew saw him and called out:

"Drive right in here. Plenty of room left."

For a while he stood by the post, talking with Andrew. When the latter had to be on his way Peder sauntered off towards the part of town where Father Williams lived. The farther he went the more deliberate did his strides become. Within him his resentment for the priest broke like a storm.

I'll bet the old devil has been putting queer notions into her head! . . . Wouldn't be surprised if he's been trying to make a nun out of her. He's had plenty of time! . . . What will he think when he sees me coming? Most likely

"And They Shall Be One Flesh"

he'll have it figured out that now the saints have put me in such a hell of a fix I've got to give in. Well, he has another guess coming! Here's one fellow he can't budge . . . and he'd better not try to! . . . Peder clenched his teeth and walked past the parsonage on the opposite side of the street. . . . I'll let it look as if I got an errand down this way. . . . No one can stop me from going where I want to go!

The parsonage stood next to the church and was easily recognized. Because he stared so fixedly at the house that his eyes watered, he barely noticed the church door was ajar. The door of the house was closed; no one came out and he walked more slowly. At the next corner he came to a dead standstill, looking back at the house. . . . This was certainly mysterious! . . . Could they all be asleep in the middle of the afternoon?

He crossed the street and came back on the other sidewalk, treading lightly; his mouth had opened; the sound of his own footsteps disturbed him. In front of the house he stopped, looking around undecided. Not the slightest sound did he hear. No signs of life either within or without. . . . I've got to talk to her; the worst he can do is lecture me for a while . . . guess I can stand that. Anyway, here goes! . . . With his face set he strode up the steps and rang the doorbell.

Moments passed and not a stir inside. By and by his ears caught the sound of shuffling footsteps in soft, loose-fitting slippers. The door opened slightly; the witch-face of an old woman that appeared in the opening eyed him cunningly. There was a wicked look in her eye.

Peder smiled into the face.

"My name is Peder Holm; my wife is supposed to be staying here. Would you please tell her that I'd like to see her?"

The face in the doorway took on an expression of deviltry and scorn; the lips puckered and sucked into the mouth:

"They're out!" hissed the mouth. The door closed with a bang. He heard the key turned inside with a sharp snap.

He stood there staring at the shut door, utterly dumbfounded. . . . Now I've at least been here! he thought. He hurried down the steps, and as he passed the corner of the house he again noticed that the church door was standing open. . . . So that was where the old bugger was holding forth? . . . Well, he had nothing untalked with him! Peder caught a new breath, hastened to his horse, and raced off at top speed toward the Doheny farm. . . . To-night he'd have Susie and Petie back home with him again!

A feeling of wonder and apprehension took hold of him as he drove into the Doheny yard. The air of abandonment that hung over the place choked him, he couldn't draw a full breath; his heart pounded violently; his eyes blurred from staring so hard. In a frenzy he rushed up to the door and rapped madly. Even then he refused to believe that the place was deserted and ran to the barn, calling Charley's name. The emptiness of the echo had a haunting note. When he was finally convinced that there was not a human being to be found on the whole farm, a helpless rage surged through him. . . . Now, by God! he'd go right back to town and wring the neck of that old she-devil!

Driving homewards he let his horse loiter along as it pleased. His eyes fixed dully on the road ahead, seeing only emptiness—cold, grey emptiness that made him ache with distress.

His mother had already finished the chores and sat by the table, reading, waiting for him. Keeping his ill-humour to himself, he went to the washstand. Beret rose and put the food on the table.

"How is everybody where you've been?"

He slumped down on the chair.

"Oh, same as usual, I guess."

"Isn't he getting any better?"

"Doesn't seem that way."

"Oh no! When blood-poisoning once has gotten started it's liable to keep him in bed for a long time," sighed Beret. "Are they still staying with the priest?"

"Where else could they have gone? . . . Have you coffee?" He handed her the cup. "Anybody been here?"

"And They Shall Be One Flesh"

Thoughtfully, with a heavy face, Beret filled the cup:

"How is Lisj-Per?"[1]

"Oh, him!" said Peder as though the question required no answer.

His mother's face grew eager:

"I s'pose he has grown?"

"Hm, grown! He hasn't got much else to do these days. . . . Pass the cream."

Peder's curt remarks invited no further talk, but her thoughts would not leave the boy.

"Just so she doesn't forget to change him. Such little folks don't stand much."

Peder ate on in silence.

"I don't s'pose they know when they will be coming home?"

"Didn't sound that way."

"It's kind of the priest, I must say."

Peder rose abruptly and went upstairs.

II

In the morning he awoke with the same thought he had fallen asleep over: Why did that old bitch have to lie to me? Why didn't she tell me where they were? But now he saw the whole incident in an entirely new light. What had been beyond all comprehension yesterday was to-day no mystery at all. . . . Only natural for Susie to be out . . . how could she know he was coming? You couldn't expect her to sit around in that musty old house all day long. . . . He'd have to hold his horses and take it easy. Now he'd just show her how nicely he could get along without her! There lay a sweet revenge in this thought. . . . Yet to think that she, his wife, couldn't see how downright idiotic this was . . . taking the boy and staying away for months at a time! Was she to run off and play nurse-girl whenever her father or brother didn't feel so well? . . . Oh well, now she can get

[1] Lisj-Per, Beret's pet name for the boy, meaning literally, the little Peder.

her fill of confessions and communions and all that sort of skullduggery. . . . If she doesn't come home soon, I'll have to drive to town and have it out with the old pope himself!

These days Peder toiled like a slave with the fall ploughing. . . . Couldn't afford to hire help, the way prices were now. Last year no crops, not a scrap to sell . . . this year an overabundance on every hand and no prices. He could see no future in this grain-farming. The joy he used to get from his work was gone. . . . Couldn't he find some other use to put the farm to? The fellows who pushed ahead were always those who had the nerve to stake their time and money on a new idea . . . they were the pioneers . . . when the ordinary man finally discovered what was going on, the idea had already grown so old that it was out of date. . . . Why wasn't he a pioneer? Saw new ideas and tried them out? Was he doomed to putter around in this same old-fashioned way all his life? He'd see about that!

On the Wednesday of the second week after he had made the last trip to town Peder received a letter from Susie. It was such a bright and happy note that, as he read, he could see her vividly before him, her dancing eyes and her queer ways.

She wrote that her father's condition had improved greatly, that they planned to return home next Friday. On Saturday evening he must be sure to come over and see his old sweetheart and court her as he used to in the good old days. They'd celebrate, and she'd be so nice to him. . . . "As it is," she had added, "I've almost forgotten what you look like!"

Peder had to impart the good news to his mother—this was too much for him to keep to himself:

"Well, it won't be long now before we have them back again. Doheny's getting along fine. She says I'd better come over and see her Saturday night. . . . Yes, sir!" His face lit up into a broad smile.

"Of course you must go and see her! What does she say about Lisj-Per? Is he all right? Won't it be nice to have him here with us again!" Beret's face was as happy as his,

"And They Shall Be One Flesh"

and in her eyes there were tears, tears that stopped and came back.

That afternoon she scrubbed and tidied the upstairs room. Saturday evening Peder dressed himself in his best, took special pains with his hair and put on his best necktie, shined his shoes and neglected not a single detail of dress. Each little task took a long time.

It was already deep dusk when he jumped into the buggy. . . . No need of hurrying. Wonder if Charley's at home tonight? There's that meeting over at the schoolhouse . . . he'll be going there, most likely? . . . Peder chatted goodnaturedly to the horse: Just take your time, Dolly, old girl. We've got the whole night ahead of us, and then some!

Driving into the Doheny farmyard, he was greeted by a light from the kitchen window. No one came out to meet him . . . Charley must have left already. Peder smiled to himself. . . . Well, we're not kicking . . . we can just as well sit out here in the buggy and pass the time until he comes back . . . just like in the old days!

The light of the lamp blinded him as he stepped into the kitchen, and he remained standing by the door, squinting into the room; his heart thumped so violently that he was barely able to hear his own words of greeting. What he saw caused a great joy to well up in him: In Doheny's lap sat Petie, half-naked, having a high old time, evidently ready to be put to bed. Over by the stove stood Susie, washing dishes, her arms bared to the elbows. She turned towards him and her eyes swept over him with a great, soft light wherein lay worlds of happiness. The next moment she had him in her arms, pressing him to her in a frenzied embrace as though she never could release him:

"At last I've got my big, bad Norwegian boy back again!"

Peder wanted to reciprocate her joy, and tried, but he could not, not right here with old Doheny looking at him. Gently he freed himself, deeply embarrassed. There sat his father-in-law, grinning at them. . . . Wasn't she ashamed to act like this in front of other people? He groped for a chair and sat down. . . . Words of surprise and of wonder cried out for voice; you could hear them plainly in the silence of both Doheny and Susie—louder in hers. Peder said:

"I was on my way to the schoolhouse . . . thought I'd just drop in and see how you folks were getting along. . . . Well, welcome home again!" His voice was low; he dared look at no one but the boy. . . . What a big rascal he was turning out to be!

Big-eyed, the boy lay staring at the stranger who had taken so violent a hold on his mother; slowly the lower part of his face puckered up in preparation for a prolonged howl; suddenly there was a frightened whimper which Peder could not possibly resist. He strode across the floor and, putting one finger under Petie's chin, he said, huskily:

"Hi there, young fellow, don't you know your own father?" When he wanted to take him the boy broke out in a scream of terror, as if the worst bugaboo were after him. At this strange behaviour of the child Susie and Doheny laughed uproariously.

There stood Peder, helpless and bewildered. When the laughter persisted he joined in disgustedly, because there was nothing else to do. He, for one, couldn't see the joke in a child's being afraid of its own father! It made him feel creepy. Stepping back from them, he said to Petie, in a loud voice:

"Just about time you got home again and learned some manners!"

"Oh, I guess there's plenty of good manners right here," drawled Doheny. "And as far as that's concerned, well, for five weeks now that boy has been living under the same roof with cultured people, people that know good manners when they see 'em."

Susie took the boy and sat down to nurse him.

"Believe me, he's learning fast!" she assured Peder, proudly. "He can talk to beat the band. You should see him crawl!"

Peder looked at her for a moment, but said nothing. Then he turned to his father-in-law and surlily asked him how he was getting along.

"And They Shall Be One Flesh"

"Can't you see for yourself? Here I sit like another cripple. Don't you s'pose that damned fool of a doctor wanted
to saw my leg off? And I was expected to pay him big money
for the job. 'Go to hell and saw off your own limbs,' I said!
Told him that if he wanted hamburger, he'd have to get it
at the butcher shop. It was Father Williams who saved my
life—God bless him! . . . No, sir, you can't have Susie
back for a while yet, if that's what you've come for. You're
not up against it like I am; you've got your mother to fry
spuds for you." A suppressed surliness made Doheny's voice
sour.

"And that's true, too," injected Susie. "It's much easier
for her with me and Petie away."

Peder could not understand what she was trying to say.

"Have you ever heard her complain?" he asked, dryly.

"Heavens, no! She'd never do that," answered Susie, re-
assuringly. "She loves Petie too much ever to think of com-
plaining. But father needs me; in her house I'm only in
the way."

Peder heard her say it and heard it not. His face darkened
and he reached for the door-knob.

"You'd better stay as long as your father needs you . . .
if there's no other way out of it? We'll have to try to help
each other as best we can." Again his eyes sought Susie's.
"Wouldn't you like to come over just for to-night?" As he
said this he felt a deep blush spread over his face and he
added, hurriedly: "I can get you back here in time to get
breakfast in the morning."

"Oh, I'm so lazy in the morning! And I've lost so much
sleep these weeks!" she begged, smiling sweetly.

"Sure, you go with him!" Doheny's surliness broke out in
full force. "I can fire up in the stove, heat the water, and
take care of myself to-night. Begad—that's no trick for a
man who can't walk! Isn't it at two o'clock we change bandages? No use spending your nights here with a good-for-
nothing old cripple like me!"

The outburst left Peder stunned. . . . Downright dirty of
him to say that! . . . How was I to know about the bandages

and that he had to have hot water? Peder's defiance had
been stirred and was mounting fast. He looked straight at
his father-in-law; the words had a hard ring:

"Hold your horses, Michael Doheny. I've done nothing
worse than ask my own wife to come home with me!"

Doheny felt highly insulted:

"Hold my horses, me eye! That's easy enough to say for
anyone who's got two good legs to run around on. Keep
your good advice to yourself! I know what's ailing you; it's
written all over your face. Susie hasn't been away more than
five weeks. You two ought to be ashamed of yourselves . . .
a couple of kids!"

Susie came quickly to Peder and grasped his arm:

"Don't you mind what he says! That's the way he is; he
has to be mean to feel good." She looked at him with a helplessness that pleaded for understanding. "Be good now and
come to see me real often. . . . Come to-morrow and stay
all day!"

For an instant Peder looked down at her, and went out,
slamming the door behind him. Beside the horse he stood
waiting awhile before untying the halter. As one thought
followed another his face hardened. . . . By right I should
go back and slap his face . . . that's what he deserves. . . .
Is that the brand of good manners they were taught at the
priest's house? . . . He'll never again get another chance to
insult me like that! Peder undid the knot and threw the
halter into the buggy box. . . . As he came by the kitchen
he stopped the horse. . . . She'll surely come out to say
good-bye? . . . Does she really intend to let me go without
coming out?

For some time he sat there staring at the door. But no
one appeared. . . . Finally he drove off.

III

While tramping behind the plough the following week
Peder could see how foolishly he had behaved on Saturday
night. It was all clear as day to him now. But that did not

"And They Shall Be One Flesh"

help to raise his spirits. No, there was a more deep-seated hurt—a groping anxiety which would allow him no peace. . . . Here were forces at work which threatened to destroy the very ties that had held Susie and him together. How could he prevent the catastrophe? Should he step in and strike the blow that would settle the affair once and for all? That blow would mean a long succession of calamities . . . smashed relationships . . . broken hearts . . . no telling where or how it would end? . . . Would the gossips prove to be right, after all? Wasn't he the commander of his own ship and wasn't he himself laying out its course? Couldn't he steer his own ship wherever he chose? His determination only grew firmer: One thing is sure, no outsider is ever going to butt in and ruin our happiness . . . just wait till I have a good heart-to-heart talk with her!

All through that week he toiled like a galley slave. His mother saw him only when he came in to snatch a bite to eat. At such times he was so talkative that she could not help wondering what had happened.

On the way home from church the following Sunday he suddenly suggested driving over to call on his brother. "We haven't been there for a long time. It's really our turn to call on them." Without waiting for her consent, he turned the horse at the crossroad.

"What if we should be getting company ourselves?" his mother objected.

Peder laughed:

"What if we should? Would that make any difference? . . . No use expecting our folks; she can't leave him for a while yet. I told her to stay as long as she was needed." Peder's tone was careless.

Beret said nothing more, and so they drove to Store-Hans' and stayed there till after milking-time.

The following week passed with no news from Doheny's. Once or twice Beret hinted that he should drive over to see how they were getting along, but each time Peder with many words brushed the suggestion aside as a foolish notion:

—Charley was busy with the fall ploughing these days.

Their Fathers' God

Susie went to bed early . . . in town she'd stayed up every night . . . she'd had a tough time of it . . . Doheny had been on the point of losing his leg. . . . In case she needed anything, the road was no longer one way than the other. Perhaps he'd run over Saturday night . . . he'd see how tired he was by that time. When he saw that his words had no effect, he became indignant: "Why do you have to go around pining your heart away over Petie? He certainly is getting all the care he needs . . . why, he's thriving like a gopher in a cornfield. What are you worrying about, anyway?" After that Peder was so cross and snappy that she hardly dared speak to him.

The days dragged by. To Peder each seemed like an age, interminable. All that week he ploughed.

Saturday evening he quit work earlier than usual, put the horses in the barn, and did the chores. He felt light-hearted because the week at last had come to an end. The evening was filled with serenity. In quiescent peace the prairie rested . . . just rested . . . dozed and dreamt of the many sun-filled days gone by. In the twilight floated a thin veil of blue with a tint of silver in it, weightless even after the smoke from many chimneys had blended with it. Silently and imperceptibly the horizons crept towards each other until the whole prairie seemed no more than a round acre. The low afterglow of a satiated evening faded slowly into deep night.

Peder was a long time in getting started. Grumpish and out of sorts he stepped into the buggy. His humour did not improve as the buggy rolled down the road. . . . Why was he going, anyhow, he asked himself. How could he ever talk to her, with others sitting there listening to every word? The old man would only think he was woman-crazy . . . that's what he was driving at last time . . . wasn't ashamed to say it right out, either. . . . And she, poor little thing, didn't see he must have her alone!

The bitterness rankling in him grew worse. . . . Did the old man mean to hang on to her until he married again? . . . There was a big lump in his throat: The child didn't even know his own father any longer! They had laughed at

"And They Shall Be One Flesh"

that . . . even she had laughed. She, at least, ought to have
better sense. About time she came to *him* for confession!
. . . Would the gossips who had been frowning and predicting the worst prove right, after all? Were they going to
get their longed-for chance of pointing their fingers at him
and saying, "I told you so!" No . . . not even if he had to
turn the whole prairie upside down to prevent it!

At the crossroad by the schoolhouse he turned the horse
and took the road that led to Tambur-Ola's. To-night he
must find some one he could talk with. . . . She had
preached to him often enough about staying home nights.
He'd show her that he could stand it as long as she could.
. . . Doggone it! let her wallow in the filth over there until
she was fed up on it!

This last summer, a niece of Mrs. Tonaas', by the name
of Nikoline Johansen, had come from Norway and was now
staying with her aunt. Peder had once heard it hinted long
ago that Lapp blood had come into the family. In Sörine,
however, no vestige of mixed race was noticeable. Yet the
rumour might be true. Nikoline was short of build and a
little stout, broad-hipped, and agile in every move and manner; there was a joyous lilt in her gait, like that of one who
is constantly hearing a cheerful tune and is fond of dancing;
the little face was round and uncommonly radiant; the skin
had a slight yellowish tinge that deepened to a brownish-
yellow whenever laughter leaped into the face; this happened
often, though she seldom laughed out loud. The deep blue of
her eyes made her complexion appear lighter than was actually the case.

Shortly after Nikoline had arrived, Peder had overheard
Sörine telling his mother about her; he had become interested
and had listened intently to the story:

—Poor girl, she is like a sea gull with a broken wing, related Sörine. She lost her father, her brother, and her sweetheart, all at one stroke, during the terrible storm on the 25th
of January in '93. It happened on the cod-banks at Varöy,
Lofoten. All three were fishing on the same boat. Early in

Their Fathers' God

the morning they had put out for the fishing-grounds and were never seen again; not a splinter of the boat turned up afterwards. Nikoline took it so hard that she had to be put to bed. For a while her mother was afraid that the girl was losing her mind. But when the spring sun arose in its glory, flooding the mountains with golden light, and the surf on fair nights sang soft songs along the shore of the cove, she had got up from her bed and made up her mind to live. Soon she was her old self again. Last winter she had written to her aunt for a ticket to America, and early this summer she had bade farewell to Norway for good.

Peder had talked with the girl twice. Both times a chord had been touched in him. Least of all would he have believed that she had been brought to death's door by sheer sorrow. The last time she and her aunt had been at Holm's, Peder had sat for a long time bandying words with her. But first she had led him to the windmill and made him climb to the top, she following close behind. "Go on, go on," she had urged him, a note of excitement in her voice. "Let's get up so high that our sight can take wing. Once more I must see the far horizons!" She was trembling with eagerness. The night was still and full of the mystery of high summer. Below them, in the shimmering moonlight lay the prairies like a vast carpet of greenish blue. Here and there, far away, glowed a dull red eye, too sleepy to wink.

There they had sat talking of things far and near. By and by they found themselves entangled in a heated argument over social conditions in America, she maintaining that the people here were in a bad way because they did not know how to enjoy life; if they tried, they went to extremes of vulgarity; or else they turned to religious debauchery like the *Lestadianers*[1] back home in Norway, and the one was as bad as the other! In attacking America she had touched Peder's most vulnerable spot; he had to gainsay her, defending his position with gusto. But she refused to be downed. She had read a lot; there wasn't a book of any consequence that she didn't know. She knew many of Mark Twain's stories by

[1] The *Lestadianers* are a religious sect similar to the "Holy-Rollers."

"And They Shall Be One Flesh"

heart; when she began relating one of them and realized that Peder did not know who he was, she clapped her hands in surprise: "Good heavens! You an American and haven't even heard of Mark Twain! What in the world do you learn in your schools over here?" Peder had tried to conceal his embarrassment by laughing it off, and had succeeded only moderately. . . . He was sure she was exaggerating; if this fellow Mark Twain was half as much as she said, he'd certainly have heard of him!

They did not come down from the windmill until her aunt came out of the house and was ready to leave.

When Peder reached Tambur-Ola's he found a celebration in progress.

"You've come just at the right time!" cried his godmother, happily. "To-night we're serving real Nordland food. Now you sit right up to the table!"

Peder, shifting uneasily, said he had just eaten.

"Oh, but you've still got room for a little *lutefisk*! Take this chair and join us."

Peder laughed and sat down at the table.

"Celebrating Christmas so early?" he asked.[1]

Just opposite him sat Nikoline.

"Norwegians celebrate Christmas the whole year 'round. You ought to know that, being one yourself." She swept him with her eyes and they seemed to him twinkling stars. He had to look up again, but did not find them. . . . This one thing he was certain of—there was not another pair of eyes like that in either Norway or America.

"You've certainly made a great mistake in coming to America. Over here we observe Lent the whole year 'round!"

The others laughed at his rejoinder. The merriment took a new spurt as she struck back at him:

"Easy to hear that you're a grass widower! . . . Lent here must be a cruel business since it forces real Nordlændings to hitch up with the Irish!"

[1] In most Norwegian homes *lutefisk* is usually found on the Christmas menu.

Their Fathers' God

Peder turned crimson:

"You should have come sooner!"

"Why didn't you come and get me?" She looked straight at him, her eyes sparkling with suppressed mischief; the natural charm of her voice and the slow rhythm of her dialect blended to make music of all she said and all she was.

He looked up innocently:

"How was I to know there was such a lovely, lonely little rose waiting for me over in Norway?"

"Why didn't you come and look? It's your father's country. . . . Anyway, you should have waited awhile."

"Why? That wasn't necessary . . . we've got plenty of roses here to pick from."

"Yes, of course." Suddenly her face sobered: "Have you ever read about the lotus-eaters?"

"Can't remember I have. What about them?"

"Well, you see," she said, innocently, "they ate and ate, and just slept and ate."

"Yes?"

"Until they forgot they were human beings. After that they lived in bliss and contentment all their days. But it was a sad sort of happiness, because they could never become human again!"

Peder laughed gleefully—now he had her cornered:

"That's heaven, isn't it?"

"Yes," she said slowly, with an odd emphasis, "for those that want that kind of a heaven."

Peder had to look at her again. His glance met hers and she did not quail; it was he who had to look away first. And when he did she laughed, low and mockingly.

The talk went on merrily and they remained sitting at the table long after the meal was finished. It felt so pleasant and so good to be here that Peder had not the least desire to get up. When at last he had said good night and was leaving, Sörine followed him to the buggy.

"There's a matter I've been wanting to talk to you about, Permand," she said in a low, kindly voice that had a touch of anxiety in it. "Now you mustn't get mad at me!"

"And They Shall Be One Flesh"

"Don't you worry about that!"

"You ought to have your boy baptized." And, as if fearing that he would misunderstand her, she added, hastily: "You know how it is with us older folks, when we get along in years, the things we learnt in our childhood mean more and more to us."

Peder was silent. Her kindliness, and still more her maternal solicitude, touched him.

Sörine spoke again, softly and with an earnestness that brought tears into her eyes:

"I've always thought a lot of you, Permand. That's why I must mention this to you. Take your child to the minister as soon as you can. We don't any of us know what might happen. And now we've got such a splendid minister, too!" She grasped his arm: "You can't believe how happy I'll be when you've had the child christened!"

He laughed at her eagerness.

"Maybe you want him named after you?"

"No, no!" she half-sobbed. Her almost frantic fear of being misunderstood made him feel uncomfortable. "Certainly you're going to name him *Peder!*" she said, more calmly. She paused, and added, quickly: "Let your mother think of a nice middle name for him. Hasn't she spoken to you about it?"

"Oh, once or twice."

"I can't understand that. She came here one day."

"Long ago?"

"Quite a while ago now."

"About the name?"

"Not exactly. But I know what she wants him named," she confided, in a low voice.

"You better tell me, then."

She was still holding his arm:

"Peder Emmanuel," she whispered, hoarsely. "That's a beautiful name. Let your mother have her way!"

Peder, ill at ease, took her hand:

"Thanks, godmother, for your advice. If I hadn't known before you were a good woman, I'd surely know it now."

Their Fathers' God

Sörine wept and could say no more. It puzzled Peder that she should be so concerned about this thing. There was a secret anxiety in her solicitude. What could it mean? It was so unlike her. With assumed unconcern he thanked her for the pleasant evening, said good night, and drove away.

The episode gave Peder much to ponder over. . . . Strange that people couldn't leave him alone? . . . Why didn't they tend to their own worries? He'd take care of his affairs . . . and never bother with anybody else's. . . . Here was Sörine worrying herself sick over Petie's baptism. Wasn't that his business? The child was *his* . . . Petie was part of his very being . . . he alone had the responsibility. . . . Why did they always fuss and fret? . . . Perhaps he'd better stir up a batter and make them a real cake . . . eh? . . . Well, no hurry yet. Anyway, that girl was worth looking at. . . . Wish he'd met her before!

IV

All Sunday afternoon and evening he was possessed by an irrepressible restlessness. If he sat down, it was only for a short while. Up he would get, and wander out-of-doors. Outside there was nothing to do. A few minutes and he would be back in the house. To try lying down was equally futile. To-day it was impossible for him to remain quiet.

This morning he had been to church with his mother and had heard the new minister. The church had been crowded. After the service he went about shaking hands with friends. . . . He'd better show them that he wasn't dying of grief simply because his wife had gone off for a little visit! Several asked how Doheny was getting along and in answer he gave long, detailed accounts of the sick man's condition.

At the church also was Sörine with her whole household. When he had greeted them he fell to bantering with Nikoline about the ministers and church life in America. It was odd to Peder that she who always questioned everything American, now grew warm in her praise of how able and democratic a man Reverend Kaldahl was. "He's supposed to

be so Norwegianified," Peder had teased. Nikoline only
looked at him, unable to understand what he meant. "Don't
you think it's a good thing for men like you to hear about
the god of their fathers?" In her question was a childlike
wonder reaching out for understanding. Tambur-Ola, who
was listening, shot in one of his cutting remarks: "Of course
there's a big difference between the god over there and the
one we've got here. Ours lives on beef and pie; the Norwegian god on herring and *lutefisk*!" . . . Peder noticed
how she coloured at her uncle's sarcasm. As soon as she had
found her answer her face broke into a bright smile: "That's
why the Norwegian god is better. Fish is a more healthful
food!" . . . "Yes," the uncle admitted, "but it always works
the other way with gods!" Suddenly it was as if a curtain had
been drawn over her whole being. She took Tambur-Ola by
the arm: "If this is how you're going to talk, I won't listen
to you. Come, let's go home."

Peder and his mother had driven straight home. At the
dinner table little was said between them. Afterwards he
changed clothes and went out to tend the cattle.

The chores did not take long to-day, and the restlessness
which was upon him soon drove him back to the house. He
threw off his work clothes and dressed himself in his best,
standing long before the looking-glass; his hair would not lie
right. His necktie looked shabby, so he changed to another.
A little while and he was strolling out in the yard again.
. . . More comfortable here than inside. Out in the open a
fellow could at least breathe!

The buggy was standing where he had unhitched, empty
and waiting for him. Dolly still had her harness on; he
could hear her every time she stamped her foot on the barn
floor. For a moment he stood gazing down the road. . . .
No, he'd wait until to-night . . . at this time of day they'd
most likely have the house full of company. For the time
being this decision put his mind at ease. He went upstairs,
picked up a book, and sprawled on the bed. He saw words
but did not read them. . . . If they had been at home now,

Their Fathers' God

he'd be lying here with the boy. Good God! how sweetly that child could smile in his sleep!

Disgusted, he threw the book aside and looked up. Some of Susie's clothes were still hanging in their place on the wall, a Sunday apron and a dress she had worn just after she had moved here. The skirt was soiled around the edges. . . . That dress ought to be washed . . . had it hung here all this time? Good thing mother hadn't noticed how dirty it was! Susie had not worn the dress after she had become pregnant. . . . Perhaps he ought to take it along to-night? That would give him an errand. He might find other things, too . . . make up a whole bundle.

The restlessness tore at him worse than ever. . . . What were they doing over there to-day? Lots of visitors? . . . Didn't she miss him at all? . . . He got up and went to the window. . . . She and Charley could easily have driven over to-day . . . the old man wouldn't have croaked on that account! . . . Funny she didn't need him? didn't cry to the heavens for him? If she had wanted him only one-tenth as much as he needed her, she would have been here long ago . . . she'd have *had* to come!

In the evening he and his mother went out to do the chores earlier than usual. Beautiful weather. Out of the south drifted a lazy breath of a wind. Peder studied the sky carefully. . . . Not so sure it might not rain to-night. Those clouds out west ——?

After they had eaten, his mother asked:

"I suppose you are driving over to see them to-night?" She seemed to have been thinking about the matter for a long time.

—To-night? His voice was irritable. No, he guessed not. He had nothing in particular to see them about.

Beret began to clear the table, her face sober and heavy with thought. Finally she ventured a suggestion:

"It is easier for you to drive over there than for her to come here. She has others to look after."

"Oh, rot!"

"No need to say 'rot' to me! I think you are behaving like

two fools! Susie has been away for nearly two months. From here to where she is is only a half-hour's ride. . . . Not that it matters to me."

"It sounds that way, all right!"

Peder shambled outside and over to the windmill. There he sat down. . . . To-night he'd have no more silly talk about this business! He clutched one of the steel cross-pieces until his hands smarted. For a long time he sat looking at the afterglow of the sunset. At last he rose, went to the buggy and pushed it into the shed. . . . If they didn't watch out, he'd go straight over to godmother's and have a chat with that newcomer girl. . . . Then Susie could stay Irish as long as she pleased!

As he came in he remarked, carelessly:

"I feel so dead tired to-night. Guess I'll go right up to bed. Hard day to-morrow again. I'll have to get the ploughing finished and start husking corn."

But he did not go to bed. He changed from his good clothes to a clean overall that hung in a corner and sat down to reread "Hamlet."

v

He had not been long at the reading before the distant rumble of an empty wagon broke through the evening stillness. The rumbling was coming nearer; a strange warmth swept through him like a sudden gust of wind that quickly dies away. He sat tensely alert. . . . Was the wagon turning into the yard? . . . Now it drove more slowly. Peder ran downstairs to see who it could be.

As soon as he recognized the horses and saw that she was alone, a dizziness came over him; his knees shook and he would have liked to sit down.

The horses halted by the post. There he stood waiting, bewildered, with his hands clasped under the apron of his overalls. Moments passed before he could get up his voice to speak:

"Is this the way you come?"

"Yes," said Susie, meekly. "Charley took the buggy and went off. There I sat looking down the road till I couldn't see. When I finally saw you weren't coming to-night, either, I just had to come over and find out whether you were dead." She made no move to come down from the wagon. "Having one man to look after is bad enough," she said, apathetically, "but it's a snap compared with having two, and those two staying miles apart." Her lassitude was reflected in her voice; yet there was no trace of complaint. Up in the wagon seat, against the darkness of the night, she appeared so tiny and so utterly forlorn.

With trembling hands he tied the horses to the post. Came back and stood beside the wagon.

"Aren't you coming down?" he asked, thickly.

"If you want me to," she answered in the same forlorn manner, and did not stir.

Peder held out his arms:

"What's the matter?" His voice was low and hoarse.

Susie put one foot on the wheel, laughing ever so little:

"Well, here I am!"

The next instant she lay in his arms:

"Are you awfully mad at me?" she whispered.

"Huh, mad!" In a frenzy he was crushing her to him.

Drunk with joy too terrible for speech, they stood thus, silent, trembling, each possessed with the same desire: to press closer to the other, ever closer, in order to give more and to get more. By and by she loosened herself from his embrace, put her arm about him, and led him off towards the barn.

"We can't talk in the house," she explained.

"No, no!" he mumbled. "Not to-night!" And suddenly he had picked her up bodily and was carrying her in his arms.

He set her down by the first stall which was unoccupied and was used only to keep bedding in. "Wait!" he whispered, huskily, and disappeared in the dark; in a moment he had returned with a horse blanket which he spread over the straw. "Now!" . . .

Tenderly he laid her down. Both were unmindful of aught

else but the passion that was upon them. To a degree they had never known before they gave themselves over to each other, she with more abandon than he; it was as though she never could get enough of him. Her passion was like the tiny whirlwind that occasionally springs up on the prairie; it rises and dies down, seems entirely gone, and then suddenly springs up again and whirls on indefinitely.

Afterwards they sat in silence, holding hands, she with her head against his cheek.

"I suppose we'd better go in," said Peder, quietly, but he did not move.

It seemed that Susie had not heard him. After a little she leaned back, resting on her elbow.

"Put your head here so I can stroke your hair. My poor, poor Peder-boy!" To-night she was more ardent than when first they found each other. And always she had more that she must give him.

They remained there for a long while. At last they walked slowly across the yard, hand in hand, satiated and stilled. As they entered the kitchen the calm eye of the lamp found their faces, casting deep bashfulness over both. Their cheeks glowed crimson. Neither could look at Beret, who came to meet her daughter-in-law. Peder did not speak; he strode over to the water-pail and drank deeply.

Susie remained standing by the door. She had suddenly stepped into a great cleanliness and knew not what to do with herself. The shining nickel of the stove glistened in many colours. The brightly polished water-kettle which had been put on to boil was sputtering fitfully, announcing that in this house a Sabbath evening was being observed . . . no loud talk, please . . . no uncleanliness of any kind . . . let the day depart in peace! With painful exactness all things had been looked after and put in order. In the wink of an eye Susie had taken in the whole scene. Timidly she greeted her mother-in-law, asking awkwardly how they all were getting along over here . . . did she still have headaches? . . . No? . . .

Beret received her as if she were just returning from a

165

long journey that had kept her away for years; the tears came into her eyes as she asked with kind concern:

"What have you done to Pete? Why didn't you bring him?" She did not realize that she was speaking to Susie in Norwegian, and she would not let go of her hand.

"What is she saying?" asked Susie, embarrassed.

"I'll tell you exactly." Peder's voice was loud and blustering. "She says that unless you and Petie move back home to-morrow we'll all be going crazy."

"Don't pay attention to his foolish talk!" stammered Beret, in English. With her apron she dusted off the seat of a chair where there was no dust and urged Susie to sit down.

Susie blinked at all this concern for her . . . it was so undeserved . . . just now so out of place. Suddenly she threw her arms about her mother-in-law:

"You're the best person in all the world! How can you manage to be so good?"

"Hush, child! You must not talk like that. Now I'll make you a cup of coffee."

Without looking up, Susie asked Peder if he would go upstairs with her? She needed some clothes for the boy . . . almost impossible to keep him dressed decently . . . now that he had started to creep, you couldn't keep him off the floor . . . soon she'd have to go to town and get new clothes for him. . . . Of course, he didn't need to come up with her . . . she knew where the things were and could just as well go alone. She had risen and it sounded as if she were asking permission to go into the loft.

Peder only stood looking at her. Twice he opened his mouth to speak, but said nothing; he could not catch her glance and so he led the way upstairs. After lighting the lamp he sat down on the edge of the bed.

Susie looked around, concentrating, it seemed, on what articles she should take along. The dress and the apron hanging on the wall were the first items selected; then she opened the drawers of the commode and pulled out some shirts for the boy and some underwear and stockings for herself. One pair she had to examine more closely. She drew each one over her hand, eyeing it critically; one had a big hole in the toe, the other was badly worn in the heel. In one of the drawers lay a few toys Petie had received as a birthday gift from Anna Marie, who was still staying with her brother in Montana—a toy horse, a rattle, a bright-coloured ball. These, together with the articles of clothing, she wrapped into the apron, carefully tying the strings around the bundle.

"Well, I guess that's about all I need now," she said aloud, talking to herself. She seemed to be checking over in her mind what else there might be to take. "Maybe I'll need another pair of stockings?" She stood with the stockings in her hand, unable to decide; finally she tucked the pair into the bundle.

Slowly, as though uncertain about something, she closed the drawers of the commode and looked at herself in the mirror. "Gosh! what a mess you've made of me! You must have rolled me in hayseed." There was a happy warmth in her voice, a touch of laughter, and a roguish glance at Peder. She began fingering her hair, could not get it as she wanted it and drew out the pins to do it up anew. She shook the long thick coils down her back and made no effort to hurry putting the hair up. Meanwhile she kept up a constant chatter, in a low, confidential tone, always with her back turned to Peder. He sat motionless, with his legs crossed, his hands clasped about his knee; his eyes stared fixedly at the opposite wall. When she shifted her weight to her left foot she could see him in the corner of the mirror.

. . . "In a few more weeks I hope father will be so well I can leave him," she said in a low, confidential voice. . . . "Poor father, he's certainly been tried in the fire! For a while we never thought he'd make it . . . that old dog-killer of a doctor didn't mind telling us, either . . . told us straight out he couldn't live. . . . I had to stay up night after night . . . it wasn't all fun, I can tell you . . . you can't imagine how I longed for you!" She gave a deep sigh. "Thank God! he's past the worst! . . . I suppose it'll be a good while yet before he's able to take care of himself." Here she crossed the floor and laid her hand on Peder's shoulder:

Their Fathers' God

"Be a good husband and come over to see me real often! Don't mind father's barking; he is that way; when he scolds it means he's in good humour." Peder sat motionless, staring hard at the wall. Suddenly she straightened up and exclaimed: "Bless me if I don't smell fresh coffee! Isn't grandma a darling? And here I'm hungry as a bear! . . . If you only knew how I hate to leave you to-night! . . . Come and be good to me just once more!" She did not look at him; she had discovered a spot on her dress that had to be rubbed out. When that was done she picked up the bundle and seemed ready to leave.

Peder rose and took the package. As he did so he bent over and kissed her hair, as indifferently as if he had stopped to pick a burnt match from the floor. Not a word did he say.

Midway down the stairs he stopped.

"Wait," he said, wearily. . . . "Oh well, never mind."

"What is it?" she whispered, leaning close to him. But now he had already opened the door to the stairway, and so she had to follow.

On the white-covered table was spread a royal feast of delicacies. Beret had carried the lamp into the front room and in its place set out two home-made candles which now shed a mellow light over the room. A visit from the minister himself would have warranted no finer preparations. Susie clapped her hands joyfully:

"How beautiful . . . just like Christmas eve!"

Deeply touched by the praise, Beret blinked; there were bright tears in her eyes, and her smile was benign.

"Now you must come and sit down. You too, Peder. The coffee is ready."

Peder already had his hand on the door-knob; he addressed his mother curtly in Norwegian:

"I'm going to hitch up. I've got to go with her." He paused for a moment, with the door opened. "She has to hurry back to look after the child. Past his bedtime already."

Susie went to the pail and drank a mouthful of water. With her face turned away from her mother-in-law she asked:

"And They Shall Be One Flesh"

"Now what did he say?"

"That he will be going home with you. He is going out to get the horses ready. But you just take your time. There's no hurry."

"Is he coming with me?" asked Susie, so frightened that she turned pale.

Beret smiled ever so little.

"I don't suppose he likes the idea of you driving all that way alone at night. . . . Here, come now and sit up to the table!" Beret poured Susie's cup, sat down opposite her, and said aloud the Norwegian prayer she always used before meals.

"Now you must help yourself! This bread is fresh. And you must taste my plum sauce. I cooked it Saturday."

Susie picked at the food, now and then putting a bit into her mouth.

Presently Beret looked up at her:

"My how thin you've grown since you left us! Poor child! only skin and bones. . . . I suppose Pete is hard on you? You haven't weaned him yet?" Suddenly her face lit up with kindliness: "Now you must tell me all about him. . . . Is he growing fast? Does he talk much yet?" There was maternal solicitude in her voice: "You must be sure to look after him and not let him lay wet. Such little folks are tender; they can't stand much. Do you remember to pot him at night? Have you still plenty of milk for him?" Beret asked and asked, question after question, all in the same intimate tone. She was less timid now about speaking English than with Norwegians present, and to-night her solicitude had overcome her natural shyness.

Susie answered in the same low tone; there was a note of suppressed excitement in all they said; at times they spoke in whispers, as if they couldn't stand to hear the sound of their own voices; though so confidential, yet they were worlds apart.

Repeatedly Susie tried to turn the talk to other subjects. She sipped the coffee and declared that never in all her life had she tasted such good coffee . . . how much egg had she

used? She stirred sugar into it and drank deep draughts.
. . . Wonderful! . . . She wished she could learn to make
coffee like that!

Beret got up and refilled the cup.

"How long will it be before you can come back?"

Susie stirred the coffee.

—She couldn't say exactly . . . not yet . . . maybe not
until after Christmas . . . it might be longer. . . . Suddenly her voice filled with warmth and she talked fast: She
had never been in a worse fix, she confided to her mother-
in-law. . . . Absolutely impossible to get decent help. Here
they had combed the whole prairie for a capable person and
couldn't find anybody. . . . She didn't happen to know of
a woman over this way? Oh no, there was nothing to do
but stay on as long as father needed her. . . . She mustn't
think she had had the easiest time of it! . . . Since father
had been sick he had been so cross and cranky that you
couldn't come near him . . . she supposed everybody in ex-
treme suffering got to be the same way, especially old people. . . . Anyway, she concluded, cheerfully, there was no
need of her rushing back here as long as father needed her
and couldn't get help. . . . Here she was mostly in the way.
She laughed a little as she said this.

As Beret listened to Susie's talk her face filled with a
great soberness:

"You must not forget that you have a husband. He
suffers and sorrows because you are staying away so long."

Susie gave a hearty laugh.

"Now you're only fooling, grandma!"

"No, no, child, that I am not. I have eyes and can see
things. I have known him since he lay under my heart. He
upsets so easily. . . . I am sure it was his intention to bring
you back the last time he went to town to see you. When
he came home I was afraid to look at him. All that night
I lay awake, listening to him twisting and turning in bed.
For days I could not get a word out of him. He is that
way; he takes things so hard."

Susie had turned her empty cup upside down on the saucer.

"And They Shall Be One Flesh"

Long ago her grandmother had taught her how to tell fortunes from the coffee grounds and often she had had great fun predicting to people what the future had in the store for them. Righting the cup again, she studied the grounds intently. . . . "Did you say the last time?" She turned the cup and searched the signs from another angle. Her face was red; not once did she look up.

"The last time, that is what I am telling you. He didn't go more than twice; the first time he didn't see you."

. . . "Let's see, how long ago was that?" She bent over the cup to scrutinize the grounds still more closely:

"The first time?"

"No . . . the second, I mean?"

Beret counted on her fingers:

"Three weeks ago last Friday? . . . Yes, three weeks ago this last Friday. I remember it well because that forenoon we had begun to husk corn. It was the first day of the season."

"Oh yes. Now I remember. That was just when father was at his worst. I had been sitting up night after night, not getting a wink of sleep. Those weeks were no picnic for me. Every day father was getting worse. . . . What did he say when he came back?" Susie was bending over the cup.

"Nothing. There was no talk left in him, like a dead man he went about his work. I feared for his reason."

"Oh!" said Susie absently, setting down the cup.

Suddenly Beret's voice quivered with eagerness.

"Why don't you let him bring the child home with him to-night? Then I can wean him for you. I still have the bottle that Peder himself used. At that time I was very low and didn't give much milk."

Susie rose abruptly, walked around the table, and patted her mother-in-law on the back.

"Thanks so much for everything, grandma!"

Beret's voice lowered:

"Don't be afraid to send the boy; it will mean less trouble for you, both now and when you come back. You need not worry that I won't take good care of him!"

Their Fathers' God

Susie pulled the door wide open:

"Well, good night!"

Beret came after her, still pleading:

"If you are going to stay away till after Christmas, you must come to see us often. . . . And be sure to bring the boy next time. The father-heart clings tenderly to his first-born, but that you don't understand . . . not yet. Wait till you have some grief to carry . . . then you will know how it is! . . . Have you a wrap? The night wind is chilly. Here . . . !" Beret tore off the shawl she had thrown around her shoulders.

Susie had already vanished in the dark.

VI

In the wagon Peder sat waiting. He had turned the horses and tied Dolly on behind. As Susie came running from the house he stood up and helped her mount to the seat. Immediately he started the horses.

She had barely seated herself before she began chatting anew in the same low tone that she had used up in the loft. Now it was about her brother and how he was making love to Maggie O'Shea. . . . Charley really meant business this time, at least it looked that way; a year ago last summer the two had been as good as engaged . . . then that big chump had started flirting with Nellie Haakensen! Maggie had got hopping mad and told him to go chase himself. . . . It would be a blessing if Charley would marry Maggie . . . she had told him so the other night . . . because then she and Petie could come home again.

"If you're going to stay away until Charley decides to get married, I'll be a grass widower the rest of my life. Maybe I should start looking around for some one else?" Peder could hold back his sullenness no longer.

Susie took this thrust as a good joke.

"Well, you just try! . . . As long as I come back once in a while to look after you, like to-night, you won't be suffering any." And in the same light manner she went on to

"And They Shall Be One Flesh"

tell how Charley had been hunting all over South Dakota for a decent hired girl and how he had been getting himself into one pickle after another. "Yesterday he drove over to see Lucy McCethrick and he found her in the back yard, plucking an old rooster, her hair and arms and clothes so full of feathers that she herself looked like the mother hen. You needn't think that he told her what he'd come for! But Lucy must have had suspicions, because she insisted that he stay until she could make him a cup of tea. Charley was in a terrible fix. 'Tea?' he had said. 'Do you think I can chase around to tea parties when my father lies there with one foot in the grave? I only dropped in to see if you'd be willing to room and board a couple of our milk cows while we're so short of help?' . . . Oh, Charley lied himself blue in the face before he managed to get away from her."

Funny how the talk runs out of her to-night, thought Peder. Here she sits gloating because they can't find a housekeeper!

Disgusted and out of patience, he cut her short:

"I don't intend to let you stay away until your father marries again. Put that in your pipe and smoke it! If you folks can't find a housekeeper, I'll do it for you."

This, too, she accepted as a joke and took hold of his arm lovingly:

"And put an end to all our troubles? Ha-ha, that's good! . . . I know I've got a mighty smart man, but he can't perform miracles. The honest-to-goodness truth is that there isn't a person to be had in all South Dakota." She snuggled closer to him and rested her head on his shoulder.

Her happy-go-lucky assurance only increased his irritation; he shrugged his shoulders so that she had to take her head away.

"Then you folks must be a darn particular lot. There's a girl staying with the Tonaas who's smart as a whip and a real worker. She's anxious to get out among Americans and learn some English. You can get her cheaper than anyone else." Immediately he regretted having said it. This was betrayal! In order to silence his misgivings he added, emphatically: "Miss Johansen is exactly the kind of girl you need, clever and afraid of nothing. My godmother told me so herself."

"Oh, her! Do you think we'd want a green newcomer girl who doesn't even know how to talk? . . . Her to take care of father!" she added, with innocent candor. "She'd do at your place because you can understand her cackling! . . . But I can tell him about her. We could try her out for a couple of weeks; I could teach her, and meanwhile we could be looking around for some one else."

Peder was stubbornly silent.

Suddenly Susie was speaking again, her voice deeply earnest:

"I can see now how wrong it was of me to leave father so soon. I oughtn't to have married so young . . . should have waited. The Mother of God doesn't look down on such acts with favour."

"Tommyrot and dead cats! How long should you have waited?"

"Until father didn't need me any longer."

Peder laughed bitterly:

"That might have been half a century." He turned his face towards her. "Do you really believe there is an old female sitting up in the sky, looking with favour on girls like you turning into old maids?" The scorn made his voice thin. "By golly—then she's a nice old hag!"

"How can you talk so wicked, Peder!" she wailed, horror-stricken, and began to weep disconsolately.

"Wicked nothing! If she isn't a witch she's something that's a lot worse. Any married woman must understand that!" . . . It made him feel good to have said this. Yet it hurt him, too. . . . Now she's sitting there crying her eyes out because she fears I'm bound for hell and eternal damnation. . . . She'll have to cry, that's all. . . . Some time or other she's got to learn the truth!

She had moved away from him as far as she could. A long time passed before the crying subsided. Finally she

"And They Shall Be One Flesh"

began to talk, picking her way cautiously from thought to thought:

"Can't understand this at all. . . . Father needs me now more than ever . . . and you don't need me at all. I can come to you and you to me as often as we want. . . . It's my own father that I want to take care of. . . . He must have help. Yet you act as if I was trying to murder you! . . . I can't understand what has come over you."

Peder forced himself to be calm:

"How long do you plan on staying there?"

"Until after Christmas. . . . That isn't very long."

"Until after Christmas?" echoed Peder. "Not on your life! . . . People aren't going to get that to jabber about!"

"Get what?"

"That you've left me . . . that the Catholic and the Lutheran couldn't get along, and you had to leave. They're hinting at it already."

"When I'm at home caring for my sick father who is helpless?" There was a strange note in her voice which he had not heard before.

"That isn't your *home*. He'll have to get himself another nurse!" said Peder, with quiet finality.

"Yes, of course," she suddenly agreed, amiably, "seeing you're so set against me staying on." She was silent for a while. Then added accusingly: "Do you think you'd leave your mother if you were in the same fix I'm in?"

"I don't have to think about that—I know it! You and I have started life together. Now it's up to us to see what we can make of it."

Of a sudden her mood had changed and she was all passionate tenderness:

"Oh, Peder, if we only had a farm of our own! Wouldn't it be great to be by ourselves with no one to interfere? I'd slave for you. And, oh, how good I'd be to you! You don't half know me yet. You've no idea how I love you."

Peder said, quietly:

"Mother's a good-hearted soul."

"Good-hearted? Have I ever denied it? She's too good-hearted, and that's the truth! She fusses over me as if I was some kind of a doll. She seems to think I'm too frail for common work. Pretty soon she'll dress me in silks and satins and use me as a parlour ornament."

"Don't talk foolishness, Susie. You know better."

"Foolishness? All right, call it what you please. Anyway, here we are back home again. . . . Thanks for the ride!" She was on her feet, and even before the wagon had come to a stop she had jumped to the ground.

VII

Peder tied the horses and followed her into the house. . . . They were not going to part like this to-night! No, sir. His face was dark and set.

A stale smell met him as he stepped into the kitchen. Doheny sat close to the stove, with his injured leg resting on the opened oven door. In his lap lay Petie, whimpering distressfully; the low wailing sounded as though he had been crying a long time and now was too exhausted to keep it up much longer. He hiccoughed spasmodically; at the sight of the stranger he hid his face and cried more loudly.

Susie snatched up the child and fled into the front room.

Peder's "Good evening" as he came in had fallen on deaf ears. He flung himself down on a chair, laid his right foot on his left knee, and tilted the chair back; his hands were plunged deep into his pockets. Thus he sat staring darkly at Doheny. Apparently Charley was not at home.

His father-in-law glanced at him, looked away, but soon turned his eyes on him once more. He stuffed his pipe, was about to light it, and found that he had no matches. "Oh, give me a match," he said, wearily. "Oh no! That's right, you don't smoke." Laboriously he pulled himself up, balanced on his cane, and bent forward to the match-box that hung on the wall by the stove. After securing a supply he turned, swung slowly back to his chair, leaning heavily on his cane. Once or twice he tottered as if he might fall. "Holy hell! what a fix to be in!" groaned Doheny as he sat down again.

176

"And They Shall Be One Flesh"

Peder let the back of his chair rest against the wall; he had locked his hands behind his head. Again there was silence in the room. Finally Peder spoke up, calmly and with certainty, as though he had thought the matter out carefully:

"Now I want to try my hand at finding help for you." He paused for a second. "This thing can't go on forever."

Doheny glanced up indifferently.

"Sure, take Susie back with you. I can take care of myself easily. Nothing at all. I'd never keep her away from you, seeing you need her so badly."

At that moment Susie returned to the kitchen with the boy. She placed him in Peder's arms and stepped aside as if to leave him there.

"There you've got him. Do you see how red and Irish-looking his hair is getting to be? He takes after his mother's family, all right."

Petie gave one look at his father and set up a fearful howl.

Like a mother eagle Susie swooped down on them and snatched up the child.

"Sh-sh, you sweet little darling!" she cooed. "Don't you like your daddy? Huh? Sh-sh! That'll do now! That'll do!"

"Give Mr. Patrick to me!" ordered Doheny, brusquely. "Haven't you got better sense than to dump him into the arms of a total stranger? Come here with him!"

As soon as the boy was back in his grandfather's arms he looked up into the familiar face, put his thumb in his mouth, and stopped crying.

"Let me tell you," said Doheny, proudly, "here's a fellow who appreciates his relatives!"

Peder closed one eye, squinting at his father-in-law with the other:

"You're not interested in getting help?"

"Aw," drawled Doheny good-naturedly, "I guess I can still do my own courting. Thanks for the offer, anyhow. One of these days I'm going to hitch up and see what I can find!"

Peder got up and said an indifferent good night. In the door, just as he left, he turned to Susie:

"I can put the horses in for you?"

She came running out after him.

"Peder!" she called, softly.

He slackened his pace without looking back.

Overtaking him, she hooked her arm in his and said, disgustedly:

"Can you beat that for a husband? Here you run away from your wife without even stopping to say good-bye! Is that all the thanks I get for coming to see you?"

Peder walked on to the wagon, stubborn and silent.

"Do you know what?" Her voice was eager, as if some new thought had just dawned on her: "I'm awfully mad at you."

Peder stopped by the wagon and looked at her. Her face was near his. Not a word did he say.

"If I were big enough I'd give you a sound thrashing!" Her voice sounded as if she didn't quite dare to let go of herself.

"Why?" he asked, coldly.

"As if you don't know! All the while I was cooped up in town my own husband didn't bother to come and see me once, not once!"

"Is that so?" he asked, scornfully. "Where were you keeping yourself the day I was there and asked for you?"

Suddenly she dropped his arm; a shoe-lace had come untied; she put her foot on the hub of the front wheel and bent over to tie the lace.

"And you ask about that?" she muttered.

"You heard me."

"You're just plain foolish. That's what's the matter with you, Peder. All of you Norwegians are the same way."

"I understand that, all right!" he said, acidly.

"You don't understand anything!" She was swallowing hard on the lumps rising in her throat.

"Maybe you were sleeping in the middle of the afternoon?"

She drew a deep breath and put her hand up to her heart,

then laughed ever so faintly; in her face the colour came
and went.

"Don't you s'pose I needed to get a little sleep once in a
while? Wouldn't you even let me have that?" She was sobbing, but talked on: "You don't know what a strain I was
under those weeks. . . . Sitting up with a dying man night
after night. . . . The doctor had given up all hope. Insisted
on amputating . . . the mean old brute . . . I'll never forgive him. He was very wroth with me. . . . There I was
all alone . . . no one to turn to. . . . Each night was an
eternity, almost as long . . . there I lay, listening to father's
agony . . . and afraid he'd die on me. . . . And you, you,
my own husband, for whom I'd sinned, you who should
have been my help and my comfort, you never came
once! . . ." She sobbed like a little child that had been
cruelly mistreated and could not forget the injustice. . . .
"Bad enough at night . . . still worse during the day . . .
then I had Petie on my hands, too! . . . Ever since the accident father's been nothing but an old crosspatch . . . he
scolds about the least trifle—you've seen how he is! . . . At
last I was all worn out . . . for ages I hadn't slept, night
or day. One day when father was a little better Annie Mc-
Bride put me to bed and made me stay there. And then you
decided to come! Can you wonder that she didn't want to
disturb me? . . . You'll never know how I felt when I
found out you had been there!" Susie could say no more.
She dropped her head on his breast, sobbing with abandon.

There Peder stood, dismayed and utterly shame-stricken.
From his eyes one blindfold after another had been torn
away until now he could see it all as clear as day. His self-
accusations lashed him mercilessly. Good God! how she must
have suffered . . . all alone, and with that old sorehead on
her hands! . . . He put his arms about her and tenderly
drew her close, closer and yet closer as though to lock her
in his bosom forever.

"My poor, poor Susie! If I had only known!"

"Known what?" she whimpered, innocently, with her tear-
stained face against his.

Their Fathers' God

And now it fell to him to tell his side of the story, how lonesome he had been without her and the boy, what he had been thinking, how he had hoped and wished and planned, how he had gone to town first once, then again, how he had to go because he had suffered so. Not a single detail could he afford to omit . . . she must see it all . . . she must understand or he'd die . . . it would never be right between them unless he could get her to understand! It took a long time, and he found himself making little progress; there was so much to tell, and she was always interrupting him with questions; to his great bewilderment, she laughed and wept and laughed again; she was so happy that she couldn't stand still and yet she wept. Over both lay a sweet solemnity that would not permit them to draw apart. Like an inexhaustible spring her tenderness was welling up.

"And now you've got to make up your mind to come home soon!" he admonished her, earnestly. "If I'm ever going to reach the Blessed Day I see ahead, you and I have got to stick together! Do you know, when you and Petie are gone I'm like Samson with his hair cut off. I'm only grinding corn among the Philistines. Can't you understand? I must have you two near me!"

"Promise that you won't leave me alone at night! I'm afraid of the dark over there. I don't dare sit up in the spooky old loft all alone, with grandma fussing around any hour of the night and making all kinds of weird noises downstairs. She slips in and out the doors so quietly; I get sick with fear and shiver all through." She hid her face on his breast and held him tighter.

"Be reasonable, Susie-girl!"

"Oh, you don't half understand," she sighed, contentedly, "because you're so Norwegian. I only see you at meal-times. You're always so busy. I can't understand a word of what you two are saying. And there I sit so full of talk that I could split. . . . Peder"—she looked up at him brightly—"couldn't we take over this farm? Charley wouldn't mind; he wants to get away and shift for himself. Then I could

"And They Shall Be One Flesh"

stay right here and take care of father? I'd be so good to you here. I just can't love you with grandma around!"

"That's impossible." He was grave and spoke slowly. "You can see how things stand. I'll most likely get the farm after mother is gone. Now I want to build it up into a real farm . . . such a farm as was never seen on these prairies . . . I want to try out new ideas. We're going to build our own kingdom—you and I and Petie together."

"Oh well," she sighed, "if it's impossible, I suppose it can't be!"

Because he could say no more he lifted her in his arms and rocked her as if she were a little child. His strength was marvellous to her. Like a well-fed, good child that had been made ready for bed she thanked him, and she was a long time about it.

Finally he drove away.

When Susie came back into the kitchen she found her father with the boy still on his lap; he was cross because she had been gone so long.

"What do you mean by staying out all the night? You a married woman! Aren't you ashamed of yourself? Come here and take your brat. And don't think he isn't wet and dirty. . . . No, lift him carefully so I don't get it smeared all over me!"

"Can't I say good-bye to my own husband?"

"Did that take you all night?"

"We had lots to talk about." She took the boy and sat down to change on him.

Doheny filled his pipe. After a few puffs his humour cleared up:

"What did he say about you having gone and baptized the child?"

"Nothing."

"Nothing, me sore leg! I don't believe it."

"Believe whatever you please," she said, cheerfully. She took the boy upstairs and returned immediately to heat water and to change the bandages.

Their Fathers' God

"I'll just bet he soaked you?" said Doheny, coming back to the subject.

"Yes, you'd think so. But he's not that sort!"

"No, I guess not! I've never seen a worse grouchy-goggly face on a human being. Bless my soul if he didn't sit here scowling at me like a mad bull. . . . I'll bet you never mentioned it to him? You didn't dare to!"

"Are you afraid that he won't find out about it soon enough?" laughed Susie, teasingly.

"There—didn't I guess it! You just wait till the next time he comes! I'll break the good news to him myself. Why, he doesn't even know the name of his own son."

"He knows plenty! Hasn't the child been baptized? And wasn't it you that insisted on having it done?"

"He'll have to kill me, then," Doheny went on, without heeding her. "There's no other way! He must be told."

Susie pretended not to hear him. Presently he suggested:

"Or I can talk to Father Williams? If he tells him, he'll get it straight!"

Susie's eyes flashed fire:

"If you ever mention that baptism to a living soul, I'll leave you for good!" She looked at him threateningly. No doubt that she meant every word. "And remember, if you ever dare to call him *Patrick* again when my husband is around, you'll have to take the consequences—now I've told you!"

"Gosh, you're just plumb crazy, Susie. You've got to let him know! Don't you see? What if he should go to work and have the boy baptized over in their church? You know how strict his mother is on religion."

"He'd never do that!" cried Susie, in consternation; apparently the idea had never occurred to her before.

"No? Why not?"

"I know he wouldn't!"

"Oh, you don't know beans! Perhaps he doesn't believe in God at all?"

"Of course he believes."

"Maybe you've married a heathen?"

"And They Shall Be One Flesh"

"You're a heathen yourself, to talk like that! . . . Are you going to sit up all night?"

"You go to bed. I have to stay up until I've thought this thing through."

That night Susie cried herself to sleep. She tried to find a way out of her difficulties, but there was none. Wherever she turned, disaster stared her in the face. She besought the angel to come to her now; she begged, she implored him to take her woes to the Mother of God and explain them to Her so that She might understand. But there was no sound, no stir. The room was full of impenetrable darkness, pitch darkness with woolly ears that heard all, heard it clearly and would not understand because the darkness had no heart.

VIII

On Monday, as Peder went about his work he looked the future boldly in the face; there was a determined certainty in his gait; the line of vision had cleared. At noon, as he lounged in the rocker, resting a little before going back to work (by the stove stood Beret, bending over the dishpan) he announced that this winter he'd feed cattle. No future in this grain-farming. There was such firm decision in the announcement that she had to look at him.

—Was he figuring on buying more cattle? They had a fair-sized herd as it was. Forty-two head in all; she had counted them just the other day. Wasn't that plenty to take care of?

—Certainly he'd buy more. He had been thinking of feeding for a long time and had put up more hay this summer than they would otherwise need. And there was always feed to be had from the neighbours. The price of corn these days would hardly pay for the hauling. Better use it as feed. Besides, cattle prices could hardly drop lower than they were right now.

Beret studied the problem in silence. . . . This must have

been on his mind for some time, she thought. She said, slowly:

"We haven't room for many more."

"I'm going to put up a straw-shed."

"What?" she exclaimed, in astonishment.

"A fellow's got to take chances. Present prices can't last forever. And if they're no better by next fall, I won't be out any more than the work."

"You had better take care that you don't bite off more than you can chew."

Peder laughed:

"I'll bite it off first and take my time about chewing it. Anyway, I'm done with grain-farming. Here we go puttering around in the same old way, year after year, and where does it get us?"

The expression of astonishment on his mother's face had changed to one of sober concern; in her voice was a queer note of humility:

"You are the boss now, Peder . . . you have taken the reins. . . . You should be old enough to know what you are doing. I hope you have thought it out clearly. . . . Have you talked to your wife about it?"

"Not yet."

"You must not launch out on an undertaking like that unless you two are of one mind. She has a right to be consulted. Let her share your responsibilities. . . . Two horses that don't drive evenly make a poor team."

A long silence ensued. When Peder spoke again it was about an entirely different matter:

"What do you say to our moving downstairs when she comes home?"

Beret bent over the dishpan, her hands clutching the edge of it; her face changed visibly, a deep flush spread over it; her eyes closed and opened slowly, like those of a person coming out of a faint.

Peder went on to explain:

"She can't always be running up and down the stairs with

184

"And They Shall Be One Flesh"

the boy; it's too hard on her. We can set the bed in the
front room until I get a chance to build onto the house."

Beret listened to him unfold his plans; a pallor had come
over her face, her lips quivered so that she had to press
them together. Not a word did she say. Peder asked, again:

"What do you say to it?"

"What do I say to it?" she repeated, slowly.

"Yes?"

"Is this her idea?" she asked with an effort, as she drew
her forearm over her eyes and reached for a plate.

"We've talked about it," he admitted.

"Oh—I suppose it can be arranged . . . as long as you
two are agreed on it."

Peder saw that she was taking it hard. But he did not
know what else to do . . . Susie couldn't be staying up in
the loft forever. What did it matter if they put the bed in
the front room? He got up slowly and went out to his work.

After he was gone Beret collapsed. She groped for a chair
and sank down on it, weeping. For some time she sat thus
. . . I'd better get used to this right away, she thought . . .
or I shan't get any work done. She rose abruptly and finished
the dishes. Afterwards she went about her tasks, muttering
constantly to herself:

—Easier for me to climb the stairs on my worn-out legs?
. . . He should have known how my heart goes! . . . Wonder what they will think up next? . . . No, old people are
only in the way . . . don't deserve consideration . . . nor
do they get any—not in this day and age. . . . And they
have planned this together? . . . Then they are agreed! . . .
They better have their way. . . . If that's her only reason
for leaving him, we can remedy that! . . . It's hardly his
idea . . . that you can't get me to believe.

During the afternoon Beret moved her personal belongings to the room Peder and Susie had occupied. She felt a
great need of sharing her troubles with some one, so she
continued talking to herself:

—Per Hansa should have been here to see this! . . . Little
did he think that I was one day to be driven out of the nest

he and I were to occupy . . . and be cozy in all the rest of our days! . . . He made it for us two . . . he sang while he was building it. . . . That summer he was full of song . . . not like the scowling that I see here now. . . . Peder says he will build onto the house? . . . Oh no, not as long as I am on my feet and have anything to say. . . . As long as I live the house is to remain as Per Hansa left it . . . the years will hardly be many now. . . . If I am to get done before Peder comes home, I better hurry. . . . Maybe he won't like this. . . . Well—I can't say I do, either. . . . Just so my eyes would stop flowing. . . . Since she came into the house life has certainly not been easy for me! . . .

By the·time Peder returned for supper she had managed to carry all of his and Susie's belongings to the downstairs bedroom and her own things upstairs—all except the table and the big chest; she couldn't manage these alone; she had dragged the chest out into the kitchen. And one more change she had made: She had taken Per Hansa's picture from its place on the front-room wall and hung it over the bed in the upstairs room, so low on the wall that she could reach it with her hand when she was lying down.

Peder got mad when he saw what she had done. . . . He hadn't meant for her to move upstairs! Had she no better sense? . . . And why hadn't she waited? He could at least have helped . . . this thing didn't need to be done to-day . . . he'd meant that they could make the change before winter set in . . . she didn't need to be quite so independent!

She listened to him awhile, her face puckering strangely:

"Why don't you use the sense you've got? If you really intend to build a barn before winter comes, and buy cattle, and get home all the fodder you'll need, you have more on your hands than you can take care of. . . . She who should be nearest to help seems to have left. . . . Here the room stands now . . . she needs only to move in. It's about time she was coming back!" There was a curious resentment in her manner.

During the days that followed Beret observed her son secretly and was greatly worried by his behaviour. Now he

"And They Shall Be One Flesh"

was just as his father used to be when his worst spells came over him, silent and unapproachable—you couldn't come near him; like a madman he flew at his work and couldn't stand to be delayed. Exactly like Per Hansa—the work had to go at break-neck speed, the whole job must be done in one mad spurt; stop for nothing, confide in no one. Sometimes it seemed to her that Peder bristled with defiance; she became frightened, and stayed awake long hours during the nights, worrying. In the mornings when she came down, and she never overslept, she found him already hard at work. What could be on his mind, anyway? . . . She had moved upstairs!

Before the week was out he had completed the shed and set up a fence around it. The corral was large and roomy. When he threshed he intended to shoot the straw over the fence.

While he was building, Beret often came out to see how the work was progressing. For hours at a time she might putter around there, insisting on helping him, but she was more in the way than she was of actual help. He said nothing, made no complaint; in fact, it seemed to Beret that the boy had lost his tongue completely. And since he did not talk, she too had to keep silent.

In the evenings he'd drive off and seldom return before midnight. Night after night she sat alone, with no idea of where he was or what he was about. Could he be at Doheny's? . . . No, hardly . . . she never saw him take that road. Anxious and uncertain, she would sit up waiting until she heard the hoofbeats in the yard. When at last she went to bed her mind was so heavy with sadness that she could find no sleep.

On Saturday twelve head of cattle came to the Holm farm, Tönseten bringing seven, Tambur-Ola the other five. Both Peder and Beret helped to get them into the corral.

"Well, there you've got 'em," said Tönseten when his seven were safe inside. "These here ain't just ordinary cows, I want you to know. Kjersti has given 'em a good bringing-up; you better treat 'em decently or I'll come and fetch 'em back! . . . What do you think about this scheme, Beret?

Hope the boy don't bump his nose on this business. The idea ain't half bad, just so he can hold on till the price goes up. You might as well go straight to the poor-farm as to try raising grain for a living these days—thanks to Wall Street and the Democratic party. If this damn rheumatism wasn't so bad, I'd start feeding cattle myself."

Beret was looking at the cattle and did not reply.

On Monday evening she was shocked terribly: As she stood filling the trough in the pigsty, unannounced James Tallaksen drove four head of cattle into her yard.

"Tell me, are these here for us?" Horror-stricken, she stared at the boy; she wanted to tell him to drive the beasts straight back to where they came from, but there was Peder coming. He shouted to James that the cattle were to go into the corral . . . yes, all four of them! And without a word she went directly to the house. Apparently she no longer had anything to say on her own farm . . . her opinion mattered not a bit!

After supper the herd was increased by four more head, brought by O'Hara. They were cows, all of them with calves, and appeared to be in good condition. Beret stood out on the porch and watched Peder close the corral gate behind them; she heard him speak in a loud, cheerful voice. And she wanted to call to him, to shout that this would never do! . . . This was madness! Her eyes filled with tears; she could not make out how many there were in this lot. She fumbled for the door and went upstairs to her room. . . . To-night she must be careful lest she say too much! She felt the danger and remained upstairs all through the evening. . . . Had the boy lost his mind? Where would he get all the money to pay for the cattle? . . . Thus it always goes when man and wife can't agree! . . . She picked up the Bible and tried to read, but got nowhere, for there on the wall was the roguish face of Per Hansa grinning at her.

In the early afternoon of the day following, Tor Helgesen came with a whole herd: two scrawny milk cows, two one-year-old steers, and one unruly heifer which, according to Tor's own testimony, was a mean little girl, always up to

"And They Shall Be One Flesh"

tricks, and so noisy—he didn't know just what could be the matter with her. Peder must have been expecting him, because he had stationed himself out by the corral immediately after leaving the dinner table.

Beret had no inkling of what was happening until the sudden uproar of long moos and lusty bellowings startled her. . . . Had the cattle broken out? By the time she reached the porch Peder and Tor were already driving the lot into the corral. A sudden pain pierced her heart and she had to sit down. Finding no relief, she hurried up the stairs into the loft. There she stood by the window, trying to count the cattle; the first time she got twenty-five, the next one more, and then she had to give up. On seeing Tor leave, she went downstairs and out into the yard.

She found Peder throwing cornstalks into the corral; he was whistling a merry tune and appeared to be in great spirits.

"Now I've got an even quarter of a hundred!" he announced jubilantly. "If I'd only thought of this sooner, I'd have started out with fifty!"

Without a word she went back to the house, her face dark and closed; she was weeping now, but was not aware of it.

He watched her go, and laughed:

Funny that old folks never can see new things!

IX

It was night and the house was still. In her bed Beret lay tossing restlessly. Her eyes smarted. The bed became a rack on which she was being tortured. She got up, sat down in a chair by the window, and listened to the slow ooing of the night wind around the corners of the house. Now and then a fit of weeping would come over her; she rocked, uttering low moans, and could not check the tears. More clearly than ever she could see how Peder was headed straight for his own destruction . . . and hers too. . . . No sane man could act this way. Oh no . . . she knew . . . she understood it all —this is how it goes when man and wife can't get along!

Their Fathers' God

Shortly after midnight long, mournful lowings sounded from the corral; at once she was all alertness. . . . Now he had better get up and look after his property! No sound came from downstairs as the lowing continued. . . . I suppose I must go down myself? . . . No peace here to-night if this is allowed to keep on! . . . She threw on a dress, took her shoes in her hand, and tiptoed down the stairs and out the door.

Vicious puffs of an angry south wind tore at the darkness of the night. In scattered groups in the corral the cattle lay resting peacefully—all except Tor Helgesen's heifer. She was standing alone by the south fence, still sending out long, distressed moos into the night. Beret went to the corncrib for a bucket of corn meal; with that in her hand she approached the animal, coaxing her in a low friendly voice to come have a taste. After some moments of hesitation the heifer sniffed of the contents, then shyly lapped one mouthful after another until she caught the sweet taste of the corn. Finally she came close enough to permit Beret to caress her. Tenderly she felt of the udder, the loins, and the small of the back. "Unless I'm mistaken, the poor beast needs attention!" she mumbled. "When they get it this way you better look after them. She is liable to give trouble . . . man and beast are alike in that!" . . . When she returned to her room and went to bed, she fell asleep immediately.

While they were at breakfast Beret announced evenly that to-day she would have to go to town. There was much she needed before the threshers arrived; she might as well get the trip over with, now that she could spare the time.

At once Peder offered to go with her.

She laughed at this proposal, kindly, as though he had been joking:

"You don't mean for both of us to leave the farm? with all these strange cattle here? There might not be many left by the time we came back. Oh no, during the next couple weeks you hadn't better go very far! . . . You didn't hear the racket in the corral last night? . . . I didn't think so.

"And They Shall Be One Flesh"

You have a heifer in the lot that is going to cause you trouble unless you look after her."

Beret got ready and drove off alone. On the way she seemed profoundly absorbed. Her face was long with soberness. She passed farm after farm and did not look up once. On the road she passed people that knew her and nodded, but she hardly noticed them.

At the general store she made the necessary purchases, and it was as if the trading did not concern her. Absently she asked the clerk who waited on her about cattle prices. . . . Did he know? . . . Would he tell her? By his astonished look she realized that this was not the place to get such information. Embarrassed, she hastily picked up her packages and made for the door.

Out on the street she stopped to collect her thoughts, quite upset because she had not learned the prices. Putting her packages in the buggy, she walked down the street to find the cattle-buyer.

"The price," said the man, jocosely, "is easily stated: One-year-olds, one dollar; two-year-olds, two dollars; three-year-olds, three dollars. For extra-fine four-year-old steers I'll give four-and-a-half. I'm not interested in calves. What have you got to sell?"

"Do you sell at the same prices?"

The buyer scratched his head:

"Sell? Well now, that's a different matter!" The man began to study her. "I have to get a little for my work, just a little, you understand. Are you buying?"

—No, not to-day. Beret left. . . . If Peder hadn't paid any more than that, she would have enough with what she had on hand. . . . Four dollars for a four-year-old steer? How could he think of feeding cattle at these prices!

Back in the buggy again, her face became as preoccupied as it had been on the way down. Her body sat in the buggy, but she was not there. Suddenly she nodded decisively to something she saw:

—Yes, I'd better try. It can do no harm. Things can't very

Their Fathers' God

well get any worse than they are. At the second crossroad she turned and took the road going west.

There was no one outside when she arrived at Doheny's; she had come so quietly that nobody had heard her. Doheny sat alone in the kitchen, reading a newspaper. As the visitor entered, his face was blank astonishment. Then as he was about to laugh, the profound concern in her expression checked him. The grin on his face vanished. Pulling himself to his feet and leaning on his cane, he limped across the floor and offered her a chair.

"It is good that I find you alone," she began. "I have a matter that I must talk to you about." She had seated herself; her hand worked nervously with a pleat in her skirt, her dimmed eyes fixed on Doheny: "It's about our children. They were married according to law like other decent people. . . . Neither you nor I liked their marrying. But we saw no way out of it. . . . That which is destined to happen must happen, I suppose."

"And now that tike of a daughter of mine has run away from your son," joked Doheny, good-naturedly. "Is that what's bothering you?"

His jocoseness embarrassed her still more.

"I hope it hasn't come to that yet. But you know what God has said, 'They shall be one flesh.' That is how *our* Bible states it. . . . You don't know Peder. He was always different from any of my other children. . . . Sometimes I am afraid of him; he gets such strange notions. I doubt that Susie understands him. . . . If they are to go on living apart much longer, things may happen that we would never forget. . . . If she isn't to come back till after Christmas, there is no telling what Peder might do. . . . In his attachment he is much like his father was."

"What's the matter with him? Has anything happened?" laughed Doheny, irritably.

"Nothing worse than that he has to have his own close to him. Already he seems bent on tempting Providence. His father was the same way." She paused while she moved her

"And They Shall Be One Flesh"

hand to a different pleat. "Once we talked together, you and I. That time you demanded much of me—nothing less than that Peder and Susie be married by a priest. I consented because I saw no way out. Now it is your turn to sacrifice. . . . I ask it, must ask it, because the welfare of our children is in danger."

Doheny straightened up in his chair, red spots coming into his cheeks:

"This certainly looks damned funny to me. Yes, sir! Peder is at home with his own mother, living like a prince in glory. What more does His Royal Highness demand? Susie's no farther away but he can see her every day in the week! Nobody's going to steal her; the boys out here aren't making love to married women. Here I sit like another cripple. She's my own daughter, begotten lawfully! Do you think she's being spoiled by taking care of her helpless father?"

"That I never thought," said Beret, quietly. "But as long as people are that way ——"

"Then, be damned! they'll have to take things as they come —just like the rest of us!" declared Doheny. "It's good for young colts like they are to practice a little self-denial. They'll have plenty of time to make love! If you don't mind me saying it, your son right now needs a good sound spanking more than anything else. Shame on him!"

Beret glanced down while she kept on stroking the pleat:

"I wonder," she faltered, "how it would work if Susie and I changed places for a few days? . . . No gossip need come of it. She could run the house over at our place as she pleased . . . the experience would be only good for her . . . it may not be long before she is left alone with it. . . . It takes practice for two to pull together evenly."

Doheny's eyes opened wide with amazement. His anger ebbed, and suddenly he burst out laughing:

"Well, if this doesn't beat the devil! . . . Gosh, no! Mrs. Holm. I hope soon to be around . . . I've got to do my own courting . . . yes, sir! . . . Just the same, I thank you for the offer!" His frame shook with irrepressible laughter.

Their Fathers' God

Blushing hotly, as though sprinkled with blood, Beret got up, groped for the back of her chair, but could not find it. More helpless a person could not be. A gulf deeper and wider than all eternity had opened between her and this house and these people. Never could the gulf be bridged over. She had come to him for the sake of their children's happiness both in this life and in the hereafter. And he laughed, only laughed at her, coarsely and lewdly, as if she had made an indecent proposal! . . . More quietly than she had entered she now slipped out of the room.

"Stop! Don't run away mad!" shouted Doheny, terrified. . . . "Susie, oh, Susie! Get up quick! We've got company! Damn you, can't you hear?" . . . He limped to the door and tore it open to make Beret come back, and his distress mounted. . . . There she goes as if the devil was after her! Now can you beat that? . . . Turning back into the room he shouted: "Can't you get out of bed? . . . Your mother-in-law is here. . . . Oh, but you'll catch hell!"

Saturday evening it was long after dark when Peder got home with his last load of cornstalks. After that he had all the cattle, the hogs, and the horses to tend for the night. Beret had done the milking and separating alone. The clock had already struck ten before they had time to think of supper.

They had barely begun eating when sharp hoofbeats thudded out in the yard. The driver stopped by the hitching-post. Both heard him come. Beret looked questioningly at Peder, who made no move to get up. Soon the rig turned and drove off again; a moment later there were steps on the porch, a hand groped for the door-knob. Peder jumped up and tore the door open. Susie, with the boy bundled up in her arm, stepped smiling into the room, much surprised to find them eating supper at this hour of the night.

"Go out and bring in my things," she said to Peder. The door had hardly closed behind him before she turned to her mother-in-law: "Terrible rush you were in the other day. Why didn't you wait till Petie and I got up and made you

"And They Shall Be One Flesh"

a cup of tea? Father was so mad he was fit to be tied! Now
he has chased me out of the house. Well—here we are!"

Beret had left her chair; she stood helplessly before Susie;
she groped for the edge of the table to steady herself.

"It wasn't much of an errand I came on. . . . Peder
didn't know I was going that way. I had to hurry home. . . .
I haven't told him I was there." There was a note of pleading in her voice. "Have you found capable help now?"

"Not the kind we want. But she'll do for the time being.
I heard you were going to have the threshers next week, so I
thought I better come home."

Peder stamped outside the door; Beret heard him and
hurried upstairs.

He came in with the bundles Charley had brought, and
dropped them in a corner behind the door.

"Well, welcome home, little girl!" he said, boisterously.

Susie had seated herself without removing her coat, still
holding the boy in her arms.

Peder looked at her, his eyes blinking:

"Don't you want to take off your coat? You're going to
stay awhile? Not that I want to urge such swell company!"

"It doesn't sound that way!"

Beret came back into the kitchen; she had put on a clean
apron.

"Peder, are you stone blind? Why don't you bring in the
cradle so that she can put the child down? These menfolks
don't see anything!" As if the house were on fire she ran
into the bedroom and came back, dragging the cradle.

"What! Have you been using the cradle in *there*?" cried
Susie in amazement.

"Heh-heh!" chuckled Peder. "So we have . . . now the
old folks are moving downstairs!"

"You don't mean to tell me we're going to have that bedroom? I'll never dare sleep in there!"

"Then you'll have to clear out of here. On these premises
is no place for little fraidie girls!" There was an untamed,
almost brutal abandonment in his joy.

Their Fathers' God

"I was going to ask," said Beret, timidly, coming up to Susie, "if you have had your supper? You will have a cup of coffee with us? I have fresh cake."

Peder went into the bedroom and lit the lamp.

"Come here!" he cried.

Quietly Susie slipped into the bedroom and closed the door behind her.

"Tell grandma I don't want anything to eat . . . this is fast-day for me. And bring back the cradle; I must put Petie to bed right away."

When he came back she was sitting on the edge of the bed, getting the boy ready for the night. Peder bent over them and stood winking and making funny faces at Petie.

"Did you see that? Look at him now!" he cried, jubilantly.

"See what?"

"How he's laughing at me!"

"You people are funny!"

"Sure thing. Good heavens! how fat he's gotten! . . . Does he talk much yet?"

"No thirteen-months-old child talks!" she corrected him.

"Not Irish children—of course not!"

She glanced up quickly, with a safety pin in her mouth: "You think Norwegians can do anything we can't?"

"Aw, I'm not so sure about that!" He crossed the floor and leaned his elbow against the commode. "Did you happen to notice my new barn when you drove in?"

She bent her head while she unbuttoned her dress to lay the boy to her breast.

"Listen to that fellow smack his lips!" Peder came half-way across the floor, watching them, fascinated.

"What were you saying?" she asked, absently.

"I was only announcing that pretty soon you and I can count ourselves among the well-to-do. . . . Look at that rascal help himself! . . . I've started on my own hook now; from now on you'll see a man that can do some work!"

She turned her head towards him, with a far-away, questioning look in her eyes.

"And They Shall Be One Flesh"

"Last week I bought twenty-five head of cattle. Pretty good, eh?"

"Twenty-five head?" she repeated, dubiously.

"Bet your life!"

"Are we going to have still more milking?"

"Nope. I bought them for feeding."

She looked at him absently, as if she had not heard what he said. Suddenly her eyes brightened:

"Peder, to-morrow morning I have to attend Mass. Will you let me take Dolly?"

Peder went back and leaned against the commode.

"I'll conduct Mass for you!"

The boy was asleep now; Susie laid him down and, kneeling beside the cradle, she tucked the blankets around him and hummed softly. When she was sure he was sound asleep she looked up:

"I've promised the Mother of God from now on to lead a holier life." Her voice was full of sweetness; her eyes, looking right at him, were dreamily distant. Now she was in the hold of an unseen power.

Peder forced himself to speak calmly:

"Certainly you can take the horse; mother and I can use the lumber-wagon. If you want me to, I'll go with you." All at once his face darkened. "But I tell you, Susie, this is all nonsense!" As if this were not convincing enough, he added in a firmer tone: "Father Williams is only an old chicken-head. Not one bit more does he know about the Holy Ones than I do!"

As though she had felt a cold draught in the room she pulled her dress together.

"I'm going to bed right away," she said, sleepily. "I'll have to leave here before daylight."

With hands folded under the apron of his overalls and still leaning against the commode, Peder watched Susie prepare for bed; he was silent and black-browed; when she was ready he wound up the clock and set the alarm to ring at five.

No more talk passed between them that night.

Their Fathers' God

x

A worse gluttony than was going on down in the corral Peder could not imagine. This was terrible; no matter how much feed he threw in, it was gone before he had time to turn around. Lest he should be caught short of feed before spring came he went to Tambur-Ola and bargained for all the corn he might need at the same prices the elevators were paying.

Meanwhile he continued to haul home hay and cornstalks. On Monday after Susie's return he was up before dawn, warmed the coffee, ate a slice of bread, and was off to work. When Beret and Susie came out to do the milking he was already unloading the first load. He stacked both cornstalks and hay so near the corral that he could pitch them over the fence right into the enclosure.

On Tuesday bad weather set in. In the morning a thick mist hung over the prairie; by and by rain began to fall, and soon it settled into a steady downpour. When he had finally unloaded and had come in he was soaking wet.

After shedding his outer clothes on the porch he ran into the bedroom, where he pulled off the rest. All dripping wet. He rubbed and massaged until his whole body shone crimson before warmth returned. In dressing he took his time. . . . Cozy in here to-day. The bed spick and span, clean spread put on. . . . Susie was a gem! She must have learned a lot while she was away. His sense of well-being mounted. . . . Now, by George! he'd go in and show that young man a good time!

Suddenly he stood in the middle of the room, staring at the wall, on his face an unbelieving, faltering smile. . . . Well, I'll be jiggered! He strode over to the wall and chuckled. There, to the left of the bed, had been hung a black-painted cross, about a foot long; on it was the image of a crucified man . . . dead . . . the eyes were closed, on the face a look of intense pain. Peder noticed the nose; it was Jewish through and through, big and crooked, too big

"And They Shall Be One Flesh"

for the face; the image was made of white porcelain, now grimy with dust and dirt—especially the nose; above the head was a crown, at least it resembled a crown, on which were inscribed the four letters, *I N R I.* . . . Peder laughed outright: With him as a roommate I'm afraid our nights are going to be kind of gloomy! . . . He must have moved in here since I got up?

Thoughtfully he buttoned up his breeches and finished dressing. He scrutinized the crucifix once more and then looked around the room.

"Are there ghosts in here?" he cried, and did not realize he was talking aloud. In three strides he was over by the door. On the wall to the right had been hung another marvel, a white glossy plaque with a small basin at the bottom; on the plaque was another cross with a crucified human form on it; here the facial features were so indistinct that the look of suffering was gone; the basin was filled with water; a somnolent fall fly, weary of seeking a warm nook, had ventured too close and had fallen in and drowned. Peder crooked his finger and plucked the fly out.

He studied the font of holy water until he felt cold shivers running up and down his spine; the muscles of his face twitched violently. Shivering, he crossed the floor and stopped; he wanted to dash to the door and shout to Susie, but checked himself. Instead, he only stood there, dumbfounded, staring at the crucifix. From here the nose appeared grotesquely large. "Now you had better be careful, Permand," said a voice in him clearly in Norwegian. "If she can find any joy in such idolatry, then certainly you're man enough to put up with it."

Before he left the room he searched it for more tools of black art. On the top of the commode he found a large volume which had not been there before; in gilded letters on the cover was the title, *The Lives of the Saints.* He laughed, as if he had suddenly gained the upper hand on the force that was near to strangling him. "Won't the powers of darkness look sick when they come in and see how well fortified we are!"

Their Fathers' God

He took his time in the bedroom. Coming into the kitchen, he still felt chilly and stood with his back to the stove. His mother had just livened up the fire and was beginning to prepare dinner. Susie sat darning socks; Petie was in a rocker in front of her, with a belt across the front of the chair to keep him from falling out. Susie laid the darning aside and got up to help Beret. Petie disapproved of her leaving and started to whimper.

Peder went over to him.

"There, there now, Mr. Holm," he said, in a cooing voice, "you're too much of a man to care about a little thing like that!" He lifted the child tenderly and began walking the floor with him. The crying ceased. To ingratiate himself in a big way he carried the boy to the window and held him up so that he could look outside. He talked to him in Norwegian:

"Now look at our farm! . . . You'd just better get down to work and grow big and strong. . . . Lots of jobs waiting for us out there. . . . You see our big herd? One of the steers is named after you." He rocked him in his arm.

Not a peep was heard from the boy.

"Does he understand you?" asked Beret, in a happy voice.

"Huh . . . of course he understands!"

Soon he left the window and sat down in the rocking-chair. Anxious to cement the feeling of good fellowship between him and Petie, Peder began singing the little lullaby *Ro, Ro, Krabbeskjær.*[1] Satisfied and pleased, the boy looked up into his father's face and nestled more snugly in his arm. The Norwegian hymn, *O Jesus, Sweet and Lowly,* which Beret had sung to Peder thousands of times, came to his mind, and now he sang it through. The hymn called up others, and there he sat, singing Norwegian hymns until the dinner was ready. When they called him to come to the table he took the boy with him.

To-day the youngster was going to sit with his father and learn some manners! Susie wanted to take the child, but Peder wouldn't hear of it; with a supercilious air he brushed

[1] Literally, Now we row us a-fishing.

her aside, and began to feed the child with food which he himself first chewed into a cud. The two seemed to get along famously. Beret, observing them from the opposite side of the table, laughed until tears rolled down her cheeks —Peder could not remember when last he had seen her so pleased.

"Where in the world did you learn that?" she asked.

"Hm, this? Haven't I known it all my life?" he answered, proudly, and continued to feed the boy.

Again Susie came around the table:

"Now give him to me!" she snapped.

"Go and sit down, woman!" he ordered, gruffly. "Can't you see how nicely we're getting along?" He noticed an unnatural flush in her cheeks, but that did not bother him now.

In the evening when they were ready to go to bed, he picked up a newspaper and sat down in the kitchen to read. The door between the two rooms stood open. Not until he was sure she was in bed did he turn down the lamp and go in.

. . . Surely she'd be all through with her idolatry by this time!

IV. On the Way to Golgotha

I

DESPITE the pinch of hard times that year, the families of the Spring Creek neighbourhood celebrated Christmas as never before. Once let loose, the festive spirit went the rounds of the settlement.

At Tönseten's the preparations had been going on the longest, and so it was only natural for him to start the festivities. And well prepared he and Kjersti were to receive their guests. On a trip to Sioux Falls late in the fall, at a certain grocery store he had come upon a shipment of the finest dried cod he had ever seen; the temptation proved too great, and he had laid in a goodly supply of the cod. On the second Sunday in Advent he had set the fish to soak; "and afterwards," so Kjersti told her guests when they overflowed with praise of how fine the fish was, "he had fussed over that pesky fish as though it had been a cranky woman in her last days of pregnancy!"—And there was more than just the fish; the dinner table sagged under the load she put on. Shortly before Christmas they had butchered a yearling steer that Tönseten had been fattening since early fall; from it she had prepared the savoury meat balls and delectable *rullepölse*. Since the middle of Advent she had been concocting mysteries of delicate cakes. With the coffee she served *fattigmand* and *sandbakelse*, and with the rice pudding, *krumkake*, and *berlinerkranse*. From her well-stocked pantry shelves she had brought out jams and jellies and many other kinds of preserves. No matter how loudly the guests protested, to-day they had to taste of it all.

Nor, if the truth must out, was the house completely dry— oh no, not the house of Syvert Tönseten! The day he brought home the fish he had handed Kjersti a jug for safekeeping, full and securely corked. The jug had been put into the bedroom, where she could give it a watchful eye. This was for Christmas and was not to be touched, no matter how much Tönseten coughed! She knew his infirmities and had obeyed him literally.

But there was one secret he had not revealed to Kjersti, not as much as given the least hint about—the womenfolks needn't poke their noses into everything! In the far-away corner of the barn where never a living soul came, among some other junk stood an old liniment bottle, all dusty, spotted with horse manure and splashings of machine oil, all grown over by spider webs and other nastiness. This bottle was the trump card which Tönseten held up his sleeve for the big party.

At the Christmas morning service Syvert and Kjersti went about inviting their guests. Tambur-Ola and all of his family were asked to come, all of the Holms, "with and including the Irishers and the other respectable folk married into the family," and also Mr. and Mrs. Gjermund Dahl. For help Kjersti had secured the promises of Nikoline Johansen and Anna Marie, who had come from Montana to spend Christmas with her mother. It turned out to be both a large and a jolly gathering.

When the men had come into the barn to put up their horses Tönseten stole up on them; holding an old, dirty bottle up to them he asked concernedly if they wouldn't please sample of this here liniment? "My God! can you imagine Christian people mixing up such medicine for cows?" He carefully wiped the dust from the neck of the bottle and handed it to Gjermund. "Here, you're a Democrat and used to belong to the Norwegian Synod;[1] now I give you the job of interpreting the Scriptures for us."

Gjermund tasted of it, and took a couple of draughts.

"Surely this o'erpasseth all understanding," he reported,

[1] The Norwegian Synod was a Lutheran church body known for its strict orthodoxy. It became part of the Norwegian Lutheran Church of America by the union in 1917.

seriously, smacking his lips. . . . No, this could hardly be
Democratic doctrine. To make sure he sampled it once more.
. . . But it might have to do with Predestination? . . . Perhaps *intuitu fidei*? The strange liniment bottle was half
empty before the men emerged from the barn, and then they
were in a jolly mood. But not until they had come inside
and Kjersti had passed around the drinks did the fun begin
in real earnest. After they had eaten both long and well the
host served punch "made after the prescription Grover
Cleveland himself uses." During the evening the merriment
ran high; all the men except Peder, and the women with
them, sampled Tönseten's Christmas brew.

The next evening found the same persons gathered at
Tambur-Ola's. Here Henry Solum and his family had also
been invited. The host had in readiness a pint bottle of
brandy, which though it did not last many rounds, nevertheless unloosed the good cheer among the guests.

After the dinner Gjermund and the host fell to recalling
Civil War days. Both were veterans of the Union Army;
Gjermund had been with Sherman on his famous march to
the sea and Tambur-Ola a prisoner in Andersonville. Their
conversation soon drew the others about them. The two
men seemed under a spell; they told of incredible sufferings,
they were describing scenes of unbelievable horror, yet they
sniggered continuously. But in spite of their low, staccato
laughter both had tears in their eyes; their faces were flushed
and shiny, their eyes bright with a moist gleam; their voices
were so husky that their listeners could hardly understand
them. Though they were sitting right here in the room, they
seemed not here at all because they were oblivious of everything about them. The excitement grew with the coming on
of dusk. Sörine, being unable to bear the strain, went out
and came back with the lamp. The light made all sigh with
relief.

On the Sunday between Christmas and New-year's the
party was gathered at the Holm farm; it was Beret herself
who planned it and did all the inviting. Here the merriment
was slow in getting started; there was no appeasement pro-

On the Way to Golgotha

vided for dry throats, and to make matters worse, Reverend and Mrs. Kaldahl were among the guests. Peder had frowned at his mother's inviting the minister, for a learned man Kaldahl's English was downright terrible, and in addition, he insisted on talking Norwegian. Short-spoken and moody, Peder received the guests. . . . It's funny, he thought, mother never can see the fitness of things! Why should she have the minister here to-day? . . . Now the Irish will get plenty to snicker about!

The minister was tight-lipped and swarthy, stocky of build, with a head set firmly on a pair of broad shoulders; his beard was black and full; his hair combed back into a flowing pompadour; the eyes, cold and grey, examined carefully into things before pronouncing judgment. He had not been long in his present call and was seldom seen abroad except on occasional sick-calls or in response to an invitation such as to-night. His parishioners had not yet been able to make him out; all they could say with certainty was that his sermons were unusually well prepared, that he stoutly defended everything Norwegian, and that he was punctilious in the performance of his duties.

The dinner finished, Reverend Kaldahl went about thanking the hostess and all her family, shaking hands with each one. He talked long with Beret and was extravagant in his praise of her excellent dinner. After a while he came into the front room where the guests had gathered; those who smoked were already puffing their pipes. He smiled a refusal of the rocking-chair which the others had let stand for him, strode to the opposite wall, and stationed himself there with his arms folded over his chest.

When he entered, the talk in the room died down. He felt the men were waiting for him to strike the note of the conversation, and so he began telling about Christmas in Norway, slowly, trying to determine how his remarks were being received. He dwelt particularly on the Christmas customs of the country districts. By and by this led him into a discussion of how "the race" (he used the phrase often) had lived in olden times.

Their Fathers' God

Tönseten could not restrain himself for long. Gosh! here was a subject worth discussing!

"Them vikings were boys you couldn't sniff at!" He struck his knee a profound slap. "Dandy fellows, I tell you!" His remark aroused laughter, and more so because of Tambur-Ola's quick rejoinder:

"If you, Syvert, had been living in those days, I'll bet you'd either have been a king or a pirate!"

The minister took his lead from Tönseten's remark:

"Fine men they were, some of them; daring and deed-hungry, unafraid to risk their lives on a great adventure. Yet we must not believe that the Norwegians of that day and age, taken as a whole, were any worthier than they are now. It is the sensational in their deeds, the things unheard of, that catch the eye as we now look back. But their deeds were, after all, the accomplishments of a meagre handful. The great mass of Norwegians stayed snugly at home with their porridge-bowls between their knees; that was as far as their vision carried them. That part of our race has always been in the great majority. The same holds true for us Norwegians in America. Here, too, the porridge-bowl type of viking predominates, and it is that kind that lends colour to all our life and activities." A bitterness had crept into his even voice; he had crossed his legs and was toying with his watch chain.

"So also with the Norwegians of that time; there were those in whom the urge to cope with the greatest difficulties and to reach the last horizon could not be downed. They must sail the far seas. In the spring when the blue mountain-tops lay goldening in the sun and fair winds set the surf singing, these men would hoist sail and set out down the lane of the fiord for the open unknown that tossed and rocked and gave promise of high adventure. For them there was no recourse; their urge was too strong, and they went. Likewise to-day. Among the hundreds of thousands of Norwegians in America there have been a few who have felt the old urge and have heeded it. They aren't many, but their deeds will live."

On the Way to Golgotha

Now and then the minister glanced up; the grey eyes studied the faces of his listeners; in his even calmness was a warm glow:

"There is nothing in all history comparable to the deeds of our viking ancestors. Their expeditions, to be sure, show forbidding, gruesome aspects, and plenty of them, but I am convinced that never in all the world's history has man's courage spanned higher and overcome greater odds. If we claim relationship with them, we would do well to remember that fact."

It so happened that Peder was standing directly opposite him. Involuntarily the words leapt from his tongue:

"And what on earth did they accomplish?"

In silence Reverend Kaldahl fingered his chain. Moments passed before he looked up; a suppressed petulance disturbed the evenness of the voice:

"You have been entrusted with a rich inheritance, an inheritance built up through the ages. How much of it, what portion, are you trying to get? Isn't it your irrevocable duty to see how much of it you can preserve and hand down to those coming after you? *A people that has lost its traditions is doomed!*" The pronouncement bore the ring of prophecy. He didn't wait for Peder to answer, but more calmly began describing the viking expeditions, tracing their journeys into the North Sea and out into the North Atlantic, from one group of islands to the other, from one colony to the next. Finally he came to Iceland, where he dwelt long. He told his small group of listeners of the world's oldest republic which soon could celebrate its one thousandth anniversary. Their own race it was who laid the foundation and who built upon it. They could do that because since time immemorial the spirit of democracy had glowed in the Norsemen's hearts. Rather than pay taxes to self-acclaimed rulers their old ancestors had chosen the pioneer's lot out on those inhospitable isles. The development the minister sketched stirred his own enthusiasm; he grew eager and spoke with power; the dark, bushy eyebrows arched under the tenseness that was upon him:

Their Fathers' God

"We pride ourselves on our accomplishments in this country, and in a way we are justified. But we must not forget that all through the nineteenth century we have followed the crowd; we were not the leaders; it wasn't our people that blazed the trail. Not so in the ninth and tenth centuries. Compare the means of transportation then and now! Nor must we forget that at that time our race numbered less than 400,000 souls; when Cleng Pierson in 1825 set out from Stavanger we were more than a million. But in spite of this small number the Norsemen of old achieved deeds that will be remembered to the end of time. Why? I ask you. How did it come to pass?" The minister's voice was challenging, like that of a man who has been wronged and is demanding redress. "Those deeds were made possible simply because the men who performed them remained true to their traditions and went on building and achieving as their forefathers had done before them. What do we do to-day? We turn up our noses at the inheritance that has come down to us. We cast on the scrap heap the noblest traditions of our race. We set higher value on aping strange manners and customs than in guarding our God-given heritage. So wise have we become and so far-seeing! God's command to the Israelites means nothing to us. We are ashamed of the age-old speech of our forefathers. And we find it embarrassing to admit our Norwegian ancestry. Such an attitude can never, I tell you, *never* build a nation. Like dead timber we go into the building. We may harm, but we cannot be of much help!"

The unmistakable passion in the minister's words struck fire in those of his listeners that understood Norwegian, but with each one differently: Gjermund's lower lip had grown inordinately long; Peder's face was clamped shut and silent; Tambur-Ola's head was cocked, like that of one with an ear for pure tones, listening to a meadow lark singing out in the dusk; Tönseten puffed furiously; he had got up and was tugging at the belt line of his trousers. . . . Preacher or no preacher, by jimminy! I got to get a word in here! . . . Let's see now, which of the Olafs was it that fell in the

On the Way to Golgotha

battle at Svolder? . . . Let's see, now? . . . Doheny, who had not the faintest notion of what the long harangue was about, had pulled his chair far into the corner and was dozing peacefully; Charley stayed in the kitchen with the girls. . . . Great sport teasing Nikoline and making her answer in English!

Peder broke the silence:

"We're Americans here!"

All sensed the hot challenge in the tone of his voice, and looked at Reverend Kaldahl.

"Yes, sir, so we are," he agreed, good-naturedly. "Seems to me I've heard that saying before. May I ask you, does the leopard change his spots by coming into new pastures?"

"I agree with Peder," said Gjermund, thoughtfully, before the other could answer. "As Norwegians we'd never get very far in this country."

Reverend Kaldahl bit his lips; the eyebrows crept closer together:

"And I maintain just the opposite. If we're to accomplish anything worth while, anything at all, we must do it as Norwegians. Otherwise we may meet the same fate as corn in too strong a sun. Look at the Jews, for example: Take away the contributions they have made to the world's civilization and you'd have a tremendous gap that time would never be able to fill. Did they make their contribution by selling their birthright and turning into Germans, Russians, and Poles? Or did they achieve greatly because they stubbornly refused to be dejewed? See what they have done in America! Are they as citizens inferior to us? Do they love this country less? Are they trying to establish a nation of their own? Empty nonsense! But they haven't ceased being Jews simply because they live here in America, and because they have adopted this country's language and become its citizens. Do you think their children will become less worthy Americans because they are being fostered in Jewish traits and traditions? Quite the contrary! If they, as individuals or as a group, owe any debt to America, the payment can only be made by their remaining Jews, and the

Their Fathers' God

same holds true for all nationalities that have come here. One thing I can see clearly: If this process of levelling down, of making everybody alike by blotting out all racial traits, is allowed to continue, America is doomed to become the most impoverished land spiritually on the face of the earth; out of our highly praised melting-pot will come a dull"— he paused to hunt for words—"a dull, smug complacency, barren of all creative thought and effort. Soon we will have reached the perfect democracy of barrenness. Gone will be the distinguishing traits given us by God; dead will be the hidden life of the heart which is nourished by tradition, the idioms of language, and our attitude to life. It is out of these elements that our character grows. I ask again, what will we have left? We Norwegians have now become so intelligent," he continued, scornfully, "that we let our children decide whether we should preserve our ancient tongue!"

Peder's reply burnt his throat:

"It would be folly to try to build up the different European nations over here. The foundation is new, the whole structure must be new, and so it shall be!"

"In that you're greatly mistaken," declared the minister, coldly. "The foundation is not quite as new as you think. If you dig deep enough and look around a little, you will find some good old timbers, materials that have been brought here from far away. Where did the Puritans come from? Mostly from eastern England. Was that mere accident? Not at all; there, too, cause and effect worked hand in hand. It was in that part of England that the Scandinavians, and not least the Norwegians, exerted their greatest influence. By nature the Puritans were nonconformists; an imposed system of worship was to them unthinkable, just as it was to your own forefathers. Suppose you look at this a little more closely: What did the framers of our Constitution have to work with? First and foremost two priceless documents which supplied the very groundsills for their structure, the *Magna Charta* and the *Bill of Rights*. Where do you suppose the basic principles set forth in these two documents came from? The seeds came from the Scandinavian peninsula,

On the Way to Golgotha

some directly to eastern England, others through Normandy, and still others, perhaps, by way of the Western Isles. There is no getting away from the fact that in no place on earth has the desire for liberty and individualism glowed brighter and more impelling than in the Scandinavian north. Read your people's history and see for yourself. This fable," continued the minister with quiet indignation, "that America more than any other nation is 'the land of the free' is only romantic schoolma'am nonsense." He looked searchingly at Peder. "Come over and see me some time. I have books that might interest you."

"Why don't we find these things in our school-books?" asked Peder, incredulously.

The minister became more sober:

"There are many, many things that don't get into your school-books. I venture to say that your teachers taught you that the Pilgrims came to America seeking religious liberty, or am I wrong?"

"What else could have brought them here?"

"I thought so! But that dogma is only part of the truth. From England the Pilgrims first went to Holland; there they enjoyed all the religious liberties they could ask. But those men were not fools; racial traditions were of vital importance to them. That's what eventually brought them to realize that if they remained in Holland their children would become Hollanders, and what was worse, they would soon lose their mother tongue. Rather than suffer such an irretrievable loss they made ready and sailed for New England."

"Can that be right?" asked Peder, dubiously.

"Right?" shouted Tönseten enthusiastically. "Why, them are the pure facts; I've read it many times myself!"

The minister had pulled out his watch. He glanced at it now and seemed terrified.

"Here I've stood talking away the time. I was to call on old David Johnson, who has been sick abed all through the holidays!" He went about the room shaking hands with all.

211

Their Fathers' God

To Peder he said: "Come over to see me as soon as you can. I'd like to have a talk with you. Bring your family."

Beret, sitting on a chair near the door in the kitchen, had followed the discussion from the beginning; she pressed fold upon fold in her apron; her eyes were wet, her hand toyed with the edge of her apron. An old saying came to her mind and she mumbled it to herself: "Now lettest Thou Thy servant depart in peace!" When the minister was ready to leave she hurried upstairs. Once last fall she had placed a ten-dollar bill in her Bible and there it had since remained; lately she had been using it for a bookmark; bringing the bill down with her now, she stuck it into the minister's hand with a request that he give it to the missions.

On New-year's day Gjermund Dahl was the host. Doheny and Charley were not there, nor the minister; nevertheless, the gathering here was larger than any of the others because Gjermund had invited several of his nearest neighbours.

Before and after the meal the host served his guests with strong home-brewed beer, in an old ale-bowl which his father, Old Gjermund, had brought with him from Norway. Except for this beer, there were no drinks served.

That, however, placed no damper on the merriment. Tönseten felt this was too good an opportunity to let pass without taking Gjermund to task for having gone astray politically:

"No question about it; if we can't throw your gang out of office, the whole country will soon be in the poorhouse! Can't you see how them big robbers down in Wall Street are sucking the blood right out of us common people? Why don't Grover grab 'em by the scruff of the neck and heave 'em out?" Tönseten made a motion as if he were pitching bundles to the top of a stack. "Ain't he got the power, maybe? If this is allowed to go on much longer, you won't be seeing any *lutefisk* on your table next Christmas!"

That ominous declaration kindled the blaze. All the worries and the grief that had been staring the men in the face since spring were lost sight of in the furious debate that developed. Once it had gotten started, there was no

On the Way to Golgotha

way of stopping it. Out on the floor the men had formed into two lines, the Republicans in one and the Democrats in the other. But in the ranks of the Democrats there was a break, formed by the one Populist present, Nils Pedersen, who single-handed fought all the rest. Tönseten talked Norwegian and English alternately, and often both at the same time. Susie was the only one to notice this, because the others spoke the same mixture. When Mrs. Dahl, late in the afternoon, came in to announce that lunch was ready, no one paid any attention to her. This party was by far the noisiest of all they had had so far.

But when they again were seated around the table the discussion died down. The arguments had been exhausted, the men were tired of shouting at one another. For a while Gjermund sat silent and stirred his coffee. After some time he looked up at Susie:

"Next fall I'll be through for good as county commissioner. What do you say to our electing your husband in my place? Do you think you could round up some votes for him out your way?"

"If you take him, I won't have any more bother with him!" she laughed; in her cheeks spread a furious blush.

Gjermund sat silent and preoccupied; he spoke thoughtfully:

"Unless I see wrong, Peder is cut out for public life; he likes politics; he is young and unafraid, and has a mind of his own." Gjermund continued to stir in his cup. "I think we ought to elect a young man from up this way, one who has it in him to grow into bigger things later on. Plenty of offices both in state and nation. I never could figure out just why we should hand them over to Jew and Gentile and not seek any for ourselves. . . . My successor will have to be either you, Peder, or Andrew Holte."

Tönseten sprang up and tugged disgustedly at the band of his trousers.

"Andrew Holte!" he fumed. "To think that you, a grown-up man, can sit here with such blasphemous talk in your mouth! If you think we want that goody-goody dis-

senter to spend our money and make laws for us, you're
going to be fooled! By God! if my rheumatism wasn't so
bad, I'd run, myself. . . . I might do it, anyhow!"

"Listen to that old scarecrow!" shouted Kjersti, beside
herself. "No, then it certainly would be better that I ran!"

Now the merriment broke out anew; laughing and joking,
the guests left the table; Gjermund, however, remained.

"Step into the bedroom with me," he said to Peder. "I
want to talk to you."

II

It was late that evening before Peder came out of the
bedroom and could get started for home. Susie, holding
Petie on her lap, sat with Beret in the back of the sleigh.
Up in front Peder stood alone; all were well bundled into
shawls and blankets, though there was no cold to speak of.
The winter night, deep, and ponderous with many stars,
domed over them. Livelier grew the music of the snow
creaking under the runners as the horses quickened their
pace. Conversation was impossible without shouting, and
Peder was grateful for that. He gave the horses free rein.
To-night he could not have sat down if it had cost his life.

A mighty mood was upon him. . . . To-night the Call
had laid a hand on his shoulder and spoken clearly, unmistakably, determining his course from now on. . . . And this
was only the beginning! Hereafter he would be thinking and
planning for the welfare of a whole county. . . . Sit in
council with older men and show them ways and means that
they themselves had never thought of. . . . Later. . . . He
was fraid to let his thoughts run on. . . . "Many offices both
in state and nation." So Gjermund had said. . . . You bet!
he said aloud, his lips closing tightly after the words. The
feel of loose snow spraying against his flushed face was
sweet and soothing. . . . Did he possess the gift to lead
others? The loud *yes* that rose from his soul forced him to
drive faster.

On arriving home he first helped his mother from the

sleigh. "Hold him tight!" he warned Susie, and promptly lifted her and Petie together to the ground with such exuberant recklessness that she had to stop and scold him.

Beret was tired from the long day and soon went up to bed. Peder put more wood on the fire and opened the bedroom door wide so it would be comfortable there when they were ready to go to bed. Susie dressed the baby for the night, rocked him to sleep, and tucked him away in his cradle.

All the time Peder sat waiting for Susie to ask about his conference with Gjermund. It had lasted so long; she had been angry because of the delay. . . . Wasn't she interested in knowing what Gjermund had said? It seemed not. Though she was bubbling over with cozy talk, she failed, strangely, to touch upon the one subject that was uppermost in his mind. She mentioned the dinner Mrs. Dahl had served, asked about some of the dishes, and marvelled at the cooking of the Norwegian housewives; she had heard bits of gossip from Kjersti and Sörine which she retold to him, mimicking Kjersti so perfectly that Peder could not help laughing. He said he didn't know much about women, not to-night, anyhow. He changed the subject and talked at length about Gjermund, of what a capital fellow he was, about his ability to reason independently and at the same time correctly; he planned to run for the Senate next fall; doubtlessly he would be elected, and the Senate was where a man like Gjermund belonged. Wouldn't it be great to have a U. S. Senator right from this neighbourhood?

Susie listened to him until she yawned long and drawn out, and patted her mouth.

"Good heavens! I'm sleepy! Could you ever have guessed it?" she said, suddenly, still patting her lips. "We're going to have another baby!"

"Aw, you're just fooling!" Peder got up and stood over her. "Can't you and I turn around without something going wrong?"

"It isn't my fault. Not only mine. You can't say that!"

"No, I guess not!"

Resigned, she held out her hands to him.

"Help me up! . . . Heavens! what a life! Now my face will get so grey and ugly. . . . Just so it's a girl I won't mind." She snuggled close to him. "Every night," she confessed, whimpering, "I pray the Mother of God for a girl." She pressed her cheek tightly against his. "Don't be angry," she begged languidly; a dull light burnt in her eyes. "You've got to be just awfully good to me during the months that are left. I'm so afraid . . . much more afraid than the first time." There were tears in her voice. "What will grandma say? I suppose she'll think it a sin and that it is all my fault."

Peder lifted her in his arms and carried her into the bedroom.

"You're not so glad as you were the first time," she reproved him, poutily. "I can see it on you."

"Glad?" he pooh-poohed. "There can't be too much fertility on this farm to suit me. You produce kids, and I cows. . . . If you want to race, you'll have to go some!"

"Just so you don't get angry," she sobbed. "If it's a girl, we'll call her Susannah? . . . Or Susan?" She listened for signs of disapproval.

"Not by a damn sight!" he assured her, warmly. "Her name is going to be Virgin Mary, seeing it's she who runs these affairs."

Susie wept plaintively, like a child that has been mistreated and has no one to go to for comfort:

"Why do you always have to be mean and make fun of me? . . . Do I make fun of your faith? . . . What's going to happen to our children, growing up in such ungodliness? . . . Don't you think God hears what you say?"

"If I have any say in this house, our children are going to learn to use their common sense. That's what they got it for."

Susie crawled into bed and drew the blankets over her head. Her weeping grew more lugubrious and was hard to stand up under.

With a face of steel Peder looked at her, just watching

for her next tantrum. After a moment he walked over and sat down on the edge of the bed:

"Sit up, Susie. Now I want to talk with you!" In his voice was an unnatural calm.

The weeping stilled. She permitted him to throw the blankets back, but she made no move to turn to him.

"Sit up. You and I have got to talk these things over sometime. Might as well do it right now. A grown-up woman who herself is a mother should be ashamed to be afraid of shadows . . . that's all that's bothering you. Now sit up!"

"No-no," she whined. "I don't dare. I know how your eyes look. Now you're going to say something terrible again. It's right on the tip of your tongue. I can hear it in your voice!" She flung herself over on the other side and curled up under the blankets.

A sudden gust of anger brought him to his feet; in a flash he was around the bed, picked up the bundle, and sat down with her on his lap.

Susie struggled frantically until she was out of breath; she tried to tear herself free, jerked and twisted, panting heavily.

"I'll scream!" she groaned, kicking her feet.

"Go ahead. Scream all you want!"

"You are killing me."

"Oh no!" He tightened his grip on her: "Now will you listen?"

Suddenly she sat stark still, her body limp like that of one whose will has been shattered.

"Can we talk now?" he asked, with an effort that made him gasp for breath.

"Put me down . . . I'm getting sick. . . . Let go of me. . . . Gosh—you're choking the life out of me! . . . Let me go . . . can't you hear!" Again she struggled fiercely to free herself, twisting and squirming like an eel. But the former closed his grip. He said:

"Nobody's going to hurt you; you're safer right now than you've ever been in your life," his voice was cold.

Their Fathers' God

A great wave broke through her, followed closely by another, then sob upon sob . . . heartless, cruel sobs . . . too much for one to endure. Never before had he seen her like this. Tenderly, as if she were a stricken child, he laid her down.

As she touched the bed her feet beat fast against the mattress, her fingers clawing the pillow; out of her rose a long whine—half weeping and half a trapped beast's hiss. Then followed a fit of hysterical crying, worse than all the rest to listen to.

Peder stood bent over the bed. With a hard hand he grasped her shoulder and jerked her towards him.

"Look out, now!" he said, hoarsely, and could not let go his grip. "Don't carry this show too far!" he added in broad Nordlandsk, not realizing that he was talking Norwegian. He still held her by the shoulder. Now he shook her.

An unbelievable thing happened. Susie's body went slack, like a taut rope that snaps; the deep flush flowed quickly from her face and a ghastly pallor remained; a couple of quick gasps for air, and she lay unconscious.

Peder could not believe his own eyes; his sight blurred. He felt of her forehead—it was moist and cold. Like a drunken man he stumbled out into the kitchen, saw the water-pail, groped for the dipper, and drank.

Breathlessly he listened for sounds of life from the bedroom. His eyes burnt with a terrible smart. On the clock shelf he saw the Norwegian newspaper which his mother had glanced at before going to bed. Clutching the *Skandinaven* to him, he sat down by the table and opened it wide. Not a word could he see. Only the grey, blurred columns. Out of them rose a dark voice, deep and sober-spoken:

"To-night we come to grief . . . yes, we come to grief."

"Can't help it," he wearily thrust back at the voice. . . . "Got to be decided whether common sense is to be the master in this house." This bit of reasoning struck him as being so sensible that he had to listen. He wanted to follow it farther, but was disturbed. Shuffling, questioning footsteps came down the stairway. A moment later his mother stood in the middle of the room, staring at him, and from him to the bedroom door:

"What's going on here? Was it Pete who screamed so?"

"Heh-heh," nodded Peder.

Beret turned and left. Just as she opened the door to the stairway the bedroom door closed with a light bang. Peder's blood ceased flowing; death-like he sat there, listening. . . . Who closed that door? . . . Or was it only the draught?

He had no idea of how long he sat there, all ears, trying to catch the faintest sound. But when he finally was sure that Susie was up—he heard the cradle go—his blood rushed to his heart so violently that he had to clasp his hand over his breast. Then he chanced to glance at the clock. It said 10:30. Instantly he concluded that the clock had stopped.

Before he could convince himself that he ought to go to her, the bedroom door opened quietly and she came out, fully dressed, with her coat on; she had tied one of Beret's kerchiefs around her head and looked for all the world like a little girl who dresses in mother's clothes to play grown-up; the face was white and expressionless, the eyes looked straight at the door. She walked past him as if she did not see him sitting there. As her hand took hold of the doorknob he leaped to his feet:

"Where're you going?"

The snap of the lock-spring was the only answer he received. But by that time he had seized her arm:

"Where're you going?"

"Home," she said like one who opens his eyes in heavy sleep and speaks absently.

"You're not, Susie-girl!" he mumbled, with difficulty. "You're not leaving this house to-night." Gently he pushed her back and leaned himself against the door.

For a moment she stood there quiet, her head slightly bent as if considering. Then she turned and went back to the bedroom, closing the door behind her. Before he left the kitchen door he turned the key and put it in his pocket.

Their Fathers' God

III

In after-years when Peder recalled that night there would
come before him a long series of pictures, some of them
dull and distant, and others so clear-cut and insistent that
he could scarcely get rid of them. They popped right out
of the columns of the *Skandinaven*: "Herring Fishers Reap
Rich Harvest in Vestfjorden.". . . "Storms Rage Along
West Coast.". . . "Three Boats Go Down Near Björn-
öyvær.". . . "Man Kills Self.". . . "Strange Sect Creates
Stir in Finnmarken." There were others that stood out
more clearly. In a new settler's shanty out West in Kings-
bury County a mother is washing clothes; it is early evening
of a December day; the lamp stands near-by on a chair;
a little girl is playing on the floor; she wants to get up, and
grasps at the chair; the lamp topples over and instantly the
shanty is a mass of flames; the father has gone to town
with a load of wheat; when aid finally arrives mother and
child are a clutter of charred bones.

A warm wave of sympathy swept through Peder; he had
to go to the bedroom and make sure. . . . Susie was sometimes so careless in putting out the light. He opened the
door quietly and held his breath. The silence in here stunned
him. On the commode the lamp was burning low; Petie slept
peacefully, with red cheeks; on the bed lay Susie, fully
dressed and sound asleep; the colour had come to her face
and she seemed natural; a corner of the blanket had been
pulled over her shoulder. Apparently she had thrown herself
down with no intention of sleeping. Timidly he drew the
blankets over her, blew out the lamp, and left the room.

To-night he was suffering from an unquenchable thirst;
his tongue was so sticky that it clung to the roof of his
mouth. Again he drank from the dipper, put more wood on
the fire, and sat down to read. It was hard for him to
gather his thoughts on anything; in his head hammered
a ceaseless pounding; never before had he heard a clock
make such racket.

On the Way to Golgotha

The scene in the bedroom was, in some unaccountable way, connected with the next series of pictures that rose out of the columns of *Skandinaven*. Now it was an account of a gruesome Mississippi lynching: A negro sits in jail, charged with raping a white girl; an enraged mob gathers and storms the jail; the mob overpowers the guards, drags the man out and hangs him; as if that is not punishment enough, they heap firewood under him, drench both him and the wood with kerosene, and light the blaze; police officers, powerless and terrified, stand looking on. . . . The account closed with an intimation that the man hanged was perhaps innocent.

The hint of the man's innocence gave Peder a peculiar feeling of satisfaction; he smiled wryly to himself. . . . Hadn't he known it all the time—supreme justice can be attained only through vicarious atonement by an innocent! . . . Otherwise the world would go to rack and ruin. . . . All society is borne up by the suffering of the innocent. . . . Isn't it the majority that always determines what is to be right and what wrong? But what has that to do with justice? The mob down there in Mississippi was in the majority; they killed the poor fellow, the excitement died down, and people went back to their homes; society could again breathe peacefully.

Peder knit his brow, grimly determined to get to the bottom of this question of justice.

—The priests and parsons had agreed on what the common man should think and believe. If he dares adventure beyond the paths laid out for him, he'll either be hanged here or burnt eternally in the hereafter, perhaps both . . . to hell with that kind of justice! That's no better than among cattle. The stronger brushes the weaker aside and stuffs himself until the belly is tight as a drum. . . . In the prelates' feed-trough it is even worse; those fellows feed on warm, aching hearts. For a whip they use fear, that deadly poison which gradually disintegrates the noblest elements in man's nature! The bitterness of his thoughts drove Peder to his feet; he had to go to the water-pail for another swallow.

—This question of right and wrong was utterly impos-

sible. . . . always it eluded him, always it drew back only
to reappear immediately in an entirely new light. What was
right in one case was the vilest conceivable wrong in the
next. . . . Was there, after all, no unchangeable, eternal
principle of right and wrong? He slumped down on the
chair and sighed.

—Here I go trying to force my views on her! He raised
his head, drawing his eyebrows together—still that's another
matter; I do it out of kindness; I want to help her get rid
of fear. It's my duty because I can see the truth, and I am
the stronger. . . . Duty? he groaned. To-night I all but
killed her . . . that's the kind of saviour I am! . . . She
lives in fear, breathes it, feeds on it . . . that's all plain
as day. Fear and superstition are her gods. If I succeed in
taking them from her, she'll have nothing to live on . . . she
will die. *Can* a human being live by feeding on lies? Like a
turtle in the mudbottom of a creek, or a fly on the manure
pile? . . . One thing is sure—she has the same right I
have! . . . How can I tell what is right? The decision made
him anything but happy. Weary and befuddled, he let his
head drop into his arms and sat bent over the table, staring
down into his thoughts. The tangle was more hopeless than
ever.

He sprang up and paced the floor.

—Is she going to have the right, then, to stuff the minds
of my children with all these old wives' tales? Nursery
stories of inherited sin, hell, devils, and purgatory? . . .
Let her befog their minds by teaching them the necessity
of confessing to stupid priests, and to believe in an old
witch up in the sky who decided whether they were to be
born girls or boys? . . . Must I, the father, stand by and
watch her inject this poison into the hearts of our own children—my children? . . . Where does my right come in?
Isn't there such a thing as *duty*? . . . His face grew harder
and colder the longer he pursued these thoughts. . . . What
did that document Father Nolan had made him sign really
say? Something about "the children are members of the
One True Church"? . . . At that time such things had

seemed so far away and unreal. . . . Different now! . . .
Had he, the happy-go-lucky boy he was, sold the souls of
his unborn children? . . . Peder could have thrown himself down on the floor and screamed. O God! he groaned,
have mercy on me!

Not until he heard his mother stirring upstairs did he
pick up the milk-pails and abandon his watch. His face was
grey, and he walked bent over with the shuffling steps of
an old man that has walked a long way to no purpose.

At the breakfast table everything was as usual save for
the tension in the air. Susie said she had no appetite. While
the others ate she sat by the stove, tending Petie. There was
a forced note of jollity in her talk. In a high-pitched voice
she chattered on and on; for no particular reason she would
break into a noisy laugh. With the glum silence of the
others as a background, her behaviour appeared so unnatural
that it became uncanny.

Now and then Beret glanced up at her daughter-in-law.
When she had finished eating she cut thin slices of bread
and toasted them with much care, boiled a small panful of
sweet milk; after she had it all ready she bade Susie come
and try.

"This I think you can stand," she said, quietly. "It's well
this comes on at a time of year we don't have it so busy.
. . . The smell of food is nasty early in the day. After this
you stay in bed mornings till we've finished with the breakfast. That will make it easier for you."

Peder gave his mother a grateful look. . . . Now Susie
wouldn't have that to fret over! . . . Queer how mother
understood everything. . . . How did she know Susie was
pregnant?

He pulled on his coat and went out. To-day he must grind
corn for his herd. More and more the enterprise with the
cattle fascinated him. Last fall he had carried on a little
investigation unbeknown to the women. Through men he
could trust he had gathered information about prominent
cattle men. He had written to a few. Shortly before Christmas he had received an encouraging reply from one:

Their Fathers' God

"No period of economic depression has yet lasted for-ever; it's unlikely that this one will. The man who has a well-fattened herd on hand when times get normal again will be certain of making good money. If you can secure fodder at a low price, you need not hesitate about investing in more cattle."

The letter had pleased him greatly; he had showed it to Susie. She had only laughed; the possibilities at which the letter hinted made no apparent impression on her.

"Listen," she had suggested, innocently. "Next time I go to confession I'll ask Father Williams to come out and bless our herd."

In amazement he had asked her what she was driving at, not sure that she wasn't joking. But when he finally realized that she meant just what she said, he had asked:

"Do you mean that we should get him out here to *read* to the cows?"

"Certainly; then we'll have better luck with them."

"Why?"

"That's how it is with everything that's blessed." Never before had Susie confronted such dense ignorance, and she added, exasperatedly, "Can't you understand that much?"

He had laughed until the tears came:

"Yessiree, that's exactly what we'll do! We'll cart the old geezer out here to pray for our cattle. Then the steers will quit eating and the cows blossom out with two calves apiece . . . in a year or two we'll have money to burn!"

Not till it was too late had he understood how deeply his joking had offended her, and by that time his anger had flared up. . . . Damn it all, there must be a limit to a grown-up person's folly! He had told her so bluntly and had walked away. Afterwards she had stubbornly avoided him; for some time he couldn't come near her.

To-day he was trudging along behind the horses, around and around the feed-mill. Now and then he cast an eye on the house. . . . Wouldn't she look out? . . . She could at least walk past the window? . . . Where had she intended to go last night? . . . Was it only a fit of temper? Just to scare him? . . . Couldn't she see that she was the last person in the world whom he'd ever want to harm? . . . When he went in for dinner he was determined to offer to hitch up Dolly for her. But mother never left the room . . . she was to be spared the agony of this quarrel!

Toward noon a slight thaw set in, but the snow around the mill was tramped down so hard that the sun there made little headway. By four o'clock it was freezing again; the path got iced and bumpy, making the tramping wearisome for tired feet. Peder, however, kept working until after dark. Before he went in he took a turn over to the corral. The sky was dark and lowering. No telling what the night might bring. When he at length came into the kitchen he was so stiff and sore that all he could do was yawn; even that was a great effort.

IV

The farm which Tor Helgesen left in order to seek his fortune elsewhere had been taken over by the twin brothers Tom and George McDougal. They had farmed for a while over in Yankton County, but last fall while here on a visit with relatives they heard about the Helgesen farm being for sale and had gone over to look at it. Right then and there they had bought the farm. A week later they had returned with all their belongings and taken possession. Soon the neighbours saw the brothers hard at work breaking new fields; day after day they toiled unceasingly, from early morning until late at night. In the spring they planned to plant flax on all the new breaking and make a real scoop.

Old Annie McBride was their aunt. Both of them were bachelors, looking for fun wherever there might be any hope of finding it. By nature the McDougal boys were happy souls, easy of manner, trusting to luck and believing unfalteringly in all things Catholic. Both were good-looking; Tom should, by right, have been the handsomer, and had enjoyed that distinction until a year ago, when a burly Scotchman, in a saloon brawl at Vermilion, had knocked his nose askew.

Their Fathers' God

In return the Scotchman had received all the thrashing that is good for a man, and perhaps a bit more; and that was not all; later the law had ordered him to pay Tom a neat sum for the damages done to the nose. The doctor who had tried to repair the injury had bungled the job badly, for when the bandages had been removed the tip was pointing to the side, with the result that every time Tom laughed and tossed his head, it looked for all the world as though he were trying to smell his left eye. "Don't shed salt tears on account of that darn nose!" his brother had consoled him. "Wait till you have a wife; she will straighten it for you!" They had had much fun over the nose, Tom no less than his brother; the damage money had been put in the bank for safekeeping while Tom continued to look for a doctor who could straighten the nose for him. It was with this money the brothers had bought the Helgesen farm.

On the evening of January 2nd the brothers got the idea that they ought to have a little fun in order to start the new year right; during Christmas they had been in Yankton, where they had celebrated in true McDougal style. Returning home one day, they ran into Charley, who happened to be in town; at once they wanted to know about the season's customs hereabouts. . . . Any parties being planned? . . . Didn't people care to dance the old year out and the new in? If so, would he do them the favour of rounding up a bunch of girls, real ones with some ginger in their legs? . . . And would Charley bring his little Norskie with him? . . . The floor would have to be scrubbed soon, anyhow . . . they might as well get it properly dirty. . . .

Yes, Charley would come and otherwise assist in every way possible.

About eight o'clock the night of the dance Charley stopped outside Peder's door; he had Nikoline with him in the sleigh, had hung bells on the horses, and was in great spirits:

"Hurry up, you slowpoke," he commanded Peder, after stating his errand. "Go in and tell Susie. . . . We haven't got all night!"

On the Way to Golgotha

The invitation kindled no enthusiasm in Peder; he stood there, listening mutely. . . . He going to a dance to-night?

"If you don't come with us, I'm going straight home to aunty!" threatened Nikoline, in her native dialect.

Peder came closer to the sleigh, as if wanting to hear better what more she had to say.

"Oh, please, do come along! Please, *please!*" She seemed distressed because he hesitated, and added, "I'm going right home to aunty, unless you go along."

Is this the way matters stand here? Peder wondered. . . . Is she afraid to be alone with him? All at once his own troubles seemed heavier to bear.

"What's ailing you? Have you lost your tongue?" shouted Charley.

"You got to come!" begged Nikoline.

"I'll have to see what Susie says." With that he went in and told Susie who was there and what they wanted. In a voice dead with tiredness he asked if she cared to go, adding quickly that it looked like they'd have a snowstorm . . . if they went, they might not get home to-night. . . . Imagine Susie and him dancing to-night!

She sat by the table, sewing on a new dress. Instantly she threw her work aside and was again the old Susie:

"Gee! that will be fun! Will you take care of Petie for us, grandma?"

Unbelievingly he stared at her. . . . Did she really mean it? Could she actually get herself to go to a dance now, after what had happened between them last night?

Without waiting for an answer from Beret, Susie went to the bedroom to get ready.

Peder walked back and forth across the floor; he stood by the water-pail, drank, and leaned against the wall. Finally he, too, went into the bedroom.

The first object to meet his eyes was Susie's wedding dress, which lay spread out on the bed. The dress was cream-colored and sewed with Spartan-like simplicity. She had been rushed that time and had had to make it herself. Peder liked it immensely because it fit her so perfectly; in it she was just the foolish little girl for whom he would gladly give his life, just his old dear Susie. Since the wedding she had seldom worn it. In the first place, because it was her wedding dress, and secondly, because she had had to skimp on material and, as a result, the dress reached no farther than to her ankles, which made her appear immodest.

"Are you going to wear that to-night?" he asked, in a quavering voice.

"Don't you like it any more?"

"I think it's great. Haven't I told you so?"

"To-night I'm dressing to please you!" She was quick in her reply. "Do you know, I haven't been out for a real good time since we were married." She stretched her arms to pin up the braid. Standing thus her bosom raised into proud curves. She took a pin from her mouth and stuck it into her hair. "That's more than two years ago now." There was no trace of reproach in her words; she only said them.

"All that time you've been imprisoned," he said, bitterly.

"God only knows how hungry I've been for a little fun!"

"With me you never find any? . . . No, I suppose not." A great helplessness had come over him; he was going to put on his coat and couldn't get started; he stuck his arm into the sleeve and pulled it out again.

"Not any real fun. You Norwegians don't know what that means."

Peder had combed his hair and went back to the kitchen. His mother looked up from the newspaper:

"Will you be gone long?"

"Aw . . . it'll be a while."

"Why don't you stay home, since you're so tired? Can't she go alone? Her own brother is with her."

Soon Susie appeared; she was ready, and they went out together.

"Let me sit with you, Charley!" she asked, in a way that made Nikoline get up at once and take a seat on the box which had been put in the rear of the sleigh. Charley growled good-naturedly about old women's crazy notions. "Here we were settled snug as in Paradise; then you have to come

On the Way to Golgotha

and spoil it. Listen here. I'm a Catholic and don't believe in divorce. . . . Hop in, Peder! What are you standing there dreaming about?"

Charley's words wrenched Peder out of his feeling of forsakenness. He drew a deep sigh. A funny scene was before his eyes: a man on his way to hell . . . deserted by those whom he for years had been trying to teach the virtue of goodness . . . now he was hounded to death by the very people he wanted to give eternal life . . . they jeered at him . . . he was hell-bound, and there was no way of escape . . . Peder could hear the jeers plainly.

"Are you coming?" shouted Charley.

Inwardly Peder froze so bitterly that he had to hold onto the edge as he climbed in.

The bottom of the sleigh was covered with loose hay; an upturned grocery box had been set in for seats. Nikoline occupied part of it. Peder mumbled something to the effect that it was swell to get such fine company . . . a maiden right out of the midnight sun . . . they didn't have many fairies here. His voice was dull and very tired.

"You're not feeling good to-night?"

"I have felt better. . . . But I guess it'll be all right."

"Are you sick?"

"No-o, I don't think so."

"Oh, but I'm glad you came!" She bent over and pulled the blanket better over his knees.

"Are you?"

"Was that why you came?"

"No . . . I don't suppose it was."

For a while she said no more. Peder could not understand how anyone who sat so still and silent could reach so deep into his heart. Never before had he felt a person's nearness more forcefully. She was sitting here in the dark, she didn't say one word, still she filled his whole being completely, and it felt so good to have her inside him.

Susie chattered incessantly all the way to McDougal's, on and on. Not a thing but that she had to ask about it.

. . . Where had Charley been during the holidays . . .

which girl did he have with him that time? . . . Had they
really got permission, to dance at McDonald's? . . . Were
both cows still milking? . . . Had he found time to fix that
oven door? Then he'd better hurry, or the hired girls would
be quitting before they got started! . . . Would anything
come of the Dennis and Maggie affair? . . . Why didn't
he get down to business and try to get Maggie? Was he
going to let Dennis snatch her away from him? . . . How
was father—possible to live in the same house with him
now? . . . Was he figuring on marrying again? What's
that? She bubbled over with laughter and swallowed her
own words. No room for anyone but her to-night. She
leaped from one subject into the middle of the next, constantly, no stopping her. For Charley's remarks she had
always some pert comment in readiness; the words seemed
to drop from the tip of her tongue. To-night there were only
bright sunshine and hilarious fun in Susie.

When they arrived the dance was in full progress. The
house rocked with merrymaking. Only young people. Everybody laughing and talking, with not a care in their soul.
Some of the men had brought their holiday flasks and had
already exchanged compliments. Dennis caught sight of
Peder and Charley and came over to shake hands. Winking
significantly, he told them he had to see them in private for
a moment. Peder said, no, thanks. Charley asked him to
wait a minute; just then the fiddler was striking up a merry
tune. He grabbed his sister's hand and instantly disappeared
in the whirl.

Peder and Nikoline were the only Norwegians present;
she felt embarrassed and clung close to him. She did not
know the quadrille and had to refuse the young men who
invited her to dance. Floor space was at a premium. Before
long they had been washed up into a corner, to which Peder
did not object.

"I should have stayed at home to-night," she said, timidly.
"You go ahead and dance; don't pay any attention to me."

Before Peder had found an answer, the fiddler had picked
up the strains of a waltz. Instantly her face brightened up in

a smile as if she unexpectedly had come face to face with
an old friend. He noticed the change come over her.

"What you say to us trying this one?"

Trustfully, as if they had played together all their lives,
she came into his arms. The movements of the waltz carried them away. Peder forgot all worries and surrendered
himself to the dance. The hubbub around him had stilled
. . . an evening in May . . . over the prairies soughed a
balmy wind . . . the air was tender with spring and it was
great to be alive. . . . Everything was as it should be. Once
he raised his head and looked about. Close by, Susie and
Tom danced past. For a second his eyes caught hers; they
sparkled like shooting-stars and were gone; he barely sensed
it was Susie and forgot her instantly. Never before had he
had such a partner. Light as a feather she floated on the
rhythm, always sure of her step, responsive to the least
impulse, the very incarnation of the waltz itself.

"You like to dance?" he asked, giddily.

"Yes. . . . Don't talk now."

"Why?"

"It's so beautiful!"

"Do you think this is sin?"

"No!"

"Lots of Norwegians do."

"That's because they're afraid."

"You're not that way?" he asked, low.

"No!"

"Why are they that way?"

"They're afraid of themselves."

Peder laughed gaily:

"Afraid of themselves? Others are that, too!"

"Are you laughing at me?"

"I am."

"Why?"

"You're the best little girl I've ever known."

For the first time she looked up into his face:

"You mean it?"

"Don't you believe me?"

"Now I believe it!"

"Are you glad I told you?"

"Yes." She rested her cheek against his shoulder.

"What are you thinking about now?"

"Of the summer nights in Nordland."

"What's that got to do with this?"

"They're more beautiful than anything else."

"Then I want to go there!"

"You must. Not till you have lived there can you know what beauty is like."

"I've seen you, haven't I?"

"You mustn't say that!"

"Why?"

"Because then everything will turn into ugliness."

Peder grew silent; a tender mood flooded his mind, and he felt a deep desire to cry . . . it would have been good just now to have had a real cry!

"Are you mad?" she asked, innocently.

"I was only thinking of Nordland."

She laughed softly:

"Come, let's go!"

"When?"

"As soon as the sun returns."

"So soon? Don't you like America any better than that?"

"That's not it. Only I'm so cold here."

"You'll have to dress warmer," he laughed.

"That won't do any good."

"Are we so terrible here?"

"No. Only you're so foolish!"

The next dance was a polka. Then Charley snatched her and flew away with her. Through the rest of the evening he clung close to them, insisted on teaching her the quadrille, joked a great deal and assured her that the quadrille was the easiest thing in the world. He had tasted of Dennis' bottle, talked glibly, and couldn't stand still. When his efforts to persuade her met with no success, he crossed the floor and

On the Way to Golgotha

whispered to the fiddler. The next dance was a waltz. Charley had taken hold of her arm before the first notes had sounded.

Darkly Peder watched them dance, his face hard and set. . . . Never shall he be allowed to ruin her life . . . nor she his!

Susie was on the floor for every dance. Usually with Tom. She danced with passionate abandon. No sooner was the bow raised from the strings than she clapped her hands, called for more, and was noisy as any of the men.

Peder observed her and crept farther into the corner. Acquaintances that chanced to see him came and wanted to know what was the matter. Why didn't he dance to-night? Was he sick? In his replies he was curt and evasive. Just before midnight he told Charley that now they must go home.

"Go home nothing!—Can't you stay till it's over? It won't be long?"

"No, I can't. Mother is home alone. It'll be late enough as it is. I'll tell Susie to get ready." He spoke snappishly.

While they were hitching up, Nikoline climbed into the sleigh and took the seat she had had before. Peder noticed that she hurried to get the seat.

"Now you can sit with your husband," said Charley to Susie. "That's what you've got him for. Here, you drive, Peder!" He was going to toss the reins to his brother-in-law. But Peder got ahead of him, jumped into the sleigh, and sat down beside Nikoline:

"Not on your life! You drive your own plugs."

"Aren't you ashamed of yourself! You, a married man!"

"Not a bit. You just get started."

Though she could not understand all the words, Nikoline sensed the friction that was in the air. And now not a word came from the two in the front seat. She lowered her voice:

"Are they mad now?"

"Let 'em be mad. They can stay that way, for all I care."

Suddenly she asked in a hushed voice:

"Can they understand Norwegian?"

"Not unless they've learned it to-night."

233

She was quiet for a moment:

"Was it you who got that job for me?"

"Oh, I don't know about that."

"I'm quitting soon."

"Aren't they good to you?"

"Too good."

"Is he after you?"

"Look out! They may hear what you're saying!"

"I'll kill him!"

She laughed.

"No, you mustn't do that. He's such a good boy!"

Peder sat struggling with something he wanted to say, but it was eluding him; he couldn't find the right words; in Norwegian it sounded so different. When he had said it, it wasn't what he had meant, not exactly, and he couldn't tell whether Nikoline understood him.

"Do you know what a *mirage* is?"

She laughed quietly:

"You ask me that? I who grew up by the sea and in golden summer nights? We call it *hilder*."

"*Hilder*? That's right, now I remember; mother has told me about it. What is *hilder* like?"

"You mean real *hilder*?"

"Heh-heh."

"When the summer night is clear and warm and still, when you hear only the deep breathing of the big sea, then the skerries, the holms, and all the islands stand on their heads in the air—they just float there. The ships sail with their masts pointing down; up in the sky, you understand. Oh, you can't imagine how beautiful such nights are! . . . It's fairyland and you aren't a bit afraid. . . . All space is a magic mirror . . . you see only phantasms floating in a great stillness . . . you don't dare breathe for fear they'll pass away."

Susie turned and bent over the back of the seat:

"What in the world are you two up to? Secrets?"

"We're telling ghost stories," announced Peder, curtly.

On the Way to Golgotha

"Can't we hear them, too?"

"Aw, let 'em alone!" said Charley, gruffly. "They're only jabbering!"

"Are they mad now?" wondered Nikoline. From her tongue the Nordlandsk dialect flowed musical and slow.

"Far from it. They've never felt better! . . . *Hilder*, then, are things that look different from what they really are?"

"Oh no! It's the magic mirror. The mermaid holds it up whenever she doesn't want the mermen to see her."

"That's how life is too, only *hilder*!" nodded Peder, darkly.

"What are you trying to tell me? Don't I know what life is?"

Peder did not hear her:

"He's a good fellow, all right. And as kind as they make 'em. He'd take care of you, I'm sure. Still, you and he could never be happy together," he had lowered his voice, "for he hasn't the magic mirror."

"And we're not going to try it, either." Her voice was warm, and again he had the same feeling, she seemed to speak from within his own heart: "That's not true what you said about life."

"I've tried it."

"So have I! But you're an American!"

"What difference does that make? Isn't life the same for Nordlændings, too?"

"No; not exactly. We know when we see *hilder*; we can tell it and make allowance. You Americans believe all you see until you run your heads against a stone wall; then you don't believe anything any more."

"And so you won't take him?"

Her answer came very slowly; there was a deep certainty in her voice:

"He and I aren't tuned to the same key."

"How can you tell?"

"I can hear it."

"Then you got better ears than I had," he said, heavily.

"You're an American, you saw *hilder* and believed it!"

235

Their Fathers' God

They neared the entrance to the farm. What Peder was going to say caught in his throat and his whole body numbed. Up by the corral he saw a light rise out of the very ground; the light had got its eye out and cast a glimmer over the white surface of the snow.

"Drive on!" he shouted, hoarsely. "Drive—for God's sake, hurry!" He had sprung up and clutched Charley's shoulder; his eyes stared until they saw only black. In the snow near the corral stood a lantern, askew as if it had been thrown there and then been left. Out by the south fence a cow blared out its long melancholy mooings. Otherwise all was still. So unearthly still.

Peder had jumped to the ground before the sleigh stopped. . . . Something's gone wrong here to-night! screamed a voice within him. A benumbing fear drove him toward the lantern. . . . Wasn't somebody lying there? A skirt ruffling in the wind? Good God——!

In a flash he was there.

"Mother!" he cried, and threw himself down beside her.

Beret stammered faintly:

"Look out . . . don't frighten . . . Susie. Tell her . . . carefully . . . my hip is broken . . . I can't get up."

He put his arms under her back to lift her up.

"No! . . . Not that way . . . you'll kill me!" she whimpered. "Lay me in your coat . . . get Charley to help carry me. . . . Tell Susie first!"

That was not necessary; the others were already standing beside him, Susie kneeling down by Beret.

"Hurry! get the corncrib door, Charley; carry her on that. Wrap your coat around her, Peder!" She clasped her mother-in-law's cold hands in her own, breathed on them, and pulled off her own mittens to put them on Beret. "How did it happen, grandma?" An anxious sympathy glowed in all that Susie said and did.

"The cattle were so noisy . . . I came out to look after

them . . . and slipped on the ice . . . it's that bull-crazy heifer."

"Have you lain here long?" Susie was bending over her.

"Just a little while . . . Pete is asleep."

Peder wiped his eyes, but there were no tears, and he clenched his teeth.

Together they lifted her onto the door that Charley brought and carried her to the house. At the kitchen door Peder took her alone. Susie opened for him, letting him go in ahead. He stopped in front of the door to the loft, waiting for her to open there, too.

"Do you mean to lay her in the icy loft? You haven't much sense!" She went to the bedroom door and opened it wide. "Bring her in here. Now we must get the fire going!"

Peder laid his mother on the bed and wrapped blankets around her.

"I'll go for the doctor right away!"

"I can do that," volunteered Charley, who stood behind the others. "You can be of more use here."

Peder straightened himself and looked at his brother-in-law, his eyes blinking fast:

"Will you?"

"One of us got to go."

Peder grabbed his coat that had been flung on the bed and went with it to Nikoline, holding it open. Their eyes met and it was only for a second, hers beaming with eagerness.

"Get into this coat. You go with him! The winter night is tough if you have to buck it all alone." He held the coat for her while she got into it. When Charley was opening the door to leave, Peder slapped him on the shoulder:

"Now hurry like hell, old boy!"

After they were gone the house settled down to an aware quiet. Peder sensed there was something unspoken between him and Susie . . . she wouldn't be carrying on like this unless some worry was upsetting her. She was bustling about with such ado that it was impossible to come near her. She heated an iron and buried it under the blankets to warm Beret's feet. She drew up a chair with the back close

Their Fathers' God

to the stove and hung a quilt over it; as soon as it was warmed through she placed it on the bed and got another; then she boiled a cup of sweet milk, brought it into the bedroom, and raised Beret's head so that she could drink the milk. Susie was so quick and certain in all her movements that Peder could only keep out of her way.

He remained standing by the warm stove. . . . Funny to see her in the wedding dress . . . so tiny and fairy-like . . . so quick and sure in every turn. . . . As in a big, downy blanket he felt himself swathed by the warmth from the stove; soon all the chill had been driven out of his body. The shivering ceased and a heavy drowsiness came over him . . . nice to stand here so full of sweet sleep! But all the time he was crying . . . there were no tears now, either, no tears that came to the surface, yet he was crying just the same.

When Susie had got Beret warm and had begun to undress her Peder went to the bedroom to see if he couldn't help. In the doorway he was met with a determined: "Go to bed, *Peermend*; you need sleep to-night!" He smiled a sick smile. Why did she try to call him by that name when she never could say it decently? She pushed him out of the room as if it were unseemly that he looked on now. He could hear how his mother struggled to subdue her sobs. Submissively he turned, went back into the kitchen, and slouched down in the rocking-chair.

When, some time later, Susie stood beside him, shaking him to bring him back to consciousness, he did not immediately realize that he had been asleep. Gulping with laughter, he looked up at her, wanting to know what kind of monkey business she was up to? . . . Where was he . . . anyhow? . . . What did she want? . . . Couldn't she leave him alone when she saw he couldn't make any headway? He was so full of laughter that he couldn't get a word out.

The dream he came out of was too idiotically funny: Light summer night; he was in a great garden standing underneath an apple tree of stupendous size; in the branches hung a placard bearing a funny inscription, *The Tree of Life*.

On the Way to Golgotha

Under the tree sat God the Father Himself, with Nikoline on his arm; He had crossed one knee over the other so that he could flap His foot; He had on golden sandals which curled up at the toe. Peder was bent on getting to the tree in order to have a look at the apples which in the late sunset hour glistened like gold, but he couldn't get anywhere; as soon as he took a step forward God flicked His foot, and, pop—Peder bounced back a step. Again and again it happened. Never had he seen anything so funny. He tried to explain to God that he was not a thief, that he would not even touch the fruit, that he only wanted to come so close that he could have a good look at it, but he laughed so hard that he could not get the words out. And right beside him stood Susie, egging him on: "Can't you get me just one apple when there are so many?"—"Sure, get you an apple! Go and get one, yourself. Can't you see that darn foot? You beat that for a foot! That's where He keeps His omnipotence!" . . . Susie was angry. "I sure thought I had more of a man than that. Can't you slip by that old fozzle?"— "More of a man? Don't you see Who it is? Are you trying to tease me into a scrap with God the Father? . . . Did you say mother was here? . . . Mother . . . well——" With an effort he pulled himself to his feet and there stood Susie in front of him; he noticed she had tied Beret's old kitchen apron over her dress, and realized where he was. In the room floated an aroma of strong tea; the table had been set for two, with bread, butter, and cold meat. . . . "Mother?" he yawned. "All right." Still wabbly with sleep he went to Beret.

Susie had turned the lamp low; the room lay in semi-darkness. Peder stood beside the bed, rubbing his eyes.

All his mother wanted was to remind him that after she was gone he must not neglect to teach Pete Norwegian; her voice faltered with concern. . . . Children that turned their backs on their fathers' God were an abomination in the eyes of the Lord.

"No, mother. That job you better take care of." He was

yet groggy with sleep. . . . "I've got another problem on my hands now!"

Beret looked up:

"What can that be?"

"Oh, just one of Susie's crazy notions!" He patted her on the cheek and returned to the kitchen, because now he was hungry as a bear.

"If you've got tea ready, let's have a cup."

Susie filled both cups and sat down. She wanted to know what he had been struggling with in his sleep.

The mood of the dream was upon him still:

"It's the funniest thing I've ever been up against. You and I were in Paradise; you dared me to steal apples from the Tree of Life; the Lord Himself sat there blocking the way, I just couldn't do a thing against Him; you were cross and called me names; you were dead set on having me steal apples. . . . Did I talk in my sleep?"

"Is it such things you dream about?" Over in the cradle Petie stirred restlessly; she got up quickly and turned him on his other side, stood for a moment humming to him, and went to the stove to move the teapot farther from the fire. After she returned to the table her face was like that of one preoccupied with weighty matters:

"What did Dahl have to talk about last night? It took him a long time. Mother and I thought we never would get started."

"Didn't you hear it?" Peder looked up at her.

"I wasn't in the bedroom with you!"

"No . . . I guess that's right; I forgot that!" He spoke slowly and shoved his cup away.

"If he really means it and you can spare the time, why don't you take it? The commissioners get good pay." She spoke with business-like promptness.

Peder's face reddened. . . . Why couldn't she have said this last night? . . . She continued to eat without once looking up. Suddenly he rose and went to the stove. He lifted the cover of the teapot and shook it:

On the Way to Golgotha

"We'd better add more water. They'll be needing something warm when they get back." He spoke uncertainly.

. . . "Besides," she continued, "I don't see what right he has to decide who's going to be his successor."

. . . "Shall I add a couple of cups of water?" He was peering into the kettle.

"I'll do that. . . . They say Dahl's farm is all run down because he spends all his time at meetings."

"Is that so?" he asked, with forced calmness.

"So they say. I can't see why he should need let his farm go to rack and ruin. If he's earning good money, he can afford to hire help?"

Peder looked up at the clock, which now showed fifteen minutes of three. . . . They should be here any time now?

Susie was busy removing the dishes from the table.

"If father hadn't fooled away so much time in politics, our farm would look a lot better, that's sure. But then he couldn't afford to hire decent help."

Peder pretended he did not hear her; he went into the bedroom and sat down.

Shortly after three Charley and Nikoline arrived, Doctor Green following close behind in his own rig. They drove right on home, the hour being so late.

The doctor threw off his fur coat and the great scarf he wore about his throat and stood by the stove, warming himself. As he looked about the room his face lit up in surprise; the cleanliness and Puritanic orderliness in which he found himself in this farmhouse seemed to mollify him.

"So here's where you live?" he asked Susie. "Where's your father?"

"At home."

"At home? Aha! Then you're not running this house? I thought so!"

Susie blushed furiously.

"If you have a cup of tea, I'll take it right away." Without waiting for an invitation, he sat down at the table and

241

watched her fill his cup. While sipping the tea he asked Peder about the accident. Instantly his anger flared up:

"So that's it, eh? You let your mother slave outside while you yourself stay in bed. Fine treatment, I call it!"

Peder felt a peculiar pleasure in being thus taken to task. He was standing in the middle of the floor, grinning broadly at the angry man:

"It isn't quite that bad."

"Well, just how bad is it, then?"

"We happened to be away."

"Out raising Cain, I suppose? And you let your mother sit home alone?"

"Yes," admitted Peder, frankly, "we were at a New-year's party."

"Good thing it wasn't a prayer-meeting!" growled the doctor. "I've heard the Norwegians out this way are great at that sort of thing. . . . I'll have some more tea." He held his cup out to Susie. "How big a farm are you working?"

"Three hundred and twenty acres."

"Good soil?"

"As good as you find around here."

"Homestead?"

"One quarter."

"I suppose you're praying every night for a buyer?" asked the doctor, acidly. "You should get rid of the farm. You don't want a homestead. Sell it and move to town with the rest of the hoodlums!"

"Hadn't thought of it yet." Peder stroked his hair back and came nearer. "Not yet, anyway."

Doctor Green turned to Susie:

"Did your father get well again?"

"He's all right now," she admitted, timidly.

"That's good. If it had gone the other way, which well it might, I'd have had that darn priest arrested for manslaughter!" he announced, grouchily.

His words were drowned in a deafening clatter from the stove; Susie had dropped a lid and was having great diffi-

culty in getting it back in place, dragging it back and forth.
With a flaming face she brought the teapot.

"Thanks, no more." Undisturbed, he returned to his subject. "That Father Williams is the kindest ass I've ever
known. And certainly the silliest. It's a wonder he didn't
send your father to the grave. Never have I heard of an act
more insanely foolish!"

"Mother wants you—she's calling!" said Susie, grasping
Peder's arm and drawing him forcibly into the bedroom. She
trembled in every limb, ran from one thing to another; she
turned up the lamp, went into the kitchen, and was back instantly. Bending over Beret, she stroked her cheek, whisper-
ing: "Now he'll soon be here. Don't pay any attention to
what he says!" Then she tidied the bedclothes, which needed
no tidying.

She was right, Doctor Green was soon in the room.

He took his time in making his diagnosis. Having set the
broken hip and bandaged it securely, he sat down on the
bed to study this case. In the deep-carved lines of her face
and in the eyes following his every move so attentively he
saw signs that made him proceed cautiously. And there was
a dignity over this worn-out farmer woman that, for once,
made him keep his temper. The pulse was very irregular.
Having counted the beats several times, he got up to make
an examination of the chest.

At last he was through. Peder followed him to the kitchen
and helped him with his coat.

"That hip won't cause much trouble," he said, "providing
she doesn't catch cold. There are worse things. Her heart is
completely worn out; she must have absolute quiet. No worries of any kind; the least mental disturbance might prove
fatal. By the way her heart is going now it should have
stopped long ago." Doctor Green had raised the collar and
tied the scarf in place; his fur cap was drawn so low that
the only visible parts of his face were his eyes.

"These prairies," came a growling voice out of the huge
bundle, "give abundant harvests. Soaked as they are with
warm blood, they ought to yield generously. A hell of a price

we've had to pay for this empire, and still we can't call it our own. Next time you want some one to rant at your Fourth of July celebration, just call on me! . . . Be careful that she doesn't catch cold."

The doctor was barely through the door before Susie clutched Peder's arm—she had her own way of doing this no matter whether she was in fear or in need of expressing affection:

"Mercy me, what a man! He must be possessed—honestly! Father thinks so, too. . . . Did you see his eyes? . . . I hate him!" She choked a sob.

Fearing that she might break down entirely, Peder put his arm around her back. Like a frightened child seeking a place of refuge she snuggled closer. But he did not respond. With a feeling of disgust he shrugged his shoulders:

"Control yourself," he bade her, coldly. "You will have to stand the truth about the priest. You can see now that others have the same opinion as I have."

"No, no, it isn't that! . . . He's so mean, so terrible! You don't know him yet. A devil cast out of hell, that's what he is. Don't you suppose I know? You must get another doctor for grandma. He's no good, anyhow. Father'll tell you the same thing!" . . . The storm abated, and she looked pleadingly up at Peder: "We don't want a demon like him to take care of mother."

"We can talk about that later. You'd better get to bed."

Susie would not hear of going to bed.

"You go right upstairs and lie down. To-night I'm going to stay up. You'd only fall asleep. . . . You know how it is with me, I sleep best after it starts getting light. Be a good boy, now!" she begged, tenderly, "and do as I say. I'll call you in time for the chores."

Beret had been listening to their quibbling; she was cross and wanted to know what this meant? . . . Wasn't there going to be any peace at all to-night? She'd hear no more silly talk about staying up . . . they were both going to bed . . . she needed no one to stay up with her . . . the idea of staying up on her account! . . . She would call them in time for the chores.

That night Beret had her way.

VI

The next morning Peder and Susie slept late. She awoke first, and when she noticed the hour she shook him frantically.

Coming downstairs, he went to the stove and stirred up the fire. Beret was lying wide-awake. In the grey light of the cold winter morning she appeared spent and weary.

. . . No, she had not slept, she announced, with a sigh . . . it didn't matter much with her, anyway . . . she was used to unslept nights. . . . But she had many admonitions for Peder concerning the outside work: He mustn't forget the small calves, those in the east pen . . . they could have only fresh milk . . . better to give them too little than too much . . . one of them was so bashful and fidgety . . . for the older calves he must mix bran with the milk . . . the measure she used was standing by the feed barrel. . . . He mustn't hurry the milking with Dropla! If the cow didn't feel just right she might hold the milk for long spells . . . a little petting wouldn't hurt . . . she never saw such a cow— more particular than a human being! . . . One of the hens had begun to lay . . . he would find her in the empty crib on the south side. . . . During the night she had been wondering whether it wouldn't be possible to heat water for the cattle he kept outdoors . . . the poor beasts would stand the cold better, and they wouldn't need so much feed. Hans Olsa had brought a big kettle with him from Norway . . . it was standing in Sörine's granary, they never used it over there . . . perhaps he could borrow the kettle? Beret's eyes roved from one object to another . . . she would have to get word to Sörine some time, anyway . . . she needed her here . . . to . . . to help her with her bodily needs . . . she would have to get up . . . she couldn't ask a stranger to help with

245

such things. Tears were running across her cheeks. . . . "God look in mercy to me that this doesn't last long!"

"Fiddlesticks! You mean to tell me we've to get outside help for such trifles? Haven't you two grown-up people right here in the house?"

But she would not be budged, she must have Sörine come over.

"The Irish are not going to carry out after me!" She wept much and seemed very depressed.

She left the breakfast untouched, but drank the coffee. As soon as Peder had eaten he went over to Sörine. She was glad to come, and stayed all through the day. On leaving she promised to be back in the morning.

For a long while that evening Peder sat in the bedroom with her. She was restless and complained of much pain in the back. Again she mentioned several things that should be looked after. She must have the minister over, and get word to Store-Hans. Mentioning her son's name made her cry. . . . Queer about Hans . . . no one quite like him . . . though she had naught but good to say about any of her children. God had looked in mercy to all of them! . . . Too bad Anna Marie left before this happened. Had she been here now they wouldn't have had to trouble outsiders.

For some time she lay thinking. . . . Did he know of a Norwegian lawyer? She needed to see a lawyer . . . no telling how this would turn out. . . . Would it be possible to have a lawyer come out here? Maybe Hans would have to make a trip to town one of these days. In that case he could probably bring one out with him. . . . "You see," she confessed with an effort that seemed to give her pain, "I lie here thinking that I must make my will. . . . Before Per Hansa passed away he willed everything to me—that was done the fall he built—and now it's high time I do something about it. . . . What the law is in these matters I know not. . . . God grant I haven't waited too long!"

All Peder said to put her at ease only served to make matters worse; she only became more stirred up; her anxiety shone through every word. Finally he kept his tongue. But thinking it might be easier for her to drop off to sleep with some one near by, he remained in the room a long while. Before bedtime Susie came in and tended her for the night. She undid her hair, combed and braided it, smoothed the pillow, and straightened the sheet under her. Peder looked on in silence. . . . She certainly has a handy way with sick people! he thought.

Not that night, either, would Beret have anyone sitting up with her.

The next morning she appeared much weaker. When she talked, her breathing was fitful and difficult. Peder got the impression that she had passed another sleepless night, but didn't care to ask. As he stood beside the bed, looking down into his mother's weary, care-worn face, a dimmed memory drifted through his mind—a picture of a scraggy old cow they had had on the farm while he was still a mere youngster. The cow had died, finally, of old age. Her name, he recalled, was Rosie, and she had been a part of the caravan when his parents moved west. He could imagine nothing quite so helpless as old Rosie during the last year of her life. And now here mother lay, looking much the same! At that same moment he was struck with the realization that now there was no time to be lost. He must act, and act quickly. He rushed through the morning chores, hitched Dolly to the cutter, and sped away to his brother.

—How did it happen? asked Store-Hans, reserved and slow-spoken as usual.

—Well, just how did he suppose such things would happen? Peder replied, curtly. Mother had slipped on the ice. He had had the doctor once, and was now on his way to town to get him out here again. Store-Hans had better hurry and go over to see her. Susie was alone at home. Peder was in a rush and didn't have time for many words.

When he got home, shortly after noon, he found his brother and sister-in-law sitting in the bedroom. Peder reported where he had been, and said the doctor would be here later in the day. He noticed his mother was pleased with what he had done.

"That is fine of you, Permand. . . . Not that he can help me any. . . . The old clock has run down." She seemed pleased with her last remark and smiled kindly at them. After a pause she added: "Now, Hans, to-morrow you must go to town for a lawyer. . . . I won't get any peace until I've arranged these matters . . . and you must be with me when he comes. Afterwards you must send for the minister. . . . Too bad that Ola and Anna Marie are so far away."

Hans asked if she wanted them to telegraph the others to come.

Beret lay considering the suggestion.

"You might as well," she said, finally. "I suppose they will be coming for the funeral, anyway. As it is they will hardly reach here in time, and perhaps it's just as well. There's small pleasure in watching an old boat sink." A weeping spell seized her. Minutes passed during which she was unable to speak. When calm again she sighed heavily. "How I have loved you all! . . . All of you went your own ways . . . that made it no easier for her who was your mother. . . . Peder, what do you think about telegraphing?"

Peder only nodded; he stood leaning over the foot of the bed. It was decided that Store-Hans should go to town to see a lawyer early in the morning and at the same time send the telegram.

Late in the afternoon Doctor Green arrived. Strange to say, he neither shouted nor raged; on the contrary, he showed the greatest patience with Beret. He left a powder with Peder, with instructions to give it to her before going to bed. In the morning he would prepare some medicine if some one would call for it. As he stood by the kitchen door pulling on his coat, he told them frankly that there was no hope of recovery. Her heart must have been in a wretched condition for many years; now it was worn out completely. She might drop off any moment—the heart could not hold out much longer.

After finishing supper, Peder moved the rocking-chair into the bedroom.

"What is the meaning of this?" asked Beret, suspiciously.

On the Way to Golgotha

"Nothing, I only want to sit here and rest myself awhile. Don't you want me to read for you?"

His offer touched her so that she wept.

"Thank you, Permand! . . . Take the hymn-book. Read number five hundred and seventy for me."

Peder turned to the hymn, looked down the page a moment, and began to read the Norwegian hymn, in a calm, sonorous voice:

> "I know of a sleep in Jesus' name,
>   A rest from all toil and sorrow;
> Earth holds in her arms my weary frame,
>   And shelters it till the morrow;
> My soul is at home with God in heaven,
> Her sorrows are past and over.
>
> "I know of a peaceful eventide;
>   And when I am faint and weary,
> At times with the journey sorely tried,
>   Through hours that are long and dreary;
> Then often I yearn to lay me down,
> And sink into blissful slumber.
>
> "I know of a morning bright and fair,
>   When tidings of joy shall wake us,
> When songs from on high shall fill the air
>   And God to His glory take us,
> When Jesus shall bid us rise from sleep—
> How joyous that hour of waking!"

When he had read the first stanza he paused briefly before continuing. As he had read on, the profound austerity of sorrow and the simple Christian faith which the lines expressed gripped him. Without being aware of it, he let himself go in the reading; the purity of the mood and the irresistible sweep of the poetry was carrying him along—his voice was deep and warm with sincerity as he continued:

> "O that is a morning dear to me,
>   And oft, o'er the mountains streaming,
> In spirit its heavenly light I see,
>   As golden the peaks are beaming;
> Then sing I for joy like birds at dawn
> That carol in lofty lindens."

249

Their Fathers' God

Susie came rushing into the bedroom; she had Petie in her arms and appeared greatly frightened.

"What on earth are you doing in here?" she broke in on his reading. "You must go for help right away!"

He paid no attention, only continued to read with increased earnestness:

> "God's Son to our graves then wends His way,
>   His voice hears all tribes and nations;
> The portals are rent that guard our clay,
>   And moved are the sea's foundations.
> He calls out aloud: 'Ye dead, come forth!'
> In glory we rise to meet Him."

Bewildered, Susie stood there, with the boy in her arm, her glance shifting from one to the other. She saw Beret's folded hands, her moving lips; she heard Peder's awed voice and guessed that he must be saying prayers. . . . Was she dying now? . . . And was he performing sacred rites given only a priest to perform? And suddenly she cried out:

"Go get the minister right away. She must get the Last Sacrament. Don't call the curse of God upon yourself this way!"

Peder drew a deep breath, letting himself go with greater abandon, a note of joy coming into his voice:

> "Now opens the Father's house above,
>   The names of the blest are given:
> Lord, gather us there; let none we love
>   Be missed in the joys of heaven.
> Vouchsafe Thou us all a place with Thee;
> We ask through our dear Redeemer.
>
> "O Jesus, draw near my dying bed,
>   And take me into Thy keeping,
> And say, when my spirit hence is fled:
>   'This child is not dead, but sleeping.'
> And leave me not, Saviour, till I rise,
> To praise Thee in life eternal."

The silence that fell when he had finished was so potent that it cried for words. Beret muttered, disgustedly:

"Here she comes rampaging in on us while we're holding our devotion! . . . Some people haven't much sense!"

On the Way to Golgotha

"What is she saying now?" asked Susie, terrified at Beret's angry tone.

Peder got up. Without a word he flung the hymn-book on the commode and went out into the kitchen. There he took the powder the doctor had prescribed and fixed it.

Susie had followed him.

"Are you sure you're doing right, now? Didn't he tell you a *full* cup of water?"

Her question lingered in the silence. Peder shot a glance at her which said unmistakably:

"If you don't shut up now, I'll strike you!"

Involuntarily she drew away, trying at the same time to hush Petie, who was dressed for bed and now wanted to go to his father to say good night.

Coldly Peder disregarded her, and went into the bedroom with the medicine. The powder worked quickly. Soon Beret lay in a heavy sleep which looked as if it would last for some time. Peder returned to the kitchen, stirred up the fire, and added more fuel. Later he wrapped himself in a couple of quilts and sat in the rocking-chair that night.

VII

Early in the afternoon Store-Hans returned from town, bringing with him a Norwegian lawyer. Meanwhile Peder had gone to get the minister. He did not find him at home, but Mrs. Kaldahl had promised to send him as soon as he returned.

Store-Hans had been sitting with his mother for a while before Peder came. To-day she was breathing more easily and seemed livelier in her talk. Peder asked if she wished to be left alone with the lawyer.

"You might know I don't wish that. I want all of you with me . . . Susie, too. We'll have to agree on how this is to be done."

Peder carried in more chairs, asking the lawyer and Susie to come into the bedroom. For a while Beret lay thinking.

"Now it's best we come to an agreement first. Then he can

251

write it down later," she began, thoughtfully. "If there is
anything he doesn't understand, you will have to help me
explain it." Again she lay quiet for a while, thinking, after-
ward talking slowly and with many pauses:

"I've intended that Permand should have the farm just as
it stands, with buildings, live stock and equipment . . . he
has struggled the hardest with it . . . was born here and
has lived here all the time. . . . He is to pay Ole and Hans
two thousand dollars each . . . and Anna Marie fifteen hundred dollars. . . . That's fifty-five hundred dollars altogether, isn't it? . . . That's a great deal of money . . . a big
load for anybody . . . but I want it so. . . . There should
be about a thousand dollars left after I have been laid away.
. . . Of that money the two oldest boys are to have three
hundred dollars apiece and Anna Marie two hundred dollars.
. . . That is to be subtracted from what Peder owes them.
. . . What is left after the eight hundred dollars have been
taken out shall go to the poor people in my home parish in
Norway. . . . You can send it to the minister in Nesna . . .
he is to distribute it."

They watched her in silence. Peder was hanging over the
foot of the bed. Susie was leaning against the door. Of all
her mother-in-law said she got only the names. After a while
she went out into the kitchen and began setting the table.

"He is to pay Ole first," continued Beret, "because he is
my first-born son. . . . If he hasn't paid him in full within
three years, he is to pay him interest . . . not over six per
cent . . . I want that written. . . . Ole may ask less . . .
that also I like to have written. . . . When the first three
years are up, he is to begin paying Hans, if he hasn't already done so. After that he is to have three years to pay
Hans, on the same conditions as with Ole. That must be
written plainly . . . I mean, he shall not pay you, Hans,
interest until the end of the seventh year. . . . After eight
years have passed Anna Marie's share is due . . . if he has
not paid her out already and cannot pay her then, he must
pay interest on whatever remains unpaid . . . the condition
for the interest is to be the same in all three cases. . . . If

in the meantime any of the heirs should die, that share is to go to the other two . . . or, if any of them, or both, is dead, to the nearest relatives. . . . If Anna should die unmarried, before he has paid her, her share is to be divided equally among her brothers then living. . . . Tell me now," she turned to the lawyer, "will this be according to law? . . . Can I do it this way?"

The lawyer looked up from his writing and nodded. There was nothing to prevent her from making these stipulations.

"Peder is not to have the right to sell the farm outside the Holm family as long as there is any of them willing to buy. . . . By that I mean this: In case Peder should get a notion to sell and there is any one left of Per Hansa's family, that person, or those persons, must be given the first chance to buy. . . . When the day comes that there is talk of selling, the three nearest relatives shall appoint three appraisers to determine the value of the farm. . . . If none of the Holm family cares to buy, Peder is to have the right to sell to whomever he pleases . . . in that case he himself can determine the price. . . . If Petie lives and wants to be a farmer, I would like 'to see that he get the farm after his father . . . that I want written in the will, but it must not be said as a stipulation." She grew silent and lay in deep thought. . . . "This farm has cost much more than money can ever pay . . . I like to see it remain in Per Hansa's family."

Her eyes had closed. By and by she opened them and looked at Store-Hans, who sat nearest her:

"Now I want you to tell me true, am I being fair?"

Hans cleared his throat; he was slow in answering:

"The way times are now you are placing a heavy burden on one so young and untried."

Beret nodded:

"I ask you, Would you have taken the farm on the same conditions?"

"Mother, I cannot say. It seems to me that you should leave him free to sell when he pleases and to whom he pleases. . . . He shouldn't be bound to ask others about that."

"No," said Beret, decisively, "that I will not agree to. . . . Then I better set down the price. . . . Now tell me honestly, Permand, will you take the farm on these conditions?"

"Certainly I will," Peder answered, quickly, and straightened up.

The bright smile spreading over Beret's worn-out features made her face so pleased that it became beautiful.

"Come here . . . both of you," she whispered. . . . "Now shake hands that it is all right."

The brothers did as she bade them, and she laid her thin hard hand over their clasped ones:

"I have done my part," she mumbled, faintly . . . "now may the Lord do His!" . . . For a while she did not withdraw her hand: "Now I have only one more thing to ask of you: You're to lay me on the left side of Per Hansa . . . as close to him as you can . . . that is how he always wanted me!" She removed her hand and lay there weeping quietly. . . . "Now you must all go in and have coffee. . . . The minister should soon be here?"

In the kitchen Susie bustled about alone preparing the lunch. She spoke to no one and no one spoke to her; it was as if she were the hired girl in the house going about her everyday tasks. No one offered to help. The lawyer sat by the table, writing; Store-Hans was helping him interpret the stipulations Beret wanted in the will; Sofie was still in the bedroom with her mother-in-law. Peder had hurried out to do the evening chores. . . . This promised to be a queer wake! Susie thought. Every move she made was marked by impetuous resentment. She slung the dishes on the table, rattled the lid of the stove, and when Petie whimpered she told him to shut up. . . . Didn't they know that where a person lay dying there must be made certain preparations? . . . Where was the minister? She slung the bread-plate on the table. . . . Or perhaps Peder would play the priest to-night too! . . . God alone knew what they had been up to all afternoon! She thumped the cream-pitcher down so hard that the contents spattered on the cloth. . . . What was she going to serve this town dandy? Most likely he was as finicky as the rest of the Norwegians!

VIII

Reverend Kaldahl arrived at seven o'clock. Store-Hans had gone home to do his chores, but had promised to come back as soon as he could.

After having talked with Beret privately awhile the minister opened the door to the kitchen and asked Susie and Peder to come in; their mother wanted to speak to them. He had set out the paten and the chalice, and had put on his canonical garb.

A great uneasiness had come over Beret. In her thin cheeks burnt an unnatural flush; her temples were splotched with crimson; her glance roved constantly from one object to another; the right hand groped nervously over the quilt as if seeking something. She seemed in great pain; her breathing was distressed and her voice, when she tried to speak, was so feeble that, at times, it died in the breathing.

"We are ready," said the minister, solemnly.

No one spoke. Peder stood at the foot of the bed; Susie leaned against the door. From the kitchen came the gleeful voice of Petie, who sat in his cradle laughing and chattering to himself.

"I have a confession to make to Peder and Susie." Beret gasped for breath and could not go on.

The minister waited with folded hands.

In a moment Beret began speaking in English, pausing often to hunt for the right words:

"That time I thought I was doing what was right. . . . God pity me, it was the only thing I could do. . . . Now it seems the blackest sin. . . . Before I . . . partake of the body and blood of Christ . . . I must confess." She was too weak to continue. The minister spoke encouraging words, reminding her of the Lord's gracious promise to all who repented their sins and confessed their guilt before men. It was of these it was said, 'They had come out of great tribulations.' For such He had grace in abundance.

"No, no," she objected, wearily, "that is for the pure of heart . . . those who had never faltered along the way." The tears trickling across her cheeks gave her trouble.

"Absolutely not," declared the minister, convincingly. "The pure of heart are not to be found in our earthly existence. All mankind is under the ban of sin. 'For the good that I would I do not; but the evil which I would not, that I do,' says the Apostle Paul. But the Lord is full of compassion for struggling souls. There are those who must creep to the Cross because they are too weak to walk. Sometimes I wonder if the Lord does not rejoice more in them than He does in the others." The minister reminded her of Moses and David, of Peter and Paul, and of the holy Augustine. All had been under the yoke of sin which it is given to no man to cast off as long as life lasts. "But be the transgression ever so great," he concluded, "there is always grace abundant. Confess the sin that is troubling you, Mrs. Holm."

"Per,"[1] she panted in Norwegian, "bring me a cup of water."

He went into the kitchen for the water and held up her head so that she could drink. But she could not swallow a drop and motioned him away. She looked about for her daughter-in-law:

"Have you put the boy to bed? . . . I should see him once more. . . . Is he asleep?"

Susie brought Petie to the bed. At once he held out his arms to Beret, babbling "Gamma!" and wanted to get down into the bed.

"There, there, my little Petie-boy!" murmured Beret, patting him on the head. "God bless and keep you all your days!" A spell of weeping came upon her, causing her great distress. Several times she tried to raise her left hand, but could not get the hand up.

Susie took Petie away and stood as before, leaning against the door.

[1] Per, common dialect form for Peder.

On the Way to Golgotha

The pastor cleared his throat:

"Don't excite yourself in this hour." He came near the bed and waited.

Beret sighed pitifully:

"It's Susie . . . Susie!"

"Is it against her you have sinned?" asked the minister, kindly.

"Yes . . . God help me!" She wanted to turn her head to look at her daughter-in-law, but the muscles refused to respond to her will. . . . "Her priest . . . came here one day . . . a year ago last summer . . . I heard what they said . . . I . . . could not . . . let it happen . . . I could not! . . . I talked to Peder about it . . . begged him to have the boy baptized . . . he heeded me not . . . wouldn't listen. . . . To have my innocent grandchild made a Catholic . . . Per Hansa's grandson! . . . How could I stand idly by and let it happen? . . . How could I ever meet Per Hansa face to face and tell him? . . . And what would God think of me? . . . I know," she moaned . . . "that time I was a tool in the hands of a Higher One. . . . There was no other way out . . . none, I tell you. . . . O God! why did You let me do this wrong! . . . It is the mother-right I have sinned against!"

Beret shoved herself back on the pillow. With a super-human effort she went on; her face was terrible to look at:

"I have had the boy baptized!" she groaned. . . . "Had him baptized without the mother's knowing! . . . God and man have mercy on me! . . . Peder Emmanuel is his name." She lay still for a moment. "I begged Sörine to do it. She—she is without blame. . . . She said the ritual as it stands in the book. . . . It was on the eighth of October . . . a year ago last fall . . . the same day the rain came." Her eyes closed. It looked as if she were retreating into herself. Each time she released her breath she struggled violently to recapture it.

The minister stood close by the pillow. A profound solemnity was upon him, yet he spoke kind, encouraging words:

"I see no wrong in this act except that you have kept it

secret from the parents. They are here and will surely forgive you. Beyond that you can rest assured that you have in no way sinned against God's holy Law. Though performed by a layman the baptism is valid, beyond all question. The child can be brought to church to receive the official blessing any time. That, however, is only a pious custom and in no way affects the validity of the act. Don't let this worry you. Through holy baptism your grandson has been made a child of God and a member of the Lutheran Church. If you were afraid the parents would neglect the baptism, unquestionably you acted right."

Beret's face was distorted with pain; the right corner of her mouth was drawn upward, her lips apart; the right eye was closed and the left lay half-open; out of it shone an unearthly fear.

"It's . . . against Susie . . . I have . . . sinned . . . can't you see . . . against . . . Susie. . . . She is . . . the mother! . . . Oh, oh, Susie . . . have you . . . forgiveness for me?" Again she tried to turn her head and could not.

When Beret had begun her confession Susie had come quickly to the bed. . . . What was this? Grandma had things on her mind that must not be spoken except in private with a Man of God! Susie bent over to bid her stop, to lay her hand on her mouth . . . she mustn't go on . . . this was only for the minister's ears! . . . What was that? Suddenly she was struck dumb. . . . What? . . . She had had Petie baptized? The devil she had? . . . Had stolen his soul . . . Petie's soul! . . . Susie tottered back to the door, stood there staring at the apparition in the bed. . . . Was the devil loose here? . . . As she listened to the confession she saw a demon in the bed, an evil spirit that had set itself up against God and all His saints and maliciously led them by the nose! Could Susie at that moment have flung herself upon her mother-in-law and torn her to pieces she would only have felt that she was doing an act that was pleasing in the sight of God, the crime was so heinous, the sin so unspeakably wicked. With a stifled cry she vanished into the kitchen. She threw herself down on a chair, crushing the child so violently that he let out a piercing cry. She sprang up and dashed with him into the front room; there the darkness frightened him still more and he cried all the louder. "Shut up, you imp!" She crushed him to her and fled up the stairway into the loft.

Peder had not noticed her leave the room. When he turned to look for her she was gone. Roughly he shoved the minister aside and grasped his mother's hand:

"Don't excite yourself so, mother! You can't stand it. . . . Everything is all right . . . Susie doesn't care about a little thing like that!"

Beret lay deathly still. Her breathing grew more feeble and disrupted. Her throat seemed to be clogging up. The lips moved, but sounds were slow in coming:

" 'In . . . quietness . . . and . . . in . . . con-fidence . . . shall be . . . your strength . . . and . . . ye . . . would not.' . . . Susie!"

There came a sigh that stuck fast in the throat and ended in a feeble gasp. Then a few short puffs. . . . And all was over.

Both men stood motionless. Finally the minister knelt beside the bed, laid his hand on the lifeless forehead, and repeated slowly the Aaronistic benediction:

"The Lord bless thee, and keep thee. The Lord make His face shine upon thee, and be gracious unto thee. The Lord lift up His countenance upon thee, and give thee peace."

The minister rose and held out his hand to Peder:

"Now one of the Lord's chosen has gone from us. The Lord hastens to gather His children home. May your mother's death prove a blessing to you, as I am sure her life was."

Peder stood facing the minister. He did not hear what he was saying; did not see that he took off his canonicals and wrapped them and the holy vessels up and put them into his grip; did not hear him bid good-bye; nor did he notice the minister leave. When at last he realized that he was alone, that the minister was gone, he threw himself down on his knees beside the bed and grasped his mother's worn hand:

Their Fathers' God

"Open your eyes, mother!" he dry-sobbed. "Don't you hear me?" Relentlessly his agony lashed him, piercing deeper and deeper. Like a mighty swelling torrent his self-accusation broke through him and he had to defend himself. " 'Tisn't true—I didn't kill you. . . . It isn't my fault!" Suddenly his blood went cold, his muscles stiffened. His mother's left eye was half-open, staring at him in a cold, glassy quiet.

IX

He was in a daze. Before his mind's eye shone a single concept: She is dead! Could it really be true? Was it possible? Until now his mother had been the one unchangeable thing in his existence. Whether cheerful or in the sad mood that had been habitual with her, it was her foresight, her concern for him, that had drawn the circle of reality in which, up till now, he had been moving. Now she was gone—gone never to return. . . . Into the land where she had fled, he could not follow. . . . And it was all his fault, that too he saw clearly. . . . Out of consideration for Susie he had neglected to have the child christened . . . hadn't thought it could make much difference one way or the other. . . . For the sake of a silly New-year's party he had left her alone at home that night. . . . And now she lay here, dead! Could divine retribution be so merciless?

Finally he had to leave the room. Couldn't stand it there any longer. Unless he found some one to share his burden with, he'd die!

The kitchen was empty. Bewildered, he looked about. . . . Where had Susie gone with Petie? From the loft came the child's persistent whining; he seemed to be teasing for something and couldn't get his way; but there was no sound from her. Suddenly the thought struck Peder: She is frightened because of what has happened and has fled upstairs . . . poor, poor Susie! His own need of sympathy filled him with pity for her. He took the stairway in three leaps. Inside the door he stopped abruptly; from the table the lamp cast a dim light; the chimney was smutchy; in lighting the lamp

On the Way to Golgotha

she must have turned it up too high; on the bed Susie lay, fully dressed, with her head toward the wall; Petie, half-undressed, was straddling his mother's shoulders, tugging at her and begging her to get up; his cheeks were purple with cold.

No sooner had Peder sat down on the edge of the bed than the boy left his mother; he came scrambling into his lap, locking his arms about his father's neck. At the touch of the child's cold cheek against his own something gave way in Peder; he began to weep, at first by violent spurts that broke down barrier after barrier, then in long sobs that were laden with agony. Petie could not at once understand this behaviour; letting his head drop back, but still holding on, he stared wide-eyed at his father. Slowly he drew back his right hand and pushed his forefinger against his father's eyelid:

"Papa wet . . . papa dry diapers . . . mamma mad . . . papa big, big 'pank . . . *this* big!" The chubby little hand struck a blow on the father's cheek. The next moment Petie was overflowing with sympathy; he hugged and caressed; perceiving that this didn't do much good, he resorted to kissing and there was no let-up. When Petie once got into his love-making mood he was apt to become annoying.

"Bless you, little Petie-boy!" moaned Peder in Norwegian. "Give me a bear-hug . . . you know. . . . Then maybe I can stop!" . . . The weeping became more quiet.

Susie had not stirred; she seemed not to know that he was sitting there. Suddenly she leapt out of the bed like a wild animal taken unaware:

"Aren't we ever going to have peace here to-night?" She stood out on the floor. "Has she confessed all now?" And without waiting for answer she went over to the mirror to tidy her hair just as she always did before going downstairs. "That a person should want to *steal* innocent souls . . . that's worse than the devil himself!" . . . She put a hairpin in her mouth while she tucked a loose wisp under a braid. "Never had I thought that she'd stoop so low. . . . Now you two can have a good laugh on me, can't you?" The seeming carelessness with which she spoke made her speech inhuman.

261

Their Fathers' God

Peder freed himself from Petie's arms. . . . Had she gone mad? How could she say this evil thing about a person who lay here dead? He wanted to go to her . . . reason with her . . . explain the circumstances . . . take all the blame on himself. But he only looked at her. . . . What use of him trying to talk now? . . . Reason had vanished from the face of the earth!

"Mother is dead," he muttered.

"Dead?" She turned sharply. "Dead, you say? Then God be merciful to her soul!"

Peder sprang to his feet and came across the floor:

"Can't you understand that she *had* to do it? That her God demanded it of her? . . . That she had to do it to satisfy Him?" His voice was shaky. The boy sensed there was something happening between his parents and began to cry. No one paid any attention to him. Susie faced Peder and stepped up so close that she could burn him with her eyes; she bent forward for added emphasis:

"No God ever demanded her to steal my baby's innocent soul. You two have certainly treated me nice!"

They stood thus for a moment, he with cold sweat glistening in his ashen face. All the while his eyes begged, begged her to use sense, to try to understand that his mother had only done right. What difference did it make as long as the baptism had been performed correctly? But Susie faced him cold and unyielding. And he thought he could feel how she slipped away from him . . . . farther and farther away . . . and was lost. In desperation he raised his hand to stop her . . . to make her see. The seconds lengthened into years, eternities . . . still he stood there begging, imploring her. . . . Down on the porch trudged heavy steps; boots kicked against the casing to get the snow off . . . opened the door and came in. Without a word Susie turned and disappeared down the stairs.

Some time passed before he came after with the boy. She was then going about her work in the kitchen as usual; Store-Hans sat on the edge of the bed, beside his mother's dead body; he had placed a half-dollar on the lid of the

On the Way to Golgotha

half-open eye and this struck Peder as the kindest act he had ever seen, because the lid had closed. Sofie had retreated into a corner with a handkerchief pressed to her eyes.

Later the brothers sat in the kitchen, talking over the arrangements that would have to be made for the funeral. To-night Store-Hans was so frank and considerate that Susie had to look twice at him.

Silent and sunken, Peder sat listening. Once he pulled himself out of his lethargy with:

"We'd better buy a ready-made coffin for mother. Makes no difference what it costs."

His brother considered the suggestion for a while.

"I'm not so sure about that. She wasn't particularly fond of all these American notions. I think she'd like it better if we have Tomaas Berg make her coffin. Tomaas has been our neighbour since coming to America; he has made the coffins for practically all the old Norwegians around here."

Peder had again retreated into himself. The brother regarded his silence as an approval and got up to leave.

Susie saw them pulling on their coats and asked, sharply:

—Who did they intend to have at the wake to-night?

—Wake? Peder looked up blankly. . . . At the wake?

—Sure! Didn't he hear what she said?

Store-Hans and his wife looked at Susie until the silence became awkward.

"We Norwegians haven't that custom," explained Store-Hans, quietly.

"We're Lutherans!" added Sofie, righteously.

"Do you intend to let your mother lie here like a cow? Like a"—Susie was so beside herself that the words eluded her—"like a pig that's been knocked dead?" She glared at her sister-in-law: "Then I'll sit up with her myself!"

Store-Hans had pulled on his mittens and came over to Susie, speaking slowly:

"Our custom is different. Mother was tired of life. We aren't going to mourn her soul. If anyone has ever tried to walk with God, it was mother." His voice sank away in thoughtfulness. "No, I don't think we need worry about her soul. . . . Well"—he turned to Peder—"early in the morning I'll drive over to Tomaas. He may have a coffin on hand. . . . Do you know, Peder, I'd just as soon help him make one for her?" It sounded as if he were asking permission There was no reply from Peder, and so Store-Hans mumbled good night, opened the door for Sofie, and followed her out.

Peder sat beside the stove, with Petie undressed and fast asleep on his lap. Not one word had he spoken since his brother left. His back was hunched like that of an old man weary with the burden of many years. A thought hovered in his consciousness: Now you are on your way to Golgotha . . . yes, so you are—on your way to Golgotha! . . . Of a sudden he heard his mother's warning voice, low, yet with fearful distinctness:

"We don't keep wheat and potatoes in the same bin."

. . . No, I guess that's right, he sighed. . . . You may be right about that . . . they shouldn't be kept in the same bin. . . . Good Lord! won't we ever get ready for bed tonight? He lifted the stove lid and laid some more wood on the fire.

Susie moved about busily and seemed never to be ready. She had set the dishes away and now was wiping the table. The next minute she was in the bedroom, came back quickly for a basin of lukewarm water, and again disappeared into the room. After setting the water aside she bowed before the crucifix, making the sign of the cross on her forehead and on her breast. Her lips moved. And straightway she began bathing the dead woman's face. It took her so long that Peder came and stood in the doorway. She had removed the half-dollar; still the eye was closed. When she at last was through she remarked, curtly: "Some one else might have helped me with this!" With that she went out into the kitchen, where she remained a long time. The lamp had to be refilled and the chimney polished. When she brought the lamp back she again made the sign of the cross.

Peder got so tired of waiting that he went upstairs with the boy. In being laid down Petie half awoke, and to keep him quiet his father threw himself on the bed, humming

low and stroking the boy's hair. Soon sleep was painting
roses in the cheeks of the child. A sadness so sweet that it
brought tears filled Peder as he lay there caressing him.
Involuntarily he folded his hands and repeated the stanza his
mother had taught him in boyhood:

> "O Jesus, sweet and lowly
> Take Thou my heart to Thee
> So that it might Thy holy
> Abode and temple be.
> Lead Thou my mind and show me
> To shun the worldly wise.
> Teach me to love and know Thee;
> That wisdom will suffice."

His mood only grew heavier. . . . He was the child that
had strayed far . . . that was hopelessly lost!

After a while Susie came up into the loft.

"Have you gone to bed?"

"Yes." He sat up on the edge. "You must be good and
tired by this time. . . . Better get yourself to bed now." He
got up. "I'll just go downstairs for a second."

"What are you going to do down there?"

"Nothing."

It took him longer than he had thought. The kitchen lay
in semi-darkness; she had moved the lamp into the bedroom,
and placed it on Petie's stool, which had been set on a chair
at the foot of the bed; the table had been placed beside the
head; on it stood the other lamp. He did not pay much attention to these changes. To make doubly sure, he bent over
the bed to see if the eye really was closed, and he drew the
sheet away from the face. . . . Yes, thank God, everything
was all right! . . . He thought it more natural to see her
with her face uncovered, and folded the sheet under her
chin. He felt sure she would have disliked two lights; so he
took the lamp from the chair and returned it to its usual
place in the kitchen. The other light was too close to the bed
. . . it must be hurting her eyes. . . . He moved the table
back in place.

Their Fathers' God

"You've arranged it beautifully down there," he said, absently, as he stood undressing upstairs a little later.

The kind tone in his voice made her collapse.

Peder let her cry undisturbed. . . . What was there to say?

She controlled herself and sat up in the bed:

"Are you really going to let her lie there alone? After all, she's a human being and your own mother!"

This touched him. . . . Now fear is making her see shadows, he thought.

"Don't you know mother any better than that? What good do you suppose we could do her by sitting up to-night?"

"We should light her soul on its way . . . make merry . . . and . . . keep the powers of darkness away!" she said, passionately.

"Remember her in your prayers to-night. Not that she needs it . . . I can't believe that."

To Susie this sounded so terrible that she threw herself down and gave herself over to crying.

Peder had undressed. Now he pulled on his coat again. Despite the fact that the doors were standing open, admitting heat from the kitchen, there was a cold draught up here, draughts that felt raw and heavy. He only glowered at her. When she at last had cried her fill and sat up, he threw off the coat and went to bed.

Susie lay on the outside, with the boy between her and Peder. Before retiring he had turned the lamp low. He had no thought of going to sleep. But during the past week he had had little rest and hardly any sleep at all; to-night his head no sooner touched the pillow than his eyes closed and he was fast asleep.

Susie's eyes remained wide open. The fact that he slept made her misery all the greater. . . . Now she was left alone with it all! Over and over she said her prayers; with audible words she begged the guardian angel to come; she stuck her thumb in her mouth and sucked just as a little child in going to sleep. But she was being disturbed because she had to listen; her ears lapped the air for sounds. The

On the Way to Golgotha

heavy gusts of the winter night stirred around the corners, with low, moaning sounds.

—Sh! . . . Wasn't that footsteps she heard just now? . . . On the other side of the house? She raised herself up on her elbows. . . . No, she was only imagining things again! . . . Peder was right . . . she was too foolish. To quiet herself she exaggerated her foolishness beyond all bounds. . . . She was absolutely the craziest person on God's green earth! Of course he was right. . . . How could he help it—he so sensible and fearless, and so strong? Steady and sure of himself he plunged into the thick of every danger . . . stood there like God himself. . . . Oh, there was no one like Peder! . . . Listen to him now—snoring innocently just like a child!

. . . Still, when it came right down to it, they too certainly believed! . . . Hadn't she gone to work and had the boy secretly baptized by a Lutheran? . . . A new thought brought Susie great comfort; she was luxuriously pleased with herself . . . no danger with little Petie . . . grandma could have spared herself that worry . . . he had been baptized by a priest in the one true Church, and with water from the holy River of Jordan, to boot. . . . No, sir, you fooled yourself that time! Susie chuckled with glee. It was this thought which earlier to-night had given her the courage to care for the dead body. Now the thought hovered near again, sprinkling her with security. She continued to lie there, talking to herself: Happier days would now be in store for them. . . . She'd be running the house alone . . . she'd have Petie to herself. No longer would she need fear grandma and her black art. . . . When the new baby came everything would be perfect! . . . Maybe it would be a girl, too! . . . She prayed earnestly to the Blessed Virgin to bless her with a baby girl, and she felt that her prayers were being heard.

By and by she got drowsy. Lay there wavering between consciousness and slumber. Her fear was gone, almost. But in order to have both ears in readiness she lay flat on her back.

Suddenly she gave a start. Some one spoke into her right ear:

"Do you lie here rejoicing because I am dead?"

"No, I'm not," she replied, fearlessly. . . . "But maybe Peder and I will get along better alone. . . . You can come back, if you want to."

Beret's broken English became unmistakable:

"A moment ago you went here happy because you had stolen Pete's soul. You should look out! We Norwegians ——"

The voice was lost in a shuffle of other disturbances: Sounds of footsteps from the front room, footsteps that moved laboriously across the floor, shuffling steps . . . now they were right at the foot of the stairs . . . hesitating.

In a flash Susie was out of the bed and across the floor to the doorway. She peered down. . . . A light in the kitchen! A power, not of the flesh, drew her down the stairs. A lamp was standing on the kitchen table! Who had put the lamp there? The same mysterious power pulled her to the bedroom door. There lay her mother-in-law, with face uncovered, as if she had just gone to bed and closed her eyes. She had pushed the table away!

A piercing scream penetrated the house from corner to corner. Then another scream that faded away in a gasping moan.

When Peder came hurrying downstairs he found her wandering helplessly out on the floor, stooped; she had clamped her hands over her ears; her nails had torn the skin so that blood came. Terrified into speechlessness, he grasped her by the arm and shook her roughly:

"See here now, if you don't cut this foolishness out, I'll spank you!"

"Oh, oh, oh!" she wailed. With hysterical intensity she thrust herself on him. "Save me! save me!" Her embrace was so violent that it threatened to strangle him.

"Shut up! . . . You hear me?" He caught both of her arms and wrenched them loose.

On the Way to Golgotha

Again she sprang at him, an insane fear driving her to seek protection.

"Save me! O God, save me!"

Holding her off with a hard hand, he shook her as if she were a naughty child, shook and shook. "Now will you behave?" His harshness staggered her and she came out of the daze. Roughly he picked her up and carried her back to bed.

That night Susie had a miscarriage. A hemorrhage started and the flow of blood would not stop.

V. "Father, Forgive Them—!"

I

FOR weeks afterwards Susie lay wavering between life and death. The glittering March sun found her in bed, still too weak to get up. But the crisis had come and gone and she had been the winner. Slowly, almost unnoticeably, her strength was returning. It was a queer gospel Doctor Rask preached to Peder: "Can't you think up a little amusement for your wife? She's a comely woman, if you really want to know it. A couple of youngsters like you should think of getting a little fun out of life. A fellow can't go a-Maying in November. First thing you know you'll be an old man huddling around the stove like all the other greybeards, sighing: 'Soon the night cometh when no man can work!'" Doctor Rask laughed as he recited the old phrase. He was himself a jovial soul, bubbling over with funny sayings, and seemed to know a good deal about human nature. Peder liked him immensely.

He did not hesitate about putting the doctor's advice into practice. Often he would drop his work and go in to share a few moments with Susie. Sitting on the edge of the bed, he would take her hand in his and study her wan, shrunken features. At such times he might challenge her, gaily: "Now if you'll just drink a little milk, I'll give you a great big kiss, one that they'll hear clear down to Tönseten's!" . . . To this she would be likely to answer: "Make it two and I'll try!" And even though the thought of milk made her stomach turn, she would valiantly close her eyes and swallow a few mouthfuls, ostensibly to win the vaunted kisses, but in reality to hear him brag her to the skies for her pluck.

"Father, Forgive Them—!"

He could become so good-naturedly jovial that she laughed till it hurt.

One day he came in and stood beside the bed, his face full of mischief:

"Got another calf this morning. Now this whole farm is creeping with life. It, and every living thing on it, belongs to you. You are the Mother Superior. Now, by Joe! it's about time you're getting up to look after your property! And here's spring coming on . . . see how the days are getting longer and longer?"

"All of it mine, did you say?"

"Certainly."

"And I can do with it just as I please?"

"Bet you!"

"Get right down on your knees so I can get hold of you!" And she took first the one, then the second, and finally the third just to see if there were any more left.

Peder made himself brusque and called her a shameless spendthrift. . . . What did she mean by such lavish expenditure? Now he had no more left and couldn't come back for a whole week! . . . "If you keep this up, we'll soon land on the poor-farm. Then what'll you do? . . . Here's one more for you. But for that you'll have to empty the cup!"

There were times when the words were fewer. Susie would just lie there looking herself happy at him. The strength she felt coming from him was of greater help to her than all the medicines the doctor brought. Her surrender to him was complete and unconditional, like that of a slave to his master, and yet as tender as that of a little child that must constantly sun itself in its mother's nearness.

The night of Beret's death and all things relative to it were never mentioned between them. And a night of all nights it had certainly been. He had had to tie her to the bed before he left, tie her mercilessly, feet and arms . . . there was no other thing he could do. He had driven the horse as he had never driven before. It was in the nick of time that he returned with the doctor.

Their Fathers' God

Nor was the funeral ever mentioned, either. At first he had refused point-blank to attend, had carried on like a madman, and had asked defiantly if it wasn't more important to save a life than to see a corpse dumped into the ground? What were they fussing about? Had they all forgotten what the Bible said about letting the dead bury their dead? People had stood dumbstruck, listening to his wild talk. But finally Sörine-godmother had brought him to reason: He must not bring disgrace on himself by refusing to attend his mother's funeral! "Now you go! I can be of more use here than you can!" At last he had yielded and gone along.

Afterwards he had himself assumed the command, and in such a manner that none dared oppose him. That night of terror had brought him to see certain things more clearly. These weeks had added years to his age. The day Doctor Rask had stood here assuring him that Susie would pull through, that there was no longer any danger providing he would exercise a little patience with her, he had experienced transfiguration. The joy of these tidings had made him straighten up; within his heart he had felt a benign warmth; he had actually stood by the burning bush and heard words that he could understand; and his vision had cleared so that he could see far, and he was filled with a new confidence. Since that day he had literally fought her back to life; the battle had been a terrific struggle, but he had come out victorious. One day, standing before the mirror combing his hair, he made a discovery which he refused to believe; above the right temple he noticed a hair, silvery grey in colour. After plucking it out he had studied it for a long while. "Now let 'em try to call me a boy!" As if it were a patent of nobility, he put it away in an envelope for safekeeping. . . . He'd have to show this to Susie as soon as she was up!

After the funeral the neighbours showered him with good will. Sörine-godmother was kind; Kjersti, who lived nearer and had less to do at home, was almost worse. Doheny insisted on loaning him Nikoline for a few days, for there was not a smarter housekeeper to be found in the state!

"Father, Forgive Them—!"

Peder thanked him. Said he'd have to think it over. It turned out that he said no to the offer.

But some help he must have, so he looked about him and found it waiting close at hand. With the Tönsetens lived Jacob Fredrik, a younger brother of Kjersti's, whom she had provided with an ocean ticket this winter. Jacob Fredrik was a queer sort, more woman than man; there was not a household task he could not perform fully as well as any woman; he was a past master at cooking, but except for the chores he was useless for outside work. In Norway he had attended an agricultural school and was fond of cattle. Peder, thinking that Susie might feel easier with Jacob Fredrik in the house than with a strange woman, had hired him. The choice proved to be a wise one.

Reverend Kaldahl called often, but never stayed longer than to exchange greetings and to ask how things were going. There was no trace of obtrusiveness in him. Peder felt a growing like for this man who was ordinarily so silent and self-contained, and yet so profoundly concerned about the welfare of others.

On one of the first days of March Father Williams came to the farm. Peder was busy grinding corn; seeing the priest drive into the yard, he left his work and went over to meet his visitor. Even before the priest had stopped, Peder had gripped the horse by the bridle. There was a cold determination in his manner. He announced curtly:

"We're having a rather tough time of it here."

"So I hear. You've lost your mother?"

Peder paid no attention to the remark:

"Susie's been very low, but now it seems she is going to pull through."

"So?"

The priest sat studying him.

"I suppose I can go in and see her?" He made a move as if to step out of the buggy.

"No, you cannot. Not to-day." Peder looked him straight in the eye: "As soon as she gets well again I want you to come, for her sake. I'll let you know when you can come."

"That might be a long time. Don't do what you later will regret," said the priest, kindly.

"Don't let that worry you!"

"No?" replied the priest, smiling. "Not that, either, may I do? It's a rich man who can afford to turn his back on the good will of his fellow-beings. Pride is a deadly sin, Peder Holm."

Peder tightened his grip on the bridle, his eyes still fixed coldly on the priest.

Father Williams' next remark had a sting in it:

"If you will be kind enough to let go of my horse, I'll depart as peacefully as I came. But I want you to know that where one of my parishioners is ill it is both my right and my duty to go in. I shall appreciate it greatly if you will greet your wife from me." So saying he clucked to his horse and was gone.

II

All that afternoon Peder avoided the house. But in the evening when he, with the boy on his lap, sat in the bedroom keeping her company, he asked quietly and without looking up if she did not wish to have the priest call on her before long. The question came so unexpectedly that it repeated itself in the silence that followed. He added, cheerfully: "I haven't mentioned this before because the doctor insists on your having absolute quiet. Now I guess you'll soon be able to stand 'most anything."

The voice that came from the bed was low and trembling: "Has—has he been here?"

"Yes, and I promised to send for him as soon as you were strong enough and wanted him."

"And you promised him that!"

"Sure I did. Why shouldn't I? It's up to you to say when. You're getting along wonderfully now. But I'd prefer you waited a week or so yet."

The boy was playing with a toy horse; a hind leg had come so loose that it was dangling; he could not get the horse to

"Father, Forgive Them—!"

stand up and wanted his father to help him fix it. Peder lifted him to his other knee in order to see better. Susie watched them awhile, laughed at their clumsiness and asked them to move over to the bed—she'd fix that horse! But no sooner had they settled themselves there before she forgot all about the toy, grasped Peder by the hand and wanted to tell him a big secret; her voice was low and affectionate. Like an eel Petie wriggled down from the lap, snatched the toy out of his mother's hand, and toddled off in search of Jacob Fredrik . . . there he'd have some chance of getting results!

Flushed with joy, she looked at Peder. Her great secret was that to-day she had gotten much, much stronger! When he failed to come in and give her the milk she had had to call Jacob Fredrik. And, now listen, she had drunk *a whole bowl of milk!* Wasn't he glad?

Peder looked up innocently:

"Wasn't it a whole barrel? . . . That's what the rascal told me!"

She laughed so that she had to cough.

"You mustn't let him fool you like that! Come to think of it, it really wasn't more than a pail, but it was *full*. You didn't come; I had to pass the time some way!"

"That's good. But to-morrow I'll bring in the milk myself. And you'd just better watch out so you don't mistake your hired man for your husband! There's a law against that sort of thing."

"I thought the afternoon would never end. Besides, I've so much fun with Jacob Fredrik. You should hear us talk together! Why didn't you come in?"

Peder sighed:

"Don't forget I've got twenty-five gluttons out there to fill up. If spring doesn't settle down to business soon, they'll strip us clean; you and I will have to live on boiled old shoes and pickled toads."

"You poor, dear husband!" She laid his hand up to her cheek.

"I need all the sympathy you can spare."

Their Fathers' God

"Will you really send for him?"

"For whom?"

"Father Williams?"

"Certainly." His face was big with suppressed mischief, like that of one bantering with a little child.

She wept quietly. He could feel how happy she was and stroked her cheek, said nothing, only stroked and stroked, and the tenderness between them was heavy with sweetness.

A moment later she picked up courage to make a confession:

"Do you know," she said, timidly, "whenever I can't sleep at night I lie here telling Her about you."

"Telling her?"

"Yes, the Mother of God. I tell Her that you're the best person in all the world. I have to thank Her, don't I?"

"Of course!"

"You're not getting mad at me? I know you——"

"Mad? At a child of God like you . . . that drinks a whole barrel of milk?"

"A pail," she corrected him, timidly.

"Yes, but the pail was full?"

"Not *heaping* full."

"Of course not, because then Jacob Fredrik wouldn't have found the handle."

She had to laugh at him. But then he grew serious:

"I want to make a bargain with you, Susie-girl: Hereafter you and I aren't going to talk any more about these matters. Let's shake hands on it! . . . It's wrong for one person to want to destroy another's feeling of security. You're going to church as often as you please. If you're not in condition to go there, the priest will have to come here. That's your right. I have an eye for the funny things in life. When something strikes me that way I've got to joke about it. They tell me my father was the same way. . . . If I ever forget myself in the future and blurt out things I shouldn't say, you and the Virgin will just have to exercise patience. . . . That will be your cross to bear, just as it will be mine to have two womenfolk on my

276

hands. And now let's consider that subject closed forever. If you want Father Williams here to-morrow, I'll go and get him myself." Peder had said it at last, and he felt easier of mind.

She wept quietly. But so forcefully did she feel his strength that this time the sobs did not come. She had to draw his head down into her arms in order to thank him properly. A sublime tenderness filled the room and it was nice to be there.

At mid-forenoon of the following day, when he dropped his work and went in to her, she drank the whole cupful without a murmur, stated her price, and demanded prompt payment.

"Now don't you think I'm smart?" she beamed.

Peder scratched his head, admitting that if she got much worse, he would be at his wits' end.

"Suppose you take another cupful?"

"I was wondering whether I could stand a pail. You aren't after having me turn into a calf?"

"Nope; we've got more calves now than we can handle. . . . Well, here's your pay—don't be too greedy!"

That afternoon Jacob Fredrik called him in for coffee a bit earlier than usual. On entering the kitchen he found her sitting near the stove with one of his mother's old shawls thrown about her shoulders. He had to stop before he could cross the floor:

"I'm out looking for a hired man. Could you start in to-morrow morning? The pay is good; you won't have to wait for it, either." His voice was husky with emotion.

"I might try, begory! Providing, of course, I won't have to milk!"

"Milk? You don't for a moment think I'd let you milk? Why, you'd drink up every drop in sight!"

"And you'd have to butcher all your calves."

"So I would. And what should I do with Goldenlocks that I'm keeping here in the house?"

He was happy beyond words, and she still more so for having made him so happy.

Their Fathers' God

—This, thought Peder, when at last he was outside, can mean but one thing: To-morrow I'll have to go and get the priest for her. But who cares about that as long as she soon will be her old self?

The next day passed without anything in particular happening. There was no mention made of the priest. From now on she sat up for a while every day, gradually prolonging her kitchen visits with Jacob Fredrik. Fun to sit here watching him work. Little by little her appetite awakened. Soon she was asking for a little more than the usual fare, and then a little more. March had run its course and now the April winds were sweeping the prairie clean. Still Susie had made no mention of the priest.

Peder could not for his life understand it. Now she was so well that he could easily take her to town if necessary. . . . Should he offer to go to Father Williams and ask him to come? Tell her about it beforehand? . . . Why didn't she speak up? . . . So long did he go about puzzling over the problem that at last an unreasonable solution presented itself: She is making this sacrifice just to please you! Oh, Susie, Susie! He was so touched that he had to wipe his eyes. Quickly he cast the thought aside. No, impossible . . . that wouldn't be Susie. . . . She simply *could not*! But the joy the thought brought was too great to be dispelled. That day he sang at his work, in a loud, strong voice.

The morning of the first Sunday in April he was awakened by Susie's restlessness. No sooner had she settled on one side than she had to turn and try the other. All at once he discovered that she lay there fighting back the sobs. Terrified, he sat up and asked what was wrong.

—Oh, nothing. Only that she hadn't been able to sleep at all. She seemed much depressed . . . she never would get well again . . . she wasn't gaining! . . . Why had they ever met? She was only a burden . . . would never be anything else. . . . If they hadn't married, he might now have been governor! Peder tried every artifice to cheer her up, but all his efforts glanced off on the armour of despondency that

"Father, Forgive Them—!"

now encased her. All forenoon she sat in her chair, shrunken and depressed and had little to say.

During the following week her humour shifted repeatedly between genial sunshine and disconsolate darkness. Peder regarded it as a good sign. Her recovery also made itself apparent in other ways; each afternoon she helped with the work so Jacob Fredrik could have time to do more of the outside chores. Peder had begun the spring work and each day he toiled in the fields from dawn to late evening.

But the next Sunday morning Susie was unable to leave the bed. It was her back, she complained. She hadn't slept a wink all night. When Peder brought in the breakfast she only shook her head and motioned him away. And when he coaxed her to drink a half-cup of milk she vomited it up immediately.

"Can't you leave me alone," she moaned. "Can't you see how sick I am?"

For a long time Peder wandered back and forth between the windmill and the corral, his face set and preoccupied. Right now he could have thrown himself down and boo-hooed like a baby. . . . Easy enough to see what the trouble was: No Mass, no Communion, no Confession since Christmas. Now she was worried stiff over the consequences! . . . Can a person actually commit suicide by simply being considerate towards another? . . . Do you intend to let her do it? The torture became too great to bear; he had to brace himself by clutching a crosspiece on the windmill. "Remove this cup from me!" he groaned, and it seemed to him that now he must surely die. . . . He did not return to the house until Jacob Fredrik appeared in the door and called dinner.

Along in the afternoon they got a visitor, and it was none other than Doheny himself; then suddenly Susie was all right again. Jacob Fredrik made coffee; she sat down at the table with the others and ate like a person in good health.

Doheny was out of sorts. Yesterday Nikoline had quit her job and moved to town! he reported, grumpishly.

"Has she really quit?" asked Susie.

"Yes, child, that bird's flown for good. Nice thanks I get

for bringing her up to be an American; last fall when I got her she couldn't even grunt, now she preaches like a full-fledged priest!"

"How did it happen?" Susie wanted to know.

"Happen? Ask your brother how it happened! You s'pose that confounded upstart could ever leave her alone? But she was as adamant as old Joseph himself. Good thing she got away before anything went wrong. One Norwegian in the family is bad enough! . . . Say, Peder"—Doheny turned to his son-in-law—"wonder if you'd do us the favour of dropping in and talking some sense into her? You'll find her at Tom Murphy's; he lives just a little way from Father Williams. How long do you suppose such a rose of innocence can survive in town, that Sodom of sin? Better that she settles down to business and marries Charley. Funny how stuck-up these Norwegians are! Do you suppose she expects to land the President of the United States? . . . You figure this out for yourself—how would you like to be left without a woman on the place, with the spring work just starting in?"

Peder took it all in without a word one way or the other. After her father had left, Susie's despondency returned; she sat in her chair, silent and depressed; the supper she did not touch but went right to bed. In the night she had spells of weeping, and struggled so hard to overcome them that she kept Peder awake. Not knowing what else to do, he got up and lit the lamp. He sat on the bedpost, holding her hand until she was fast asleep. After that she slept soundly all night.

III

The rest of the night Peder lay awake. After finishing the chores Monday morning, he set out for town and drove straight to Father Williams.

Mrs. McBride met him at the door. Upon hearing that he had come to see the priest her face puckered up into a grimace; her eyes shone small and pointed out of the many wrinkles. . . . Was Susie well yet? And how was the

"Father, Forgive Them—!"

youngster getting along? . . . God a-mercy, what a world!
. . . Why didn't she ever come to town? Had she quit
going to church? He wasn't making a heathen out of her,
was he? For then he'd have been better off with a millstone
tied around his neck! . . . With this ominous pronouncement she showed him to the study.

There Peder got a new impression of the priest. Surrounded by these sombre walls, the striking childlikeness of
the face was transformed to a faith not of this world. Long
rows of books looked silently out of the shelves, requesting
that here you speak reverently; there were many of them;
on the table two ponderous tomes lay opened; the crucifix
on the wall and the frayed stool of penitence beneath it
heightened the impression. What affected Peder the most
was the musty trenchant smell of stale tobacco smoke and
the peculiar odor of a human body. Since the first day of
creation God's wind and gracious sunshine must have been
shut out from this retreat. At the table sat Father Williams
in a green lounging robe, yellowed with age.

The priest invited him to take a chair.

Peder's eyes met his; he remained standing. Evenly he
announced that Susie was now well enough to have him
call. Would he please come out as soon as possible?

"Is she all right again?"

"No."

"Did she send you?"

"No. But I can see she needs you."

"And so you came?"

"Yes."

The priest looked at him long and searchingly.

"Can it be you now are beginning to see God's great wisdom? Then praised be His Holy Spirit! Fearful and wonderful are His ways in dealing with man; first He took your
mother from you; then He led your pious wife to the very
door of death. Now He is returning her to you! Do you
have sense enough to thank Him for His loving-kindness?"

Peder cleared his throat:

Their Fathers' God

"Can you come today?"

The priest's eyes did not leave him for an instant:

"Yes, certainly. And now I want you to remember that where God's grace is accepted in faith His blessing shall be tenfold."

"I'm not the one who's sick!"

"Not nice of you to say that! You two are one. When the one member suffers, the other member suffers also. It may have been for your sake that He made your wife go through these tribulations."

"That's a queer sort of justice!" Peder's face twitched with scorn.

His eyes blinking fast, the priest came around the table and laid his hand on Peder's shoulder, his voice trembling and low:

"Tell me, Peder Holm, what wrong have I done you?"

"Nothing." Peder turned the door-knob; the spring clicked sharply.

"Then you are not being fair with me! You knew at the time you married her that Susie was a Catholic. It isn't my fault that you chose her." The kindliness of the voice was becoming annoying: "Some day the living God will find you out. That will be an evil day for you. Not because He deals with you unjustly, but because your eyes will be opened and you will see how grievously you have sinned! Humble yourself now!"

Peder stood there, all colour gone from his face, his upper lip curled in scorn; his head was drawn back, in his eyes burnt a strange light—as cold as that of the stars on a frosty mid-winter night, his hand closing around the doorknob so hard that the knuckles whitened. Again that feeling of aversion which the priest always engendered in him was upon him. Not a word did he utter, but his eyes never left the face of the man.

Something in his looks fascinated Father Williams, and his eyes begged with kindness until they watered, imploring him to seek God's mercy ere it should be too late.

"Father, Forgive Them——!"

"Susie will be expecting you this afternoon," Peder said gruffly, still holding on to the knob.

"And what about you? . . . You yourself? Methinks you need me more?"

"One thing I ask of you"—Peder was speaking with great difficulty—"You leave me alone. . . . See her . . . she seems to need you . . . that is, she thinks she does. But beware of what you say and do! Beware that you don't mix into the relation between her and me. If you do, I shall have to kill you, grind you under my heel as I would a venomous snake. I tell you now, once and for all, that your God is not my God!" The words fell slow and were spoken with a terrible earnestness. With a jerk Peder opened the door and went out.

The priest called after him, said something which he did not hear. He saw only one thing—to get out of here quickly. Mechanically he got into the buggy and spoke to the horse. He froze so that his teeth chattered. . . . Never again! his mouth shut. . . . There's a limit to what one person must endure for another!

For a while after dinner he stayed near the house, waiting. But at last his impatience became unbearable. He told Jacob Fredrik he was going out to sow, he might be working late, and they shouldn't wait supper for him. Would he please look after Susie, and do as much of the chores as he could? Likely as not they'd have company.

He did not return until long after supper-time; then he had worked himself out of the doldrums.

The door to the bedroom was open. While he sat eating he listened to the talk that went on between Susie and the boy; Petie was ready for bed and both he and his mother were in high spirits. Every night now the boy slept with his toy horse in his arms. To-night he couldn't find the horse. His mother lifted him on her lap and told him about St. Anthony. . . . Whenever he had lost anything he must always remember to pray to St. Anthony . . . St. Anthony was helpful with such things . . . many, many a time he had helped her,

and she repeated for him the little rhyme she had said so
often in childhood:

> "Saint Ann, Saint Ann,
> Give me a man ——"

She showed him how he could change the prayer to fit
every occasion. At last she set him down and told him to
hunt behind the bed. And sure enough, there lay the horse!
Petie was very happy over the remedy and could not let go
of the rhyme; with a sleepy, contented voice he lay in the
bed, toying with it and the horse.

Peder listened until he forgot to eat. Jacob Fredrik mentioned that they had had company this afternoon. Peder said
he already knew about it and resumed his eating.

"Did the priest stay long?"

"Till dusk. He must be a kind man?"

Peder did not answer. As soon as he had finished eating
he went out to care for the horses. He let it take him a long
time. Having come in again, he pulled off his coat and went
into the bedroom. Susie had gone to bed and the smile
she greeted him with betokened a pleasant evening; she lay
there with flushed cheeks; her eyes had the mischievous glint
of old days:

"Come here. I got a surprise for you!"

He sat down on the edge of the bed.

"I was talking to Father Williams about you to-day," she
began cheerfully. "Haven't you the least little pat in that
big hand of yours? Here you've been gone all day long;
I haven't seen as much as the heels of your shoes!"

Peder bent over and caressed her, spiritlessly; he had an
absent look and didn't say anything.

"Now you'll surely get to be governor.—Oh, let me hold
your hand! Holy Mither! what a dead husband I've got!"

"You're off the track there," said Peder, thoughtfully. "It's
the President's chair I'm headed for!"

"But first county commissioner; you have to start in
some place, you know. I told him Dahl wants you for his

successor and that you're crazy about politics; I said you're
better fitted for the office than any one else around here—
that, too, I told him! I asked him straight out to help you in
the campaign. If he gets behind you, and I know he will,
you're sure of election! Once you're in, the rest will be
smooth sailing. . . . What's there to prevent a man like
you, you who's read so much, from becoming governor?
Pretty soon I'll be well again; Jacob Fredrik and I will run
this farm like a clock. You haven't any idea of how smart
a little farm-wife you have, Mr. Holm! . . . And you'll be
drawing such a big salary, we can afford to hire all the
extra help we need. . . . But when you're governor you
needn't think I'll be satisfied to stay here digging in the dirt!"
Her eyes shone warm and affectionate.

Peder got up and began pacing the floor. Uneasiness had
come over him. Now and then he raised his hand as if he
were making a speech, and he seemed greatly agitated.

"Don't you think I'm smart?" asked Susie. "You could
never guess what a big help I'm going to be to you. I'm telling you, Peder, you don't half know me yet!"

"You smart?" he came over to the bed and kissed her.
"Pretty soon you'll turn into a miracle-worker. People will
be flocking here from all over the country; we'll be crowded
right out of house and home . . . there will be great pil-
grimages!"

"Whups! don't go too far, now!" she exclaimed gleefully.
"You always exaggerate so."

"I mean every word I say!" He had turned towards her.
"You and I, we together, could work miracles, Susie, I've
known that all the time. Haven't I told you we're bound for
the End of the World?"

"Lots of times, but you've never said what we're going to
do when we get there."

"Do? So you actually want to know what we're going to
do at the End of the World?" he asked, with an eloquent
sweep of the hand. And suddenly he laughed: "Well, then,
I'll tell you now: We're going to eat manna from on high;

at every sunset-time we're going to dance dreamy waltzes on floors of shining gold. It'll be good-bye to all drudgery . . . no more tugging at dirty cow teats, no more danger of being eaten alive by hungry flies! You want to come along, Susie-girl?"

"I suppose so, if it's going to be as grand as all that!" She sat up in the bed and laughed to him. "Good heavens! what a husband! Always slipping right through my fingers! . . . Now you come right here . . . you hear me?"

He laughed giddily, clapping his hands.

"Yes, sir," he went on, "out there at the End of the World, that's the place to be. That's where men catch visions and dare try them out, and that's life eternal! There the Blessed Day lasts forever, 'for the first heaven and the first earth are passed away. . . . And He shall wipe away all tears from their eyes; and there shall be no more death, neither sorrow, nor crying, neither shall there be any more pain, for the former things are passed away . . . these words are true and faithful.' "

"I wonder if that can be the place for sick women?" Susie sighed, timidly, throwing herself back on the pillow; and a shiver went through her as though she had been exposed to a cold draught.

"That I can't tell you. But this I know, that as soon as you are all right we must be on the way. Here we have fooled away two and a half years! It's a terrible waste, I tell you. If it isn't the place for sick women out there, we'll make it so—and without consulting either priest or pope!"

Often she had heard him hold forth on this theme, but never with such enthusiasm. To-night he seemed beside himself. . . . Was he superhuman, perhaps? She drew the quilt over her shoulders and hid her face.

Having flung off his clothes and blown out the lamp, Peder jumped into bed. Tenderly he drew her close:

"If you have a little love for me, Susie-girl, you better give it to me now!" . . . What was this, now, did she lie here shivering?

The priest's visit was never again mentioned between them.

"Father, Forgive Them—!"

IV

Owing to all the attention the cattle required Peder fell behind with his spring work. And now Lent was here to make matters all the worse. As they were retiring Tuesday evening (Peder was already in bed and she ready to blow out the lamp) Susie asked, suddenly, as though the thought had just occurred to her, if he could let her have one of the horses in the morning.

"If you're going out to harrow for me, you'd better take more than one!" He thought she was bantering and made a joke of it.

But instead of a merry rejoinder there came a reply that was all seriousness:

"To-morrow is Ash Wednesday—didn't you know that?" She puffed out the light.

"What about it?"

"That's when you go to church and make promises of penance. . . . You're blessed; in that way you get the help of the saints to keep your promises."

Neither spoke. Peder lay wide-awake, thinking. . . . Hanged if he could spare the time for a trip to town to-morrow! The neighbours were all getting ready for planting, and here he'd be idling away precious time. The problem called forth other thoughts. Casually he asked:

"Will you have to make more trips after that?"

"I s'pose so," she yawned.

It was quiet for a while. Then he asked, gingerly:

"When?"

"Thursday of Holy Week is Communion. And nobody would ever stay away on Good Friday. I don't want to be an Easter bird . . . they show up only once a year." Her voice sounded sleepy.

Before he could check himself Peder was thinking aloud:

"Three work days lost! At that rate I'll never get the planting done this year!" His bitterness made the words large and luminous. He realized it and bit his lip. "I suppose you'll be going Easter Day too?"

"I s'pose so. Norwegians go then, too, don't they?"

The boy stirred in the cradle and she was up in an instant to see if he had kicked off the quilt.

Settled in bed once more, she said, cheerfully:

"You don't need to lose any sleep over it. At home I'm of no use, anyway. You can certainly spare one of the horses? I don't need any one to go along. . . . I'll take Petie with me."

"Not as long as I have a voice in the matter! You haven't been out of the house since New-year's and now you want to make that long trip four times in six weeks?" He fought back his ill-humour. "Couldn't you make one trip do, say on Good Friday? . . . What time do you have to be there Easter Sunday?"

"We surely can't afford to forget Our Lord's sufferings . . . what the Mother of God had to go through during those days." A touch of reproach had come into the voice.

"Can't one do that right at home?" he blurted out. "We have a Bible here!" He could not restrain himself from adding: "How I am going to fool away three good work days without committing a greater sin is more than I can understand!"

"Oh, well, if it is so impossible! . . . Only it seems funny to me . . . when it's entirely unnecessary for you to come along. . . . You don't have to drop your work on my account. Why shouldn't I go alone? I've done it thousands of times!"

He didn't say another word.

Nor did she speak again. But he could hear how she lay wide-awake. Neither of them slept much that night.

He rose before dawn and hurried out to feed the horses. The morning breeze sent chills through his body, making him run from one task to another in order to keep warm. As soon as it was light enough to see he was on his way to the field with the seeder. By eight o'clock he had done a good half-day's work and felt better.

"Father, Forgive Them—!"

On the way down they sat silent, she with the boy well bundled in her lap. They passed farm after farm; everywhere men were hard at work, so busy that they couldn't look up.

He let her off outside the parsonage. Many rigs were already lined up along the street; others were arriving constantly; people climbed out of them and went into the church.

"It won't take me long," she assured him in a business-like manner. "Be back as soon as you can."

"Then I might as well stay right here?"

"Don't do that. You'll only get tired of waiting!"

He didn't care to say any more and drove on down the street.

It was now nearing ten o'clock. Suddenly he caught sight of a girl scrubbing the porch of a near-by house, recognized her, and stopped his horse. . . . So this was where she was working? A smile spread over his face.

Nikoline glanced up. Dropping the washrag, she came out to meet him.

"Are such callers abroad to-day?" She rolled down the sleeves of her dress. Her hair was mussed and the breeze was toying with stray wisps over the temples.

"So you're a city girl now?"

"I couldn't turn hermit simply because I wasn't good enough for you."

Each was enjoying the sight of the other.

"It's no use to wish for things you can't have." Since his mother died he had seldom spoken Norwegian; today he enjoyed it thoroughly; the old idiom sounded rich and good to him.

"Doheny said you refused point-blank to have me. You wouldn't even consider it. . . . Can't say it was nice of you!"

" 'Thou shalt not covet thy neighbour's wife, nor his manservant, nor his maidservant, nor his cattle.' Don't you know your Commandments?"

"Oh, I see—so that was the reason?" She laughed and tucked a few of the wisps back in place; her breasts stood

289

out large and full like two rosebuds ready to burst open. "You needn't have minded the Commandments. I'd rather be working for you than for these people."

"At my place you'd only have frozen to death!"

"Is it really that cold?" A deep seriousness passed over her joviality like a dark cloud blotting out the sun: "How is Susie?"

"Aw, well enough. Right now she's in church getting ready for Lent and penance. . . . So I thought I'd better drop in and find out when we're leaving for Norway."

"Norway?"

"You promised last winter you'd take me along."

A great joy broke vivaciously on her face:

"Now it will soon be summer. Out in the west the sun will be hanging low on the sea. . . . Come, let's go! I want to show you what beauty really is like." The vision of a distant land, of her childhood home, gripped her so strongly that she let her tongue run loose: "I'm so glad to see one of my own people I could hug you!"

"Go to it . . . suits me all right!" He made a move as if to jump out of the buggy.

His joking passed unnoticed:

"To-day I've been sick with a great homesickness. Now it's Easter-time at home. By this time the kildeer has returned. Soon the Lofot men will be back from the fisheries. Down by the shore they're burning tang . . . I can smell it now. Up in the mountain the sun dreams golden dreams, and the nights—O God!" She sighed, lost in visions. . . . "To think that you can be such a fool!"

Peder squinted at her, breathing hard:

"*Hilder* again!"

"No!" she declared, firmly. "I knew what I was doing. Only I didn't believe it could be quite so bad."

"So cold, you mean?"

"Yes."

"The *hilder* fooled you, too!" nodded Peder. "Now listen. I'll explain the great riddle of life to you: People think they can see, but they're stone-blind, the *hilder* fools them all."

"Father, Forgive Them—!"

She cocked her head while looking at him:

"I can't understand the cause of your misery. You got what you wanted?"

"Certainly. And if you had gotten it, it'd have been exactly the same with you."

"No. There was no *hilder* in my case . . . I had the magic mirror."

Peder saw some one come to the door.

"We'll argue that out some other time. To-day I'm here to make love to you for Doheny. He wants you back; he asked me to see you."

"Now you're fooling."

"I'm not!" He lowered his voice: "Don't you think you could stick it out at Doheny's? With you over there the days wouldn't be quite so empty for me!"

"Is it really that bad?" She laughed ever so little, and reddened furiously.

"More frankly I cannot say it!" He gripped her hand and pressed it. Then he left.

He drove on down the street and had no idea of where he was. . . . Where was he going, anyhow? Oh yes, that's right . . . had to see the cattle-buyer about the prices.

Shortly before noon he was back at the church; now the whole neighbourhood was cluttered with wagons and buggies. People were still coming, tying their horses and vanishing into the church. Others were coming out; their heads bowed, they climbed into their buggies and left. Very few stopped to talk.

Susie had evidently been waiting for him. No sooner had he stopped the horse than she appeared at the door of the parsonage, leading Petie by the hand.

Peder stared at her. . . . What kind of monkey business was this, anyhow? Her hat was pulled far down over her face; from where he sat only the chin was visible.

"See, it didn't take me long!" Her voice was bright and she spoke rapidly. "I've been waiting all of half an hour. I don't feel a bit tired. To-morrow I'll drive in alone."

Their Fathers' God

As he bent over to lift up the boy he caught sight of her face, and he had to look a second time.

"What the devil have you stuck your head into? Your forehead's all black with soot?"

She stepped into the buggy and settled down in the seat. For a while she sat silent.

"Aren't you going to wipe off that dirt? We might meet somebody."

"That's my mark of penance. I should have remembered you Norwegians are too good for that sort of thing." There was peevishness in her voice now. She made no move to adjust her hat or to wipe off the black mark on her forehead.

"Do you folks have to smear yourselves up with dirt in order to be decent?" he said sucking the breath through his teeth. "To me that sounds doggone ridiculous if you want to know it."

"And so you get a chance to have some more fun at other people's expense—just because you don't understand the customs in use by others than the Norwegians . . . that can't be so terrible smart!"

By her voice he could tell that she was near to crying, and he let her talk go unanswered. As his indignation receded, a dull indifference settled in its place. His expression hardened.

"Only, I didn't believe it could be so bad," said a voice in Nordlandsk. The voice was soft and musical and spoke right in his ear. He answered it: "That was wisely said. . . . I didn't believe it, either."

Meanwhile a state of war had developed between Petie and his mother. At first the boy had wanted to sit with his father and hold the reins, but finding little fun in that since his father had become both deaf and dumb, he turned back to his mother and began mewling for food. Susie shook him. "Now sit still—you imp you!" This made Petie so mad that he struck at her. Angrily she snatched him up in her lap and held him tight. Now thoroughly incensed, he rebelled in earnest, kicked, slugged, and scratched. "Can't you make him

292

behave?" she asked, crying. "Don't you see how he's pester-
ing me?"

For a while Peder sat listening to the racket, his face dark
and foreboding. Unable to endure it any longer, his arm shot
out and, grabbing Petie by the collar as if he had been a
kitten, he lifted him over on to his own lap. Not a peep was
heard. The boy stuck his thumb in his mouth, but was too
astonished even to suck. It was nice to sit in the crook of the
arm. Soon he had forgotten all his difficulties, became
drowsy, and pattered to himself, over and over:

> "Saint Ann, Saint Ann,
> Give me some food!"

Peder's face was cold and grey; he stared straight ahead
of him.

. . . "Only, I didn't think it could be quite so bad," persisted the soft voice in Nordlandsk.

v

That evening he received an unexpected caller. He had
worked late with the seeding; he had just had his supper
and had come out to finish up the chores. He was feeding
the cattle in the corral when Gjermund Dahl drove into the
yard.

Gjermund tied his horse to the windmill and came over
to look at the cattle.

"What's this you're up to here? Must say you're a nervy
fellow; you start feeding when the rest of us are giving
our cattle away. Why, the county ought to subsidize your
undertaking. I'm going to propose it!"

Instantly Peder was in good humour; he talked and explained until his face beamed:

—This many loads of stalks had he stuffed into them,
and that many bushels of corn; the hay he had not kept
track of at all, but it was a fright what they had gotten
away with.

"So you're keeping a record of it, eh? That's what they

293

call scientific farming. Yes, sir, I think this is splendid. Take
a bit of advice from me: Don't sell this fall, even if you
can get your money back; rather buy twenty-five head more.
I'll sell you a bunch on time. You plant all the corn you
possibly can cultivate. Unless old signs fail, good times are
coming. Can't say just when they'll be here, but they're on
the way. Next fall the Republicans are bound to win."

"Does that mean better times?" laughed Peder.

"I think so." Both leaned against the fence, Gjermund
with one leg across the other.

"I thought you were a Democrat?" exclaimed Peder.

"And so I am. But if we should win, which we won't,
it will mean restless times, with great economic upheavals.
Such a pigpen as this needs a thoroughgoing cleaning; a few
shovelfuls won't help much, and you never saw capital and
disturbance out walking together."

"You think they'll win?"

"I think so," said Gjermund, thoughtfully. "The Republicans are arming to the teeth, they got a sly old fox for
leader, and they're going to put on a campaign the like of
which you've never seen before. For them it's a question
of life or death; they're ready to spend no end of money.
Doubtlessly they'll win." Gjermund paused. "Tell me, just
where do you stand?"

"Of all the parties, the Populists are advocating the most
sweeping reforms; they've a great program. For that reason——"

"For that reason you should stay clear of them!" laughed
Gjermund, slapping him on the shoulder. "The great progressive ideas never win out overnight; they must fight long-
drawn-out battles. It is always that way, for the masses are
too slow-moving; among them new ideas germinate slowly.
When a progressive measure wins out it is usually being
pushed through by the conservative cud-chewers; by that
time the idea is no longer new." His voice was low and confidential: "I came here to-night to talk politics with you.
And now listen to me—I advise you to run on the Republican
ticket! I've never seen such a mix-up as we're in now. By

"Father, Forgive Them—!"

fall there'll be four different political parties in the field. That means fishing in troubled waters!"

"How do you figure four?"

"Oh, you don't know? Here you've got the two old stand-bys. Don't let it surprise you that the Populists aren't over-anxious to join forces with us; if they do, they're done for, and they know it; and this stunt the temperance people are up to strikes me as being sheer madness. You haven't heard they're organizing their own party and this fall will enter the field with a full set of candidates from governor down?"

Peder was amazed at the news:

"And so you advise me to turn cud-chewer?"

"Yes, I do," laughed Gjermund. "If I were in your boots, with a long life ahead of me, I think I'd take that course."

"And chew the cud the rest of my life?"

"No, you need not do that, not at all. There are lots of forward-looking Republicans; they're the boys I now would line up with. I've been keeping my ear to the ground; I'm pretty well acquainted with South Dakota; I've learned enough to know that we've all got a conservative devil in us, even the Irish, though they always make the most noise."

"The Irish!" exclaimed Peder. "The priests've got them by the nose!"

"Of course! You haven't forgotten what happened at that rainmaker meeting? Our state will most likely be voting conservatively for a long time to come; both blood and religion are steering us that way. These prairies are dear to me; I want to see them governed by men who are progressive-minded." Gjermund's voice grew warm with enthusiasm: "Do you see what an endless amount of work remains to be done here? Good Lord! We haven't even started yet! Our roads are still unfit to travel; we haven't even thought of draining our lowlands; we let speculators grab our natural resources, or we ourselves squander them. We're simply groping in the dark. We don't know what it's all about yet. Where are the pine forests that ought to be standing here now? We've been puttering around with cotton-

woods and willows, and should have been planting pine
and spruce; the fir and the pine would in time have meant
good fuel and excellent lumber, and would have been a
thing of beauty in both summer and winter. See what we've
got! Why don't we do it? Simply because we haven't the
foresight. And so it is wherever you turn." His voice was
low and intimate. "We've been milking cows ever since
the state was settled. Where are our creameries? We don't
know what a creamery looks like. We don't know beans
about coöperation; we don't know the word even. You see
the same thing wherever you look. Take our schools, for
example. What do they amount to? What can you expect
of a lot of giddy twenty-year-old girls? Out in the settlements there's not a library to be found. No signs or thought
of providing talented youth with the education they should
have. Can't you see we have become a living example of
spiritual poverty and hot air? The dawn is still a long,
long way off! . . . You, Peder, have the gift to see clearly
where the masses move blindly; for that reason I advise
you to take the road that is the surest of bringing you to
the front. Certainly here are man-sized jobs to be done;
yours it is to breathe life into dead bones!"

"You don't think the Populists will get anywhere?"

"Not unless they join forces with us, and then they're
as good as dead. There's too much noise and not enough
reason in those fellows. But I admit some of their ideas
would be worth while trying out."

"How do you advise me to proceed?" asked Peder, wonderingly.

"Use your head and never preach more wisdom to the
voters than they can stand."

"Isn't that betrayal?"

"Not at all! Which is better, evolution or revolution?
Never tear down any faster than you can build up. Otherwise you'll soon find yourself without a roof over your
head. It's through and with human beings that you have
to build. . . . Listen here. I've just been over to see Tön-

seten. He's only a parrot; you won't see any new ideas coming from him. But he's valuable because he wields a certain influence. He wants to be elector from this district. Fine and dandy. He will work for you. I want to have a chat with that Holte boy up north here."

"You're a Democrat?" Peder's eyes were shining now.

"Why should that bar me from talking to Republicans? I want to see our minister, too; that man's got a head on him. If you can only get the nomination, the rest will come of itself."

For a long time after Gjermund had gone Peder stood leaning against the windmill. He was utterly lost in a chaos of visions. Once, years ago, a pedlar had stopped with them overnight, an old greybeard full of stories and much queer talk. He had told him an Indian legend, "The Night of the Shooting Stars," the man called it. For Peder this was such a night; stars flared and stars sparkled; all space was full of them; stars popped out and went a-shooting. Though the air was so quiet and mild, he felt shivers pass through him. It was so unbelievable that the prophet had chosen to let his mantle fall on him, and with it—a world of good will. . . . Here was a man whose every thought was directed for the good of a people, some of whom would gladly have seen him hanged!

. . . Well, he'd better be going in. All at once the visions and the many stars vanished. . . . In? He began to walk, back and forth between the windmill and the corncrib. . . . What did he have to do there? Before he was aware of it he had fallen into a black sea of melancholy. The soft voice of the spring night no longer reached his ears; he was in the grip of a tugging undertow. . . . Adam didn't stay long in Paradise! he mumbled, dead-tired, and went into the house.

Susie was already asleep and Jacob Fredrik had gone up to his room. Peder went into the bedroom, picked up his nightshirt, and went to bed in the spare room up in the loft. In the morning he explained that he hadn't had a decent

night's sleep for the last week or so . . . thought he'd try
sleeping alone for a while . . . at least he wouldn't be
disturbing anybody.

After that he used the room in the loft regularly, but he
kept all his clothes and belongings in the downstairs room as
before.

VI

From early summer to Thanksgiving Day there raged a
terrific storm over the length and breadth of the land. Crazed
and befuddled, men of all ranks were tossed about by it;
they saw visions and caught the spirit of prophecy, and it
happened that they spoke in tongues. Some, in whom the
spirit was too weak to be audible, fired it with whisky until
the gift of eloquence fell upon them, too. At last people had
found the solution, the cure-all for all misery—through
politics the Promised Land was to be reached!

A raving madness was smiting the country. Everywhere
men spoke with prophecy. . . . Now the wretchedness re-
sulting from bad government had come to an end . . . the
blood-suckers would be brought low, get their just reward
. . . at last, finally! Wall Street was to be crushed, smashed,
ground to dust like the golden calf of old . . . and the
guilty made to pay now as they had done at that time. And
the people, that is to say, the farmers and the laborers, but
especially the farmers, would gain the power and reign
eternally—just wait and see! Out of the West he shall
come . . . there young David goes now; he's gathering
stones on the hillsides of Nebraska . . . soon he'll have his
pouch full, and his sling has been made ready. . . . I tell
you Wall Street, that scarlet whore, is doomed . . . the
patience of the Lord is exhausted!

With hot words one man aroused the next:

—Can't you see how the false prophets have been betraying us common people? Who was to blame for the panic
three years ago? Who, I ask you? Who has been growing

fat and sleek on our toil? Now the deluge is sweeping down on them . . . to hell with them! . . . See the dawn how fair it is . . . in glory the Party of the People marches victorious o'er the earth . . . see how Justice waves her banner triumphantly. . . . I tell you the day is at hand!

Thus spoke the Populists.

The Democrats did not answer them directly; they were too overjoyed at receiving such miraculous aid. And not so easy to answer that kind of talk . . . certain points required lengthy, involved explanations. For the past four years the country had been sailing under the colours of the Democratic party . . . they had ruled and were ruling still. The Populists would probably find it difficult to understand the reasoning. They were a good sort, these Populists, but, thank God, they lacked the right kind of leaders! Poor fellows, they got so easily excited . . . sometimes they'd let their tongues run away with them! And so the Democrats only stirred in the embers in order to keep up the fire. Occasionally they would stick in an innocent question: Who ruined the prices for you two years ago and robbed you of the just fruits of your labor? Wasn't it Wall Street, I'd like to know? . . . And isn't the devil himself the king of Wall Street? . . . You just listen to the cutthroats down there preaching about their false god, the *gold standard*. As if the United States need beg old, out-lived Europe for permission to use the money standard it must use! "We can't go it alone," they shout at us. I say, *Rot!* . . . Let me tell you: If we wanted to, we could coin *iron*, because we have the power. . . . Their mouths gush forth filth. Why? They want to keep all the gold for themselves . . . you keep the dirt and the drudgery! . . . The gold they have already. But now they're scared stiff . . . because they know that once we get free silver, sixteen-to-one, and free trade, there will be such an abundance of money among the people of this glorious land that it will be utterly impossible for them to scoop it all into their private coffers. In that they're right: If we once get the money, we'll also have the power . . .

then we'll do the whistling! Just wait . . . out of the West
a man is coming!

Unto the Tabernacle of the Congregation did all the Republican chieftains betake themselves for to hold council.
There was plotting, and much black prophecy and the shouting of great shouts. With a new heart they went back, ready
for battle. Never had the hope of victory been brighter, for,
thank God, the enemy was divided! . . . And how wantonly
the Democrats had betrayed an honest people . . . how
they had swindled and played crooked—thank God for that,
too. Now anybody could see. . . . What were the custodians
of the law doing? Gambling and growing fat on the spoils!
. . . My dear friends, if we once more return these cutthroats to power, the whole country is ruined. (Tönseten, to
quote him correctly, said *runified*; and Kjersti, hearing her
husband use the term so often, adopted it also, as is only
proper for a loyal helpmate.) Again and again the Republicans charged: Will you let yourself be hoodwinked by a
pack of fortune-hunters? Who, we ask, have been running
this country? Take a look at it and see how you like it.
. . . For four years now Tammany Hall has been our
king . . . and still you say you're going to vote the Democratic ticket? . . . You take care. Lot's wife refused to
heed the warning from above, and there she stands now,
a lump of salt! You look out!

Among the common people there were some who had
only a hazy idea of what the hullabaloo was all about. There
was Kjersti, for instance, who to the last held the belief that
Wall Street was nothing but an imaginary bogey man put
up by the Democrats to scare the rest of the country with.
Kjersti died in that belief. Tönseten himself was not so much
better off; for a while he would have sworn before God
that Tammany Hall was a monster down in New York, the
very incarnation of satanic crookedness, perpetually at war
with eternal justice. But from a speech he one night heard
in the Tallaksen schoolhouse Tönseten came home with uneasy misgivings as to what the monster really was. After
that the word Tammany never passed his lips.

"Father, Forgive Them—!"

With ever-increasing fury the campaign raged on. After the conventions had been held and the candidates chosen the visionary joy of the crusader seized the fighters; the battle was no longer a thing of this earth, not a question of politics, of who should be elected President, but the last stand for eternal justice. This assurance shed an unearthly glory over all existence, like the evening sun, big and blood red, breaking through a storm-riven sky; men saw the sign and fought with the reckless courage of the berserkers. On the memorable morning when the papers brought the news of the Populists' decision to join with the Democratic party a shock of wonder passed through the whole nation. The sacrifice was so stupendous. Here was the most powerful third party in history willingly sacrificing itself on the altar of the People. Now, surely, the millennium could not be far away!

Up and down the land went Bryan, letting his mighty voice ring out over thousands and tens of thousands. From everywhere people flocked to hear him. Many travelled great distances, sat on slivery planks and wept in approval of his great message. . . . Look—there's the commander of the Army of the Lord, the Lion of Juda!

None escaped the magic spell of the campaign. Often it happened that busy housewives, gathered at the monthly meeting of the ladies' aid, left both heathen and orphan to shift for themselves and engaged in hot dispute over Bryan and McKinley. Even the school children were mustered into service; toddlers, still too young for school, went about witnessing unto the truth. The Republicans had played a smart trick. Campaign caps made of red and white cloth, with pictures of McKinley and Hobart in the tops of the caps, were distributed right and left among the children. This was too much of a taunt for the Democrats to let pass unnoticed; in due time there appeared on the streets caps of blue and white; in the tops of these sat Bryan and Sewall, their eyes fixed soberly on the deviltry the Republican children were up to.

Their Fathers' God

One Saturday evening Peder brought one of the Republican caps home from town. As he came in he tossed it to the boy:

"Now put that on your head and show your mother what full-fledged Republicans look like."

This splendour was greater than any Petie had ever dreamt of possessing; wild with joy, he ran to his mother to show her the wonder-cap.

"Look! Two mans!"

"That's your grandpa and your uncle," explained his father. He was brimming with mischief.

"How can you stand there lying to the child?" Susie had taken the cap and was looking at it.

"Is it them?" cried the boy.

"Heh-heh," nodded Peder. "They're so long in the face because this fall they'll have to vote the Republican ticket."

"Oh, I don't know about that," drawled Susie. "You'll hardly get them to vote for you . . . not with Tom McDougal running against you."

Peder shot a glance at her. . . . Was she sitting there rejoicing over the fact that both her father and her brother might vote against him?

"I'm not planning to ask them, either. That job I leave to you."

"If they don't want to, I don't suppose I can force them. Father's been a Democrat all his life. . . . Let me see the cap once more. Begory! if it isn't clever! . . . That jigger got a regular bull's face."

The parents said no more about the subject.

Coming from work Monday evening, two weeks later, Peder found the boy waiting for him. As soon as Petie saw his father he started off on a run to meet him.

"Ride horsey, papa. Ride horsey!"

Peder stood there staring at the boy.

"Where did you get that cap?"

"Father, Forgive Them—!"

"From mamma. . . . Let me ride!"

"When?" He took the cap and looked at it, forgetting what the boy had asked. . . . She must have got hold of this yesterday? . . . Most likely from Charley? . . . She shouldn't have given it to him . . . not that it makes any difference.

Petie begged and stamped his feet:

"Ride horsey!"

Peder lifted him up:

"You think this one is prettier? . . . Take a good hold now!"

"Make 'em run!" In his excitement over the horses the boy had forgotten about the cap.

Peder let him ride clear up into the stall; there he lifted him down and set him on the partition. When he had unharnessed and fed he picked up Petie and sat down on a stool with him.

"Let me see that new cap of yours. My, how we're primping up around here! When did she give it to you?"

Now the boy had time to give this matter attention:

"Mamma says nicer." He pointed at the faces in the top. "This grandpa. That uncle."

"Heh-heh," nodded Peder. "And do you know who those fellows are?"

"Presidents!" answered Petie, proudly, pulling the cap down on his head. Now he remembered he was hungry and wanted his father to go in with him.

Coming into the kitchen, they met Susie with the basket on her arm, ready to make the evening round for eggs. Her face brightened comely at the sight of them:

"Here you are already. That's fine! Supper's waiting. You sit right down, I'll be back in a minute."

. . . To-night she seems in great spirits. It doesn't take much sometimes! Peder set the boy down and washed. He asked Jacob Fredrik to pour the coffee because he had little time. He hurried through the meal. Hearing her out on the porch, he went into the bedroom and started to change his clothes.

Their Fathers' God

Susie poked her head in:

"Going away again?"

"Heh-heh."

"Far?" she stepped into the room, picked up the work shirt he had thrown on the bed and hung it on a hook.

"To the schoolhouse."

"Who's speaking to-night?"

"Why do you ask about things you know already?"

"How can I know who is speaking?" Her tone was light and innocent.

Peder did not answer.

"I never go anywhere. And you never tell me what's going on. I don't suppose I can get things out of the air?"

"You were away yesterday. I'm sure you know about the meeting to-night!" he retorted.

"All right, then," she said, simply, and remained standing in the middle of the room. She added, slowly, as if she were puzzling over some problem she couldn't understand: "Is this how it's going to be at the End of the World?"

As if suddenly stung by a sharp pain, Peder faced her:

"Yes, by golly—just like this!"

He snatched up his coat and left. On the way over to the schoolhouse he sat sunken together in a corner of the buggy. By and by he straightened himself and clutched the edge of the box. If he only could have stretched out his hand and smashed things to smithereens, smashed and smashed! . . . O God! he groaned. Is this to go on for ever?

The array of rigs around the grounds brought him to his senses. It took awhile before he found room to tie his horse. Other men were arriving with him; they were in a hurry to get inside. The house was already packed to the door. Through the open windows drifted the sound of the speaker's voice, sonorously and full of unctuousness.

As he elbowed his way through the door Peder's heart beat faster, a pleasant quivering passed through him; he threw his head back; his face was bright, and he sniffed as a wild animal that has found the scent. Inside the door

304

"Father, Forgive Them—!"

he stopped to have a look at the room . . . who might be here to-night?

He knew all and smiled to himself . . . these fellows will save the world, all right, for they see green and think red . . . now they get the pure gospel! . . . Reverend Kaldahl must have come early; he sat in the centre of the middle row, his mien thoughtful and ponderous, his white necktie shone immaculately clean under the fringe of black beard. Peder left the sombre figure and found Gjermund Dahl. Just now his face seemed longer than usual—Peder nodded to it and passed on. The Irish had taken possession of the row of benches to the right; Doheny and Charley sat far to the front; just behind them the McDougal brothers, Tom with his nose high in the air; he must be feeling good to-night because he was smiling so pleased. Peder hunted for Dennis and did not find him. . . . Too bad Dennis wasn't there . . . I'll have to have a talk with him soon as possible . . . he's got to help me among those fellows!

Lloyd Gill presided. Herman Angell, candidate on the Populist ticket for the office of State Superintendent of Schools, was the speaker of the evening. He was an eloquent man, speaking with much feeling. Peder could not see the face from where he was standing and began working his way down the aisle; he did not stop until he reached clear down to the corner; there stood Tambur-Ola alone, grinning. He gripped Peder's hand:

"Here's where you get the unadulterated gospel!"

Peder only nodded and craned his neck to see the speaker better.

Apparently Mr. Angell was making a good impression. He got a touching note into his exposition of "sixteen-to-one" and the era of glory which was bound to come, once this measure had been embodied into law.

Peder knew the whole lesson by heart; the amusing childishness of its reasoning had caused him to remember it. He squinted at the speaker and his fists clenched. Tambur-Ola whispered something in his ear, but that he did not hear.

. . . Now he's lying, he knows he's lying . . . no man in

305

his position could be that asinine blind! Involuntarily his shoulders raised; he looked about him and sniffed. . . . Here are all these people wasting their time listening to this imbecility! Why doesn't some one get up and tell him he's a liar? . . . Just wait, boys! . . . Here we'll have some fun!

When Mr. Angell at length was through, Lloyd arose to thank him for his great speech; that done, he asked his listeners if there was anyone who wished to add a word to what already had been said.

"You bet your life there is" came Peder's warm, cheerful voice. The whole room turned to look at him. He was on his way to the front, and met the many faces exultantly. As he came up the crowded aisle he talked by spurts like one whose joy is too great for coherent speech:

. . . "The evening's still young. . . . This is a public meeting. . . . We'll be keeping on here till after midnight. . . . Simple-minded country folk have gathered to get information on questions they know little about. . . . Just stay in your seats, please . . . it'll only take me a minute." The eyes of the audience followed him in wonderment. Would he actually match wits with an educated man?

There stood Peder on the platform, drawing back his shoulders and talking all the while; his words came in a deep, thrilled voice sweetened with the joy of battle which now filled him. Here sat the men who were fighting him—Charley, that trusting child whom anybody could fool and his father-in-law—oh, well, who cares about him? By George! if he didn't have to laugh at Tom! Was it with his nose he was weighing the arguments?

. . . "Never," continued Peder, "have more important matters been put up to us voters. A day of visitation is over this land. Now we better pray for bright weather and a keen sight; for that spirit of humility which alone can enable us to choose as leaders men with the greatest possible vision. . . . Hatred of one party for another never brings forth good fruit. It keeps you rooting about in the mire; it warps your minds and makes you see cross-eyed. It's the devil's own way of getting his work done. . . . These are times that try men's souls. We're up against great difficulties. Who dares point out the guilty one and say: There he is, that's the man? We farmers have been blocked and bucked on every hand. Now we're looking for ways and means of getting out. A strange mirage has come into the air. Beware of it. It makes you see things upside down without you yourself knowing it."

Lloyd and Mr. Angell sat beside him, Lloyd squinting at him, wondering what he should do with this lunatic. . . . Best, perhaps, to leave him alone as long as he stuck to generalities.

Peder was oblivious of them. He saw words glitter in the air, sharp and steel-pointed, words that he had been hunting for all his life, words that would cut clean through a fellow; they were coming faster than he could handle them, joining with each other and forming golden chains that sparkled brightly in the sunshine. . . . God! what a treat to stand here to-night! He noticed restlessness in the audience and raised his hand in warning:

"Take it easy, friends. Listen to a word of truth; then go home and think it over . . . in order to think, you need to be alone with yourself and to have silence about you . . . Jesus went out into the desert . . . so did John and Paul . . . they didn't run around to political rallies. . . . Chuck all fancy frills, and the phrases you've been hearing, on the manure pile. No, no, not there, because they'd only infect the fertilizer, and we've got plenty of weeds as it is!"

One by one he tore up the assertions that Mr. Angell had nailed down, turned them inside out and held them up for all to see, toyed with them in gladness until he had shown every absurdity . . . then he passed to the next. His face shone with radiance; never before had he felt so supremely happy.

Lloyd was at a loss what to do and scratched the back of his ear. . . . The devil of it was that there was so much good sense in what the jackass was saying!

. . . "Take for example all the hokum we've been hearing here to-night," continued Peder, chuckling. "Can't you

Their Fathers' God

smell how rotten it is? Ha-ha-ha! I can see your noses turning up! Here comes an educated man and tries to tell us
that it doesn't matter in the least what we really are worth,
but what we claim we're worth. Have you ever heard worse
nonsense? We are almighty gods. I don't mean the old
hayseeds in the fairy-tale stories, but honest-to-goodness
gods. It's amusing, too . . . I rather enjoy hearing myself
glorified like that! Here he stands assuring us that if we
want to, we can coin iron, and that the world at large will
kneel humbly at our feet; it'll take our iron coin and re-
gard it on par with its gold dollar. No country, he says,
would dare object, because we are the all-powerful! Why
should we go to all the bother of digging iron out of the
ground? Why engage in useless work? Besides, iron is heavy;
it wears out our pants pockets. No iron for me! Why not
coin dry horse dung? How about it, Tom, why shouldn't
we? Of course, there might be unpleasant consequences. We
import our tea from China, our coffee from South America,
our sugar from Cuba, and our *lutefisk* from Norway. How
far do you think you'll get when you come to China with
this sixteen-to-one dollar of yours and want to buy tea?
The Chinaman has as much sense as you've got, if not
more; he'll take your dollar, look at it, and give you sixteen-
to-one tea for it." Peder took a step forward.

"Good Lord! what asininity! Can't you understand that if
we could compel the countries we trade with to accept this
sixteen-to-one dollar, we'd be almighty? Why stop with the
money? Why not make them take our blue jeans in exchange
for their fine silks? Why not swap our farm women for
princesses and fairies? It's all the same, the one thing would
be just as easy as the other.

"That's how it is with practically all the articles of faith
that the Populists are dishing out to us. Pity those who pro-
claim them! God have mercy on us if we put trust in their
fables. I tell you they are nothing but fables. The dream
of riches has made us drunk. Now we're reeling about
with our heads in the clouds. We've stared ourselves so blind
watching the blue emptiness above that we no longer can

see our poverty-stricken homes. Let's have no more silly talk about world politics! What we think about world problems, which we don't in the least understand, will never build up this county. Let's start in at home. If we're to start over in Norway, or Great Britain, we'll never reach South Dakota. And that's a shame, fellows, because right here we have the chance to build up a kingdom above all other kingdoms!"

Peder walked back to the corner where Tambur-Ola was standing. No one called for the floor and so the meeting broke up. A great hubbub ensued; men spoke with loud words, jostling their way out; neighbour shouted to neighbour; outside horses neighed and snorted.

Tönseten came back to the corner and patted Peder on the shoulder:

"Permand, Permand, if you ain't a devil of a fellow! Yes, sir, now I can safely go home and go to bed. . . . Some day you'll be President, see if you don't!"

Peder stood there, smiling queerly; he was still trembling; his eyes searched eagerly about the room. . . . Was there no one else with a good word for him? . . . What became of Gjermund? . . . Did Charley intend to leave without even shaking hands? His nostrils dilated, and he had to support himself against the edge of the nearest desk.

VIII

By day he toiled in the fields; in the evening he barely had time to snatch a bite to eat before setting out to attend meetings or call on voters. He saw the whole mess, understood it all clearly: People's minds were in a muddle . . . they had quit using their brains and were being whisked about like leaves in the wind. . . . No sense, no reason. As soon as they they saw a firefly they'd swear it was the morning star! It was clear as day to all who followed the campaign that the race for commissioner would be a real scrap. Peder realized it better than anyone. Sitting out on the doorstep talking with Dennis O'Hara one evening, he learned that both Doheny and Charley were working against him and that Father Williams had said that he for his part would have to vote for Tom McDougal. When he heard this Peder got up and laughed:

"Saul slew one thousand, David ten thousand. Never fear, Dennis. If they're going to mix religion into this mess, we'll beat them to dust!"

Given time to think it over, his confidence was less sure. Susie's attitude puzzled him. . . . Did she wish him to win or did she not? She had promised to enlist the pope himself for his cause! . . . Should he tell her what Dennis had said? . . . Not a single word did he breathe to her. At home he went about silent and unapproachable, ate little and slept poorly. His face grew thin and haggard, and took on the preoccupied expression of one who goes about struggling with an impossible problem.

That fall the corn ripened early. These days he was busy cutting and shocking, providing winter feed for the cattle— he had bought ten head more. On afternoons when the weather was right he would take Petie with him to the field, set him on top of the shock, and talk Norwegian to him. Since moving to the room in the loft he saw Susie only at dinner and supper. There was one puzzle he could not solve: for two Sundays in succession she had neglected Mass and during the past month she had made only one trip home. Why? . . . Is she afraid of herself? Or is it for me she fears? Doesn't dare to hear what people say about me? . . . Ask her about it? No . . . I'll wait till I can show her that in a political row the Virgin Mary has no more to say than a dead herring . . . no sir, not a bit more!

"What are you saying, papa?" asked Petie from his perch on the shock.

Peder had to go over to him.

"I said, *du e en kjæk glönt!*[1] Can you say that?"

"*Tjæk glönt!*" said Petie, after him, and laughed gleefully.

On the Sunday following Peder's speech (the episode had

[1] *Du e en kjæk glönt*—You're a dandy boy!

"Father, Forgive Them—!"

set the whole settlement talking) Sörine-godmother arranged a little farewell party for Nikoline, who had given up her place at Murphy's and to-morrow was leaving for Norway. Peder and Susie were at the party, likewise Store-Hans and his family, and also Tönseten and Kjersti.

In spite of his repeated efforts, to-day Tönseten could not get any fun started. They had eaten both well and long, had already come to the pie and the second cup of coffee, and still there they all sat, long-faced and silent, with no talk and no life in them. Never had he seen the like of this for a party! He looked at Nikoline and winked:

"Now I'll tell you what we'll do. You go straight to town and sell that ticket of yours, then I'll get a divorce. When Peder gets to be governor he'll find me a swell appointment; that'd be the least he could do for all the help I've given him. Ha-ha! . . . you and I'd make an ideal couple; we'll live like two peas in a pod!"

"Then she certainly would better herself!" Provoked, Kjersti laid her fork down. "To think that an old fool like you can sit there talking so silly!"

"Don't mind it, Kjersti," laughed Nikoline. "I won't take him away from you."

"Oh no! God pity me, that'd be too much to expect!" She sniffled and wiped her eyes. "Now you go to Norway and pick out a real fellow; then you come back and rent our farm. . . . Here I sit alone with the old fool. . . . We ain't got none of our own to help us. . . . And now I'm worn out and can't work like I used to!" Suddenly she got up and left the room.

The party was more dismal than ever; the silence was heavy in the room. Tönseten could think of nothing fitting to say, and the others held their tongues, waiting for him. Sörine was out of sorts because the only one of her family that had come to America was leaving her for good; to-day no words in Tambur-Ola; he only grinned wryly to anything that was said; Store-Hans was taken up with his own thoughts; the sisters-in-law sat beside each other, both speechless. What could Sofie find to say to a Catholic, any-

311

how? She had read *The Black Prophet* and knew what kind
of people the Catholics were; and Susie sat as cold and
stiff as a statue, getting only a word now and then of the
conversation. . . . Why did Kjersti leave? Why should
Susie have to make a fuss over this greenhorn Norskie who
had snubbed her brother and now strutted around here like
a cocky rooster?

Peder had not come home until three o'clock this morning; he ate slowly, now and then stealing a glance at the
girl who was going straight back to the very place she had
fled in desperation. He was the first to leave the table;
without a word to anyone he slipped outdoors and wandered
about the yard behind the house. Back here, in his day,
Sörine's first husband had planted a considerable orchard—
plums, apples, and many kinds of berries. Most of the plums
had been picked already, but there still were a few left.
Peder picked one and ate it.

A little while later, as if by agreement, Nikoline appeared; she carried a pail and called out gaily that he must
not eat the trees bare.

Peder met her and took the pail:

"What makes you do this?" he asked, looking intently
at her. "Why do you leave?"

They picked from the same tree.

"That's easy to understand. When you see you've taken
the wrong road, you turn back. What else can you do?
. . . Pick only the nicest ones!"

Peder tasted of one.

"Are you so dead sure you've taken the wrong road?"

"Oh yes."

"You didn't think so when you came here."

"But now I've tried it and know. I'm not so stupid as I
look."

"And so you simply turn back? . . . Here!" He held
out the pail for her to empty her hand. "What if you should
be taking the wrong road now, too?"

"Mother's alone there. I have her!" At once she was

like a changed being; all mischief was wiped away. "Mother's exceedingly kind."

"Not all can do as you," he bent over and picked up a big, ripe plum from the ground.

"Don't you turn back when you see you're on the wrong road?" she asked, innocently.

"What would you do if you were in my shoes?" He moved a step nearer, looking at her keenly.

She met him beamingly:

"In your shoes?"

"Yes?"

"I would keep on going straight ahead till I was governor of South Dakota. Unless you do, I shall disown you!"

Peder's hand shook:

"If I had some one along, one that found pleasure in the going . . . one that could watch out for dangerous places . . . and also see the beauty in the landscape ——"

"You don't need that. You're not afraid of the dark!" she burst out. She faced him and seemed agitated. "You should know by this time that Success and Happiness don't live on the same road! Why don't you use your magic mirror? If you want the one, give up seeking the other. . . . How much coddling does a man need in order to pick up his bed and walk?"

The plum in his hand was worm-eaten; he turned it over, studying it, his face was knit.

"Did you ever drive a team with one of the horses hanging back all the time? There was nothing the matter with him, only that he was afraid of his own shadow; no matter what you did, whether you whipped or coaxed, there was no life in him, the other horse had to drag him along. You had to get there, remember. What would you do?" Peder flung the fruit away.

She turned her face away; her voice had the sweet nearness peculiar to her when she became really intimate:

"I don't think I'd pay any attention to him. Why bother? Better to whip up the fast horse. Otherwise you might get caught in the rain and never get there."

"Somehow, that doesn't seem right. . . . I'm fond of horses."

"Now you see *hilder* again!" she laughed, stepping around to the other side of the tree.

A silence settled over them.

"You mean, then, that Success and Happiness can't be hitched together?"

"I've never seen it—that is, except in slushy story-books. Do you believe it?"

"I was only asking. . . . Let's go to another tree."

She came after, walking fast to catch up with him:

"It's queer with you Americans, you want heaven, and aren't willing to pay the price. Do you think heaven can be reached by eating ice-cream and going to dances?" she laughed, teasingly. "Why don't you eat ice-cream, go on dancing, and never bother about the rest? . . . On the way home you take a bottle of pop?"

"Because I want both."

"Then you may have to hunt a long time!"

"I know now it can be done."

"Yes, in the fairy tales. There the hero slays the monster and gets the princess. The only trouble is that just at that point the tale ends."

Peder's face was red and he spoke in a low voice:

"I want to ask you a question. What was it you were hunting for when you came here? Tell me honestly."

Many plums lay on the ground where they stood; she squatted and began gathering them into her hand; she laughed ever so little:

"For life, I suppose. . . . That's what some of us are hunting for. . . . They're bigger here, aren't they? Oh, look at this one!" She held out a big, ripe plum to him. "Eat it."

Taking the fruit, he searched in her eyes:

"And now you want to go back and hunt there? That's foolish, if you want to know it!" His voice trembled and he took a step nearer.

"I'm going home to mother." Abruptly she got up and

went around the tree. Rays of sunlight danced on the leaves that partly hid her face.

"Are you through, then, hunting for life?"

She stood motionless for a moment; on her face played shadows of a branch moving in the afternoon breeze, her words hardly audible:

"Now I am through hunting."

Peder came to where she stood, so radiant that he could hardly speak:

"Why?"

She turned halfway from him:

"I have seen Paradise . . . I know I can't get in!" Her voice got steadier:"Now I think we have enough . . . they won't eat more than this."

"Was it beautiful in Paradise? . . . Come here and help me pick these off the ground . . . we can't leave all this ripe fruit!"

When she came they squatted down and gathered plums into the pail which stood between them, she with slow movements.

"Beautiful . . . and terrible, too."

"What you say—terrible in Paradise?"

"There was one standing there, one with a flaming sword."

"And you were afraid?"

"I wasn't allowed to get in!"

"Was"—he had to clear his throat—"was it in Norway you saw it?"

"No," she said, quietly, "it was here." She had turned her head so that he could not see her face.

"And you go and leave it all behind?"

"Yes."

"For good?" he asked, hoarsely.

"Now we must go in"—she looked into the pail—"they won't eat any more." She took a few steps, hesitatingly, then turned towards him without looking up: "Thank you . . . Peder . . . for everything!" She bent her head as if she had spoken indecently and walked away.

Their Fathers' God

He came hurrying after her; he had something he must tell her, something she must hear before she left.

"Wait—wait!"

He was stopped by hearing his own name called from the other side of the house, where Susie was hunting for him. They met at the corner.

"Where have you been keeping yourself all afternoon?"

"What's the matter now?" he asked, darkly, and went past her.

"Some one's here looking for you. . . . Can't you tell me where you've been?"

Peder pretended not to have heard her; he saw a saddled pony bound to the hitching-post, on the doorstep sat a boy whom he did not know; his first impulse was to turn and go back to the orchard.

The boy handed him a letter; he said he had been asked to wait for an answer.

Peder opened it and read, failed to grasp the meaning at first and began over again; his hand shook so violently that the words blurred.

Susie stood beside him, reading over his arm.

"Now look at that!" she cried.

The letter was from the chairman of the State Republican Committee and bore a singular message:

—Through reliable sources, it read, they had been informed of his able and timely reply to Mr. Angell. First of all they wanted to thank him for his manly conduct; and next to inquire whether he would accept a speaking engagement from the State Central Committee. Would he during the remaining five weeks travel for them and give the same speech against "Sixteen-to-one"? They would lay out the route for him. As compensation they would pay him $100 plus his travelling expenses. Could he come at once?

Absently he handed her the letter and started to walk down the yard, entirely oblivious of what he was doing. . . . "Wonder if that's the road to Paradise?" he said, half aloud.

"Don't you understand?" exclaimed Susie. "Now try to

tell me miracles no longer happen, and the Mother of God doesn't hear my prayers! We must hurry home so I can get you ready." She was beaming now. "Jacob Fredrik and I can easily do the work while you're gone; don't let that bother you. . . . I'll bet Tom hasn't got any offers like this from his party! . . . We must hurry home right away."

Peder said:

"Has the boy had anything to eat? Go in and ask Sörine to warm the coffee." The last trailed away in an absent-minded voice. . . . I simply must see her once more! he thought. He followed Susie to the house; there he waited until she had gone in, and slipped around to the kitchen porch and sat down on the steps.

When Susie came in she found the others in the front room; Nikoline was providing each one with a saucer, asking them to help themselves to the plums. Susie flourished the letter.

"Do you want to hear what a smart husband I've got?" she asked, proudly, and without further ado proceeded to read the letter aloud to them. "I know he'll be elected now!" she added, with childish joy.

"Elected?" shouted Tönseten. "Why, good Lord, woman! he'll have a walk-away!" He put his saucer aside and shook his fist menacingly in her face. "But let me tell you one thing: The more of the Irish you can swing over to our side, the safer he'll be. You tell your father and brother I said so. . . . Of course he'll be elected!"

Nikoline brought the pail back to the kitchen, saw Peder's face through the screen, and gave a low cry. Setting the pail away, she listened for a moment before slipping over to the door:

"You must go in and join the others; we can't talk here. Please, go in!"

"It was only this I must tell you," he said, heavily. "I too have stood at the gate and looked into Paradise. What I saw was not *hilder*. The flaming sword does not frighten me. What I've been hunting for all my life I've seen with my own eyes, I know it exists. And now I think that I can make

317

the journey alone. May I shake hands with you before you leave?"

Her head drooped; the eyelids raised ever so little.

"When we meet the next time!"

"Then you're coming back?" he asked, gravely.

"I thought you were coming to Norway?" Again he was conscious of her nearness, but the voice was so low that he barely caught the words.

Quickly she vanished into the hallway and fled upstairs.

IX

For four weeks Peder stumped the southern part of the state for the Republican cause. The fifth he felt he was needed at home and quit at the end of the fourth week. As he came driving into his own yard on the late Tuesday afternoon before election, it seemed eternities since he last saw this place. All day long as he had jogged along in the buggy, just resting—half asleep most of the time—a mass of hazy memories had hovered in his mind: Memories of strange places scattered over a prairie so vast that it must reach the ends of the earth and beyond; of run-down places from which poverty and distress stared grimly at you the moment you came near; and of prosperous farms with stately barns and palatial homes—unmistakable evidences of how richly these prairies could reward a man for work well planned and faithfully done; memories of a people that toiled and fought on bravely, won and lost, just like himself. There were many other scenes, too, hosts of them. To-day he had relived every scene—scenes of dimly lighted schoolhouses packed solid with brawny men in overalls whom he had addressed with the sincerity of one called to witness before the very throne of God . . . good faces some of them, faces that beamed at all he said and gave him ten men's strength and twelve men's wits; but also dark, ill-boding faces ready to charge at any moment; not soon would he forget the den of Populists he had stumbled into down in Lincoln County, how they had pelted him with snarling questions and how they finally had booed him out . . . Norwegians every last man of them . . . plenty excitement that night! And there were scenes of sleepless nights in filthy hotel rooms where he had lain reliving the day's experiences, and delivered again his speech on "A Greater Justice Among Men"; memories of nights when droves of bloodthirsty bed-bugs had sent him scurrying out of bed to grope for matches. As he now saw his home a great swell rose in him, sweeping all away. Only one remained, and that did not belong to the series: A woman squatting low under a plum tree, telling him how she had found the way to Paradise. Like a sweet odour of sanctity it had followed him on his journey and had kept up his courage to go on.

The sight of home made his eyes blink fast. There were the buildings, the windmill, and the cattle in the yard; the soft melody of the autumn evening lay sweet in the air; the meadow lark caught it and trilled lustily; from down in the pasture the old herd came ranging over the hill, the milk cows lowing in the lead; those in the corral lapped their corn meal and switched their tails contentedly; from the pigsty rose a wild tumult; Jacob Fredrik was pouring into the troughs. As Peder beheld it all he felt his heart swell with peculiar warmth. To-night he would climb to the top of the windmill and have a good look at his king-dom . . . this was his, his very own! . . . Wonder if the mistress is at home? Ha! here's where we clinch a vote or two. . . . "Hello there, Jacob Fredrik. To-night you'd bet-ter give them an extra drop!"

He had not stopped the horse before Susie came out, leading Petie by the hand. . . . Then she'd gotten his letter and was expecting him?

As soon as the boy saw his father he tore himself free and ran to meet him. Peder had climbed out of the buggy and stood waiting.

"Can you talk Norwegian to-night?" he demanded, huskily.

"Talk Norwegian to-night," cried Petie, gleefully, in Nor-wegian. . . . "Sit on horsey; I sit on horsey, papa!"

Their Fathers' God

Peder sniffled, and had to wipe his eyes before he could lift the boy up.

Susie stood near them, smiling bashfully; at first she couldn't get her voice up, but finally she managed to ask if he didn't have the least little welcome for his Irish girleen?

Peder cleared his throat. . . . Did you ever hear the like of a woman? . . . What did she expect? . . . "Come here." In the buggy seat lay a few packages, gifts he had bought for her and the boy; picking up two he handed them to her.

She paid no attention to the packages, but threw her arms about his neck and pressed him to her. "Oh!" she murmured, and would not let go; after she had kissed him on one cheek she had to kiss the other, too, and then she hugged still tighter, for now she hadn't seen him for ages and ages and was man-hungry!

There Peder stood with one package in each hand; he was helpless, could neither reciprocate nor defend himself. Seeing Jacob Fredrik approach with the milk-pails, he laughed good-naturedly:

"Now you can see what kind of reward we Republicans are reaping. . . . You come and take care of the boy; he might fall down and kill himself!"

Jacob Fredrik laughed till the tears came.

Still Susie would not let go.

"Now take *this*! . . . That's what you get for not talking so that your wife can understand what you say. . . . And *this* . . . Gee! how hungry I was!"

Outdoors as well as indoors serene peace reigned. No sooner had Peder eaten than he had to go out and look around. The boy clung to one hand, Susie to the other arm. In order to free the arm he stooped and picked up the boy. It felt so good to stretch a bit! . . . His being filled with a sweet calm . . . he was home again . . . and he hadn't failed in his mission. . . . This was his farm, the boy was his, too . . . all was his. Like a silken garment the oncoming twilight enveloped them.

Beside him walked Susie, full to overflowing with confidential talk of how things had gone while he was away;

she told of how smart she and Jacob Fredrik had been, of how they'd planned and worked . . . they hadn't let the grass grow under their feet—not they, oh no! The field he had begun cutting on before he went away they had both cut and shocked . . . yes sir, they had, the whole field!

—What's that? Peder hadn't been listening.

—How many times must she tell him what a smart wife he had? And that field wasn't all; they had half-finished another. Jacob Fredrik had done the cutting, she had shocked; they'd had Petie along to do the bossing; one day when it rained they had pitched in and done two weeks' washing so as to be ready for the good weather when it returned. Now wasn't that smart?

The words flowed, on and on:

—Last Sunday she had made a trip home; she had used the lumber wagon and had taken Jacob Fredrik with her . . . a devil of a fine fellow, Jacob Fredrik was. She paused for a brief moment. . . . "I think Charley will vote for you, though you can't get him to say so . . . you should have heard me preach to 'em! I told them they ought to be ashamed of themselves not to back their own relatives, because you might get to be governor in time . . . then they'd be ashamed!"

"Did you really say that?"

"Uh-huh, sure I did; you know very well you will be governor some day . . . Father's awfully proud of you, I could tell it on him; I'll bet he'll be voting for you, too!"

"Did he say so?"

"He? Oh no, he'd never say it, not if you killed him; but when he says no that way he always means yes. I know him. He asked me what we were going to do with all our cattle this winter. Cattle? I said. We're going to buy twice as many head more because now you had money and Jacob Fredrik was so smart with the work; I told him that next year the cattle prices would be way up, and he wanted to know how I could be sure of that, and I said the Republicans couldn't help winning this fall, and as soon as the elections were over the prices would start going up. . . . You should have heard

him then—he was so mad he popped! I thought he'd go
crazy. You talk about fun! I know he won't vote for Tom;
he thinks it's a sin to vote for anyone but a Democrat."

"I suppose you've been to church?"

"Yes, once. The first Sunday you were gone. I took Jacob
Fredrik with me so he wouldn't have to sit here all alone.
He's a good man, that fellow, and so clever and kind-
hearted! If he only would learn how to talk. . . . He
thought it was lots of fun to go to our church."

Peder grew more and more interested. . . . To-night she's
got some worry on her mind. Wonder what it is this time?

"Have you been to confession?"

"No," she said, cheerfully, "not while you were gone.
What have I got to confess now? I've hardly stirred from
this spot all summer, I haven't seen a single soul, and every
night I've said my prayers. . . . The Sunday we went to
church I dropped in to see Mrs. McBride. Oh, but she's
good and mad at you! She's scared pink you'll beat Tom.
He's her pet nephew, you know; she took care of him for a
while when he was a little tot; she wanted to count for me
all who had promised to vote for Tom, but I didn't have time
to listen and so she got mad at me, too. She isn't real funny
before she gets good and popping, but then you can laugh
yourself sick. She's sure Tom will be elected."

They had been to the top of the Indian Hill; there Peder
had surveyed his kingdom while with half an ear he had
listened to her chatter; they had talked their way down again,
and now the increasing chill of the deepening dusk drove
them indoors.

Jacob Fredrik had taken the *Skandinaven* and gone up to
his room. Petie was sleeping with his arms locked about his
father's neck. The peace and the stillness were profound.

"You better put him to bed. Poor little man, I'm afraid
he got cold!"

"Just a minute." She put some wood on the fire and
opened the bedroom door wide . . . to-night she wanted it
warm and cozy in there. She took the boy, undressed him,
and tucked him into the cradle which stood ready in the bed-

room. To-night there was a dexterous agility in all her movements, and she stepped so lightly.

Peder stood by the stove, warming himself.

"Guess I'd better sleep downstairs to-night. I don't suppose my room has been aired out since I left?" He stretched and yawned.

"I'd like to see you try to run away from me to-night, too!" She gave him a quick glance, loving and secretive. "What do you suppose I've got a husband for? You come when you're ready—I'm going to bed right now."

When he came into the bedroom a little while later she was undressed and stood combing her hair.

"Any of my nightclothes down here?" he wondered, drowsily.

"Get under the quilt or you'll catch cold. I'll run up after your nightshirt later." She slipped into bed.

"Last night," she confided, intimately, after he had joined her, "I had a queer dream. I dreamt I gave birth to twins, two big red-haired boys. We called the one Peder and the other Mikey. I wasn't the least bit sick, now wasn't that smart of me?"

"We've already got a Petie," he said, sleepily.

"Oh, you're so foolish! It was in a dream we called him that, don't you understand?" She snuggled close to him, had to get her arms around him in order to draw him closer to her.

That night Susie's wants were insatiable.

x

Late Thursday evening Dennis O'Hara rode into the yard. Susie and Jacob Fredrik had already gone to bed, but Peder was sitting up, looking through the newspapers that had collected during his absence. Since his mother's death he had begun reading *Skandinaven* and was often surprised at finding so much of interest in its columns both from this country and from abroad. When he heard the rider come into the yard he got up and went out to meet him.

Their Fathers' God

Dennis wanted to see him for only a minute and was not to be persuaded to get off the horse. He had heard Peder was home again, he explained, and came to ask whether he knew that Tom was slated to give a speech over at the schoolhouse next Saturday evening?

"Are you around with invitations?"

"Not exactly," laughed Dennis. "But I'll bet you'll hear things you never knew before. He's going to shoot his big gun at you."

"At me?" Peder patted the horse.

"Bet your life! His subject is 'The Republican Candidate for Commissioner in Our District.' As far as I can figure out, that must mean you."

"Can it be possible? . . . Then Tom must be scared."

"That's what the announcement says. I wasn't sure whether you'd heard about it, so I thought I better drop in and put you wise."

"Well, he's picked a good subject!" Peder shrugged his shoulders.

"And he'll certainly make the most of it!" Dennis put a peculiar emphasis into the declaration.

"What do you know about it?"

"Nothing certain."

"Do you think I ought to go?"

"Depends on how much your stomach can stand. Tom can be darn reckless. Especially after he's had a drink or two, and he'll hardly overlook that on this occasion. Couldn't you get Gjermund Dahl to be there? He's a dandy old fellow; I hear he's been saying a lot of nice things about you."

"You mean I should go get a Democrat to defend me? Not on your life, Dennis. Then I'd better smear on some war paint and go myself!"

"You ought to have some one there. I'm no good for that sort of thing, and no one can tell what Tom might have up his sleeve. He has a faithful supporter in Father Williams."

"Does the priest have anything to say about this?"

"Not at High Mass!"

Peder stood patting the horse. Suddenly he asked:

324

"Father, Forgive Them—!"

"You think the Doheny's know about this meeting?"

"Why, of course! Tom was out last Sunday, announcing it. I talked with Charley last night. He asked me if I was coming."

"I'm not counting on a great deal of help from that quarter," admitted Peder, darkly.

Dennis laughed:

"Well, according to the looks of things, I guess you'd better not!"

"What have they got to say? Have you heard anything?"

"Only that no self-respecting Irish Catholic would ever disgrace himself by voting for a Norwegian Lutheran, that seems to be the slogan. . . . If you say so, I'll mention this to Gjermund Dahl. I have to go over that way to-morrow, anyhow."

"Do as you please about it. But don't tell him that I sent you!" He slapped Dennis on the thigh. "Well, thanks, old boy, for coming over. I won't forget this favour!"

For a while Peder sauntered about out in the yard. The lamp in the kitchen was still burning. Coming in, he picked it up and went into the bedroom.

"Are you sleeping?" he asked, coldly, setting the lamp on the commode.

"No." It sounded as if she awoke with a start. She rubbed her eyes. "What's the matter? You look so queer!" Alarmed, she sat up in the bed.

He rested his elbow on the edge of the commode; his eyes were fixed on her and he folded his hands:

"Did you know Tom had called a meeting for Saturday night?"

"Is that anything to bother about in the middle of the night? Forget your old politics for a while and come to bed." She tried to act provoked, but her voice didn't sound right.

"You've heard about it?" he persisted, imperturbably.

"Now when you mention it, I think Charley did say something about it." She lay thinking for a moment. "Did you say Saturday night? Wasn't it to-night?"

"No."

Their Fathers' God

"I'm sure it wasn't Saturday night."

"Do you know what he's going to talk about?"

"How silly of you! Here you come pouncing on me in the middle of the night—as if I kept track of Tom and his crazy stunts . . . I haven't seen Tom for years. Get yourself to bed so we can have peace!" She threw herself back on the pillow to indicate that now it was time to quit talking and go to sleep. She turned away from him and pulled the quilt over her shoulder.

"You might as well out with it. Don't you suppose I can tell you've been hiding something from me? Speak up, Susie-girl!"

Not a word from her. To make it still clearer that now she wanted peace she drew the quilt over her head. Silently Peder watched her, waiting for an answer. Moments passed. With slow movements he took the lamp, went upstairs and to bed.

The door to the room he had left half open. In bed he had lain for a long time, struggling with his thoughts; downstairs the clock struck twelve; now he lay half asleep, but not so far gone as to have lost all consciousness.

Suddenly the door pushed wide open; a white-clad figure stepped into the room, stood motionless for a moment, closed the door noiselessly and stopped again. Peder became aware of its presence, turned his head to look, but was too sleepy to determine whether the apparition was flesh and blood or only a dream.

It tiptoed over to the bed:

"I had to make sure you'd found your nightshirt," it whispered in an unearthly voice, and remained standing there.

Involuntarily he moved over and the white figure slipped under the quilt. Again he moved a little. By her breathing he could tell that now he had better be careful.

"Was the bed made up?" she whispered, in the same unearthly tone.

"Yes," he coughed, moving over once more.

Two, three times she gasped frantically for air:

326

"Father, Forgive Them—!"

"Don't you know ... this is ... unchastity? ... We're committing it wilfully. ... It's a mortal sin!"

"It's what?"

"That married people don't sleep together. ... The saints don't look with favour on such married life!"

"What the saints think doesn't interest me in the least," he said, in a cold, hard voice.

... "All summer long I haven't meant a thing to you. ... Here I go ... I never think of anything but you. ... You've been gone for weeks ... you come home and sail into me like a wild man because—because ... I can't tell you what Tom's up to! ... You carry on as if you were the Lord God Himself and I ... the blackest ... sinner!" Still her voice was rasping with awe, and she spoke in gasps.

"If you have any more to say, you'd better say it now," he answered, with the same icy calm. "Yet you haven't told me what he's going to talk about. I know you know it."

She was crying now. He turned away from her and lay motionless, as if he were oblivious of her presence.

When he awoke at sunrise she was sound asleep. At the breakfast table she asked if he intended to use the buggy to-day? She had some errands to do in town ... she needed things for the house ... she had saved a few eggs ... could he spare Dolly? Peder noticed nothing unusual in her manner. He told her that she could take the horse.

Having harnessed Dolly and hitched her to the buggy, he drove the rig to the door; poking his head in, he asked Jacob Fredrik to tell her the buggy was ready.

"Thank you, Peder!" she shouted, cheerfully, from the bedroom. She took the boy with her and was gone till nearly supper-time.

That night he again slept up in the loft and she downstairs. When he came in for breakfast Saturday morning she was still in bed; this struck him as being peculiar ... she seemed all right yesterday. The bedroom door stood ajar and he could hear that she was awake. Before going out to work he stepped into the room and asked what the trouble was.

327

Their Fathers' God

She seemed tired and worn out:

"You ask Jacob Fredrik to keep an eye on Petie." She paused. "Last night I was on the verge of having another hemorrhage."

"Then you'd better stay in bed." With that he left her.

She raised herself on her elbow and listened to his footsteps. . . . He'd surely come back! . . . Did he take this as a joke? . . . Heavens! what a husband! She sank down on the pillow; laid thus a long time with her eyes closed. Suddenly she raised her head and called:

"Jacob Fredrik, run and tell him I want to see him."

Jacob Fredrik's sunny face appeared in the doorway.

"Oh well, it can go till noon. Is there any coffee left? I'm getting up right away."

When Peder came in for dinner she was up and helping with the work, silent and preoccupied. Otherwise she appeared to be quite all right; she didn't eat with the others, but waited till they had left the table.

That evening he worked late . . . thought he'd better finish up the field before calling it a day. In the kitchen a feast awaited him . . . stewed chicken and potatoes that had been cooked just right; they were boiled in their jackets, and so mealy and nice that the skins had burst. Susie had been doing the cooking herself; she was an expert at preparing a chicken this way; Peder had often praised her for it, and said she was a wonderfully able cook.

To-night he sat silent at the table, helping Petie to more than he ate himself. Furtively Susie watched him. Suddenly he glanced at the clock, got up hastily, and went to the washstand.

"Going away?" she asked, in surprise.

"Heh-heh." He finished washing and went upstairs to dress.

A moment later she too came up, stood with her back to the door, on her face a questioning look:

"Where you going to-night?"

"Oh"—he pulled the shirt over his head—"I suppose I'd better go over and hear what Tom has to say."

"That's not to-night!" she exclaimed, laughingly.

"No?"

"Begory! that'll be a good joke on you! I talked with Mrs. McBride yesterday, and she said he was to speak last night."

"She did?" he asked, evenly, and buttoned his shirt.

Susie drew a heavy breath.

"That's what she said. . . . He certainly raked you over the coals!"

"That's fine. . . . What did he say?"

"Huh! nothing you need worry about! . . . You know how Tom is. He said you were a Lutheran and a good friend of the minister here . . . you two were scheming to make the whole county Lutheran," she related, cheerfully. "I nearly cried my eyes out laughing at her."

"She actually told you all that, eh?"

"Sure she did." She forced a laugh. "You should have seen old Annie when I told her that you didn't care a snap of your fingers about those things, and that you and the minister could hardly be called friends, at least not *good* friends!"

"You ought not have said that."

"Why?"

"Because it isn't true."

"Well, I declare, isn't that true, either?" She clapped her hands together in childish surprise.

"I think a lot of Reverend Kaldahl. He's a man of honour. He doesn't pry into other people's affairs. He has never bothered you?"

"Me? Not at all; he knows better!" She took his remark as a joke and laughed. . . . "Wait, I'll help you. You aren't to run off with your necktie upside down!" She crossed the floor and stood before him, trying to straighten his tie; unable to get it as it should be, she pulled it off and tied it on anew; it took a long time before she could get it just right.

He noticed that her hand trembled and that her expression was strangely unnatural.

"*There!* You aren't a bad-looking man, if I must say it." Suddenly she laid one hand on each of his shoulders, but without looking up. "You could make me happy to-night!" She kissed him hastily. Her lips were dry and hot.

He only looked at her with the same cold, hard expression.

"Take me along with you and drop me at home on the way over . . . that won't be much out of your way . . . you can call for me on your way back. It's so lonesome to sit here all alone with a strange man in the house . . . one I can't even talk with!" Her eyes were inordinately large. Standing so close to her and with the light shining right in her face, he could see the blue under the brown in her eyes more clearly,[1] and it looked as if the blue were quivering.

Peder pulled on his coat. He had to get started, and that right away, or he'd be late. Slowly he went down the stairs. . . . Now she was most likely boo-hooing again! . . . Why wouldn't she tell him what she knew? Did she think he was afraid? . . . Down in the kitchen he paused for a moment to tell Jacob Fredrik to look after the boy. . . . Susie wasn't exactly well to-night; he'd better keep an eye on her, too.

XI

The schoolhouse was crowded when Peder arrived. Men thronged the hallway and jammed the stairs. The windows had been thrown open; he stole up close enough to one of them so he could both see and hear without himself being seen.

Tom had just begun. His voice was joyous, the face afire with enthusiasm; the words came in an even stream. He was telling stories, had just finished one and straightway launched into another. . . . He is just warming up to his subject, thought Peder . . . he'll soon be getting there.

And so Tom did:

—He, for his part, was only an uneducated man, he confessed, cheerfully. Free trade and money standards and all that highfalutin stuff was as much Greek to him as it was to them; he didn't aim to set himself up as an authority on such complicated problems. Never had he traded free or

[1] See Peder Victorious.

"Father, Forgive Them—!"

minted money either of gold or "dry horse dung." He'd leave such things for his worthy Republican opponent to rack his brains on! He himself had to pay for everything he bought, with hard, cold cash, earned in the sweat of his brow. The stray pennies he got hold of now and then were worn so thin that they slipped through his fingers before he even had a chance to look at them. And as for the problems of coining money and deciding what metal should be used, the county board didn't have a blooming word to say! For emphasis Tom's first pounded the desk; his face had a challenging look.

—Nor would these be the issues the voters would decide when they went to the polls to elect a commissioner next Tuesday. His Republican opponent was only an ordinary farmer like himself. So far Mr. Holm had never broken the law, at least not to the extent that you could put him in jail —not yet, anyhow! From the way Tom flung his battered nose into the air it was clear as day that it was only a question of time when the jailing would come to pass.

—Mr. Holm's mother had been a lunatic, announced Tom, happily. No use worrying about that, since it couldn't be proved that such infirmities always run in a family. Her son might be a good man, for all that. He wondered if all Norwegians were not lunatics? Once lunatics were safe behind the bars, they couldn't do much harm!

—He s'posed, said Tom, his listeners knew that all Norwegians were Lutherans? But had they heard the God's truth about these Lutherans? Did they know that Luther himself was a possessed monk who got so unruly that at last the pope had to kick him out of the True Church? Yes, sir!

—This Mr. Holm was not even a good Lutheran, explained Tom. He was a freethinker and didn't give two whoops for either God or the devil. That's how smart he was! Was that the kind of man they wanted to look after their roads in this county? To build their bridges? All right, then they'd better watch out so that they didn't get left sprawling in the ditches! . . . Tom found great delight in the fact that his opponent was a freethinker and that they intended to elect

331

that kind of man to look after their public affairs. Suddenly
his tone changed, became serious and very much concerned:

—They'd better look twice, he warned them, before select-
ing their public servants; otherwise they might wake up some
fine morning to find themselves in a devil of a hole. In na-
tional affairs it didn't matter so much, he explained, because
there the rascals constantly devoured one another, yes, sir,
so they did.

—They'd do well first to look at a man's private life before electing him to public office—yes, sir, for saints were
saints, and devils devils and their private life showed them
up. Mr. Holm had taken unto himself a Catholic wife, the
only sensible thing he had ever done. But in spite of the fact
that she was a member of the local congregation here, Father
Williams was not found worthy to perform the marriage
ceremony. Think of it, men! This man who walked among
them as a shining light and a holy example was not good
enough to marry a freethinking Norwegian Lutheran! And
that's the man they wanted for their commissioner? Not that
Tom cared; in time the devil would get his own!

—But pity the young woman who had fallen victim of his
tricks! Tom was touched to compassion when he thought of
her. She was the one who had suffered innocently. Here
was what happened: In the fullness of time a child was born
to them —— Hey, hold on there! One couldn't really call it
the *fullness* of time, no, hardly that! But of course this was
none of Tom's business; he only mentioned it. What did Mr.
Holm do after the baby had come? Tom cocked his head
and repeated the question.

—Did he bring it to the House of God for holy baptism as
he had once solemnly promised to do? Oh no, not Mr. Holm!
Every time his wife mentioned the matter he'd start some
kind of rumpus, because he was through with such nonsensi-
cal old-fashioned institutions. Yes, sir, that's exactly what
he called it, Tom had it on good authority. But because she
was the kind that always tried to walk in the paths of the
just, his wife finally had to sneak the child away and have

it baptized *secretly*! Tom gave his audience good time to think this over before he went on with his speech.

—What did they think of it? How did they like it? Here was a father who positively refused to have his own child brought to holy baptism. So obstinate was he that his wife was utterly helpless. For fear of her husband's wrath she did not dare—Tom sucked the air—did not dare to do the only right thing by her own child. Driven to desperation, she at last had to take the child and have it baptized secretly! Tom thrust his hand forward dramatically and paused to let the words sink in.

—He admitted that he was not in a position to tell them exactly how the father had taken it when he finally found out about the baptism. But did they know that all spring Mrs. Holm had been in bed deathly sick and that the sickness, or whatever it was, had come over her all of a sudden? The word went around now—no doubt they'd heard it—that she was being held a prisoner out there on the farm, but as to that Tom couldn't say. . . . Was that the type of commissioner they were looking for?

Peder heard no more of the speech. He had dragged himself over to the wall so that he could lean against it; he had to steady himself because his knees would no longer carry him. A feeling of nausea had come over him, he wanted to vomit but could not; worst of all was the dizziness; everything inside his head was whirling around and around; he saw things and heard things which he knew were impossible . . . they were not there, couldn't be there, and it bothered him that he couldn't get rid of them. Here stood his mother talking to him, her words coming clearly and unmistakably; she was being unreasonable, and nagged him so that he had to argue with her.

"Now you go straight home and to bed!" she said. . . . "Not by any means, not till I've given Tom the licking he has coming!" . . . "You're going right this minute; a man's wrath never accomplishes that which is right in the eyes of God. Mind me now!" . . . "You're crazy, mother! Didn't you hear him say so?" . . . "Go now!" He felt some one pushing him and he started towards his horse. "I might as well. She who's to blame for all this is at home. I can take care of Tom later."

Dolly sniffed for caresses, poking her silky muzzle into his face, whinnying low and drawn-out. Involuntarily Peder threw his arms about the horse's neck and hung there, crying distressfully till his heart was breaking.

On the way home he sat crumpled and utterly empty, only the nausea persisted, now and then making him gulp. Thoughtfully Dolly jogged along; at the crossroad where she was to turn, she took the right road and went on, by turns throwing her long ears forward and back.

From the south bedroom window the tired eye of the lamp met him as the horse turned from the main road into the yard. He caught the gleam and his head cleared. . . . To-night is Saturday night . . . now you go in and clean house . . . it's about time! he mumbled, darkly.

On the bed Susie had been lying fully dressed. Upon hearing the buggy enter the yard she jumped up and darted to the window, stood there behind the curtain while he put in the horse; she shook so violently that she had to catch hold of the window casing to steady herself. She saw him shove the barn door shut, and for one moment she hesitated, then fled to the bedroom where Petie lay sleeping peacefully. Without a word she snatched him up, shaking him pitilessly. The boy's eyes opened wide; instantly he set up a wild howl.

"You shut up, will you!" She pinched him and gave a twist before she let go. "Shut up . . . you hear me? *Shut up!*" When Peder tore the door open Petie was shrieking like one possessed.

"What's going on here?"

"How can you ask! How can I tell what's going on? He's been keeping this up all night; you must hurry for the doctor right away!"

"Give him to me!"

"To you!" Brushing him aside, she made for the kitchen. He caught her by the arm and held her:

"Father, Forgive Them—!"

"Don't you hear me?"

Once she swept him with her eyes, and then once more:

"Hold him while I warm the water!" Dropping the boy into his arms, she flew into the kitchen. In a moment she had the fire roaring and the water-kettle on.

She stayed in the kitchen till the water was warm. Returning to the bedroom, she brought with her a handful of rags, the wash-basin and the water-kettle. She was high and mighty in her manner and so commanding that without a murmur he handed her the boy.

Peder had succeeded in quieting him, only echoes of the sobs were heard. But no sooner did Petie realize that he had been transferred to his mother than he howled worse than ever.

"Mercy me! it's the cramps!" she groaned. "Can't you see that it's the cramps? That's what killed Mrs. Flaherty's baby. She told me exactly how it started." Susie had laid Petie over her knees and was rubbing him over the abdomen. "Set the basin here. Good Lord! can't you see?"

Peder handed her the rags, filled the basin and set it beside her chair. He remained standing behind her and every moment it looked as if he would strike her. Not a word did he say.

Deftly she applied the warm applications, removing them and putting on new ones. Meanwhile she cooed to the child:

"There, there, my little honeybunch! . . . Now it'll soon be all right. . . . Tush, tush, darling, don't cry! . . . Oh, is it worse again?"

In terror Petie looked up at his mother's face, and couldn't understand. . . . Wasn't she mad any longer? Feeling that it would be safer to be with his father, he stretched out his arms, begging:

"Sleep with you, papa!" and he sobbed pitifully.

Without further ado Peder bent over to pick him up. Susie objected and held on, the boy squirming and howling as if he had been stabbed.

"See!" she stormed, angrily. "It's the cramps. . . . Get away from here. . . . Let me do this!"

335

Their Fathers' God

With the boy in his arms Peder went into the kitchen and paced up and down the floor. Like an enraged tigress she was after him.

"Give him to me. Can't you see it's killing him? You got to go for help . . . I won't take the blame for this!"

He pushed her away so roughly that she reeled backwards. Not a word did he say.

She picked herself up and ran into the bedroom, slamming the door shut behind her.

Peder sat down in the old rocking-chair; he tried to talk, but no words came, only a low cooing sound that came in spurts and rose from way down in his chest; with a shaking hand he stroked the boy's cheek, stroked and patted, Petie moaning pitifully. The caresses continued, got so tenderly intimate that Petie had to stand on his knees in order to lock his arms around his father's neck. Gradually the sobs stilled and the little body relaxed, at last resting peacefully against Peder's breast. Soon Petie was sound asleep.

For a long time Peder sat there staring into darkness. Arising finally, he tiptoed up the stairs and laid Petie down in his own bed. Waiting long enough to make sure that the boy didn't awake, Peder came down again, just as noiselessly, his face glistening with a cold sweat.

With a sharp thrust he opened the bedroom door wide and stepped in.

The lamp was still lit. On the bed lay Susie, half on her side; she was fully dressed, her right arm was thrown across her face.

Stark still he stood there, looking at her. . . . Was she asleep? Hardly! We'll soon find out, he thought, and strode over to the wall. The white porcelain figure of the crucifix appeared yellow in the dull light of the lamp. His hand stretched out and tore it off. There was a snap, and the trickling of small grains of plaster falling to the floor. Turning the crucifix over, he studied it for a moment. He had hold of both ends, and suddenly there was a sharp sound. He dropped the pieces to the floor, stamped on them and ground them under his heel. Slowly, deliberately he did it.

"Father, Forgive Them—!"

Horrified, with eyes and mouth wide open, Susie sat on the bed, staring at him; the muscles of her throat worked frantically but there was no audible sound.

. . . *Crunch, crunch!* came from under his heel. He was aware that she was watching him, and felt pleased . . . hm, didn't he know she was awake! A cold grin broke on his face and he nodded to something he saw. And the next moment he was standing by the other wall; his hand swept down and the vessel of holy water clattered on the floor. The vessel didn't break and so he applied his heel there too.

. . . *Crunch, crunch!*

In the excitement earlier in the night Susie had laid her rosary on the commode and had forgotten it there. Picking it up Peder studied it long. "Here's the root of all the evil." Suddenly he was picking the rosary to pieces. A terrible calm was upon him. Holding the rosary in one hand, he picked methodically with the other, bead after bead. And when there were no more left he emptied his hand on the floor and applied his heel. The beads were more brittle than the crucifix and the vessel of holy water and gave a sharper sound.

Creak! it said from under his heel. *Creak-eak!*

"Now we're through with the idols in this house, Susie!" he said, very quietly. "There'll be no more of it." He took a step towards the bed as if now her turn had come. "God pity you!" His face was ashen, his words so low-spoken that they were hardly audible. Abruptly, as though overcome by a sudden pain, he turned and staggered out of the room.

Dumb-faced, Susie sat staring at the door; her eyes were unnaturally big; but there was a silly grin on her face as if she had seen into horror itself, was seeing it yet and could not believe it; from her throat rose gurglings, as if she were trying to laugh, had to laugh, and could not get the laughter out. Her head began to droop and she sank over in a swoon.

XII

Along towards morning Peder fell into a deep sleep from which he did not awaken until far in the forenoon. He was much surprised at having slept so soundly; he felt well rested and easy of mind. Jumping out of bed and looking around, his surprise increased. Petie up already? The little rascal—and I didn't even hear him! On seeing what time of day it was, Peder laughed in dismay . . . he certainly hadn't intended to leave them alone with the chores!

When he came down, Jacob Fredrik was busy in the kitchen; his face seemed red and swollen and refused to meet Peder's. On seeing Peder make ready to go out he came and gave him a folded paper:

"She asked me to give you this," he said, huskily.

Peder opened the note and read:

"Now I've lived the Blessed Day, I've been to the End of the World and have found out what it looks like. I'll never go near there again, because it is an accursed place. I remember a holy word, 'Father, forgive them,' and I say it here, not that it will do any good. I'm taking Petie; the horse and the buggy you'll get back.

"Susie."

For a while he stood looking at the note. Having read it once more, he tore it up and threw the pieces into the stove. And going to the corner back of the door he began hunting among the clothes that hung there, aimlessly and with slow movements.

"Looking for something?" asked Jacob Fredrik.

"That old cap of mine," he answered, absently, and continued turning the clothes. . . . "What time did she leave?"

"This morning, shortly after I came down," gulped Jacob Fredrik.

Peder found the cap, which all the time had hung in plain sight, put it on, and went out.

THE END

338